FOLLOWING THE DREAM

"You are a woman who follows her heart."

Evelyn's smile faded at the words, so insightful. She found it amazing that this supposedly wild Indian renegade could be so easy to talk to. "It's strange that you would say that. My mother has always taught me to follow my heart, but to be careful." She felt her cheeks growing hot. "She said that sometimes the heart can lead a person into danger." Evelyn wished she could look away from him, but it would do no good. He surely knew exactly what she was thinking, and she could see by his eyes that he was thinking the same. To love each other could be dangerous for both of them.

"Your mother is dead now," he finally spoke up softly. "Perhaps her spirit lives on, in you. And perhaps, as you suggested yourself, Wild Horse lives in me. Would that not mean that the two spirits who could not be together in life should finally be together, through us? Could that be the meaning of your dreams, and my vision? Perhaps if we came together ourselves, the vision would be fulfilled. Then when our hands touch in the dream, neither of us would disappear. . . ."

ROSANNE BITTNER
FULL CIRCLE

ZEBRA BOOKS
KENSINGTON PUBLISHING CORP.

ZEBRA BOOKS are published by

Kensington Publishing Corp.
850 Third Avenue
New York, NY 10022

First Printing: September, 1994

Printed in the United States of America

Dedicated to a people whose whispers can still be heard on the wind, whose moccasined footsteps now lie beneath pavement, whose spirit still lives in Grandmother Earth and in the animals . . . crying to be free again.

Author's Note

As with all my books, the historical background and locations in this story are based on true events; however, the characters are fictitious, except for Agent James McLaughlin, who plays a minor role in my story. I based Mr. McLaughlin's personal situation and how he might have reacted to incidents in my story on information about his history that is a matter of public record.

Inspiration for the heroine of *Full Circle* came from two real-life women who dedicated their lives to helping Native Americans. One was Alice Fletcher, called "The Measuring Woman" by the Nez Perce. The other was Mary Clementine Collins, missionary to the Sioux and highly respected by them. Mary was called *Wenonah,* meaning "Princess." I have used this detail for my own heroine, Evelyn Gibbons; however, it must be noted that Evelyn's personal story is entirely fictitious and not at all related to either of the women mentioned here. It was only their hard work and dedication to helping Native Americans that inspired me.

Many of my readers, when they are finished with my books, are convinced that the characters really lived. Who is to say there were not people just like Evelyn Gibbons . . . and Black Hawk . . . whose lives might have taken the same pathways.

Once our flesh and blood were a part of the earth;
Our spirits were joined with the animals
And with the air we breathe.
Life was one great circle, birth, life, death . . .
Life again, through our children,
And through our children's children.
They carried on . . . the flesh, the blood, the spirit,
The way of the People.

Then came the white man,
And the circle was broken,
The earth torn, the air tainted.
Our children were taken from us to learn a new way.
The spirit left us, but we will find it again.
We will relearn the old ways,
We will feel Grandmother Earth and the animal spirits
Live in us again.
We will teach the children about the Circle of Life,
And it will be whole again.
It will be so.
Hechetu alo. It is good.

Introduction

June 1892

"You've lost your mind!"

Evelyn Gibbons turned away from her fiancé, wondering if perhaps he was right; but the dream would not leave her. She knew that until this moment she had only been living the life that was expected of her, not the one she really wanted. Her back to Steven, she smiled when she realized she had her mother's independent spirit to be herself and not live as others dictated.

"If I don't do this, Steven, I'll never be happy."

"And what about us?"

She lost her smile, turning back around to study the man she had promised to marry. Steven was as ordinary as could be, son of a Wisconsin dairy farmer, a good man, hard-working. He had brown hair, brown eyes, was rather short but had a sturdy build and was pleasantly handsome . . . and he was a quiet, gentle man. He would make a good husband for any woman satisfied with living on a farm the rest of her life.

"I'm sorry, Steven. When we met last year, I had finished college and got my teaching job here in Waupun. I met you and fell in love, and I thought marrying you was all I wanted in life. I thought I was ready for marriage and children and settling, but I wasn't having the dreams then, or feeling this restlessness. You remember I told you the same thing happened to my mother when I was very small, and she and my father had some problems, mainly because she had married him because everyone expected her to. She had never been free to live her life a different way if that was what she wanted."

"She was the wife of a *preacher!* How could they have had problems?"

The memory was so clear. Evelyn could still see the Cheyenne Indian called Wild Horse talking with her mother at the pond, their secret meeting place. She was only four then, and her family lived in Oklahoma near a reservation where her father had preached to the Cheyenne for eight years before moving back here to Wisconsin.

The memory of Wild Horse had never left her. At her mother's deathbed just six months ago, she admitted to Evelyn that she had loved the dashingly handsome, dangerous Indian man. The things he had taught both Evelyn and her mother were still with her.

"Being the wife of a preacher doesn't guarantee a blissful marriage, Steven," she answered. "All that matters is passion—utter devotion. How much money a man has, what he does for a living, his station in life, none of those things really matter if the passion isn't there." How clear were her mother's dying words, the same words she repeated to Steven now. *Be sure, Evy,* Margaret Gibbons had warned her. *Be sure. Follow your heart, your dreams. Don't ever do something because it is expected of you.* "Steven, isn't it better to be *sure* than to marry and end up in a loveless match that makes both of us unhappy?"

"Are you saying you don't love me then?"

She saw the hurt in his eyes. "I *do* love you, but I am realizing that maybe I don't love you enough, and that maybe that fact will only make me more restless and unhappy living on your farm, where I couldn't experience new things, challenge my teaching abilities."

"And you think that going to live and teach among a sorry, drunken, broken tribe of Sioux on a remote reservation that probably has no modern facilities is going to be a challenge to your *teaching* abilities?" He sniffed and shook his head. "The only challenge will be how to manage to take a bath, how to keep yourself from being violated by some drunken Indian. Those people don't want our help, Evy. They don't want to learn our ways. They aren't even *intelligent* enough to learn!"

Not intelligent? Wild Horse had mastered the English language easily, and he'd had a wisdom that far surpassed that of any white person she had ever known when it came to common sense and exploring one's spiritual path. It was Wild Horse who had taught her and her mother, rather than the other way around. She saw a side to Steven Hart she knew she could not tolerate. Ignorance of the beauty of another race. She had not noticed any of that until she had mentioned wanting to delay their wedding so she could go and teach at the Standing Rock Reservation in South Dakota.

"They are *very* intelligent, Steven, in ways you could never imagine. Your attitude only shows me I've made the right decision. Why is it so wrong for a woman to want to stretch her wings and experience more of life? Why is it so wrong for her to have dreams and goals beyond milking cows and baking bread and birthing babies?"

Steven met her eyes, so blue. When he'd first met Evelyn Gibbons at a dance, he had been instantly consumed with the desire to have her for himself. He studied her blond hair, hair that, when worn loose, hung in thick waves nearly to her waist . . . hair he had imagined seeing spread out on a pillow beside him. She was twenty years old and a beauty, a graceful young woman with an exquisite face and a body that would turn any man's head. She was a virtuous young woman with a tender heart, but as he came to know her better, he had begun to see a side to her that was difficult for him to tolerate in a woman, an independence that just wasn't natural. His own *mother* had been content to live on the farm and raise ten children, for heaven's sake.

But Evy was certainly nothing like his mother. Much as he loved and desired her, he realized more and more she was probably right about one thing: looks, station in life . . . none of those things mattered in the end. A man had to ask himself if a woman was truly going to make him happy. Maybe Evy couldn't do that after all. If they married, and she grew miserable with the life she led, then he would be miserable, too.

He blinked back tears and turned away. "What a waste," he muttered.

Evelyn felt a lump forming in her throat. "It is never a waste to go out and explore, Steven, to be sure what you are doing is right, to know your own heart. Our spirit paths are not the same. You are content to have a farm and a wife and a lot of children and never leave Wisconsin. There is nothing wrong in that. I'm just not sure it's what *I* want for myself, and I feel this dream I have been having is some kind of message."

He turned to face her, quickly wiping at one tear that managed to slip out of his eye. "I really love you, Evy." He sniffed and forced a grin. "But I'm not so sure I could put up with you." He waved his arm and walked past her. "All this talk about spirit paths and dreams and feeling a calling to go teach a bunch of drunken heathens." He threw back his head. "Go ahead, if that's what you need to do. But I won't wait for you. There probably wouldn't be much sense in that. I can name two girls right now who would like to marry me. And you know who they are."

Evelyn felt a tinge of jealousy, but it was mixed with relief to know that already he was thinking about going on with his life and finding a woman better suited for him. She knew he was talking about Kathleen Hage and Jessica Wilson, both young women who always flirted with Steven at socials. She couldn't blame Steven for wanting to marry and have children. After all, he was twenty-seven years old and came from a big family.

"You do what you need to do, Steven. My mother told me once to follow my heart. I care very much for you, and I want you to be happy. I thought at first we could find that happiness together, but now I just don't think we can. It's better this way." Evelyn looked around the parlor of the pleasant farm home Steven had built with his own hands on a piece of land his father had sold to him. Maybe she *was* crazy. A woman could have a pleasant, sedate life here, but a restlessness inside told her *she* could not settle for that. She had driven herself here from town in a buggy, a very long drive, and one Steven didn't feel she should have made alone. *But then, you aren't like other women,* he had said. *You fear nothing.*

Except perhaps not being free, she thought.

"What does your father think of all this?" Steven asked.

She smiled rather sadly. "After living with my mother all those years, he's not surprised. He knows I'm just like her. And he certainly understands about a person feeling a calling to do something God wants them to do."

"Is that how you think of it? *God* is calling you to do this?"

"I don't know. Maybe it's just old memories from when I was little. It just seems to me that when a person has the same dream every few nights for weeks, it has to mean something." She turned away, the dream always vivid in her mind—a warrior on a spotted horse, both he and the horse painted. Whether the colors were his prayer colors or war colors she had no idea. Sometimes she thought the man in the dream was Wild Horse's spirit come to visit her, trying to tell her something. "There is something the man in the dream wants from me," she said aloud, "but I don't know what it is."

"You never had the dreams until your mother died. They probably have something to do with losing her and will go away after awhile. You're just upset over your loss, Evy. You and your mother were very close. I think it's foolish of you to put more meaning into those dreams than there really is."

She faced him again. "I think there *is* something to them. The vision is so real, Steven, and then when the missionary from the Standing Rock Reservation visited my father's church, talking about how badly teachers were needed because most of the Sioux wouldn't let their children go to white man's schools off the reservation, it was like an answer. I can't ignore the compelling need to go there. I'm so terribly sorry it hurts you, but this kind of hurt isn't near as damaging as the kind we might both suffer if we marry for the wrong reasons."

He ran a hand through his hair and sighed. "When do you leave?"

"In three days. I'll be traveling with the missionary, Janine Phillips. We're going to Milwaukee first to meet a preacher and his wife who are being sponsored by Mission Services. We'll need to get written approval for me to go with them to the reservation to teach, but there should be no problem, with my father being a preacher, let alone the fact that I have a teaching degree from Ripon College." She swallowed, sometimes as surprised herself that she was doing this as some others were. "From Milwaukee we go to Chicago and then take a train into Nebraska to Fort Kearny, where someone will be waiting for Janine with a wagon and horses. They'll take us to the reservation." She blinked back tears. "I'll write you, Steven, and if I think I want to come back after a year or two, I'll let you know. I might even come back sooner than that for all I know. Either way, if you're married to someone else, I'll understand."

He reached out and touched her cheek. "God knows *you'd* have no trouble finding someone else. You're a beautiful woman, Evy, and I'll miss you dearly. I know this is important to you, I just don't fully understand it, and I still think it's wrong. I'll worry about you."

"The Indians are nothing like you imagine, Steven. I told you about Wild Horse. I have nothing but fond memories of him, and because of the impression he left on me, I have studied Sioux and Cheyenne customs and languages for years. It surely was all leading to something. I can't ignore any of this, and I can't ignore my promise to Wild Horse that I would never forget him. This is something I can do in his memory, even though he was Cheyenne and not Sioux. Both tribes were very close."

"And both were at the Little Big Horn, where a lot of soldiers died."

"That was a long time ago. Everything is so changed for them now. They have nothing left; in some cases, not even their dignity. I feel there is something I need to do, *have* to do." She looked down at her hand and removed her engagement ring, handing it out to him. "You will always be dear to me, Steven. I wish you the best in life."

He sighed, taking the ring hesitantly, holding her gaze. "And I for you. I just don't see how you'll get the best going where you're going. Be careful, Evy." He leaned down and kissed her cheek. "I'll drive you back myself. It's getting late, and I don't want you on the road alone after dark. I'll go check on your father's horse, make sure he's cooled down enough to make the trip back."

She nodded, and he closed his fist around the ring and turned away. "God be with you, Evy." He left the room, and Evelyn closed her eyes. She could see the vision again. In the dream the warrior would come so close. He would reach out, as though to grab her and whisk her up onto his horse. But just before he could grasp her hand, he would disappear, and she would wake up in a cold sweat.

Was it Wild Horse riding toward her, calling for help? Or was it someone else? She could not help feeling that somehow, if she went to the Standing Rock Reservation, she might find the answer. She was giving up a comfortable life, a good job, marriage . . . leaving her father. But none of those things mattered. She had to go.

One

Seth Bridges tipped a bottle of fine bourbon and swallowed, allowing himself a moment to savor the satisfaction of letting it slip and burn over his tongue and throat and into his stomach. He grinned through yellowed teeth, then smacked his thin lips. "Good stuff, boys. You tell whoever pays you to bring this stuff in that my own payment for helpin' you find a way past the soldiers is very acceptable."

Luke Smith laughed lightly, scratching at his dark, unkempt beard. "It's the ones like you, who help us get through, that get the good stuff. The bottom of that there wagon is stuffed with cheap, rot-gut whiskey—good enough for the Indians, but not for a white man who knows his liquor."

Seth joined him and his partner, young Marty Able, in more laughter. The campfire around which they sat flickered light against their faces, faces the gray-haired, unshaven Seth had come to know well. As long as he could keep getting his own supply of good whiskey, he would continue helping these men sneak it onto the reservation, as long as he had the cooperation of Sergeant Jubal Desmond, who could be easily bribed into looking the other way when patrolling for whiskey smugglers.

Luke was dark and hairy, his beard reaching to his big belly and mixing into thick hairs on his chest that came clear up to his throat and stuck out of where his shirt was left open because of the warm night. The crinkles around his nearly-black eyes showed he was a man in his middle years who had spent a good deal of time out of doors.

Marty was much younger, and forty-nine-year-old Seth, whose thinning hair was almost completely gray now, envied that youth. Marty was not a bad-looking young man, Seth thought, although he wondered why the boy bothered to keep himself so clean and closely shaved out in these parts. His sandy hair was neatly combed, and the kid was always rubbing baking soda over his teeth.

Seth considered cleaning his mouth and teeth a waste of time. Whiskey made a good enough mouthwash, and as for shaving, he only did that every few days. "Hey, boy, you like women, don't you?" he asked Marty. He took another drink and wiped his lips on his shirtsleeve as Luke guffawed and Marty just grinned.

"It's the other way around, Seth," Luke told him with the strong southern drawl of a man originally from Kentucky. "It's the women that love Marty. Every place we go up and down the river on my steamer, the whores are waitin' for Marty at every stop along the way. There's even a couple of married women down in Kansas City who open their back doors for him when their husbands are gone."

Seth grinned, and Marty drew deeply on a cigarette, shaking his head as though embarrassed; but his blue eyes showed a cocky pride. "Sure I like women," he answered Seth, "long as they're pretty and layin' in my bed . . . or I'm layin' in theirs." He flashed a bright smile and rubbed at his privates. "You got a reason for askin' that, Seth?"

Seth shrugged. "Maybe. I got me two adopted daughters. The older one, Lucille, is broke in. She's sixteen, real pretty. I broke her in myself. For some extra fine wine, I'd consider lettin' you have at her."

Marty took a swallow from his own bottle of whiskey. "I'll think on it. Next time me and Luke bring the riverboat back up, maybe we'll have a case of French wine along. You like red wine? White wine?"

"I like *any* wine. Good wine and good whiskey. It's worth the risk of gettin' caught by the Army, helpin' you two get that wagon onto Indian land. And sharin' my daughter don't bother me. I'm thinkin' on somethin' different in my bed anyway. Her little sister is startin' to sprout in all the right places."

Luke chuckled. "How old is the sister?"

"Katy's twelve. A mite young yet, but watchin' her grow up has got me wantin' her."

"How in hell did you end up with adopted daughters?" Marty asked. He took one last drag on his cigarette and threw it into the campfire.

Seth held his chin proudly, enjoying what he considered his own cleverness. "Easy. Four years back I heard about an orphan train comin' west to find homes for kids from back East. My own wife ran off on me years ago, took a couple of kids with her. I wanted a woman in my bed, but I sure as hell wasn't gonna go takin' another wife; and I needed a woman around the house to cook my meals and help with chores. I went to Omaha and met the train, cleaned myself up real nice, gave them a real sad story about bein' a church-goin', Christian man who had an ailin' wife who couldn't have no kids of her own and always wanted daughters. I said it would probably help make her better if she had a couple of girls to keep her company, help take care of her and be like daughters to her. The man from the orphanage who brought the kids out believed my story. I swear to God the fool had tears in his eyes."

They all laughed and gulped more whiskey.

"So he just handed over the two girls?" Marty asked.

"Pretty as you please. They were eight and twelve then. I wanted them young so's I could do the job myself. I waited till the older one was thirteen."

"They got some surprise, didn't they?" Luke joked. "I bet

they thought they were goin' home to some nice woman who needed their help."

Seth grunted in a laugh and took a cigar from his pocket. He pulled a burning stick from the fire and used it to light the cigar, then puffed on it a moment, remembering how much he had enjoyed that first time with a struggling Lucille. She didn't bother struggling anymore. "They got surprised, all right. He studied the cigar. "They're good workers, too, if you deal them a hard hand. They learned real quick."

"I'll see if I can't get one of our suppliers to throw in some good wine next time," Marty told him. "You try to bring your daughter along when you meet us."

"I'll think on it."

"I'm not so sure how much longer we can keep doin' this without gettin' caught," Luke put in. "Word is the government might send out even more soldiers to patrol the reservation borders."

"We'll find a way," Seth told them. He had never asked just who the actual whiskey suppliers were. That was something he knew Luke and Marty had sworn not to tell. The two men were simply the couriers for people of much greater wealth. Luke had a family back in Omaha, or at least he claimed he did. He owned a steamboat, and Marty, a kid who had been on his own most of his life, worked for Luke on the steamer, which Luke took up and down the Missouri River, picking up and delivering supplies from and to Omaha and Kansas City. Seth did not doubt that the man made his biggest money from land-grabbers and businessmen who wanted to keep the Indians drunk and in a helpless state in order to swindle them out of more land and also keep them too weak to ever try making war again.

Besides being paid by outsiders to smuggle whiskey onto the Sioux reservations, Luke made money from the Indians themselves. Those who were addicted to the watered-down whiskey Luke brought them would spend their last government cent and trade their last government-supplied blanket and pan for just one bottle of the stuff, which was only worth a few cents to begin with. Seth himself figured he did pretty good supplying food from his farm to the reservation trading post and to the Army at Fort Yates. His daughters did most of the hard chores, and he enjoyed the profits, always tacking on extra for anything he sold to the Army. It pleased him no end that the government didn't seem to keep very close tabs on what it was getting for its money.

"I have real good connections," he told Marty, "You bring the whiskey, and I'll—"

The man's words were cut off by a piercing war cry, and before any of them could react, a spotted Appaloosa horse came charging through their camp, its rump painted with red-and-yellow stripes, its rider's face smeared with red-and-white war paint. He wore only buckskin pants, his dark hair hung loose nearly to his waist, and his eyes looked more frightening in the firelight because of the white circles painted around them. His chest was bare except that it, too, was smeared with war paint.

All three men jumped back, and Luke reached for a rifle, but another Indian moved in from the darkness and rode his horse into the man, knocking him down. The first and most frightening-looking warrior charged them again, galloping his spotted horse right over the fire and sending embers flying.

"Black Hawk! You sonofabitch!" Seth Bridges cussed.

The one called Black Hawk turned his horse and pointed a lance at Seth, resting the tip of it on Seth's shoulder. By then, the second Indian, much older than Black Hawk, had dismounted and picked up Luke's rifle. He held it on Luke and Marty, and Marty shivered visibly with fright. "What the hell is goin' on here?" he asked, his voice squeaking.

"Ask this goddamn bastard!" Seth sneered, glaring at Black Hawk.

"Do you think I do not know what is in the wagon?" Black

Hawk growled in the white man's tongue. "These men bring the
firewater that makes my people sick and weak, and *you* help
them get in!" He whirled the lance around quickly to slam the
butt end of it across Seth's chest. Seth grunted and fell backward.
Black Hawk quickly pressed the pointed end of the lance against
the man's chest while he lay on his back. He looked from Seth
to the other two men, whose terror was evident in their eyes.
"You will not move!" he ordered. He let out a coyotelike yip,
and four young men rode into the light of the fire. They tied
ropes to the buckboard wagon, which was stacked with blankets,
and tipped it on its side. They then dismounted and began chop-
ping away at the bottom of the wagon with hatchets.

Black Hawk grinned wickedly at the sound of whiskey bottles
breaking. The four young warriors who did the damage had been
eager for some excitement, and Black Hawk understood their
pent-up anger. He glanced at the old man who held the rifle on
Luke and Marty. Night Hunter was a priest and medicine man
who liked to tell stories about the "old days," when the Sioux
under Red Cloud and Crazy Horse and Sitting Bull chased everyone with white skin off their land, even the soldiers. He
grinned victoriously at the old man, who nodded in reply with
a sly grin of his own. It felt good to spoil the plans of these
white men who made money by filling the Sioux with rotgut
whiskey.

"You can't do this!" Luke growled.

"Who will stop us?" Black Hawk asked Seth. *"You?"* He
laughed. "I do not think so. The soldiers? We are doing what
they *should* be doing. They should be *glad* we are doing this.
Will you report me to Agent McLaughlin? How can you? You
would have to tell him why you were out here. They would come
here and find the whiskey bottles and would know you help
these men bring the firewater to my people!" He poked the lance
just enough to startle Seth and bring surface pain to his skin.
Now Black Hawk could see real fear in the man's eyes, and he

enjoyed it. "Do you think I am stupid? These men are paid by other white men who want our land! They think they can get *all* my people to depend on the whiskey, which makes them weak. It is easy to talk a drunk Indian into selling some of his land for firewater!" His dark eyes flamed with rage. "Not *this* Indian! There are some of us who will not touch the demon in your bottles that robs us of our powers! I cannot stop all of it from getting in, but any that I *can* stop helps my people."

The men destroying the whiskey bottles laughed and whooped as they smashed every last bottle hidden in the bottom of the overturned wagon. Then they began grabbing blankets, each taking an armful to give to mothers and grandmothers. Black Hawk watched with a note of sadness in his eyes, thinking how this was all that was left of once-proud warriors who fought enemy tribes and once successfully fought the whole United States Army. Now they destroyed whiskey wagons and stole blankets. He looked back down at Seth.

"I will not kill you this time." He looked over at Luke and Marty. "But if I find any of you on this land again, I will slice your bellies open! The soldiers will come after me, but I will make the sacrifice to see all of you holding your insides in your hands!" He let out a shivering war cry, holding his lance in the air, then rode off into the dark night, followed by the four men loaded down with their supply of blankets.

The old man who held Luke's rifle on him and Marty stood there grinning. He backed up, then leapt onto the bare back of his horse with the agility of a much younger man. He kept hold of the rifle, then raised it and nodded to Luke. "Thank you for the gift," he said with a wry grin. He turned and rode off after the others, sounding another war cry.

Marty let out a sigh of relief. "Damn! This is the last time for me. I'm not coming back here," he told Luke.

"Who the hell *was* that?" Luke growled at Seth.

Seth kicked at the fire. "He's called Black Hawk. He's one

of them goddamn bastards that won't come into the agency and settle like he's supposed to. He lives out in the hills with a son. Most times the soldiers can't even find him. They gave up—figured if he didn't cause any real trouble, they could leave him be." He turned away and stomped a foot. "Shit! The sonofabitch knows I can't report this!"

"Well, *I'm* gonna be out a lot of money for not bein' able to deliver the goods!" Luke fumed. "The men I work for aren't going to like this. *I* don't like this! I was *countin'* on that money!"

"I hate that cocky redskin!" Seth seethed.

"Let's get out of here!" Marty told Luke. "It's a long way to where the boat is docked. The quicker we get away from this camp and back to the boat, the better, before soldiers or scouts find this mess and link it to us!"

Luke sighed, leaning down and grabbing up his hat to plunk it on his head. "You're probably right."

"And *I'm* not comin' back, Luke! You can fire me if you want, but I'm not comin'!"

"What about my daughter, and the wine you promised me?" Seth asked, stepping closer to the boy.

"Mister, your daughter isn't worth me gettin' caught, or gettin' my insides ripped open by that crazy warrior out there!"

"Black Hawk won't really kill you. He knows he could never get away with it."

"Well, he looked pretty goddamn sincere to *me,* and I don't aim to come back and test him out! I never have liked comin' onto Indian land. I don't trust the heathens. It wasn't that long ago that they were still killing whites."

Luke began packing some of his gear. "Get your stuff together, kid, and let's get going. There's enough moonlight to see our way back to the boat."

"Wait a minute!" Seth stood in front of Luke. *"You're* comin' back, aren't you? We made a deal—"

"To get through the soldiers' guard," Luke interrupted. "I didn't expect an attack to come from Indians. I'll have to talk with the men who pay me. If we come back, they're going to have to pay me a hell of a lot more to do it." The man opened a leather bag and began angrily ramming things into it.

Seth could see no argument was going to make them stay, and with all the whiskey destroyed, there was no reason for them to be here. He had already been given his own supply of the good whiskey, and he was glad Black Hawk had not looked into his own saddlebags. His biggest worry was that it would be harder to get his hands on more if Luke did not return. He clenched his fists in anger at Black Hawk, then turned and walked over to where his horse was tied, still saddled and carrying all his gear. He mounted up, watched Luke and Marty scramble to get their own gear together. He vowed then and there to find a way to get back at Black Hawk for interrupting what could have proved to be a very profitable business deal that would have kept him in good whiskey and wine for some time to come.

He turned his horse toward home. It was a long ride, but he decided he did not care to camp alone out here with Black Hawk prowling about. Besides, he had to keep a good eye on Lucille, who had tried to run away once. He figured he had probably taught her a good lesson that time, but he still didn't trust the brat. She might try again. "You let me know if you need my services again," he told Luke.

Luke glanced up at him and nodded, then returned to packing. Marty couldn't seem to get his own things together fast enough, and Seth shook his head and rode off. Maybe he could force some whiskey down Lucille's throat again. She didn't fight him as much when he managed to make her drink first.

Evelyn stood watching the old mantel clock a moment longer, listening to its familiar tick, thinking how she had been listening to it for as long as she could remember. Her mother had had the clock clear back when they lived in Oklahoma, only then it had sat on the mantel of a much more rustic fireplace in a simple log cabin. She realized she would be going back to that kind of life when she went to South Dakota. Janine Phillips had told her how primitive life there still was for most people. There was no electricity yet, no telephones, no decent plumbing. The government was not eager to spend any more money than it had to on conveniences for the Indians.

She had lived in Wisconsin since she was twelve, in this modest but comfortable and tidy frame home that belonged to the church where her father preached. Now that her mother was gone, she had taken care of the house herself, living and teaching here in Waupun since graduating from college. "Will the church provide a housekeeper for you?" she asked, turning away from the clock to face her father, a slender man whose hair was still thick, though quite gray now.

"Oh, I'm sure they will work something out. Since your mother died, several of the older widows in town have offered to help."

The man grinned wryly, but Evelyn saw the aching sadness in his eyes, eyes that were surrounded with many wrinkles. Edward Gibbons had devoted most of his fifty-six years to bringing the Word of God to others. He'd had big dreams when going to Indian Territory back in '76, but he had known nothing about how to reach a people whose culture was vastly different from his own. He had supposed he could just charge right in and change them overnight, that they would listen to his teachings and quickly want to grasp a new religion.

Those dreams had been dashed quickly, and it was her mother who had shown him how to reach the southern Cheyenne, who at that time had only recently been forced into reservation life. Margaret Gibbons had in turn learned what she knew from Wild Horse, her secret friend at the pond . . . a man with such powerful influence over others that he had nearly caused her to do something the very Christian and virtuous woman would never have considered under any other circumstances. Almost losing her love was what had jolted Edward into realizing he was making his wife very unhappy by his stern lifestyle, by refusing to allow her to help him in his work, by considering joy and laughter almost sinful.

Your father was raised that way himself, her mother had told her once. *He needed to be taught how to free his feelings, how to laugh, that it was all right to express passion and desire.*

It was those things Wild Horse had awakened in Margaret Gibbons, his own free spirit helping hers to soar into new joy. He had taught her about the Indian spirit, Indian beliefs, a beautiful way of looking at life and nature. The woman had almost lost her heart to him, until the tragedy of his death helped her open up to her husband and brought a new closeness to their relationship. Edward Gibbons had been a changed man ever since, and after another sixteen years together, losing his wife had been very hard on him. She was only forty when she died.

"I'm sorry to leave you now, when you're still missing Mother so," Evelyn told him.

He breathed deeply in an obvious effort to force back his emotions. "I always said you were just like your mother, free-spirited, determined to do what you will do, no matter what anyone else thinks about it. If you feel this calling, Evy, I suppose you should act on it. I just hope you realize what you're getting yourself into. The Sioux have not been settled in for very long. Don't forget the massacre that took place not even two years ago at Wounded Knee. Some of them are still quite hostile, I'm told. Getting through to them is going to be a very difficult task. Your biggest problem will probably be getting them to send their children to school."

She nodded. "I know, but teaching is not the only reason I am going."

Edward studied his daughter's lovely blue eyes, her mother's
eyes. She was almost a replica of the woman, and seeing her
only made him miss Margaret more. "You know what I think
about those dreams, Evy." His theory was similar to the one
Steven had espoused. "Your mother has only been gone for six
months. I think it just has something to do with you missing
her. You were so close. I know how hard it was on you losing
her. I think the dreams are just memories . . . of when you were
a little girl, and you and your mother used to go to that pond
and talk with Wild Horse."

Evelyn saw the hurt in his eyes, knew he could not help but
feel resentment and jealousy whenever he thought about Wild
Horse. She closed her eyes and sighed. "I think it's more than
that, Father. It's like . . . like someone, maybe Mother, is trying
to tell me something." She faced him again. "At any rate, I feel
I won't know the answer if I don't go to Standing Rock. There
has to be a connection between the dreams, and Janine Phillips
coming here to tell us how badly more missionaries and teachers
are needed out there. In the dream an Indian man reaches out
to me, as though to ask for help. I wouldn't think so much of it
if I hadn't had the same dream so often."

Edward studied her lovingly, hating to see his beautiful daughter leave the comforts of a settled life and a good teaching job
right here in Waupun for the rugged, perhaps dangerous life she
would face in the Dakotas. Besides that, she had broken her
engagement with a fine young man who would have made a
good husband. But then, just like her mother, she would not
choose a husband for the reasons most women did, just because
the man was stable and settled. Like Margaret, Evelyn Gibbons
needed something more, a man with a vision, a man of great
passion, who saw far beyond a simple home life and babies.
Evelyn was a woman with great spirit, a quest for drama in her
life, a passionate woman who was also *com*passionate, very determined, brave, and with enough temper to make sure she got

what she wanted. He hoped that temper and determination would not get her into trouble eventually.

He stepped closer, putting his hands on Evelyn's shoulders. "You do what you have to do, Evy, and don't worry about me. The congregation has bent over backward helping me, keeping me company. The women have brought me food, offered to help with the house. I'll be just fine. *You're* the one to worry about."

Evelyn reached out and embraced him. "I'm not afraid, Father. I know I'm doing the right thing. I feel like Mother is with me. Does that sound silly?"

He stroked her long blond hair. "No. Knowing your mother, she *would* find a way to come back and keep us hopping. Heaven knows she had enough spirit that it couldn't all have died with her."

Evelyn smiled and kissed his cheek. "I'll write as often as I can. And if I think I have found the answer to the dream, I'll tell you what it is. I'll let you know everything that is happening. For all I know, I'll be back in a year."

Edward's smile was sad. "I have the very distinct feeling you'll *never* come back, except to visit. I hope I am wrong, because you are the light of my life, Evy. I will miss you terribly, but I wouldn't dream of forcing you to quell your passion and your desire to help others or to do what you feel God is calling you to do. I tried doing that with your mother, and I almost lost her." He squeezed her hands. "God be with you, Evy, just as *I* will be, in spirit."

"And I will be with you in the same way. Maybe you will end up coming out there to help."

He shook his head. "I'm getting too old to get involved in that kind of life again. I intend to stay right here and preach as long as they want me."

"They'll want you as long as you're willing to stay. The congregation loves you."

He laughed lightly. "Well, the point is, you can concentrate on whatever it is you have to do in South Dakota without worrying about me."

She kept hold of his hands. "I'm glad." Their eyes held for a moment in love, and in the pain of parting. "I'll wake you up early tomorrow and we can have a nice breakfast together before I leave."

He kissed her forehead. "I would like that." His eyes teared. "God bless you, Evy, and keep you safe."

"He will, Father, because He wants me to do this. I know it in my heart. I will find the cause of these dreams and maybe I can finally get rid of them. I'm tired of waking up in a cold sweat, with the terrible feeling that someone needs my help." She turned away, walking to the clock again. "Maybe I'll find the man on the spotted horse at Standing Rock, and then I'll know what to do."

"Maybe. Just be careful, Evy. The heart and the mind can sometimes play tricks on us, you know; sometimes they can lead us down the wrong pathway."

Evelyn could see the man on the horse so clearly, except for his face. Was it the spirit of Wild Horse who visited her in the night? She was tired of wondering and guessing. The visit from Janine Phillips could not be a better sign of what she must do. "I only know I have to go there, Father, and I'm not afraid. She faced him again. "I'm not afraid."

Two

"You made quite a sacrifice, Miss Gibbons, breaking an engagement and all." The Reverend Greggory Evans and his wife, Beverly, sat in seats that faced Evelyn and Janine Phillips. The Union Pacific coach in which the four of them traveled rattled across the Iowa prairie, much of which was now broken up by plows and planted into crops. It was unbearably hot, and Janine had opened the train window, which helped little. Not only was the air that came through miserably humid, but also filled with smoke and soot from the rumbling black engine ahead of them. Evelyn felt sticky and dirty, but there was nothing to be done about it until they reached a place where there was time to get off and find a bath house.

"I just felt I was meant to do this," she answered Evans, her miserable condition making her wonder now if maybe she *had* made the wrong decision. The fact that there would be few comforts where she was going was becoming more real, but she was not going to give up on what she felt was her calling until she knew the meaning of her dreams. She had not told these people any of this. They would probably think she was insane. "I don't really think I was ready to get married anyway."

"Well, that's good," Janine spoke up with a smile, "because there is a definite shortage of white men where we're going, except for a few soldiers, most of whom are already married or terribly un-Christian and not worth considering." She blushed a little. "There *is* one soldier, Lieutenant Teller, who does seem to be a decent Christian man." She leaned closer to Evelyn. "He comes to church whenever he can, and he's been making sure he manages to sit next to me."

She giggled like a schoolgirl, and Evelyn smiled, wondering if by leaving civilization and Steven she would end up an old maid with no prospects of marriage. Janine was herself already twenty-six years old and just now finding a man who might be interested, but then, marriage had not been something she was interested in till now, Evelyn knew. Her work with her brother, John, had been her most important concern. She was a devoted Christian, and John was the preacher at the small Methodist church on the reservation. He had sent Janine to Wisconsin to give talks at various churches and urge people to give to Mission Services and send donations of clothes and money to the reservation. Janine was a persuasive speaker, and Evelyn surmised her brother must also be very good at what he did. He would be very pleased to find out Janine was bringing two missionaries and a schoolteacher back with her. Now that he would have help, she could give more serious thought to finding a husband.

Janine took a handkerchief from her handbag and pressed it to her forehead. "Oh, it's so hot, and it's only late June. We have the whole summer ahead of us, and the heat in the Dakotas can get quite unbearable at times."

Evelyn noticed the woman always wore dresses with long sleeves and high necklines, in spite of the hot weather. Her plain, round face was unpainted, her light-brown hair pulled into a tight bun at the nape of her neck. Looking at her made Evelyn think about her mother, who all her life had valiantly gone against the rules of what was expected of a preacher's wife, including refusing to dress primly when it was hot. She remembered Margaret letting her swim naked in the cool water of their secret pond back in Oklahoma. Back then such a thing was considered sinful, even for a four-year-old, but her mother had insisted it was not. Sometimes she went into the water with Evelyn, but as far as she could remember, she had never undressed, although Evelyn was sure now she had wished that she could. It had been daring enough of her to take off shoes and stockings and unbutton the bodice of her dress and lift her skirts to go into the pond and splash water on herself.

She would never forget those days of secret pleasure at the pond, or the day Wild Horse was shot down by soldiers when all he was doing was helping her. She had not told these people about her experiences as a little girl in Indian Territory. It seemed too personal, and it still hurt to remember Wild Horse falling, his body riddled with bullet holes. Maybe that was the reason for the dreams. Maybe it was just her own guilty conscience over the fact that if she had not become lost, if Wild Horse had not been so kind as to come looking for her, he would not have run into those soldiers who thought he was stealing her away. Maybe he was coming after her in the dream because it was her fault he had died . . . or maybe her mother was with Wild Horse now, in some beautiful place where they could ride free together. Maybe Wild Horse was just trying to tell her everything was all right.

"Miss Gibbons?" Reverend Evans, a short, stocky man who was already balding in spite of being only thirty-four, was leaning forward as though to get her attention. He waved a hand in front of her face. "Did you hear me?"

"What?" Evelyn realized she had been so lost in thought that she had not been aware the man had asked her a question. She met his gray eyes in embarrassment. "Oh, I'm sorry! I was just thinking."

The man smiled, revealing one missing tooth at the left side of his mouth. "We can see that!" He put two fingers between his neck and the stiff collar of his shirt, stretching his chin to adjust what was apparently an uncomfortably tight shirt neck. Like Janine, he seemed to think a person had to dress a certain way no matter what the weather—shirt and bow tie, vest and suit jacket in his case. His wife was as stiffly dressed as Janine. Both women were very plain and rather colorless, although twenty-eight-year-old Beverly Evans had a natural beauty about her. She and her husband had no children, and Evelyn had not pried. Perhaps the woman had a physical problem . . . or perhaps her marriage had no passion.

That was another thing her mother had taught her, that a marriage should be for more than convenience or having children. She had sometimes felt flutterings of desire for Steven, but she knew deep inside it had not been enough. She could hardly imagine allowing a man to do to her what was required between a man and a wife, had wrestled with the thought of letting Steven do those things to her. She supposed that if she did not feel comfortable with even the *thought* of letting him touch her that way, then she had been right to break off the engagement.

Someday a man will come along who will sweep you off your feet, Evy. You won't give a second thought to wanting to belong to him. Wait for the right man, one who will set your spirit free and awaken a passion in you that is so beautiful . . .

"I was asking about your education," Evans was saying.

Evelyn forced herself to stop daydreaming and pay attention. She wondered if any of her fellow travelers thought less of her for wearing a light cotton dress and only one slip. The dress was yellow, and it had short sleeves and a scoop neckline. A straw hat was perched on her head. She did not wear her hair in a bun. She had simply pulled it back at the sides with combs, and the long tresses hung down her back in a cascade of waves. Right now she wished she *had* put it into a bun, just to get it off her neck. She supposed the others thought the way she was dressed was probably fine, since she was not a missionary or a preacher's wife.

"You got your degree from Ripon?" Evans continued.

"Yes. Ripon is a coeducational, liberal arts college. I attended year-round with a full load of courses so that I could finish sooner. I have degrees in literature and history and social science."

"I wish you had also studied music," Janine spoke up. "There is a piano in my brother's church, but no one knows how to play it." The woman opened a pink paper fan and waved it in front of her face to help cool herself off. Evelyn thought how, if she were alone and near water, she would strip and dive right in. It would feel so wonderful right now.

"My wife plays a little piano, but then we'll be at the Oahe Mission, too far away to help," Evans told Janine.

"I wish I *could* play for you," Beverly told them.

"Well, it's a shame," Janine answered. "We have a piano and no one to play it, and you play, but there is no piano at Oahe."

"Yes. I shall miss being able to play once in awhile. Playing hymns soothes me," Beverly answered.

Evelyn saw a strange longing in the woman's blue eyes, and suspected she was not totally happy. Beverly could be truly beautiful, if she were allowed to let her dark hair down, put a little color on her eyes and cheeks, wear prettier clothes. The few words she had just uttered were almost the only ones the quiet, shy woman had spoken since they boarded the train, and it struck Evelyn that Beverly Evans never smiled. Right now the woman was studying her intently.

"A pretty young woman like you, educated and all, it seems you would want to stay in more civilized places, Miss Gibbons," she said then, a kind of longing in the words.

"I suppose I could take the easy way," Evelyn answered. "But my parents never did, and I guess I take after them. They worked among Indians when I was small, and I never forgot some of those experiences." How could she explain about the dream, or about what had happened to Wild Horse? "God speaks to us in many ways," she added. "When Janine came to our church to talk about the situation at Standing Rock and how badly teachers were needed, I just knew I had to go. The fact remains that all of us can leave whenever we want, but the Indians can never leave. They have been forced into that life and told they must stay on that land. I feel sorry for them. The way they live now goes entirely against what is in their hearts, against their basic beliefs and needs. I think I understand them sufficiently so that I can be of assistance to them. Maybe by teaching, I can find a way to help them adjust to this new life." She took a handkerchief from her handbag and dabbed at the perspiration beading her face. "I have studied the Sioux and Cheyenne tongue. I learned some Cheyenne while living among them in Oklahoma. There aren't many books on Indian languages, but I managed to find a source on Sioux through a university in New York City. Once I get to the reservation, I intend to learn more."

"Oh, that isn't necessary, Miss Gibbons," Evans replied. "The government has mandated that we teach only English, you know. They don't want the Sioux using their own language. The objective is to erase all the old ways and get on with the new."

Evelyn felt her temper begin to rise. "I am afraid I disagree with that, Reverend. The way to reach the Indian is to first understand everything about them, their beliefs, religion, way of life. For years my parents practiced that very thing. We must respect their ways, honor their beliefs, learn their language so that we can communicate more easily. When we do those things, they begin to trust us more, and through that trust, they will listen to what we have to tell them. We cannot order them to begin living like white men overnight. It just doesn't work." She could see the irritation in Evans's eyes.

"Well, we certainly differ there, Miss Gibbons." He looked her over, for the first time showing disapproval of her appearance. "You have a lot to learn, but you'll manage. I would suggest, however, that you keep that pretty blond hair twisted up on your head and covered with a bonnet, and that you wear clothes that cover your arms and neck. I don't mean any disrespect, but there is no telling how the Indian men will react to seeing such a pretty, unmarried white woman with light hair."

Evelyn felt her cheeks flushing with even more anger. She suspected the deliberately embarrassing remark was made only because she had challenged the man. "I spent most of my growing-up years among the Cheyenne, Reverend. The men were most respectful of me and my mother. She was a lovely woman, with light hair like mine. The Cheyenne men and women both respected her because she genuinely cared about them. She learned their ways and then taught them that their own beliefs were very similar to our own Christianity." She took a deep breath for self-control. "At any rate, I have no fear of the Sioux men. They are no different from white men, and in some cases I would feel safer among Indians than among whites."

The man's eyebrows arched in surprise, and she could tell he thought she was quite a foolish woman. "Well, Miss Gibbons, I would still advise you to be cautious. As far as teaching in the Sioux language, it will do no good in advancing the Indians' education and helping them assimilate if they don't learn English."

"They also can't learn anything if they don't understand a word I am saying. I will teach them English, Reverend Evans, but I will also speak to them often in their own language, just to keep them at ease and make sure they are understanding the things I am teaching them."

Evans could see she was not a woman who often lost an argument. "Do what you wish. You are certainly qualified, but I would be careful, lest Mission Services looks upon you with disfavor. Don't forget the government will be paying you only through their approval. And that was acquired because of your education and because your father is a well-respected man, his own work among the Cheyenne most impressive. However, your personal conduct and your teaching methods will be watched."

"They will have to trust my judgment in how to teach them,"

Evelyn answered, struggling to keep her composure. She noticed Beverly looking at her lap, as if embarrassed by her husband's rudeness.

"Well, heaven knows it doesn't do any good to try to get the Sioux adults to send their children off to outside boarding schools," Janine put in. "Most of them refuse, afraid they will never see the children again, and they have good reason. So many of the little ones who are sent away die from white man's diseases, some, plain and simply, from broken hearts. Most go only because they feel they must, to appease the Great Father in Washington; and when the survivors return home, they go right back to their old ways. The ones who try to live like whites are shunned by most of the old ones as traitors. It's very hard for them." She fanned herself almost frantically. "I agree with Evelyn. If we can teach them on the reservation, get through to them by whatever means necessary, we will make a lot more headway than by ripping little children out of their mothers' arms and forcing them to turn away from their heritage. We lose the trust of the parents, and the children end up terribly confused and coming home as outcasts. Too many turn to whiskey as solace, and nothing gets accomplished."

Evelyn was glad for the words. Perhaps at least in Janine and her brother, John, she would have some support and cooperation. Janine had already told her that a little log building had been constructed near the church to use as a schoolhouse, so she would be close to people who understood what she was trying to do.

"There is one Indian you'll probably never reach," Janine added. "My brother has tried for nearly two years now, but he's afraid to stir the man's anger too much."

Evelyn again pressed the hanky to her damp neck. There would be an overnight layover in Omaha, and she hoped she could find a hotel where she could bathe. "Who is that?" she asked.

Janine stopped her fanning and just stared at the pink paper thoughtfully. "His name is Black Hawk. He was a good friend of Crazy Horse, and he is very stubborn and belligerent. He lives the old way, in a tipi, deep in a canyon on the northwest end of the reservation with his seven-year-old son, Little Fox. He refuses to bring the boy in to listen to any teaching of any kind from any white man, and most of the time he refuses to take government rations. He lives off the land as best he can, using bow and arrow. He isn't allowed to have a rifle because the agency and soldiers don't trust him with one."

"Can't they *force* him to bring the boy to school?" Evans asked.

"Everyone is afraid it will start some kind of trouble that will mushroom into something they can't handle. Better to lose one child than risk people's lives by stirring up trouble. The rest of them look to Black Hawk as a kind of hero, someone who still lives the way of the warrior. Knowing someone is still living that way seems to appease the rest of them. The only one who can go out and talk to him and always knows how to find him is his sister, Many Birds. She and Black Hawk's mother live on the reservation. Sometimes Many Birds takes food to Black Hawk that she got from government rations, and once in awhile he comes in to the agency for supplies; but other than that, the most any of us see of him is from a distance, when he rides the outskirts of the reservation like some kind of ghost, he and that spotted horse of his painted up as though for battle."

Evelyn's heart tightened. "Spotted horse?"

"Yes. He rides a gray-and-white Appaloosa. Most of the white is in spots on its rump and chest."

Evelyn quickly looked down at her lap, not wanting them to see the shock in her eyes. The man in her dream rode a gray-and-white spotted horse. A shiver moved through her at the irony of how accurately Janine's description fit her vision.

She was more sure than ever now that she was doing the right thing. She would miss her father, who was the only family she had left. There were no brothers and sisters, and other relatives lived back in Massachusetts. She would miss Waupun, her friends there, Steven; but this was where she belonged for now. Perhaps her mother was guiding her to the Dakotas . . . maybe even to this man called Black Hawk.

Evelyn grabbed hold of the bale of hay on which she sat, finding it difficult to keep her balance. She had hoped her trip to the reservation could be made in a buggy, but there were not enough funds in Mission Services for anything fancy. The wagon in which she rode with Janine was nothing more than an old buckboard, owned and driven by an ageing Sioux Indian man called Two Trees. He was accompanied by his daughter, Dancing Eagle, who had taken the white name of Maggie.

"Maggie attended the Genoa Indian School with Anita Wolf, the young woman who will be your teaching assistant," Janine had explained in introductions. "Some of Maggie's own people shun her because of her white man's education, so she and Dancing Eagle live near the church and help with chores and such."

Evelyn already liked Maggie. Nineteen, quiet, and friendly, she was a chubby young woman who seemed round all over, her body, her face, her puffy hands. She had seemed impressed at learning that Evelyn had a respectable knowledge of the Lakota language, especially the Hunkpapa dialect, the band to which Maggie belonged. Evelyn could already see that even though the woman had accepted the fact that she must learn a new way, there was still a deep pride in her soul at being Sioux. It was too bad the others could not see that learning the new ways did not mean they had to completely give up the old.

Because of the continued heat, Evelyn had been forced to pin her hair into a bun today, although pieces of it kept falling against her damp face. A light breeze helped cool her, but it came from the south, forcing dust stirred up by the wagon wheels right back onto them. The country through which they rode seemed so barren, but Janine had promised that there were more hills and grassland and trees where they were headed. The Little Eagle Station on the Grand River, the center of the Standing Rock Reservation, would be home for some time to come. They had left Beverly and Greggory Evans at the Oahe Mission on the Missouri River, a desolate, treeless place where the heat seemed worse because of the barren landscape. Still, it was at least near the river, and a chapel and school had already been built there by missionary Thomas Riggs fifteen years earlier. Riggs was the son of Stephen Riggs, a missionary from Ohio who had come to the Dakotas back in 1835 to minister to the Indians.

Evelyn could not help feeling sorry for Beverly, who did not seem at all happy with having to follow her husband here; but she was at the same time glad that Evans would not be coming to the Little Eagle Station. He was a pompous man who liked to think he was always right. She had a feeling she would have enough trouble with Indian Agent James McLaughlin, whom she knew from things she had read and heard, ran the Standing Rock Agency with a firm hand. Maggie had said that McLaughlin would not want her teaching in the Sioux tongue. Then she had covered her mouth and giggled, her dark eyes dancing, and said he didn't need to know that.

Already Evelyn could see many challenges facing her, from the way she preferred to teach, to finding the answer to her visionary dreams . . . to learning more about the elusive and mysterious Black Hawk. There was the additional challenge of growing accustomed to this new life, with its lack of modern conveniences. This South Dakota reservation appeared even more desolate and lacking in modern conveniences than even Oklahoma had been. It was obvious the government had done little to provide decent housing here, and there was no plumbing or electricity, just as Janine had warned. Their only connection to the outside world would be by telegraph and mail delivery, which was done through pickup by steamboats along the Missouri River.

The wagon jolted her again, and she brushed at dust and hay that scattered across her lap. She noticed a sagging, two-story frame house just ahead, its grounds obviously sorely neglected. The wood siding on the house was dark and weathered, some of it bowed from drying out in the sun. As they came closer, she noticed a skinny young white girl hacking at the front lawn with a scythe to try to cut down some of the grass, which grew nearly as high as she was tall. The girl wore a plain brown dress that was too big for her, and even from the distance Evelyn could tell she was sweating profusely from her hard work in the hot sun. Her long dark hair was pasted to her head, and she kept wiping her face with the hem of her dress.

When they drew closer, the girl stopped working and watched them, a forlorn, pitiful aura about her that Evelyn could feel even from a distance. A white man with gray hair wearing only coveralls and no shirt came out the front door then. He stared at them for a moment. It seemed to Evelyn that the proper thing to do would be to nod and wave to him, but she noticed Janine and Maggie looked straight ahead and did not even acknowledge him. He turned and yelled something to the young girl, and she wielded the scythe with even more energy, as though afraid the man might think she was not working hard enough.

"Who is that man?" she asked Janine.

The woman removed her spectacles and dabbed at the perspiration around her eyes. "Seth Bridges. He is a most reprehensible person, who I don't think should be allowed to live here. He farms government land and is permitted to stay because he sells his produce to the agency and to the Army at Fort Yates. John and I personally suspect he deals with whiskey traders who manage to sneak onto the reservation, but no one can prove it. God forgive me, but I cannot bear to be near the man. He is filthy, seldom shaves, and he has a foul mouth. He took in two orphan girls sent out from the East. Word is he gave the orphanage a story about his own wife being ill and needing help, but his wife ran off on him years ago, taking two children with her. I fear the man abuses his adopted daughters, at least the older one. We hardly ever see the girls except when he brings them to the agency to shop for supplies. Even then, they are quiet and overly reticent. We have tried a time or two to go to the house and see what their situation is, try to get him to let the girls have some schooling, but he threatens us with a shotgun and orders us to mind our own business."

"Dear Lord!" Evelyn looked back at the house, noticing the young girl had stopped working for a moment to watch them. "How old are his daughters?"

"I'm not sure. The oldest, Lucille, looks to be about sixteen. The younger one is eleven or twelve, I'm told, although she's built so small she seems younger. Her name is Katy. That's about all we know about them, except that we are sure they are sisters by blood. It is a sad situation."

The wagon rattled up a hill and down the other side so that Evelyn could no longer see the sorry-looking house and farm. She had come here to teach Indians, but she already knew that the memory of how the young white girl looked at her would haunt her. She decided that she would try to see the girls and talk some sense into Mr. Seth Bridges, whether he liked it or not.

Three

The old wagon in which Evelyn rode rolled into agency head-quarters on the northern section of the Standing Rock Reservation, dust billowing from under its rickety wheels.

"We are not far from North Dakota now," Janine explained. "Fort Yates is only about thirty miles farther north on the Missouri River, a good day's ride. Several soldiers are stationed right here at the agency to help keep order. The commanding officer is Colonel Alfred Gere, and he is often here. Second in command is Lieutenant Teller, the man I told you about." She blushed at the mere mention of the man's name. "Gere is quite stern and unbending, but Lieutenant Teller seems to have a little more compassion for the Indians."

"You like him very much, don't you?"

Janine smiled. "I think he is quite handsome. You will get to meet him the next time he comes to services, unless we happen to see him today." She sighed. "I don't know for certain if he feels anything special for me, but I know my own heart flutters something awful whenever he is near. I am hoping he asks me to the annual dance at the fort in August. Pretty as you are, I am sure there are any number of men here who would like to ask you, but as I said, a lot of them are not worth getting to know. John says that men who join the western army often are just criminals fleeing something back East. A lot of them are foreigners who join up just to see America and make a little money."

Evelyn retied her slat bonnet, already realizing how important it would be to always wear something on her head with a wide brim in front to protect her face from the sun. The contrast of this land to Wisconsin was almost overwhelming. She supposed it was no wonder the Sioux were not happy with what had been left to them—a flat, treeless, barren land they were expected to farm. It was miserably hot in summer, and, according to Janine, bitterly cold in winter, with nothing to break the howling winds and blowing snows. In Wisconsin, hills and trees and lakes helped keep things a little warmer in winter and cooler in summer. Already she missed the green of home, the big trees, but she refused to let the desolation here discourage her. She had promised the mission to come here and teach for at least a year, and she would keep that promise, but Janine's talk about Lieutenant Teller made her miss Steven.

Still, it was not enough to make her go back. Besides, she already felt a deep compassion for the once-proud Indians who lived here. Many of them just hung around the agency begging, or sitting quietly, doing nothing, for they literally had nothing *to* do now that their freedom was gone. Here and there naked children played, smelly chickens pecked at sparse feed, and dogs ran everywhere. In the distance a few soldiers drilled, and several of the uniformed men who were stationed at the agency stopped to stare and point or smile. Evelyn was embarrassed at how they gawked at her. She could hear the words "new teacher" and "too pretty for these parts." A couple of men just let out soft whistles, and she pulled her slat bonnet lower down over her face, irritated by their rude stares.

When first arriving at Standing Rock, they had stopped at the Little Eagle Station on the Grand River to see the one-room cabin she would share with Janine until another cabin was built for her private use. Reverend John Phillips lived nearby in a small room behind an equally small, white frame church. He had not been there when they first arrived, and they had been told he had gone to the agency to complain to Agent McLaughlin, as he had done several times before, about the free flow of whiskey on the reservation. White whiskey traders remained a continuing problem that the soldiers could not seem to stop.

After a day of rest and a bath at the cabin, Evelyn felt somewhat refreshed, although the weather was still dreadfully hot. She was self-conscious about her dusty appearance, which made her even more nervous about meeting both John Phillips and Agent McLaughlin, who she had heard ruled the reservation with an iron hand, although word had it he did try to be fair with the Sioux. Janine had told her she felt it was McLaughlin's fault that Sitting Bull was blamed for bringing the Ghost Dance religion to the Sioux, a religion that had stirred the Indians into dancing and wild chanting and singing. That in turn had frightened surrounding settlers and soldiers alike. Blaming Sitting Bull had led to an order for the man's arrest, which ended in the murder of both the great Indian leader and his seventeen-year-old son, Louis. The death of their once-great leader frightened the rest of the Sioux at Standing Rock and had ultimately led to the Wounded Knee Massacre in December 1890, where many innocent women and children and old people had died.

"Where is Sitting Bull buried?" Evelyn asked.

A look of disgust came over Janine's face. "Way in a back corner at Fort Yates, with just a little wooden cross marking the place. The day he was killed, several Indian police also died. Some of their relatives beat Sitting Bull's dead body so badly that his face was no longer even recognizable. That is another way the white man has of keeping the Indians weak: He knows how to divide their loyalties and keep them arguing among themselves." She sighed. "Sitting Bull was taken to the fort and buried in a pine box, and Agent McLaughlin showed no remorse whatsoever. He felt Sitting Bull's death was the best thing that could have happened to break the back of the Sioux and their old ways. It's his fault Sitting Bull got blamed for inciting his people to join the Ghost Dance religion in an effort to regain his leadership. In truth, Sitting Bull had nothing to do with the new religion. He even denounced it as being bad for his people, but McLaughlin continued to insist he was behind it all."

Evelyn was still weary from their nearly three-week trip by wagon from Fort Kearny north into the Dakotas, from the nights spent sleeping on the ground or in the wagon. She would begin teaching soon, but first there were many people for her to meet, including the Sioux woman, Anita Wolf, who would be her assistant.

"Actually, the Ghost Dance religion was a joyous faith that taught the Sioux *not* to make war," Janine continued. "They only danced and sang because they thought their dead relatives were going to come back to life and the land would become as it used to be—full of buffalo, unplowed, covered with sweet grass. That, of course, never happened. Others thought the Indians were preparing for war, and McLaughlin tried to get General Miles to arrest Sitting Bull, but Miles refused, saying it was a matter for civilians. Miles talked Buffalo Bill Cody into going for Sitting Bull, but I have a feeling Cody didn't know he was being used by the government to capture the man. You know, of course, that Sitting Bull was part of Buffalo Bill's Wild West shows for a couple of years. They were good friends. At any rate, when James McLaughlin discovered the plan, he was furious that Miles had refused to have the Army do it. He sent Indian police to intercept Cody, and Cody left without ever even seeing Sitting Bull. McLaughlin finally had Indian police arrest Sitting Bull. Feeling betrayed by his own people, Sitting Bull put up a fuss. One thing led to another. There was a scuffle. I suppose no one will know for sure how it all took place, but by the time it was over, six Indian police were dead, Sitting Bull and eight of his followers also dead." The woman shook her head. "It was all such a waste."

More dust rolled as Janine drove the clattering mission buckboard around several buildings. Besides an old white mare that

Janine said Reverend Phillips rode, the rickety wagon and the two aging red mares that pulled it were their only means of transportation about the reservation.

Evelyn was lost in thought, picturing the horror the Sioux must have felt the day Sitting Bull was shot down, remembering Wild Horse and his own awful death. How ironic that such a renowned, once-feared Indian leader like Sitting Bull should die so shamefully. "Why would Agent McLaughlin be so against Sitting Bull? Isn't his own wife half Indian?"

Janine brushed dust from her dress. "I feel Mary McLaughlin contributed to the feud. As with most half-bloods, she is a woman torn between two worlds. She has tried to fit in with the officers' wives here at the fort, but they are not friendly to her. She is always striving to be respected and rid herself of the title some people have given McLaughlin: "squaw man." She has little use for her Indian blood. She hated Sitting Bull since the year she could have gone with him on a world tour with Buffalo Bill to act as an interpreter and Sitting Bull changed his mind and refused to go. She felt he had cheated her out of the chance to do something that would have given her a little more status—traveling to several countries with the Wild West show."

Janine smiled then, meeting Evelyn's eyes. "I think Sitting Bull's own personality was also part of the trouble. In spite of his years of working among the Sioux, McLaughlin still does not seem to understand their sense of humor. That is very important, Evelyn. They love to joke with you and pull tricks on you."

Evelyn pushed a strand of blond hair back up under her hat. "I remember a Cheyenne Indian man I knew back in Oklahoma when I was very small. He had a wonderful sense of humor. I am familiar with that part of the Indian personality. But how did that make trouble between Sitting Bull and McLaughlin?"

Janine headed the wagon to a large house at the center of the reservation. "McLaughlin wanted Sitting Bull to give up one of his two wives. He feels that having multiple wives is sinful and only contributes to the Sioux continuing to practice old ways. Sitting Bull said that was fine. He would give up one wife, but he asked McLaughlin which one it should be. He wanted to know who would be father then, to the children of that wife." She laughed lightly. "I am sure you can see the predicament it would pose for any man with two wives to have to choose which one to give up."

Evelyn joined in the laughter. "What did he do?"

"He told McLaughlin it was impossible to decide. He said he'd make it equal and give them *both* up if McLaughlin would find him a *white* wife. Anyone who understands the Sioux knows it was just a joke, but McLaughlin didn't like being made a fool of, and he was convinced Sitting Bull meant it. That only cemented in his own mind the fact that Sitting Bull was nothing more than a dirty-minded old savage, which was not true at all."

Janine pointed out a few other buildings—quarters for the Army men present, a trading post. The agency was much bigger than Evelyn had imagined. "Mr. McLaughlin lives in this big house where we're headed, which also serves as agency head-quarters. John is probably around there somewhere. He must have decided to stay a day or two to spend time with the Indians here and try to talk them into school or church, find out if any of them have health problems that need tending. We need a doc-tor here for the Indians. The only one around is the Army phy-sician, but he's thirty miles away."

Again, Evelyn could see the government was providing only the bare necessities to the Sioux, but her thoughts were disturbed when a uniformed man rode up to the wagon, tipping his hat to Janine. "Good afternoon, Miss Phillips. Good to see you back from your trip. Who is your lady friend?"

Janine halted the wagon. "Hello, Sergeant Desmond. This is Miss Evelyn Gibbons, from Wisconsin. She has come here to teach at Little Eagle Station. Evelyn, this is Sergeant Jubal Desmond."

Evelyn met the man's pale-blue eyes, seeing a cockiness there she did not like. His hair was light brown, and his skin was burned dark and ruddy from many hours in the sun. He had a slender but strong-looking build, and she supposed he could be thought of as handsome if he did not put forth such an arrogant attitude. "How do you do, Lieutenant," she spoke up.

Desmond remained on his horse, but he removed his hat and bowed slightly. "I do just fine, ma'am, as long as I can look at something pretty as you. You watch out for those Indian bucks. If any of them gets any fancy ideas, you just come running. Jubal Desmond is at your service."

"I will remember that, Sergeant." Evelyn struggled to keep her dislike of the man from showing.

Desmond grinned. "We keep the Sioux pretty much in line now. Since Wounded Knee, they don't bother putting up much of a fuss anymore, but you never can totally trust them. You remember that. So far the older ones aren't too cooperative in letting their little skunks go get taught by whites, so you'll have a time getting the wild little savages to school."

Evelyn found it incredulous that in so few words this man could make himself look the ignorant, prejudiced fool that he was. It was also clear by the look in his eyes what he was thinking about her.

"I will do my best, Sergeant."

"Well, they aren't too smart to begin with. You'll have your hands full. Pardon me, but you look more like a lady who belongs in a city back East, being wooed by some fancy lawyer. You sure don't fit the picture of a schoolmarm come to work in a place like this with hopeless people like the Sioux."

Evelyn wondered if the man realized he had just insulted poor Janine, as though she was plain and unattractive enough to fit in just fine here. The temper she always had trouble controlling battled to be released. "And you don't speak with the intelligence I would expect from an officer, sir," she replied.

The remark wiped the smile off the man's face, and Janine put a hand over her mouth to hide her own grin.

Desmond tipped his hat again, a hint of anger coming into his eyes. "Sorry if I somehow insulted you, ma'am. You just do like I said and watch yourself, and remember where you can come if you have any problems."

The man turned his horse and rode off, and Janine laughed lightly. "What a wonderful answer you gave him, Evelyn! It is exactly what I would have wanted to say, but I don't have the courage to speak up like that."

"The man is an arrogant, prejudiced buffoon who has no business being out here around the Indians!"

Janine got the wagon rolling again, heading toward agency headquarters. "You're going to be so good for the Sioux," she commented. "I am already sure of it. I'm so glad you decided to do this, Evelyn." The wagon neared the large frame building when she suddenly drew in her breath and waved. "John!"

Evelyn watched a man approach them as Janine halted the wagon. He reached up to lift her to the ground. "I was just about to head back to Little Eagle Station," he said. "I wasn't sure when you'd finally return—" He looked up at Evelyn, and the pleasure in his dark eyes was unmistakable.

Evelyn knew this had to be Janine's brother, Reverend John Phillips. He was an average-looking man and stood only a few inches taller than Janine, who was not herself a tall woman. There was nothing ugly about him, but also nothing that could be called handsome, although his eyes sparkled with kindness. He sported a neatly trimmed mustache but was otherwise clean-shaven, and he wore a black, double-breasted serge suit jacket that looked well worn, as did his dark gray flannel trousers. She admired and respected both Janine and her brother for their willingness to give up the comforts of life and the chance at having more money and better clothing if Phillips preached in a church in some city back East. There was not a lot of money to be made in mission work. Most things they needed were provided through donations, and most money went into building and buying supplies for the church and to help supplement government rations of food and clothing to the Indians, which was never enough. The man came closer to help her down, and she noticed his shirt collar was frayed.

"Well! You must be our new schoolteacher."

Evelyn allowed the man to take her hand as she climbed down from the wagon. "I am Evelyn Gibbons, from Waupun, Wisconsin. I was teaching there when Janine came to speak at my father's church."

"Gibbons. Reverend *Edward* Gibbons? I've met him. It's been a few years, but I remember him."

"And you are apparently John Phillips."

"Oh, forgive me! I didn't even introduce myself!" John looked Evelyn over again, surprised and pleased at what he saw. When he had gotten the wire from his sister that she was bringing a teacher back with her, a single woman, he had envisioned a plump, plain spinster woman . . . not the slender young beauty who stood before him in a soft green checked gingham dress, its high collar and puffed shoulders trimmed with bands of lace. "And what brings a young, educated woman like yourself out to this desolate place?" he asked with a smile. He finally let go of her hand.

Evelyn knew the man was thinking the same thing most men thought seeing her out here. She had felt the stares of other soldiers as they had driven through fort grounds, and Jubal Desmond's hints at the fact that she would have to protect her person just because she was young and pretty and single still irked her. In the case of John Phillips, she did not feel offended. She knew he was a good man, and his eyes did not show disrespect. She felt comfortable around him already.

"I'm not even sure myself yet what I'm doing here, Reverend," she answered. "I just felt a calling. My parents both worked among Indians in Oklahoma when I was young, so being around them is not completely foreign to me. I fully understand the needs here, and the problems."

"Well, you do have your work cut out for you," Phillips was saying. "Have you met Anita Wolf yet?"

"We've only been here for a couple of days, John," Janine answered for Evelyn. "We spent most of that time resting and getting ourselves clean. I haven't shown Evelyn much of anything yet. When I found out you were here, I decided I would show Evelyn where agency headquarters are, perhaps introduce her to Mr. McLaughlin. Is he here?"

John scowled. "He's here. As always, he promised to do something about the whiskey smuggling, but with such a big area to cover, I don't expect a lot of progress. Too many of the Sioux are eager to get their hands on the firewater. They'll find a way to get it, and the whiskey dealers will oblige them. They don't care what the stuff does to the people who consume it, and they don't care that the Indians spend their government rations for watered-down slop." The man sighed, looking back at Evelyn. "Some of these men would starve before they'd go without their whiskey." He turned to tie the horses. "It's getting worse all the time, and part of the reason is that their spirits are so broken, they see no future for themselves. They drink themselves into oblivion just to ease the pain in their souls. It's a never-ending battle, Miss Gibbons," he said, taking her elbow. "We might as well go and meet McLaughlin so we can head back."

"One thing in addition to the Indian situation concerns me, Reverend," Evelyn told him before going inside. "We passed a farm home when first coming to the church a couple of days ago. Janine said it was owned by a Seth Bridges. He has two adopted girls, and the one I saw looks poorly cared for. Janine says the man won't even send the girls to school. He seems to use them like little slaves. I can't help worrying just how abused they really are. Isn't there something we can do?"

Phillips sighed. "They are private citizens farming government land and under no agency or mission jurisdiction. Bridges supplies food to the agency and the fort. I agree it's a sad situation, and I've tried to talk to the man, but he's mean and crusty, threatened me with a shotgun more than once. I feel all I can do at this point is pray for him and those poor girls. We suspect him of being involved in whiskey smuggling but haven't been able to prove it."

Evelyn had already made a secret vow that she would try to get through to Bridges. There had to be a way to help those girls. She could not get the picture out of her mind of the younger one watching her with those big, sad eyes.

As they stepped up onto the porch of agency headquarters, Phillips opened the door for them. A soldier sitting at a desk looked up, his eyes lighting up at the sight of Evelyn. He glanced at John. "Back again, Reverend?"

"This is Evelyn Gibbons. I'd like to introduce her to Jim McLaughlin. She'll be teaching over at Little Eagle."

The soldier nodded and rose, walking to another door and opening it. Somewhere in the back of the house Evelyn could hear a woman talking and children playing. She walked inside McLaughlin's office, where she saw a large man with white hair and a white mustache sitting behind a desk. "Reverend's back, Mr. McLaughlin," the soldier said. "He's got his sister, Janine, with him, and a newcomer, Miss . . . what was that again?" The man turned to Evelyn, who stepped forward, holding her chin proudly and facing McLaughlin squarely. McLaughlin had a domineering look about him, and Evelyn made up her mind right away that she would make sure he knew he could not intimidate her.

"Miss Evelyn Gibbons," she said, reaching across the desk and offering her hand. "My Father is Reverend Edward Gibbons.

He taught and preached for some years on Indian reservations down in Oklahoma. Perhaps you have heard of him?" She put on her sweetest smile, declining to appear to be someone who would fully cooperate with whatever the rules were on the reservation. Deep inside, though, she had no intention of doing any such thing.

"Well, Miss Gibbons, how very nice to meet you." McLaughlin took her hand and shook it lightly. "I believe I have heard of your father, but I've never met him. Where do you hail from?"

"My parents moved to Wisconsin when I was twelve. I attended Ripon College and have a degree in teaching." She explained what had led up to her decision to come to Standing Rock. "I have agreed to teach for one year."

"Well, that was quite a courageous decision, considering the things you must have had to give up. What do your parents think of it?"

"My mother died about six months ago. My father, of course, understands about mission work, although I am not working for the Mission Association. I am being paid through them by a special grant from the government."

"Well, I am sure that Reverend Phillips and his sister can fill you in on the situation. They have worked here for about three years now. You'll find you have your work cut out for you."

Evelyn was getting tired of hearing that remark. Just about everyone she had met so far had said the same thing, and the challenge they all alluded to was beginning to make her anxious to get started.

"I am ready to do what needs to be done," she answered. "I do have some experience already from working with my parents."

The man nodded. "You'll need it. Of course, things have been more peaceful around here since Sitting Bull left this world, but there is still a problem getting most of the adults to cooperate and allow their children to be taught. Since the majority of them won't hear of sending their children off the reservation, we have decided to set up some schooling right here, in hopes we can reach them that way. There are about six thousand Sioux here, Miss Gibbons, many of them still restless and hostile. I have a bit of a reputation for being quite stern, but it's necessary, and I do call many of them 'friend.' I try to be fair about everything. As I said, with Sitting Bull gone, things have been better, but we still have one stubborn fellow out there who keeps things stirred up. He's called Black Hawk. So far I have decided to let him be. We don't need any more disasters like Wounded Knee around here for a while. As long as Black Hawk stays out in the hills and canyons and leaves things alone, I'll let it slide."

"Yes, Janine told me about Black Hawk," Evelyn answered. "I am going to make it one of my goals to get the man's little boy into the reservation school."

McLaughlin looked at her as though she had lost her mind. "I don't think you realize what a project that would be, Miss Gibbons. You leave Black Hawk to me. Don't do anything foolish."

"Well, I can at least talk to his sister, Many Birds. I am told she lives on the reservation."

"Yes, with an old grandmother, Dancing Woman. If you can reach the sister, there is a remote possibility you can reach Black Hawk, but it isn't likely."

If this Black Hawk won't come to me, then I will go to him, Evelyn thought. She decided it was best for the moment not to voice the words. None of them understood that she had more reason to meet this Black Hawk than just trying to teach his son, nor had she ever liked being told that anything was impossible. "We shall see, Mr. McLaughlin. We shall see."

Conversation turned to other problems on the reservation, but Evelyn's thoughts kept turning to the elusive Black Hawk. Some of her weariness left her as an eagerness to get started began to grow in her soul. In spite of the hardships and deprivations she would face here, she knew in her heart she was doing the right thing. The more she heard that she had her work cut out for her and that some things would be impossible, the more determined she was to prove them all wrong. Already she knew the key to reaching most of the stubborn Sioux who clung to the old ways and refused schooling. That key was Black Hawk. If she could reach him, the others would follow. And eventually, somehow, she would also find a way to help those poor young girls living with Seth Bridges.

Four

The call was similar to a howling, yipping coyote. Evelyn could hear it in the distant hills, could see the rider on his spotted horse. She walked out to greet him as he came closer. He was a big man, his long black hair flying in the wind, his horse's hooves making a thundering sound as they beat the ground. She could see the muscles of the magnificent, broad-chested Appaloosa flexing as it charged, nostrils flaring, mane dancing. Its rider was handsome, his bare chest and arms well muscled, his dark eyes flashing with pride . . . and something else . . . something else. What was it? His eyes drilled into hers in a way that left her feeling almost hypnotized as he reached out to her. She knew she must go with him, but where? And what was that look in his eyes? Love?

She reached toward him, and just as she was sure he would take hold of her hand, he vanished. She gasped and nearly fell, and in her sleep the dream made her jump so violently that it woke her. She sat up, panting, drenched in sweat. The room was dark. The oil lamp she had lit had burned out.

Hot, so hot! And the dream was so real! She almost expected to see a wild Indian man standing at the foot of her bed. She took several deep breaths to gather her thoughts, stood up to walk around so that she could convince herself everything was all right. It was only a dream, but it was the same dream that had plagued her for weeks now. She unbuttoned the top of her flannel gown, grasped hold of the garment and fanned it back and forth to cool herself. These first few days had been ones of oppressive heat, and the nights brought little relief.

She stopped and sat still when a distant sound sent chills through her blood. It was as though part of the dream had returned, only now she was awake. She heard the same cry she had heard in the dream, like a coyote out in the hills, and she realized that real sound had crept into her dream and awakened her. She hurried to the door and opened it, stepping out onto the little porch of the small, one-room cabin she shared with Janine, who lay fast asleep. A bright moon lit the wide, lonely landscape.

She listened again, realizing it was a man making the sound. Whoever it was, he was too far away for her to see. Only an Indian would make such cries. Finally, she saw a figure silhouetted on a horse against the moonlight. He rode back and forth on a distant hill at the outskirts of the agency, yipping like a warrior in the same way she had heard in her dream. He carried on that way for perhaps ten more minutes before disappearing over the hill. The air hung so silent then that it almost hurt her ears. She turned and went back inside, wished she could ask Janine about what she had heard, but when she went to stand beside the woman's bed, her breathing was deep and rhythmic.

Evelyn sighed and turned away, deciding to take advantage of the fact that Janine still slept and remove her flannel gown to cool herself. She slipped it over her head and threw it on the bed, able to see a little better now that her eyes were adjusted to the dim moonlight that came through the two front windows.

She grasped her hair and twisted it up off her neck, walking quietly on bare feet over the wooden floor to a rocker, wearing only her drawers. She sat down, still keeping her hair up as she leaned her head against the back of the rocker. It felt good to sit with nothing on. It reminded her of the times her mother took her to that pond down in Oklahoma and let her swim naked. She thought how she would like to do that right now, if there were anyplace to swim. Her thoughts wandered as she closed her eyes and rocked, and she envisioned the cool water caressing her skin. She wondered what it would be like if a man came along and found her that way. No man had ever looked upon her naked body, but for the last couple of years she had wondered what that might be like.

In her fantasy, she imagined a man coming to the pond. Not Steven . . . just a faceless man, but nicely built. He gazed upon her nakedness as she emerged from the water, and he was also naked. The thought was both frightening and thrilling. She came closer, and he wrapped strong arms around her, pressing her breasts against his chest. He told her that he loved her and that he wanted to make love to her. She looked up into his face. Now it took form. Wild Horse!

She opened her eyes, disgusted with herself for such ridicu-lous and probably sinful fantasizing. She had only been a little girl when she knew Wild Horse. He had been her good friend, had saved her life once. Now he was dead. Not only was it sinful to think of him that way, but to even imagine letting any Indian man look upon her naked body and make love to her. She could not fathom what had gotten into her lately, thinking about men and making love. Just yesterday, when she had taken a bath alone, she had explored her body, touched her breasts, wondered what a man would think of it, how he would touch it. What it was like to open herself to a man and allow him to invade her? It would take tremendous trust and love and desire to permit such a thing. Although she had trusted Steven, she had not felt that love and desire, not enough to let him ravage her body for his own pleasure.

She got up, disgusted with her thoughts. There would be no man in her life for a while, certainly not out here. She supposed any man at Fort Yates would certainly like his chance at courting her, but she was not interested. Sergeant Desmond was totally unlikable. Janine's brother John was most certainly attracted to her. She could already see it just from working with him these last few days. He was a good man, pleasant-looking, but she felt nothing for him, except respect and friendship.

She put her gown back on, anxious to move into the cabin that was being built for her by soldiers and a few of the reservation Indians. She enjoyed Janine's company and friendship, but she preferred the freedom of having her own place and being able to do things like strip off her gown without worrying about someone seeing her. Her own cabin would be near the little one-room school, which up to now had been empty for quite some time. She was going to change that. Tomorrow she and Janine were going to get to the task of encouraging children to come to school. Janine would take her to meet many of the families at the Little Eagle Station, and she would do her best to convince the elders to allow her to teach the young ones. She was determined to prove to Jubal Desmond and James McLaughlin and all the others who had told her it was an impossible project that they were wrong. Not only would she fill her little school, but she would show everyone how intelligent Indian children were.

Again she realized that the one thing that would help her win the battle would be to get Black Hawk to allow his son to come to the school. She had mentioned to Janine that she wanted to talk to the man, but Janine had nearly fainted at the idea. *No one even tries to talk to Black Hawk anymore,* she had told her. *He is not the kind of man you just ride out and visit. You wait for him to come to you.*

The remark only made Evelyn more determined. Her mother had often joked that she was independent and stubborn, and that those traits would get her in trouble someday. Maybe so. She only knew that if she could get Little Fox to her school, the others would come. She would start with Black Hawk's sister, Many Birds.

She lay back down, wondering what her mother would do in the same situation. She would probably march right out to wherever Black Hawk stayed and force a confrontation. That would be just like the woman. Maybe that was what *she* should do if he didn't come to her on his own.

Seth Bridges rolled over in bed, completely oblivious to the foul smell of his unwashed sheets and the fact that the smell was made worse by the dampness of fresh perspiration. He rubbed Lucille's bare back, fingered her long dark hair, stringy and tangled from struggling with him. She curled away at his touch.

"Don't you be pullin' away from me, girl," Seth warned. He put an arm around the front of her body and jerked her next to him. "You know what I done told you. You start givin' me problems or try to run away, and it's your little sister who'll be in this bed with me. It don't bother me that she's only twelve." He grasped at one of her breasts. "Fact is, I ain't gonna last much past her bein' thirteen before I'll have to break her in, too, but long as you give me my pleasure, girl, I'll leave her alone, just like I promised."

Sixteen-year-old Lucille had long ago learned to shut off all feeling. She turned to look into the man's weathered, whiskered face. She could barely stomach the sight of him and his tobacco-stained lips and teeth, his ugly, bloodshot gray eyes, his foul whiskey breath. His hair, too, was gray, and receding, and as far as she was concerned, he was the most vile man who ever walked the face of the earth.

She would never forget the day four years ago when Seth Bridges had come to meet the orphan train back in Omaha. He was clean-shaven then, wearing a neat suit, looking the picture of a respectable farmer from South Dakota whose ailing wife needed help on the farm. Anxious to be rid of his wards, William Carey, who was in charge of seeing that the children he had brought west would get good homes, turned her and her sister

Katy over to Seth within ten minutes of meeting the man, asking for no references, totally unconcerned about what kind of man he might be. His job was simply to find homes for all the children on the train. The orphanage where she and Katy had lived in New York since Katy was born was overcrowded. It was time to weed out the older children and make room for the little ones.

Being taken away to a new land had been upheaval enough, as it was the only home Katy had ever known or could remember; Lucille's home since she was only four. To be placed with a man like Seth had only added to the children's horror. They were nothing more than prisoners here, terrified of trying to defy the man in any way for fear of the consequences.

"I'll go make you some breakfast," she told Seth. He let go of her and she sat up. As she rose, he slapped her bare bottom, just hard enough to remind her how much harder he could hit when he thought it was necessary. For the rest of her life she would not forget that first time. She had been barely thirteen. He had tied her to his bed and kept a terrified, screaming Katy locked in a closet until he had raped and beaten Lucille to the point where he had broken her will. She had agreed to fight him no more, and her ravaged body had become numb to his advances.

She walked into a little curtained-off room to wash his filth from her and get dressed. She had tried to run away once, but he had caught her, and when he was finished with her, she decided it was not worth trying again. Ever since then, if she did not respond to him the way he thought she should, he threatened to replace her with Katy. She had made up her mind she would kill him before she would let him do this to her sister.

She looked into a foggy mirror, wondering if anyone could ever think of her as pretty. Once people had told her she was. Her sister Katy was pretty, but she was herself so used and abused that she could not imagine ever being pretty again. Her mother had been quite beautiful, from what she could remember, and she had been good to her daughters, lovingly devoted, but the pleasant life they had shared in their simple apartment back in New York ended when their father was killed in a factory accident before Katy was born. There were no other relatives, and no money. She and her mother were quickly reduced to begging. Then her mother had died at Katy's birth, leaving the two of them orphaned. She had made a vow to her mother before her sister was even born that whatever happened, she would always take care of her baby sister and love her, as she would be all the baby would have. Her mother had lived only long enough after the birth to name the child, Katy Lynn, after her own mother, the children's grandmother, who had died several years earlier.

Authorities had taken her and Katy to the orphanage, where they had lived for eight years. Lucille had never quite gotten over the terror of knowing she was completely alone, that her mother was gone. She had ached to have a normal life, had briefly thought that she might find it by being adopted by some nice farm family who lived near a town, where she could meet people and make friends and go to school, maybe even meet a handsome young man and fall in love.

Then four years ago Seth Bridges had come. She had not liked or trusted him from the first moment she set eyes on him, and her suspicions had been right. Now there was no going back. Even if she could get away from him, what respectable young man would want anything to do with her? She probably couldn't even have children now. Seth had gotten her pregnant once, then had forced her to drink whiskey until she was so drunk she did not feel the pain of whatever it was he had done to her to make her lose the baby. He could not "allow" the baby to be born, he had cursed, or outsiders would know what he was doing. Once the whiskey wore off, there had been the awful pain and bleeding. That was nearly a year and a half ago, and she was convinced, after all of Seth's attacks since then and no pregnancies, that whatever he had done had left her barren. She was of no use to anyone now, and this big farmhouse was the only home she had. With no place else to go, and because it was too dangerous for Katy to be running homeless in a wild land full of Indians and outlaws, she had decided she might as well give in to this life and accept that things would never be any different for her.

She finished dressing and went downstairs to start breakfast. Katy came into the kitchen with an armload of wood just as she took down a black fry pan. "How long have you been up?" she asked Katy.

Katy, skinny and unkempt, dropped the wood into a woodbox. "I heard Seth in the bedroom," she said quietly. "I knew what he was doing to you, so I came downstairs and went to fetch the wood. I don't like to hear it."

Lucille felt the flush of shame come into her cheeks. "There is no way out of it anymore, Katy. As long as I lie with him, he'll leave you alone."

Katy blinked back tears. "I saw a new white lady come to the reservation the other day. She was with that preacher man and his sister. They rode past the house in a wagon, and the new lady, I could tell she was real pretty. Maybe she's a teacher or maybe the preacher's new wife. Maybe she's somebody who could help us."

Lucille picked up a butcher knife to go outside and hack some bacon from a slab hanging in the smokehouse. "Nobody can help us, Katy. We're legally adopted, papers and all. We belong to Seth, and we've got no rights. I'm going to wait till I'm eighteen. Then I'll be old enough to have some say in my life. Then maybe I can think of a way for us to run off without getting caught next time. We have to be real careful about it, because if Seth catches us again, you're the one who will suffer, not me."

Their eyes held in mutual terror and understanding, and then

Katy's gaze moved to the knife in Lucille's hand. She looked back at her sister.

"Don't you think I've thought about killing him? But what if people didn't believe our story? We could be *hanged,* Katy! Even if they *believed* us, to just walk up and kill him would still be considered murder. He'd have to be coming at us with a weapon. If they *didn't* hang us, maybe we'd be sent to some awful prison that's worse than being here. Maybe I'd be the only one to go, and we'd be separated forever."

Katy puckered her lips. "I'm going to find out who that lady is and I'm going to talk to her."

"You mind your business. If Seth gets wind of you trying to get him in trouble, he'll take you upstairs." Her eyes teared and she shook her head. "You don't want that, Katy. Please just do your chores proper and keep quiet. You let me do the thinking. I'll handle Seth."

Katy suddenly hugged her big sister. "It's not fair, Lucy! I can't hardly stand it when I hear him yell for you to come to his bed. Sometimes I throw up."

Lucille drew a deep breath, determined to put on a brave front for the girl. "It doesn't hurt anymore," she lied. "And when he's with me I just shut off my mind, stop all feelings till he's done. Right now we've got to be careful and keep things like they are."

"I don't smell no bacon!" Seth suddenly shouted from the top of the stairs. "You better get the goddamn bacon started right now, Lucille Bridges, or I'll set your bare ass in a fry pan and cook *it* for breakfast!" The man started down the stairs, and both girls charged out the sagging screen door at the back of the kitchen. Katy went to gather eggs from the smelly chicken house, and Lucille went to the smokehouse to cut off some bacon. She turned back to the house to hear Seth inside cussing about no breakfast yet, fuming that a man couldn't do his chores properly without a decent breakfast in his stomach.

She smiled in a hateful sneer. *What chores?* she wondered. The man hardly lifted a finger all day. All the chores were left to her and Katy, which was why he had adopted them in the first place. There was no "ailing wife." His wife had run off on him, and she could certainly understand why. Seth Bridges was a lazy, drinking man who just wanted women around to cook his meals and take care of the livestock and the crops. She kept the house up as best she could, but it was impossible when the man would spend no money on paint or decent furnishings or the basic necessities for keeping house. Besides, with all the cooking and washing and outside chores, there was little time left to try to make the house pretty and clean, and Seth himself certainly didn't care about cleanliness. The parlor, where he sat drinking most of the time, was a cluttered, smoky mess.

She shivered, gathering her courage to go back inside. She knew how it would go. He would scream and yell and complain about her being too slow. She would pay no attention. She would cook his breakfast and gladly go do her other chores just to get away from him.

She looked down at the knife in her hand. Yes, she *could* kill him, and she would feel not one ounce of remorse. What if she tried it and didn't quite do the job? What would he do to her and Katy then? Between that and not being sure what the authorities would do to her, she had decided to just bide her time; but if Seth began to get more serious about touching Katy, she could not be sure *what* she would do.

Evelyn walked among the village of tipis, in which most of the Indian families still preferred to live. Log cabins had been built for them, but they did not like being surrounded by hard walls and having a solid roof over their heads.

"They feel they cannot reach the Great Spirit when they are so confined," Janine explained.

"I am aware of their feelings about white man's homes," Evelyn replied. "I remember one particular Indian my mother and I befriended back in Oklahoma saying that he could not reach the spirits if he was inside a building. With a tipi, they can pray over the smoke of their fires, and the sacred smoke drifts through the top to the heavens, even in winter."

"Many of these tipis are important for more reasons than that," Janine told her. "They are sewn and painted by the women, and are personally precious to each woman for that reason. The tipi is her castle. When the Indians were nomadic and would migrate with the seasons, the tipi went with them. They didn't leave their homes behind like we do. They dismantled them and took them along. The pictures painted on them are always symbolic of their spiritual guide, or perhaps depictions of something important that happened in their lives."

The village they visited was east of agency headquarters, not far from a trading post used by whites and Indians alike. Janine stopped and nodded to a woman who was cooking something in an iron pot over an open fire. The woman smiled at Janine, but she looked suspiciously at Evelyn. "This is Red Foot Woman. We have given her the Christian name of Sara Eagle. Her husband is White Eagle, and Sara's sister, Yellow Sky, is also his wife. Sara is thirty-one, as far as we can determine. White Eagle is forty, and his other wife, Sara's sister, is twenty-four. They all understand some English, but they feel better speaking in the Sioux tongue." She turned and introduced Evelyn to Sara, who rose from the fire and shook her head.

"No school," she said, a look of fright in her eyes.

Janine started to explain further, but Evelyn interrupted, speaking to Sara in her own language. "I have not come to take your children from you," she said. "I live right here on the reservation, and if you will bring them to my school, I promise I will only keep them for a few hours each day."

Janine was glad to see that Sara seemed impressed at how

fluently Evelyn could speak her language. She and John had
never mastered it very well. They had picked it up some while
working among the Sioux, but had never had the opportunity to
actually study the language.

Evelyn smiled and gently asked Sara to tell her about her
children. She had never met a woman yet, of any race, who did
not like to brag about her offspring. Sara told her she had a
fourteen-year-old son, Hides-The-Sun, whom the "white priest,"
meaning John Phillips, had named Joseph Eagle. Broken
Feather, called Robert by the missionaries, was ten. He-Who-
Hunts, William, was eight; and Flower Girl, Martha, was five.

"My husband's other wife, my sister, Yellow Sky, is called
Sharon by the missionaries," she went on. "She has a son, Little
Feather, James Eagle. He is six. And she has a daughter who is
four summers, Buffalo Girl. The whites call her Rose Eagle."

"Could I please meet the children? Would you allow me to
at least talk to them?" Evelyn asked.

Sara shook her head. "White Eagle says no. No children to
go white man's school. Not even on reservation. You teach them
white man's ways. They forget old ways. They get bad ideas."

"No, Sara. I teach only good things, things that will help your
children for the new way they must live now. I will teach them
white man's knowledge, which will help them take care of themselves if and when they are able to leave the reservation and live
a new way. Everything is changed now, Sara. Surely you see
that. It is good that they know and remember the old ways. They
should never forget that first they are Sioux. I would never try
to take that away from them. But they must also understand the
white way now. It is the only way your people will continue to
survive."

"No." The woman shook her head. "I have seen those who
go away to white man's schools. They are different when they
come back. Sometimes they want nothing to do with their own
family anymore, or with the old ways. They scoff at us. Many

who go to these schools die, sometimes in body, sometimes in spirit."

"Not Anita Wolf. I have not met Anita yet, but Janine tells me she went away to the Genoa Industrial School and knows how to cook and sew and bake the white way. She knows how to do numbers and can read and write in English. She is a very smart girl and she understands that her people must learn the new way, yet she is proud of being Sioux. She has not forgotten old customs, and she respects them."

Sara sniffed. "Anita's father is one of the lazy drunks who hangs around the fort and the agency buildings to beg for food. He runs after the white men, doing things for them so they will pay him with tobacco, and with firewater, when he can get it. He has deserted his people. He has no pride. His wife has been long dead, and his son, Anita's brother, Broken Knife, he is as lazy and shameful as his father. Anita only went away to school because it was bad for her at home. Her father sometimes hit her and made her do all the work. Anita only turned to white man's schooling to get away from home. She is no longer Sioux at heart. She thinks the white man's way is the only way, but she is wrong."

Evelyn was anxious to meet Anita, who Janine said was gracious and quite pretty. She hoped having Anita's aid in teaching would help get others to send their children to school, since one of their own would be helping teach. This was her first day out "recruiting," and already she could see that those who told her how hard it would be were right. She folded her arms and held her chin proudly. "Tell me, Sara, what if the one called Black Hawk sent his son, Little Fox, to school? Would you send your own children then?"

Sara laughed. It was only then that Evelyn realized the woman had a tooth missing in front. "Black Hawk will never send his son to a white man's school."

"But what if he did? Would you then agree to send your own?"

A sly look came into the woman's eyes. "I will agree, because you will never get Black Hawk to agree. You cannot even find him unless he wants to be found."

"You just remember your promise."

As Sara chuckled again, a naked little girl came running up to her and grabbed the skirt of her worn, thinning buckskin dress. She stared at Evelyn. Evelyn guessed she was the five-year-old daughter called Flower Girl. She reached into her pocket and took out a piece of hard candy, handing it out to the child and introducing herself. The girl smiled and grabbed it, then ran off again. A young, pretty Indian woman came toward them, carrying a basket on her head that was filled with clothes. A little boy and girl followed close behind. Because of the heat, they were also naked, like most of the children who played about the area. The woman who appeared to be their mother set down the basket and ordered the children to stay back. She looked Evelyn over cautiously.

"This is my sister, Yellow Sky," Sara told Evelyn. She explained to Yellow Sky, who was also called Sharon, about Evelyn's reason for being there. Sharon backed away, reaching out to keep her children behind her.

"You will not take my children from me," she declared.

Evelyn felt frustrated. "I have not come here to do that, Sharon, I assure you," she told her in the Lakota tongue. "I just want to meet everyone and tell them that the school is available for anyone who wants to use it. Your children can stay right here and come home every evening. You can continue to practice your old customs when they are home. I don't want them to forget them any more than you do. Please think about it. The teaching must begin."

Sharon shook her head. "If I take my little ones to your school, I will never see them again. You will sneak them off to the schools far away, and when they come home, I will no longer know them."

Evelyn closed her eyes in exasperation.

"We all told you it wouldn't be easy."

Evelyn sighed and faced Sara and Sharon. "I am honored to meet both of you and your children," she told them. "I hope you will change your minds. I mean only good things for your children. I have lived among Indians most of my life. I understand and respect your ways." She turned away and walked toward another cluster of tipis.

"Don't give up," Janine told her.

"Oh, I'm not about to do that." Evelyn stopped walking and faced her. "Janine, last night I was awakened by the strangest sound—like a man far away yipping and howling like a coyote in the middle of the night. It gave me the shivers."

Janine smiled knowingly. "It used to frighten me, too, until I got used to it. You will hear the sound many times. It is Black Hawk. He often rides closer to the agency at night to taunt the soldiers and give voice to his stubborn refusal to comply with reservation rules. He knows his war whoops won't disturb his own people. It will only bother the whites."

Evelyn looked out toward the distant hills. "I need to talk to him."

"To Black Hawk?" Janine laughed in the same disparaging way as Sara had. "I already told you, you'll never get near him if you go looking for him. Besides, it could be dangerous."

Evelyn thought about Wild Horse, and how close he and her mother had been. "I don't think so."

"Well, first he has to be found. Why don't you just wait until you have a chance to talk to him when he comes in to the agency?"

"How often does that happen?"

"Not often. The best thing to do is befriend his sister, Many Birds. We haven't met her yet. She lives with her old grandmother in the next village. She will be sixteen the first of August. That's only a couple of weeks away. You wait until then. I am guessing Black Hawk will come in to help celebrate her sixteenth birthday. He'll bring her something, maybe fresh meat or some kind of gift. You stay close to her around that time, and you just might get to meet her brother and nephew, but don't expect to make much progress."

Evelyn could still hear the man's calls, was convinced he was the Indian in her dream. If that was true, and if Black Hawk was as spiritual as most Indians she knew, he would know when he saw her that she was something important to him. He would allow her to say her piece. He would feel this powerful vision that had plagued her for months.

Her heart pounded at the very idea of meeting him. If he looked like the ghostly rider of her dreams . . .

She looked past Janine toward a big, clattering farm wagon that was making its way toward the trading post. The back of it was stacked with ears of corn. A gray-haired man drove the wagon, and two young girls sat beside him. "Seth Bridges," she muttered. "We'll visit more of the families later, Janine. I am going to talk to that man."

"I'd stay away from him, Evy."

The younger girl that Evelyn had seen working in the yard the day she arrived at the reservation looked over at her then. Evelyn could see she recognized her, and she saw a cry for help in those big blue eyes.

She looked at Janine. "You brought medicine for a little girl you said had a bad cough."

"Yes. Little Otter is the daughter of Three Bears and Owl Woman. So far they have refused white man's medicine, but I thought I'd try once more."

"You go ahead then. How far is it?"

Janine pointed to a sagging little frame house a good quarter of a mile distant. "Out there. Why?"

"I just wanted to know so I can catch up with you later."

"Evelyn, our responsibility is to the Indians. Seth Bridges's girls are white, and he is not a part of the government program. He's just a farmer who sells food at the trading post. He can make trouble for all of us if you make him angry. He doesn't like anyone sticking their noses in his business. My brother and I already found that out. Believe me, he's a man to stay away from."

"Those girls are in a bad way, Janine. Anyone can see that. My job is to teach and to help, and those girls need both. I intend to do something about the situation." She stormed toward the wagon, determined to follow it until it came to a stop. She would find out a few things about Seth Bridges and his "adopted" little slaves! She heard Janine call for her to come back, but she ignored the plea.

Five

Evelyn half ran to keep up with Seth Bridges's wagon, following it to the log trading post run by Bill Doogan, a middle-aged ex-soldier. Doogan was a redheaded Irishman who had married a Sioux woman who, Janine told Evelyn, had been orphaned several years earlier and had been living with a brother who liked his whiskey. The brother, one of those who gave up his pride and the fight long before Wounded Knee, had literally sold his sister to Doogan for a good supply of tobacco. Doogan was a pleasant-enough-looking man who seemed to treat his family decently, but his wife was shunned by many of her people because she was married to a white man, and her half-breed children, four of them, lived torn between two worlds, accepted in neither.

Doogan operated the trading post for the government, buying supplies from whoever wanted to furnish them and sending the bill to Washington. The supplies were rationed out to the Indians, and the government repaid Doogan with an extra percentage tacked on for his duties handling the trading post. Evelyn did not doubt that he tacked on his own little extra with the original bill, making a profit much tidier than what the government paid him. No one was there to keep an eye on what Doogan really bought—a hundred bushels of corn, or a thousand. She had only been here a few days, and she could already see how easy it would be to cheat both the government and the Indians. Men like Doogan could make a killing. He dressed well, and was a hefty man who apparently also ate well.

Cheating and thievery were rampant in dealings between the government and Indian agencies. Evelyn intended to do some letter writing to Washington and see that something was done about it. Just yesterday a supply of beef had arrived by riverboat, salted and packed in lard, but still half rotten. The soldiers in charge of handing it out to the Sioux had said it was nearly always that way. Obviously the meat-packing houses in Omaha were being paid by the government to deliver good quality meat but were sending spoiled meat instead. As Janine had explained, it was difficult to pin down the culprits, as the meat packers swore their innocence and blamed those who owned the freighting services, claiming they must sell the good meat somewhere along the way and collect someone else's spoiled meat. Each person had someone else to blame, and the government seemed to have no interest in investigating the situation, even though it was they and the Indians who suffered in the end.

Seth Bridges pulled the wagon around the back of the trading post, and Evelyn marched right behind it, calling out to the man as soon as he pushed on the brake and started to climb down. He hesitated, then jumped to the ground to face her with a warning look in his blue eyes. Evelyn could feel his daughters staring at her, but they kept silent as she held a steady gaze on Bridges, refusing to show any fear. She felt sick at the way his bloodshot eyes moved over her. His whiskered face not only needed shaving but also a good scrubbing, and there were old sweat stains on the faded shirt he wore under his coveralls. He adjusted a floppy hat as he stepped closer. "Somethin' you want, missy? I've never seen you around here before."

Evelyn faced him squarely. "I am Miss Evelyn Gibbons, the new schoolteacher here on the reservation."

Lucille and Katy both watched the confrontation, both of them thinking Miss Evelyn Gibbons was just about the prettiest lady they had ever seen, both of them longing to be so ladylike and well spoken, aching to fix their hair pretty like that and wear clean, neat dresses. Katy leaned over and whispered to her sister, "She's the lady I told you I saw go past in a wagon the other day."

Lucille put a hand over her sister's mouth, quietly warning her Seth had told them not to speak if anyone approached them at the trading post. She watched in both fear and admiration as Miss Gibbons faced Seth unafraid—or at least she appeared to be unafraid.

"And just what can I do for you, *Miss* Gibbons?" Seth asked rather sarcastically, stressing "Miss" in a mocking way.

The tone in his voice and the look in his eyes readily told Evelyn what he would *like* to do with her. *You filthy old man,* she thought. What went on behind closed doors at the Bridges home? What kind of hell were Lucille and Katy living in? Bridges stood nearly six feet tall, making him seem even more imposing against her five-foot-four-inch frame, but she refused to let him intimidate her.

"I would like to talk to you about sending your girls to school," she told him. "I will be teaching full-time here on the reservation, but my students certainly do not have to be only Indian children."

The man turned and looked up at Lucille and Katy. "Quit starin' like a couple of pups and get busy unloadin' that corn!" he barked.

Both girls hurriedly climbed down.

"Go on inside and tell Bill Doogan to get some bushel baskets out here for you," Seth ordered.

They ran inside without a word, reminding Evelyn of trained dogs. Seth turned to look at her then, taking a menacing pose. "My girls don't need schoolin', lady," he told her. "The oldest is already sixteen, a woman. Katy is gettin' old enough that she don't need no more schoolin', neither. They both got all they needed when they lived at the orphanage back in New York. Besides, I need them on the farm."

The girls came back outside, each carrying a stack of empty bushel baskets. "So you can lie around and do nothing while they do all the work?" Evelyn asked Seth.

Lucille nearly dropped the baskets when she heard the bold question. She looked at Katy. Neither girl was sure what might happen next. They quietly set down the baskets, each of them taking one and pretending to pay no attention.

Seth's jaws flexed in anger. "I do my share, lady. I adopted them girls out of the goodness of my heart, and because I had a wife dyin' on me. She needed help around the house—"

"Don't try to feed me your lies, Mr. Bridges! Anyone can see why you adopted them. You needed a woman to do your cooking and cleaning and washing and most of your own chores! You chose little girls because they are more easily intimidated than a grown woman or a couple of boys. I hate to even think the *other* reason you might have chosen girls. The thought of it turns my stomach! There must be some kind of authority or law that can stop you from what you are doing, and I will find a way!"

Lucille and Katy stopped working. They stared dumbfounded at the pretty, courageous woman who faced Seth so boldly. Both of them were afraid for her. Seth leaned closer, and neither Lucille nor Katy had to see his face to know the look he had in his eyes at that moment. They were amazed that Miss Gibbons did not back away.

"Missy, you send anybody to take my girls from me, and I'll shoot them! I'd have every right! There ain't no laws can take away a man's legally adopted kids, and no law that gives them girls any rights against me." He poked his finger toward her, jamming it into her chest twice as he spoke. "And if *you* come nosin' around, you'll regret it, lady, in more ways than one!" He ran the finger down between her breasts before taking his hand away. "You'd be trespassin' on my property. Now you get away from me and my girls before I call some soldiers to come and *drag* you away. We've got work to do, and you've got your own work in store tryin' to teach ignorant Indians. You stick to the reason you came here, and keep that pretty little nose out of other people's business, or it's likely to get broke."

To Lucille and Katy's amazement, Miss Gibbons still did not back away. "Those girls had better be cleaner and better dressed the next time I see them, Mr. Bridges; and you had better start sending the younger one to school, or I can and *will* make trouble for you!"

Evelyn had no idea how she would do that, but she hoped there was enough sureness in her voice that he would wonder, at least enough to make life a little more bearable for the girls. She saw a hint of worry in his eyes, and she hoped she was doing a good job of hiding her own fear. Before he could answer, Bill Doogan came outside.

"Well, I see you've met our pretty new schoolteacher!" the man said, his already ruddy complexion reddening more with delight at the sight of Evelyn. "My own young ones are not old enough for school yet, but soon as the oldest boy turns seven in December, I'll be sending him. I promised Miss Gibbons. She's too pretty to say no to, wouldn't you agree, Seth?"

Seth still glared at Evelyn. "I'll agree she's pretty, all right." As he turned away, Lucille and Katy immediately began grabbing armloads of corn and dumping it into the bushels.

"The wife has some fresh Indian bread inside," Doogan told Evelyn. "You come and get some later for your evening meal with the good preacher and his sister."

"Thank you, Mr. Doogan. We might do that. I appreciate your wife's generosity. How are the little ones?"

"Oh, the baby keeps the wife up with feedings, and the others keep her running with the mischief they get into." He turned to Lucille and Katy. "Well, girls, you're working pretty fast there. Doing a good job. Looks like a good crop, Seth."

"Came in early because of all the rain we had last month. We could use more of that rain now. It's damn hot and dry for picking, but the girls get out in the fields early."

Doogan turned and winked at Evelyn. She realized he must have heard part of her conversation with Seth and was trying to smooth things over before they got out of hand. "You making much progress in getting any Indian children to school?" he asked.

"Not so far."

"Well, it will take some time. Maybe you should convince them that if they don't send the children to the reservation school, they risk having the children taken from them by force to off-reservation schools. It could happen, you know."

"I will be meeting this afternoon with Anita Wolf. I am hoping she can help."

"Anita has been visiting the Rosebud Reservation, trying to help out there. I didn't know she was back," Doogan answered. "She is a nice young woman. Got a good education at the Genoa school."

Evelyn realized the man was just making idle conversation, turning attention away from her confrontation with Seth Bridges.

"Well, anything you can do to help me will be appreciated, Mr. Doogan. You see a lot of them on a daily basis when they come to trade with you."

Several baskets were filled with corn by then, and Seth began carrying them into the rear storeroom. Evelyn glanced at little Katy, who took advantage of the moment and smiled at her. Evelyn started toward the girls, but Doogan took hold of her arm. "Stay away, Miss Gibbons."

Evelyn met his eyes. "I am not afraid of Seth Bridges, Mr. Doogan."

"Then stay away for the sake of the girls. If you get him riled, he will only take it out on them. Nobody around here likes what goes on over there, but there's no law that allows anybody to do anything about it. Your job here is to teach the Indian children. Stick to your business, for your own sake and for the sake of those girls."

Evelyn drew in her breath. "I understand what you are trying to tell me, Mr. Doogan, but I am not going to give up on this." She walked around the other side of the wagon, taking a quick glance at the two girls, who stared back at her. She could see how pretty they would be if they were cleaner, their hair washed and curled. Both had dark hair and blue eyes. Lucille had a lovely shape to her. Like Seth said, she was a woman in body; but what about on the inside? What kind of damage had been done to both her and her sister emotionally? "If there is anything you need," she said to them, "anything you want to tell me; if you need any kind of help at all, you come to me. Will you both please remember that?"

Lucille glanced at the door to the storeroom to make sure Seth was not watching them. She looked back at Evelyn. "Thank you, ma'am, but there isn't anything we'll be needing."

Evelyn glanced at Katy, who looked ready to cry. She started to say something to the girl, but quickly turned away when Seth came out the door. She headed toward the little house in the distance where Janine had taken the cough medicine to Little Otter. In the background she could hear Seth cussing at Lucille and Katy for not working fast enough. "We've got more to pick when we get home! Quit wasting time! Time is money, and I want those bushels filled quick as you can load them!"

She felt sick inside at what they must suffer. Perhaps, as Janine had said she must do, she should just put it out of her mind and concentrate on the Indian children. She was to meet Anita today and officially open the school tomorrow. She had a lot of work to do, and she would have to set aside her concern for Lucille and Katy Bridges for the time being.

She headed across the open ground between the trading post and the mixture of tipis and log and frame homes where several hundred Sioux lived. Actually, families were scattered all over Standing Rock, an area eighty miles long and forty miles wide. Most of the villages were on the west side of the agency, an area she had not yet visited.

So much to do. So much ground to cover. Somehow she had to find a way to reach every family, introduce herself, get to know as many of them as possible. That especially included Many Birds, Black Hawk's sister. That was another situation that needed taking care of. After what she had heard last night, she was more curious than ever about Black Hawk.

She had nearly reached the sorry-looking home of Three Bears and Owl Woman when Janine came out and stepped off the sagging porch. "Stay away from here for now," she warned. She blinked back tears. "Little Otter died last night. Owl Woman thinks it is some kind of omen, that it means the new white woman should never have come here. She is in deep mourning, and she says she will not send her other three children to school."

Evelyn closed her eyes in disappointment. "I am certainly getting off to a grand start, aren't I?"

"They'll get used to you being around, and they'll begin to realize how sincere you are. It will just take time. Come with me and we'll go visit Anita. I heard she is back from Rosebud and is visiting her father and brother. They don't live far from here, about a mile. They still live in a tipi, so Anita has to live there also. She has no place else to stay here on the reservation. She has a fine education but still must live the old way because that is all there is for her."

"It's too bad her father and brother are always drunk and don't do anything to better themselves."

"Yes. It has made life doubly hard for Anita. Half of her people shun her and don't trust her because of her white man's education, and the other half shun her because her father and brother are part of those who bring shame to all of them."

".We must go and see her today, Janine. I am so anxious to

meet her, and I need to talk to her. Maybe she can arrange for me to meet Black Hawk."

"Don't you ever give up on the impossible?"

"No."

"You're determined to do something to get you into trouble, aren't you?"

"I just think getting Black Hawk's son to school would change a lot of things."

"Of course it would. But that will never happen. If you want to meet his sister, you're welcome to. She lives with her grandmother in a village to the northwest. When we get the time I'll take you there. Right now, you have taken on enough responsibilities. How did it go with Seth Bridges?"

"Not very good. He is a vile, ignorant, uneducated man whom I detest. I am going to help those girls one way or another, Janine."

"Interfering will only hurt them, not help them. Do like I said and stick to what you came here for."

"That's what Seth Bridges told me. You can't be that unconcerned, Janine. You're too soft-hearted and intelligent."

"I didn't say I wasn't concerned, but I understand there is only so much a person can do, Evy, and I also know that getting too involved can only bring harm to those girls. If God intends for you to have a hand in helping them, He will show you the way."

Evelyn wished she could talk to her mother about Lucille and Katy, and about the best way to reach the Sioux children . . . and about Black Hawk. Her mother had always been so easy to talk to. She had considered asking her father to come to Standing Rock, but he was getting old, and this life would be hard for him. He had already donated a lot of years to the Indians.

"I'm sorry about Little Otter," she told Janine.

"So am I. They brought in their own medicine man, but when prayers and chants and special treatments failed, he claimed it was because of the new white woman who had intruded, wanting to steal away the children. Owl Woman said he claims the Great Spirit came to take Little Otter before the white woman—you, of course—could steal her away to the white man's world."

Evelyn sighed. "Oh, Janine, how am I going to fight things like that? I haven't even started yet, and they're all against me."

"God will provide a way, Evy."

Evelyn decided God had better do so soon or there would not be much reason to stay. She still believed Black Hawk was the key to reaching the rest of them. If he did not come to his sister's birthday celebration and she was not able to talk to him by then, she decided she would ride out herself into the hills and try to find the man. Somewhere deep inside, perhaps because of her dream, she was sure he would not harm her. Her mother had been afraid of Wild Horse at first, but they had become good friends, more than friends. So many times she had wanted to tell Janine everything about her mother, but she feared the prim and proper spinster-woman would never understand.

"There don't seem to be a lot of Indians around, Janine. Are they hiding inside to avoid me?"

Janine smiled and shook her head. "I found out from Owl Woman that many of them snuck off last night to a secret place to celebrate the Sun Dance."

"The Sun Dance! The government no longer allows them to go through that ritual. They're afraid it will stir them to making war again."

"Let alone the fact that it is a barbaric practice."

Evelyn silently disagreed. She had studied the Sioux culture and knew how vital the Sun Dance was to their basic spiritual beliefs. Yes, it was bloody, and in the minds of people like her father and John and Janine, it was a heathen practice, but part of her understood that it was also beautiful, a fiercely spiritual, moving experience for those who practiced it.

"Every year John preaches against it, and the soldiers try

to stop it," Janine went on. "So now they sneak away in the night to a place far from agency headquarters and from Fort Yates. The soldiers know they do it, but it isn't worth the risk of possible bloodshed on both sides to try to stop it, so they let them go. Owl Woman and Three Bears will take Little Otter's body to the secret celebration. They will include her burial in the ceremonies."

"And by the time they're through, with the rest of them all worked up over the Sun Dance, the whole nation of six thousand Sioux here at Standing Rock will be against me."

Janine smiled sadly. "There *are* a few who stayed here, including, I am sure, Anita. She no longer believes in the old ways of worship. She is a Christian. Maybe you'll feel better after you've met her. Things will change, Evy. It just takes time."

Evelyn nodded, her heart heavy with concern. "Let's get on with our task here. I'm anxious to meet Anita and talk to at least one Indian who accepts me."

The two women started walking again. Evelyn longed to witness the Sun Dance for herself. If she could see the ceremony, perhaps she could get a better grasp on its importance to these people, find a way to connect the old with the new. That was her only hope of reaching the stubborn ones . . . like Black Hawk.

Black Hawk leaned back, straining against the skewers that pierced his breasts so that they pulled at his skin until he nearly hung free. The skewers were attached only by his skin to strips of rawhide that were tied to the sacred central Sun Dance pole, around which he danced, pushing his starved body to the limit of endurance. The pain caused him to blow his bone whistle often and loudly. He kept the whistle between his lips as he pranced to the rhythmic drumming, and he felt himself falling into another world, a world where no white man existed, where the buffalo roamed so thick that a man could almost walk across their backs.

Yes, that was a beautiful time, when he was a small boy. His father used to tell him that the years before he was born were even better, and better still for his grandfather, for with each older generation there were fewer white men in the vast lands that once belonged to the Sioux. It was all different now, except in times like this, when he could dance and worship in the old way, when his people sang their celebration songs and defied the white man's government by conducting the sacred Sun Dance, even though they had been ordered not to do this.

He had already shed his blood this way twice before in his life, an offering to Wakantanka, praying that the Great One would help his people through these terrible times. This was his third sacrifice, and he was doing it for Little Fox, who he knew was watching him now. He wanted to teach his son everything about the old ways. He spoke only Sioux to the boy, and he took him along on the hunt. He talked about what life was once like for the People of Paha-Sapa, the sacred Black Hills. He had known Crazy Horse, had ridden with him at the battle of the Greasy Grass, the one the white man called the Little Big Horn. He had been only thirteen then, but he remembered it all well. He remembered how strong and victorious his people had felt that day! He longed for those times again, but since then the soldiers had come by the thousands to hunt them down. His parents and a brother had been killed. For a while he had lived in the land of the Queen Mother with Sitting Bull and several of his people, but they were soon forced by starvation to return to their homeland, where things were not much better. Now Crazy Horse was dead. Sitting Bull was dead, killed by some of his own Indian police. Everything was changed, and his biggest fear was that Little Fox would be forcibly taken from him. He would kill whoever tried to do that!

He felt his flesh tearing, and he blew even more frantically on the whistle to keep from crying out in pain. He continued dancing, the beating of the drums and the prayer songs that filled the Sun Dance lodge seeming louder now. Two of the warriors who had joined in the shedding of flesh and blood had already passed out, the skewers torn away from their breasts. Black Hawk was determined to remain dancing longer than the others. Now sounds of the drumming and singing became dimmer, and he felt himself floating in a deep trance. He rode his spotted horse, yet he could hardly feel the animal beneath him. It was as though he and the horse were one.

Fast! So fast the horse galloped, across the wide prairie, while somewhere in the distance his people sang and danced and urged him on. The land was vast, and it all belonged to him. To his left was a huge herd of buffalo, and all around the grass was green and plentiful. In the distance someone waited for him, hand outstretched. Could it be his wife, Turtle Woman, come back to life? How could this be?

The woman stood alone. As he came closer he realized she was not Indian at all! Her hair was light, and her eyes the color of the sky. Somehow he knew her. The spirits told him she was important to him. This woman was close to his heart, yet he had never met her. He came closer, ever closer. She must belong to him! Her heart was good, even though she was white. He reached out to grasp her hand, but the instant he touched her she disappeared.

At that very moment the skewers tore loose from his flesh, and he fell unconscious to the ground.

Six

Anita Wolf rode up to the schoolhouse, a little boy perched in front of her. Evelyn recognized He-Who-Hunts, eight-year-old William Eagle. "How did you do it?" she greeted Anita with a smile as she reached up to lift William down from the big roan mare Anita rode.

"I did much talking to Sara," Anita answered. She straddled the horse like a man, even though today she wore a white woman's calico dress. She flung a leg over and slid down, then tied the animal. "I told her and White Eagle to please send just one child and see that we will not steal him away or make him turn against his people."

"Well, it's a start."

"I also talked to Big Belly. He is one of the lazy ones who hangs around the soldiers and trading post." A sad look came into her eyes. "He is one of my father's friends. He does not take good care of his children, Red Foot and Bright Feather. The government has given them the Christian names of John and Linda Adams. Big Belly said he would let them come to school. I think it is only because he wants someone else to take care of them. He lives in a little shack between here and Fort Yates. They will ride here by themselves. They should come soon." She sighed deeply. "You will see. In a few more days I will have your school filled. You only have to be patient with my people. They are very stubborn and set in their ways."

Evelyn smiled. "I am well aware of that." She led William

inside the one-room building, where she had written the alphabet on the small blackboard at the front of the room. In spite of having the little school's four windows open, it was still stuffy inside. She sat William down on one of several crates that served as chairs. In front of each crate was a small, crude wooden table that served as a desk, each one handmade by some of the reservation Indians, one of the many projects the government created for them to keep them busy. Her own cabin next to the school was nearly finished, and a privy was already in place behind it, a reminder that it would be quite some time before she lived in any kind of luxury again.

She leaned down and spoke to William in the Sioux tongue, which seemed to comfort him, then handed him a beaded counting board to play with.

"We'll wait until the Adams children get here," she told Anita. She looked toward a window when the wind again carried the sound of rhythmic drumming across the hills and prairie to the little school. Last night, when all else was quiet, the sound had been very distinct. Evelyn had even been able to hear the singing. It was a sound that gave her the chills, for she had lain in bed imagining what it must be like to hear that sound and know that Indians were coming to pillage and torture and murder. She understood the reasons for some of the things the Sioux had done, but there had been chilling cruelty nonetheless, and she could understand why the soldiers and white settlers often panicked when they heard Indian singing and drumming. The saddest part was, if there had not been the same cruelty on behalf of United States soldiers, and if treaties had not been broken over and over again by the government, the Sioux might never have resorted to making war.

She and everyone else knew the drumming came from somewhere out in the hills, where those clinging to the old ways were illegally celebrating the Sun Dance.

"It has been several days since the Sun Dance was begun,"

Anita said, as though to read her thoughts. "By last night those who wanted to make the blood sacrifice would have done so. Do you know about the Sun Dance celebration?"

"I have studied about it. I find it beautiful in some ways," Evelyn commented, "but also terribly barbaric. I understand the spiritual concept of the sacrifice, shedding blood as a way of showing the sincerity of their prayers, their willingness to suffer in return for having those prayers answered."

"My people are not afraid of pain or death. They admire courage in others. In the days when they made war, it was the bravest captives who were allowed to live."

As Anita walked to a window, Evelyn thought how pretty she was, with a slender shape and an exquisite face. Her skin was very dark, but her complexion was creamy and smooth. She wore her long black hair twisted into a thick braid that hung down her back. She was very pleased and impressed with her Sioux assistant. Not only was there little difference in their ages, which was fast leading them to a close friendship, but Anita was courageous, one of the very few of her people who had learned to accept and live in two distinctly different cultures. She was a sweet, intelligent woman, and Evelyn felt sorry for her situation. She was shunned by many because she urged her people to learn new ways, and she knew Anita was ashamed of her father and brother, two of the "lazy ones" who had long ago lost their pride to whiskey.

"It is not easy to turn away from old beliefs and customs, Miss Gibbons," Anita continued. "It would be like someone coming and taking everything from you and telling you you can no longer be a Christian. The problem is made bigger by the fact that my people are very proud and unafraid."

Evelyn was tempted to tell the girl about her dream. It had returned again last night, and she had awakened to hear the drumming and singing on the night air. She had felt drawn to it, had even been tempted to follow the sound and go to where she knew Black Hawk must be.

"Please just call me Evy, Anita." She folded her arms. "Tell me something. I know that you are yourself a Christian now," she told Anita. "But do you believe in dreams and visions?"

Anita faced her. "Did not the prophets have visions? Did not Christ himself predict things that were to come, much as our own priests and medicine men do? Yes, I believe in dreams." She frowned. "Have *you* had a vision?"

Evelyn suddenly felt foolish. "It's probably nothing," she answered with a nervous smile.

Anita stepped closer. "If it is something you have seen in your dreams more than once, and if it seems very real, then it has meaning. Our people believe that dreams are very personal. They should be shared only with someone who understands these things. Perhaps you should tell Night Hunter about your vision."

"The old priest?" Evelyn had heard about Night Hunter, a wise, old respected priest and medicine man, who, Janine said, preached against white ways. "He wouldn't allow a white schoolteacher inside his tipi!"

"I think that he might. You know the Sioux tongue, and after he spoke with you for a few minutes, he would realize that you are a good person who truly cares about our people. You do not have to be afraid of the old man, Miss Gibbons. He can seem frightening sometimes, but he would never harm you. He is very wise. He sees into the heart, and your heart is good. If he knew you had had a vision, he would respect you for it and help you understand it. Does the vision involve my people?"

Evelyn felt embarrassed, especially for the fact that in the dream she was beginning to feel sexually attracted to the Indian on the horse. "Yes," she answered. "It's . . . part of the reason I decided to take this job. I felt as though I was supposed to come here."

"Have you talked to Reverend Phillips about it?"

"No. I haven't mentioned it to anyone. I would rather you didn't, either."

Anita nodded. "If you ever want to go and see Night Hunter, I will take you. For now he is at the Sun Dance. In a few days he will come back to his village. It is about a half day's ride from here."

"Thank you. I will think about it."

Anita glanced toward a window again, then suddenly became flustered. "Reverend Phillips is coming!" She smoothed her dress and pulled a piece of fallen hair behind her ear. "How do I look?" She fanned herself. "Oh, it is already so hot!"

Evelyn watched in surprise. "Anita! Are you attracted to the reverend?"

The girl drew a deep breath. "I think he is a wonderful man," she said with a sigh.

Evelyn smiled. "Does he know how you feel about him?"

"Oh, no! Do not tell him! He would never consider—"

Just then the door opened, and Anita turned away, hurrying to the front desk to look busy.

"Well, good morning to the two prettiest young ladies at Standing Rock," the man announced. "I came to see if you had any better luck today."

Evelyn put her hand out toward William. "Anita convinced White Eagle to send William. She also talked to an Indian called Big Belly. He is sending his two children."

"Lazy old Big Belly? Good. Those poor children of his are terribly neglected. If possible, try to get any children who come to school to also come to church services. I'll have Janine come over here for a few minutes of Christian lessons at the end of every day. Maybe working together we can give them an education *and* convert them."

Evelyn noticed how the man looked at her, knew from the first day she met him that he had taken an interest in her. Now that she knew how Anita felt about him, she realized she had to discourage him every way she could. Perhaps she would talk to Janine about Anita, and Janine could find a way to hint to John that Anita was attracted to him. From the look in her eyes just before he came inside, Evelyn was convinced Anita was totally in love. She glanced at the girl, who sat at the desk looking at a schoolbook. She knew she was not really reading it. She was just trying to avoid having to look straight at John.

"You have Anita to thank for getting William and Big Belly's children to come." She heard a horse outside then. "That must be them now." She hurried past the reverend to go and greet the children.

The reverend stepped closer to the desk. "Well, it seems you have been doing a good job, Anita. Thank you."

Anita finally looked up at him, wondering if he could read her eyes. "I will get more to come," she answered. "It will help when they get to know Miss Gibbons better."

"Yes, she is going to be a big help. How do you like working with her?"

"We have only just started, but I like her very much already."

Phillips smiled, and Anita felt an ache in her heart. *I love you, John Phillips.* What would a white preacher think of an Indian woman being in love with him? He was much older than she. Maybe he looked upon her as just a child. There was a time when she never would have dreamed she would fall in love with a white man, but week after week she had sat in his little church, one of only a few Indians who bothered to come, and she had watched and listened. She admired the reverend for his dedication, for his refusal to give up on her people, for often defending them when they were wrongly accused, for doing all he could to keep whiskey off the reservation. He was a good man, and since her schooling, she had learned to understand the white world, had learned not all white men were bad.

"Miss Gibbons is easy to like," he was saying. "She is a very sincere young lady. It took courage for someone her age who was living a comfortable life to come out here. I think she has never forgotten some of her experiences when her parents worked among Indians in Oklahoma. I think God chose her to come here."

The man turned to greet Evelyn when she led John and Linda Adams inside then. Both had refused to use their assigned names when they had got down from the horse they had ridden there together. "I am Bright Feather," Linda had told Evelyn. "And this is my little brother, Red Foot."

Evelyn introduced them to the reverend, and Linda watched her in wonder, for this new white teacher had readily and graciously agreed to call them by their Indian names. She had asked in the Sioux tongue if they had encountered any trouble on their ride to the school. Bright Feather had never known a white woman who knew her language, nor had she ever seen one quite as pretty as this Miss Gibbons.

"Oh, I know these two well," Phillips answered. He patted young John's head. "You will have fun learning new things here today, Son." He looked Evelyn over appreciatively. "I just know that within a few weeks this school will be full. You'll see." He turned to Anita. "Good day, ladies. Janine and I will come back this afternoon."

The man left, and Evelyn noticed that Anita looked flushed, in spite of her dark complexion. "Anita! I do believe you're in love!"

The girl smiled, but Evelyn detected tears in her eyes. "The reverend would never care for me in the same way."

Evelyn folded her arms and stepped closer. "Maybe he just needs to be told how you feel. He is not a man to be forward about anything, you know. Perhaps you need to be the first one to say something."

"No, never! Never!" Anita rose and came around the front of the desk. "We should begin the lessons. Do you want to start with mathematics?"

The shy girl's cheeks were still red, and Evelyn could see the conversation made Anita uncomfortable. "Yes, we'll start with numbers," she answered.

Anita took the counting beads from William and sat down on a crate in front of all three children. Evelyn walked outside for a moment to lead John and Linda's horse closer to a watering trough. In the distance she could see a wagon heading toward the trading post. It was stacked with corn, and she knew Seth Bridges was bringing in another load. She was still in a quandary over what to do about the situation with Lucille and Katy. She didn't want to make even more trouble for them. She decided she must talk to John Phillips about it . . . and about the fact that Anita Wolf was in love with him.

As she tied the horse, again she caught the faint sound of drums. She wondered if Anita was right that she should go and see Night Hunter. The old man would probably just laugh at her dreams.

Black Hawk could hear the gunfire, smell the smoke from burnt powder. He could hear the screams of women and children. He grabbed Little Fox and ran, searching frantically for his wife, Turtle Woman, and his other son, Small Bear.

Bullets whizzed past him as he screamed Turtle Woman's name, but there was no answer. The bullets came from the soldiers' guns. Why were they shooting at them? He and his people had no weapons with which to shoot back. They had all just been captured and surrounded by the soldiers. He wanted to stand up and fight, even without a weapon, for what the soldiers were doing was wrong. Everything was confusion and death. If it were not for Little Fox, he would make a stand, maybe kill himself a couple of those soldiers before they murdered him as they were murdering so many people around him.

Shielding Little Fox with his body, he ran with the others to try to find shelter from the singing bullets. He felt one graze across his upper right shoulder, and he grunted and fell, then got up and kept running. How could this be happening? He had fled here with Big Foot, the old Indian leader who, like he and the others, had become afraid when Sitting Bull was shot down by their own Indian police. They had few weapons, were not looking for a fight, just safety. When the soldiers found them, they had taken what weapons they had, and then there had been a gunshot. He had no idea who had fired the shot or why, but that was all the surrounding soldiers needed to believe that a fight had begun. They had opened fire. Poor old Big Foot, who had already been dying of pneumonia but had been dragged out into the cold anyway, was among the first to be killed.

He ran, clinging to Little Fox, gasping for breath. He stumbled down a small hill, and that was when he saw them, Turtle Woman and Small Bear. Turtle Woman lay dead, shot in the head; Small Bear lay beside her, where he had apparently rolled out of her arms when she fell. He had been hacked almost in half, his tiny, bloody body already stiff.

Never would he forget the horror of that moment. Never! Nor would he forget the sight of Sergeant Jubal Desmond, who sat nearby on his horse, a smoking gun in one hand and a bloody sword in the other. When Black Hawk reached out to touch his baby boy and felt how cold his little body was, he had gasped and cried out in grief, as he did now . . . in his semiconsciousness, a deep sleep brought on by pain and fasting and loss of blood from the Sun Dance ritual.

The cry in the dream came out of his mouth in an agonizing groan, and the shock of the memory startled him awake. He opened his eyes to see the old priest, Night Hunter, bending over him, waving sacred smoke over his face and chanting a song for healing. Black Hawk tried to sit up to gather his thoughts, but he felt as though he could not get his breath. Pain enveloped him, and he fell back against a pillow of straw and buffalo hide.

"You must lie still, Black Hawk," someone told him in his own tongue. It was a woman's voice. He turned to see Otter Woman sitting near him. She leaned over him, pressing a cool rag to his forehead. "You have been very sick since the Sun Dance. Your wounds are full of the bad spirits, who try to take over your body," she told him softly. "Night Hunter has treated your wounds and fought the bad spirits with healing herbs and prayer." She touched his hair. "You were the bravest of all the dancers. Wakantanka will surely smile upon you and take the bad spirits away and make you well."

Black Hawk swallowed. "Water," he mumbled.

"I will get you some," Otter Woman answered.

Black Hawk watched her move about. Otter Woman was a good friend, sometimes a lover. She was not beautiful, had long passed her youth, but she was pretty enough, plump in the right places. Otter Woman had been widowed twice, by two men who had been brothers. Now she lived with her grandmother, but often she came out to find him, offering to tend to his manly needs. Otter Woman had always been loose. She liked the men, but since offering herself to him, he suspected she had been with no one else. He did not love her or want her for a wife, and she did not expect it. She could have no children. She was simply someone to share a bed with when needed, someone to hold in the night when he ached for Turtle Woman. In return, he often brought Otter Woman fresh game, which was so much better than the rotten meat supplied by the government.

How he hated the white man's government, the white man's power and superior weapons, the fact that there were so many white men in the East that it was impossible to ever again consider defeating them. How he hated this new way of life, this helpless feeling. He hated the soldiers who patrolled the reservation, the spineless, worthless white whiskey traders who often snuck onto the reservation to sell their firewater to the Sioux. The whiskey made his people weak and silly. Those who liked the drink did not seem to see that. Some would kill for one drink of it.

Everything about life as he once knew it was changed now, and warriors like himself belonged nowhere. It felt good to suffer this way, to know it was because he had made the ultimate sacrifice again at the Sun Dance. At least he had that. He would never let go of his beliefs, of the old ways. Never!

Otter Woman bent over him and put a ladle of water to his lips. He swallowed, watching her eyes. "I will . . . live?"

She smiled. "Nothing can kill Black Hawk. He has much power. The sacrifice has made you weaker for the moment so that the body can rest and become even stronger when it is healed. I watched you, Black Hawk. You were the last to go down. I watched you blow your whistle, and, in the end, I could see you were having a vision, and that you were lost in it. I am glad. I would not want you to suffer that way without the reward of a vision. You will be even stronger now, and you will be able to carry on with courage against the soldiers and missionaries who try to change us."

Black Hawk closed his eyes. Yes, he had had a vision. It came back to him now, and he was confused by it. He had to tell Night Hunter what he had seen, but he could not say it in front of Otter Woman. A man's vision was too sacred and personal to share with anyone but a priest, who was the only one who might be able to tell him its meaning. Besides that, another woman had been part of the vision . . . a white woman. Otter Woman must not know about this.

"Leave me," he groaned. "I must . . . be alone . . . with Night Hunter."

Otter Woman wanted to stay. Surely she was important enough to him now to share his vision. She glanced at Night Hunter. The old man's piercing dark eyes warned her she must go. She pressed her lips together in anger and rose. "I will come back and take care of you until you are healed," she told Black Hawk before leaving.

Black Hawk watched her go. "Look out," he told Night Hunter then, "and be sure she has . . . gone far enough away . . . that she . . . cannot hear."

Night Hunter nodded. He waved a feather over Black Hawk's wounds, then rose to go to the tipi entrance. He looked to see that Otter Woman had walked over to speak with Black Hawk's sister, Many Birds, and his grandmother, Dancing Woman, several yards away. He turned back and came close to Black Hawk. "She is gone." He leaned over the man, lifting a cloth that had been placed over each breast to cover a packing of moss on each wound.

"Never before have you taken sick this way after the Sun Dance," he told Black Hawk. "I believe there is meaning to it. Do you wish to share your vision with me?"

Black Hawk thought a moment, not wanting to admit that a white woman had been part of his dream. Still, it was important that a man understand his visions. He had suffered much. To do so without understanding the meaning of what he had seen would go against all his beliefs, against Wakantanka, who had brought him the dream in return for his blood sacrifice. He looked up into Night Hunter's all-knowing eyes, studied the thousands of wrinkles on the old man's face. Yes, Night Hunter would have the answer.

"I rode . . . my spotted horse, Father," he said, using the term often used by his people for the old, wise ones. "I was riding very fast across the wide land. I saw a herd of buffalo to my left, but then I could no longer see them. Ahead of me there was a woman . . . waiting." He breathed deeply against the pain, and his body was drenched in sweat from fever. "I thought it was Turtle Woman . . . that I had died and had gone to be with her; but when I drew closer . . . I saw that she was white. She had hair the color of corn silk and eyes like the sky. It does not seem right . . . to have a vision about a white woman . . . but I must tell you the truth, for I do not know what to make of it." He swallowed, his mouth feeling as though he had chewed on sand. "I need . . . more water."

Night Hunter moved around him to get another ladle of water from a wooden bucket. He leaned down and helped Black Hawk drink it. "You have not told me all of it," he said. It was a statement, not a question. Outside, children played and men joined in horse racing and a bow-and-arrow contest. The Sun Dance celebration would continue for several more days before they all went back to the central agency. The soldiers had not come to stop them, but they knew that one day even this, their most sacred celebration, would be taken from them.

"No, I have not told you all of it." Black Hawk held the old man's gaze as he spoke. "I have never seen this woman before . . . not in this life. Yet in the vision, when I came closer to her, I seemed to know her well . . . and I had deep feelings for her. I do not understand this. I could never feel deeply for a *wasicu* woman. I reached out for her . . . and she stretched out her hand. The moment I touched it, she vanished."

The old man closed his eyes and breathed deeply. "I have seen things myself, Black Hawk. I have seen death . . . a white man. I cannot see his face, but his death will mean much trouble for you. This white woman with the golden hair, I do not know who she is, but there is talk of a white woman who has come here to teach the children. She has golden hair, and she is different from the others in that she speaks the Sioux tongue, and she seems to understand our ways. I do not know if this could be the woman in your vision, but I feel the meaning of the vision is that somehow that woman will help you. If you accept her, she will not vanish when you need her." He opened his eyes and looked down at Black Hawk. "Somehow I believe this woman will have something to do with the trouble you will see over a white man's death, but I know no more than that. When you feel you have found this woman, do not shun her, in spite of how you feel about the *wasicus*. This vision must be fulfilled. I do not know how it will happen. Only your own heart can tell you what you must do, and only your heart will know when you have found this woman."

Black Hawk could still see it all vividly. He could see her hair, her blue eyes, yet he could not see all of her face. He could feel a fire tear through him when he touched her fingers, and it still startled him to remember it. "I want nothing to do with any white woman," he told Night Hunter.

The old man scowled. "To turn away from our visions is to die, Black Hawk." He shook a sacred rattle made from a turtle's shell over the fire nearby. He prayed for Black Hawk's health, and for an answer to his vision. He breathed deeply of the sweet smell of the sacred smoke. "You will know, Black Hawk. You will know, and you will not be able to turn away from her."

Black Hawk closed his eyes." I would rather die."

Seven

Evelyn approached the gathering hesitantly, accompanied by Anita, who explained the ritual taking place. "Many Birds has had her first time of month," she told Evelyn, who understood that talking about such things was natural to the Indian. All aspects of life were beautiful and to be celebrated, such as a young girl's first menstruation, which in her own culture was a forbidden subject, something women only whispered about, as though it was something shameful.

She and Anita watched the ceremony from a small rise, remaining on horseback. Anita sat astride a roan gelding, while Evelyn used an old sidesaddle on the ageing white mare that belonged to Reverend Phillips. She could see Black Hawk's sister sitting below, in the center of a circle of men and women. The thirteen-year-old girl was listening intently to an old man, who was talking quietly to her, sometimes shaking his finger at her.

"The old man is Night Hunter, isn't he?" Evelyn asked Anita.

"Yes. Because he is considered sacred, he has been chosen to instruct Many Birds in her responsibilities as a woman now. The old woman sitting close behind her is her grandmother, Dancing Woman. She is the only relative left to Many Birds and Black Hawk, except for Black Hawk's little son."

Evelyn looked around the crowd, more interested in catching a glimpse of the mysterious Black Hawk than watching the puberty ritual being conducted for his sister. For several days she had contemplated whether or not she should go and talk to the rather frightening old Night Hunter, but she had not been able to drum up the courage.

"The ritual would have been conducted before this," Anita was telling her, "but first came the Sun Dance. Because Black Hawk wished to participate in that, and since he was sick for several days afterward, they waited until now for his sister's celebration."

"Sick? I didn't know he had been sick."

"The wounds from the piercing of the breasts became infected, and for a few days he was very weak." Anita patted her horse's neck to keep it calm. Today her hair was combed out long and straight, and she wore a doeskin tunic rather than white woman's clothing. Evelyn knew she did so out of respect for her people at this sacred celebration. Today Anita was a Sioux woman in every respect. She could sense her pride as she explained the ritual.

"The tipi to the right is a new one, constructed by Many Birds's grandmother and other friends," Anita continued. "Many Birds has placed her menstrual bundle in a tree to guard it from the evil influences of *Inktomi,* the Spider. Night Hunter will smoke the pipe and will burn sweetgrass and sage to ward off the evil spirits and assure that Many Birds will live a long life and bear many children."

Evelyn tried to concentrate, but she could not help wondering about Black Hawk . . . if he would come here . . . how sick he had been. She admired his courage and faithfulness to his religion and beliefs for participating in the Sun Dance, even though she personally agreed it was rather barbaric. The thought of a man willingly sacrificing blood and suffering pain stirred feelings deep inside that she would rather not admit to. She shook away those thoughts as Many Birds rose and walked inside the tipi with Night Hunter, who had first put on a buffalo headdress and a buffalo tail. The old grandmother and several others followed the two of them inside. "What will happen now?" she asked Anita.

"Many Birds will sit between a sacred altar and the tipi fire. On the altar will be a buffalo skull, a pipe, prayer wands, and sweetgrass. Night Hunter will light his pipe and blow the sacred smoke into the nasal openings of the buffalo skull, then will paint the forehead red. He will tell Many Birds she must be industrious, silent and wise, and cheerful like the meadowlark. If she does this, she will command a high price as a bride, and will bear many children. She must be wary of evil influences. She is now a buffalo cow. Soon you will hear singing as Night Hunter dances the buffalo dance around her. She will drink from a bowl of water and chokecherries, as a symbol of drinking from a buffalo watering hole. She will be told to sit like a woman, with both legs to one side of her, and Night Hunter will paint her forehead red and on up through a center part in her hair. Her grandmother will go and remove the girl's menstrual bundle from the tree, and she will be declared a woman and can leave the lodge. Then there will be a fine feast to celebrate Many Birds's womanhood."

Evelyn watched quietly, wishing she could see the entire ritual; but she knew that those below would never allow her, a white woman, inside the sacred tipi. "I wish—" She did not finish the sentence, for just then she heard the shudder of a horse behind her. She turned, and her breath caught in her throat as her heart inexplicably pounded so hard she could feel it beating. She felt the crimson coming into her face as she stared at the most handsome Indian man she had ever set eyes on. He was so like the man in her dreams that she had to struggle to keep her mouth from falling open, and she wondered at the possibility of supernatural powers having invaded her soul. He sat there tall and proud on a spotted horse, his dark skin glistening in the hot sun, his chest and arms bare except for a bone choker necklace around his throat. He wore only a loincloth because of the heat.

She forced herself to keep from allowing her eyes to move over him admiringly for fear she would appear lustful . . . yet to her surprise and chagrin, lust was exactly what she felt at this moment. She knew without casting her eyes downward that his legs would look as strong and muscled as his powerful arms.

Simple rawhide straps decorated each of his upper arms, from which dangled little beads. The necklace and armbands, and a beaded rawhide strap tied around his forehead, left him simply adorned, no paint on his finely etched face or on his chest. His black hair hung long and straight, and his deep-set eyes were dark and unreadable, his nose straight and a perfect size for the rest of his face. His lips were full and clearly outlined, and she could see his jaw flex in what she supposed was anger at finding a white woman at a sacred Sioux celebration.

Perhaps the sight of him would not have held her so spellbound if he did not look exactly like the man in her dreams. Could this man, whom she had never met before, be the same one who had haunted her in the night? Perhaps it was just the part of her that *wanted* to find that man that led her to believe this was he. Whatever the answer, she knew without asking who he was: the notorious and elusive Black Hawk.

Black Hawk felt an odd force rush through his veins at the sight of the light-haired white woman who sat sidesaddle on a lazy-looking white mare. All the words Night Hunter had spoken to him about his vision came back to him. A white woman with light hair would someday help him. Could this be she? It angered him to come face-to-face with this beauty who could very possibly be the woman who had plagued him since the Sun Dance.

"Who are you?" he demanded in the Sioux tongue, thinking to frighten her by speaking fiercely in his own language. To his surprise, she did not flinch, and she apparently understood his question, for not only did she answer him, but she did so in his own language.

"I am called Evelyn Gibbons," she answered. "I have come here to teach on the reservation."

Although the woman put on a show of calm, he could see that she was somewhat shaken by his silent and sudden appearance. It was more than that, though. He had never met this woman, yet she had not only recognized him and seemed to expect him, but she also had looked at him as though they were already acquainted. How could that be? In those stirring blue eyes he saw the same emotion that stirred in his own soul—a feeling that he already knew her, and she knew him . . . a sense of one-ness that sent a chill through his blood. The realization that this could be the white woman Night Hunter had told him he would find angered him even more. "You do not belong here!"

"I brought her here, Black Hawk," Anita spoke up. "She wants to learn all about our ways so that she can understand our people better. She has a good heart."

He looked at Anita with a sneer. "You have befriended the white man, gone to his school, taken his teachings to heart. You are not one to choose who can and cannot attend a sacred ritual!"

Anita held her chin proudly. "I am still Sioux! I still honor and respect our beliefs. I am just smart enough to understand that to survive, we must accept what is. We must learn the white man's ways. To cling to the old ways and continue to fight will mean the end of us! The battle is over, Black Hawk. The time for healing and learning a new way has come. It does not mean we must give up all that is precious to us."

He rode his spotted horse closer, tossing his long hair behind his shoulders and turning his dark eyes to Evelyn. "That is exactly what the white man would have us do. Teachers like this woman here have come to steal away all that is sacred to us. She might say she has not come to take away our children or our very hearts, but that is her mission, all the same!"

Anita started to answer him, but Evelyn interrupted, angered by his words, determined to show no fear in front of this man who was equally determined to insult her and frighten her away. "If I were here for such a thing, why would I come to witness the puberty celebration for your sister?" she demanded. "I want to understand, to find a way to teach your children what they must know to survive without their losing grasp of their own heritage. I understand more than you think, Black Hawk. I have lived among Indians most of my life. My mother and father taught on a Cheyenne reservation in Indian Territory when I was a child, and I befriended—" She hesitated, realizing now why this man looked so familiar to her. He was the image of Wild Horse. Had he returned to her in another form? Such a thought went against all her beliefs, and she felt like a fool for even considering it. "When I was a little girl, my mother and I befriended a Cheyenne warrior called Wild Horse, who taught us many things about his people that I never forgot. I saw him killed by soldiers, and I vowed then to always do what I could to help all people of the Indian race, to help them preserve their customs while learning to live a new way."

For several seconds Black Hawk's dark eyes drilled into her, and Evelyn felt as though the man could see right into her soul. Did he sense her attraction to him? His eyes moved over her, and she felt totally naked, not just in body, but in her deepest emotions. He drew in his breath when he looked into her eyes again, and he seemed to be fighting something in his own soul when he suddenly jerked the reins of his horse and urged the animal to back away. "I do not believe you!" he said through gritted teeth. "I do not want you here!"

He looked back at an approaching pony, and Evelyn moved her gaze to see a young boy riding toward him. She knew it had to be his son, Little Fox, who at seven was obviously already a good rider. The boy came toward them at a gentle lope, perched in a sure position on the young Appaloosa, his dark hair dancing in the wind. Even from a distance, Evelyn could see the boy was as handsome as his father.

"Leave this place!" Black Hawk demanded. "Do not set eyes on my son, and do not speak to him! You will not take my son from me!"

Evelyn frowned, turning her horse slightly. "I have no wish to take your son from you, Black Hawk; but if you would allow him to come to my school, it would help convince the rest of your people to do the same. You would be *helping* them by setting an example, by showing your trust—"

"Do not speak to me of such foolishness!" he interrupted her. "My son will never set a foot inside a white man's school, where they would cut off his hair, and punish him with the whip for speaking his own tongue; where they would destroy his soul and break his heart!"

"I would never do any of those things," Evelyn said calmly, forcing herself to face the man squarely in spite of his fierce determination and the threatening look in his eyes. "My school is right here on the reservation. Children who come there can go back home every day when their lessons are done. I do not ask them to cut their hair or wear white man's clothes. Talk to Red Foot Woman. Her son, He-Who-Hunts, has been coming for many days now. And Big Belly has sent Standing Horse and Bright Feather."

"Big Belly is lazy. He sends his children so that someone else will look after them! He has no pride, and his only friend is a bottle of firewater!"

"Red Foot Woman is respected by your people. Talk to her. She will tell you I have not tried to change He-Who-Hunts. I have not cut his hair or asked him to dress differently. And there are others now. More have come because they are beginning to trust me. Falling Eagle sends his son and daughter, Fast Arrow and Laughing Girl. Many Hands sends all three of his sons, Tall Buffalo, Prairie Runner, and Flying Horse. I call them by their

Sioux names because I respect the names given them by their loved ones. I know that they have also been given Christian names, but I use only their Sioux names. Why would I do this, and why would I have studied for years to learn the Sioux tongue if I did not truly care about your culture and respect your ways?"

Black Hawk found himself both admiring this woman for her courage in talking right back to him, in his own language; and hating her for that same courage, which made her speak boldly to a warrior, with a truthful look in those blue eyes that made him look and feel foolish. It only made him more determined to be right, more determined to convince himself she was lying, like *all* whites had lied to his people from the first time they set foot on Indian lands and drew up their first treaty. Little Fox rode up beside him, and he put out his hand. "Stay back from this woman!" he ordered the boy. He grasped hold of Evelyn's forearm, squeezing just enough so that he knew it hurt. "Leave now," he sneered. "You do not belong here!"

Evelyn refused to show that he had brought her pain. "I will leave, but not out of fear or because you order it!" she answered firmly. "I will leave only because I respect your reasons for wanting me to go, because you feel this is too sacred a moment for one such as I to share! You do not frighten me, Black Hawk," she lied. "It is *you* who fears *me!* You fear I might take something precious from you, but you will learn that you are wrong! And there is something more. There is something we must both settle between us, but neither of us knows yet what it is. This is not the last time we will meet. You feel it, and *I* feel it!"

She yanked her arm away and rode off, her heart pounding, feeling on fire in a way she had never before experienced, longing to stay and talk to the mysterious man who had kept her awake nights, and the sight of whom sent desire rushing through her like a waterfall. Her blood still felt hot from his touch, and she was sure now that Black Hawk was the reason she was here, the powerful force that had drawn her away from a settled life of comfort and peace back in Wisconsin. She shivered with the eerie sensation the sight of him had given her. She knew she had to find a way to get close to him again.

Anita rode up beside her, laughing lightly. "You surprised Black Hawk by standing up to him, Evy," she told her. "He tried to be mean to you, but I could tell he was greatly impressed by you! You have given him much to think about. I have never seen anyone face him so boldly! What did you mean about him fearing you, and that you will meet again? Have you had a vision about Black Hawk? You must talk to Night Hunter if this is so!"

Evelyn, more shaken than she wanted Anita to know, slowed her horse and turned it to see Black Hawk still watching her. "It's very personal, Anita. I don't know yet just what I'm going to do, but come hell or high water, I am going to see Little Fox in our school!" She turned and rode off, and Anita looked back at Black Hawk. "You have met your match, Black Hawk," she said quietly, and with a smile. "And it is not another warrior or a soldier. It is a small white woman with eyes like the sky."

Evelyn rode at a near gallop, her mind whirling with confusion. For the moment she just wanted to get as far away from Black Hawk's discerning eyes as possible. Her arm still hurt where he had grabbed it, and she did not doubt his painful hold would leave bruises. She was amazed at her own courage when talking back to him, but now she felt like a fool for some of the things she had said, not only because they had been almost intimate, but because Anita had heard her.

She headed toward her now-finished cabin, glad she had a place to go where she could be alone. She hardly noticed the group of five soldiers that came toward her from her right until they were close by and hailing her to slow down. She pulled on the reins of her horse, not realizing until the men surrounded her that one of them was Jubal Desmond.

"Where you headed in such a hurry, Miss Gibbons?" the man asked. "Something wrong?"

Evelyn began to perspire in the midday heat. The hard ride had shaken loose some of the hair she had bound into a loose bun at the top of her head. She knew she must look a mess, and she was embarrassed, as well as irritated that Jubal Desmond thought he had a right to stop and question her. "I just wanted to feel some wind in my face," she told him. "It's so very hot. If you will please go on with whatever you're doing out here, I will be on my way." She started to continue on, but Desmond grasped her horse's bridle.

"You look upset, ma'am," he said with a cocky grin. He glanced in the direction from which she had come. "Couldn't be you went to that celebration Black Hawk's family and friends are having for his sister, could it? What'd they do, chase you off?" He chuckled. "I could have told you not to go there. You're lucky Black Hawk himself didn't send you running."

"Please let go of my horse, Sergeant Desmond."

Desmond released the animal. "Long as I've got you here, I'd like to ask you to a dance, Miss Gibbons, next Saturday at the fort. Will you do me the honors?"

Evelyn scrambled to think of a way out. She hardly knew Desmond, but she detested him just the same. Still, she suspected it was best not to cross him, or to embarrass him in front of his men. "I am very flattered, Sergeant, but I am afraid I don't dance. It is against my religion," she lied. She loved to dance, although her father had always preached that it was sinful. "I hope you can understand."

The man shrugged. "You don't have to dance, if you don't want. There will be plenty of food. You can just eat and keep me company and watch everybody else dance."

"Besides, the sergeant don't dance too good anyway," one of the other men spoke up. The rest of them laughed lightly, and Desmond scowled at the one who had made the remark.

"Shut up, Henley! Go on with the rest and get over to that shindig they're having. Make sure nobody starts trouble. Black Hawk could come along and rally them together. He's been feeling his oats lately."

Evelyn watched them all ride off, and she worried for Black Hawk. "It's just a puberty celebration, Sergeant. Everyone there is quite peaceful."

The man rubbed his chin. "Maybe so. We're supposed to keep an eye out just in case. And if everything is so smooth over there, how come you were riding hell-bent out of there a minute ago?"

Evelyn prayed she would be forgiven for her continued lies. "I told you, I just wanted to feel the air in my face because of the heat. Most of them were in a tipi when I left. There was nothing to watch, so I decided to go home."

"Well, whatever the reason, I'm glad I caught you. Will you go to the dance with me?"

The man's gaze raked over her hungrily, and Evelyn shivered. She thought how strange it was that Black Hawk's grabbing her wrist and trying to threaten her had not made her nearly as apprehensive as merely being around Jubal Desmond did. "Perhaps another time, Sergeant. I am so busy, what with just moving into my own cabin, more children coming to the school every day and all. I truly appreciate the invitation. Why don't you let me think about it for the next couple of days? It's so warm, I just can't think straight right now. I would like to get to my cabin and change my clothes." To her relief, Anita rode up beside her.

"I decided to catch up with you, Evy," she told her. "I was going to stay, but I was worried about you riding back alone." Her horse shuddered and was beginning to lather. "You rode off so fast, I could barely catch up!"

"I'm just fine, Anita." Evelyn noticed the way Desmond looked at the Indian woman, as though she were nothing but a bit of trash, something to be ogled but not respected. "Check with me in a couple of days," she told the man, putting on a smile for him. "And thank you for the thought, Sergeant."

The man nodded. Evelyn could not be sure if he was upset or not. "You be careful now," he told her. "And if I were you, I'd stay away from those Indian ceremonies. It's no place for a lady like you." He tipped his hat and rode out after his men. Evelyn breathed a sigh of relief.

Anita watched after him with a frown. "I do not like that person one bit. When I saw him and his men surround you, I rode faster to get here. I thought perhaps they were giving you a bad time."

Evelyn urged her horse into a slower trot. "He asked me to a dance Saturday night. I told him maybe, only because I didn't want to embarrass him in front of his men, but I have no intentions of going with him."

Anita rode beside her. "It is best that you don't, but I fear he is someone who does not like to be crossed. He has a reputation among my people as a bully and a man not to be respected."

"I can handle the sergeant, Anita."

The woman grinned. "Like you handled Black Hawk?"

Evelyn cast her a scowl. "I hope you don't go telling Janine or the reverend about what happened, Anita. It's a personal thing. If I feel there is something they should know, I'll tell them myself."

"I will not say a word."

Evelyn looked back at the sergeant, who was headed for the site of the puberty ritual. "He won't make trouble for Black Hawk, will he?"

Anita shrugged. "I do not know. The soldiers are only to stay back and watch. They cannot get close."

Evelyn prayed there would be no trouble, but she knew she had more than that to pray about. This restless stirring in her soul and the unanswered questions she had about her dream were going to make it difficult to sleep. She had to see Black

Hawk again, find a way to get closer to him. It irritated her that she had to think of a way to turn down Sergeant Desmond. There were so many other things to think about right now, including considering Anita's suggestion that she talk to Night Hunter. Now that she had met Black Hawk and was convinced he was the man in her dream, she needed some answers that only an Indian holy man could give her.

Black Hawk flexed his hand, thinking how slender and breakable the white woman's arm had felt in his grip. He did not want to like or admire her, yet touching her had sent a tingle through his body, and her boldness had left an impression. Her blue eyes were true. He sensed that she did not lie, yet to trust a *wicasa ska,* man or woman, went against all that he was sworn to accept about his enemy, especially a white teacher.

Why had the woman said they would see each other again? What was this strange familiarity with someone on whom he had never set his gaze before? It was a puzzle, as was the attraction he felt to her. The woman in his vision had been faceless, yet he knew she had been white, with hair like yellow grass.

His thoughts were interrupted when his lovely young sister came out from the sacred tipi, wearing a white tunic, her forehead painted red. He smiled at how pretty she was, and a feeling of protectiveness came over him. She was marriageable now, but he would make sure she went only to a fitting warrior who would provide well for her, as well as could be expected now that they were forced to stay within the confines of the reservation.

How he longed to live the old way, the way he remembered as a boy, free and wild, migrating with the seasons. The white man had ended all of that, had taken away his wife and another son. "Go and join in the celebrations," he told Little Fox. Both had dismounted and tied their mounts. Little Fox ran down the hill to take part in the feast that had been prepared. Everyone had contributed something, and in that precious moment Black Hawk saw a few happy faces. He remembered how it was after a buffalo hunt, when those who downed the most animals shared their meat and the byproducts with those who were not so lucky in the hunt. A grand feast was always to be had those first few days while the women cleaned the hides and smoked more meat for winter and made pemmican. Nearly everything they needed had come from the buffalo: clothing, utensils, water bags, blankets, tipi hides, sacred rattles, war shields, jewelry, hair ornaments, moccasins. When the buffalo ran as thick as grass, they were able to live off the animals and the land. They did not need the white man's handouts.

Now all of that was gone. He seldom even spotted a buffalo anymore, and sometimes he wondered if perhaps soon there would be none left at all.

"Aren't you going to join your sister and the others, Black Hawk?"

Black Hawk turned to see Jubal Desmond and four other men sitting on horses behind him. His own eyes turned to slivers of hatred. Desmond was one of those who made him want to keep fighting, a soldier he would gladly run his knife through if he could get away with it. The lieutenant had been at Wounded Knee, and Black Hawk had himself witnessed the man shoot down several unarmed Indians. Never would he forget the sight of Desmond sitting on his horse near Turtle Woman when he found her shot in the head, Small Bear lying bloody and dead beside her. Desmond had hounded him ever since, trying to find reasons to arrest him. Black Hawk suspected it was because he had a guilty conscience. Perhaps Desmond was afraid of him, afraid he would seek revenge. He could sleep better if he knew Black Hawk was behind bars in one of those terrible prison camps in the South.

Desmond was part of the reason Black Hawk often liked to

ride near the fort or the agency at night and give out war cries. He wanted the sergeant to feel a chill down his spine, wanted him to be nervous. "I will go and wish my sister well soon," he answered Desmond in English. "You and your men need not be here. This is a celebration, not a war dance."

Desmond grinned nervously. "That's what your people said about the Ghost Dance, and look what that led to."

Black Hawk studied the man intently. "Yes," he answered. "I well know what it led to, and all because of the stupidity and cowardliness of the soldiers who were there and did not understand. You were so ready to shoot us down before you tried to understand what had happened. Go away, Sergeant! You do not belong here!"

Desmond rode closer. "Don't let me catch you making trouble, Black Hawk. Word is, somebody has been stealin' cattle and horses from white folks up north of here. You'd have a hard time provin' your whereabouts if you got blamed. And another thing, me and my men found a whiskey wagon all busted up a few weeks ago, whiskey bottles spilled out all over the place. You have anything to do with that?"

Black Hawk shrugged. "I do not know of this."

"I'll just *bet* you don't," Desmond sneered. "You stay out of soldier business, Black Hawk, or you just might stir up more trouble than you can handle!"

Black Hawk did not flinch. He gave Desmond a look that he could see was making the man shake in his boots. "When the soldiers start taking care of their business the way that they should, protecting my people from the whiskey traders and those who would steal their land from them, then *I* will not have to do the soldiers' business for them!"

Desmond leaned over in his saddle. "You watch yourself, Black Hawk. You're looking to go to prison, and then there won't be anybody around to protect that boy of yours."

Black Hawk just grinned. "You are a brave man when you

are surrounded with others who would help you, and when your opponent is not armed." He reached up and quickly yanked Desmond's hat down over his eyes. "You watch *yourself*," he said. He quickly turned and walked away, taking pleasure in the sound of laughter from the other men as he headed toward the celebrations.

"Black Hawk, you sonofabitch!" Desmond shouted. "Come back here, you red-skinned bastard!"

Black Hawk heard more laughter, then cussing from Desmond, and orders for his men to shut up. "Someday I will repay you for Wounded Knee," Black Hawk muttered. He did not fear that Desmond would try anything here, not with so many Sioux around, and not without just cause. The peace between the Indians and the soldiers on the reservation was always a tentative thing, and any time he could put fear in the heart of Jubal Desmond, or insult the man in front of others, he would take advantage of the moment.

He turned to see Desmond and the others riding away. "Until we meet again, my friend," he sneered. He thought again about the white woman whom he had chased away . . . or had he? Perhaps she really had left out of respect and not out of fear. She was a woman of great mystery, and he decided that if they truly were destined to meet again, he would not really mind; but he would not let her know that.

Eight

Lucille brushed her long dark hair as she studied herself in the mirror. It was always a blessed relief to her when Seth went off alone. Each time he did so, she daydreamed about something happening to him and that he would never come back. Since he had been gone all night, probably playing poker with some of the soldiers, he would probably show up any time now. She was finished with morning chores, and if she was lucky, Seth would be tired and want to sleep the rest of the day, leaving her and Katy a free afternoon.

She leaned forward, cocking her head one way and another. Was she pretty? She grasped some of her hair and twisted it up on top of her head, realizing it made her look older, much more a woman. A woman . . . Tears stung her eyes when she realized Seth had not even allowed her to be a child, and now that she was nearing an age when most young women married, who would want her? Would Seth even allow her to marry? Was it her place to tell a man she was not clean and pure, that her own adoptive father had stolen what should belong to a new husband?

She let her hair down and shook it behind her shoulders. Seth liked her hair this way, brushed out long. She gulped back a sob and grabbed the dark tresses angrily, twisting them into a simple bun at the nape of her neck. Why had she even bothered to wash her hair, or to wonder if she was pretty or what it might be like to have a real husband who loved her? She probably couldn't even have babies, and thanks to Seth no man would want her anyway. She rose from the wooden chair she had pulled up in front of the sagging dressing table with its faded, foggy mirror, thinking how that mirror reflected the true Lucille, faded and distorted, not clean and bright and new.

She walked to the bedroom window and stared out across the wide, barren land to the north. In the distance she could see the scattering of tipis and log houses, a couple of little frame homes. Although she could not see it from here, she knew that only a few miles away was the church . . . and the school . . . and Miss Gibbons. She already loved the woman for the way she had stood up to Seth that day at the agency.

She was sure no prettier woman existed on the face of the earth, perhaps none kinder. Since her days at the orphanage and then being literally sold off to Seth Bridges, she had never known one person whom she felt she could trust, one person who might really care, until watching Miss Gibbons the other day. For the first time since becoming the property of Seth Bridges, she saw a ray of hope. Until now, there had been no one to whom she could turn if she decided to run away. Not even Reverend Phillips had been brave enough to talk to Seth the way Miss Gibbons had talked to him. The trouble was, she knew how mean Seth could be. She did not want to visit the man's wrath on poor Miss Gibbons. She could not just run off with Katy and expect the woman to gladly take them in with Seth right on their heels, probably with a shotgun.

She had to think this through carefully. She had no particular plans yet. All she had was that glimmer of hope, and it stirred something in her, a bit more courage, even a hint of pride, something she had not felt in a long time. How she wished she could be as pure and beautiful and educated and well-dressed as Miss Gibbons. Maybe if the woman knew about her and Seth, she would be shocked and want nothing to do with her . . . but then, if she could get Katy to safety, find a way to let her sister be raised by a woman like Miss Gibbons, she would have at least saved Katy. It didn't much matter what happened to her anymore. She was soiled goods. But Katy was still good and pure and innocent. There was a chance for her to lead a normal life.

She saw Seth coming then, detested the sight of him. He slouched in the saddle, riding a sagging gray mare he had abused for years by not properly caring for the poor horse. She knew without seeing him close up that he had probably not slept more than three hours last night and would not have taken the time to shave or clean up this morning before heading home. If she was lucky, he would be too tired to give her the time of day, and too broke to buy much whiskey. Where he got it, she was not sure; but she *was* sure that a soldier or soldiers were part of the plan, probably being paid by whiskey smugglers to keep quiet and let them slip through so they could keep the Indians drunk and ignorant. She felt very sorry for the Indians sometimes, even though most of them frightened her. This land had been theirs, after all, once. As far as she was concerned, they could keep it. She would gladly move on to more civilized places, if only she could find the money and the means.

Someday that would happen. She already had some money saved, money she stole from Seth's pockets at times he was in a drunken sleep. She had it hidden in a secret place in the corn crib, a spot even Katy didn't know about yet. She would keep adding to it as much as she dared until she had enough to run away with Katy.

She glanced down to see Katy scurrying off to the chicken house. The girl had apparently heard or seen Seth coming and decided to stay out of sight. How much longer she could keep Seth from setting his hands on Katy, Lucille was not sure. If he *did* touch her sister, she would have to kill him after all and suffer the consequences. Maybe there would be a way for Miss Gibbons to help her before that happened.

She quickly ran her fingers over the dust of the windowsill and rubbed it onto her face. The last thing she wanted was to look pretty for Seth Bridges. She wore a faded blue dress that was too big for her, her hair pulled back into the plain bun. She hurried downstairs to the kitchen to appear busy, deciding to go ahead and start working on a stew for supper, even though it was only midmorning. The longer it simmered, the better it tasted; and the better meal she served, the better mood Seth would be in. She began peeling potatoes, and minutes later she heard Seth outside shouting to Katy that she had better come out from where she was hiding and tend to his horse, or he would give her extra chores.

"Goddamned lazy brat," he muttered as he came through the back door. "You'd better straighten out that little bitch of a sister, Lucy, or I'll tan her bare bottom till she can't sit down."

"She's feeding the chickens," Lucille answered without turning around. "She's just doing the chores she's supposed to do. She'll take care of the horse. Don't worry about it. Go on upstairs and get some sleep." She shivered when she felt the man move up closer behind her. He moved an arm around her middle from behind.

"You'd like that, wouldn't you? Get me out of your hair for a while?" He yanked at the bun at her neck, and with one painful jerk he tore out most of the pins and the ribbon that held it. "You know I hate it when you wear your hair like this!"

Lucille stood rigid, refusing to turn around. "It's hot. It feels better away from my face. Let go of me, Seth. Can't you see I'm trying to peel potatoes? Do you want a good supper when you get up later? You must have ridden most of the night if you came all the way from Fort Yates."

He moved a hand over her breasts before finally releasing her. "I'll want more than a good supper." He chuckled, then walked over to the wood stove to pour some hot coffee from a blue-speckled metal pot into a tin cup. "I made some plans for you, girl, somethin' that ought to please you."

The remark brought a tingling alarm to her blood, and she stopped peeling and turned to face him. "What plans?"

He grinned, showing teeth stained dark from too much chewing tobacco. Some of those teeth were missing. "You get to go to a dance at the fort. What do you think of that?"

Lucille knew the man too well to think he was allowing such a thing so that she could have a nice time. "Why?" she asked.

"Why!" He wiped at his nose with his shirtsleeve. "Now, that's a pretty stupid question! I figured you'd like to go, that's all. Wouldn't you like to get all prettied up and go dance with some of them nice young soldiers? Wouldn't you like a good time away from here? There will even be a beef roast. You won't have to cook—just eat and enjoy. Don't that sound nice?"

Lucille watched his filmy gray eyes warily. "What's the *real* reason, Seth?"

He slugged down the rest of his coffee and slammed the cup on the table. "I *told* you the reason! I even fixed you up with a date, that fine, handsome Sergeant Desmond. He was gonna ask that bitch of a schoolteacher, but the stuck-up, prissy snob turned him down. When I told him I figured you was old enough to go to a dance with a man, he lit up like a full moon and said he'd much rather take you anyway, says you're lots prettier than that old maid Gibbons. Now, don't that make you feel good? Wouldn't it be fun goin' to a dance all prettied up, bein' escorted by a sergeant in the United States Army?"

Lucille knew Seth too well to think that was all there was to it, and no man in his right mind would think she was prettier than Miss Gibbons! Besides, she was not terribly fond of Sergeant Desmond. She had met him a few times when he and Seth talked whenever they ran into each other. She didn't like the looks Desmond gave her, and she suspected he and Seth were in some kind of deal together involving whiskey smuggling. She could understand why Miss Gibbons had turned him down. She was much too good for the likes of Jubal Desmond. *But I'm not,* she thought.

There was something Seth was not telling her, but to question him was to ask for trouble. She forced a smile. "That sounds real nice, Seth, but please let me take Katy. She would love going to something like that. If the sergeant is a man of honor and respect, he won't mind my bringing my sister." She prayed inwardly he would agree. Her biggest fear was that the dance was just a ploy to get her away so that he could force himself on Katy while she was gone.

Seth scowled, and for a moment Lucille thought he would refuse her request in a explosion of curses, but then he only shrugged. "Sure, you can take her. Just make sure she understands that she ain't to dance with any of the soldiers. She's too young. And if the sergeant wants to be alone with you a time or two, tell Katy to mind her business. She can help with servin' the food or somethin'. I'll be there, too, so if either one of you messes with another man, or if I see you talkin' to that Miss Gibbons, you'll suffer for it, understand?"

Lucille turned back to the potatoes, breathing a sigh of relief that at least Katy would not be left behind alone with Seth. "I thought you said Miss Gibbons wouldn't be there."

"I said she turned down the sergeant's invitation. That don't mean she won't be there with somebody else. I expect there's plenty of soldiers who'd like to get under that woman's skirts and get a feel of her. You can bet somebody else will ask her."

Lucille gripped a potato tightly in her hand, hating the way the man had of making everything ugly. "When is the dance?" she asked.

"This comin' Saturday. You've got that one pretty yellow dress that fits you good. You wear that. It shows your shape real nice. And wear your hair down long." Seth walked toward the back stairs. "I'm goin' to bed. Wake me when supper's ready."

"I will." Lucille listened to him climb the stairs. She looked down at the knife in her hand, thinking how easy it would be to sink it into his heart while he slept; but if he awoke and caught her, he would most likely wrest the knife from her and put scars on her that would never go away. Worse, he would vent his wrath on Katy. No. There would be a better way. Someday she would figure out what it was.

She raised her head and watched out the window. Katy had untied the gray mare and was leading it to the barn. She wondered about the dance. Why did Seth care that she might want to go to something like that? Why had he even set her up with the sergeant? There was more to this than Seth suddenly allowing to let her go out and have a good time. Was he just trying to show others what a "considerate" father he was, showing off his lovely, young daughter? Was he considering getting someone else interested in her so he could marry her off and have Katy all to himself? And why the sergeant? There were lots of other soldiers at the fort who would probably love to have a date for the dance, men much younger than Jubal Desmond.

She returned to peeling potatoes, her mind racing with questions that she knew would not get answered until the night of the dance. She was not sure if she should be happy about going . . . or if there was some unknown reason she should dread the occasion.

Otter Woman awoke, taking a moment to allow her eyes to adjust to the moonlight that filtered into Black Hawk's tipi through the opening at the top. Because of the heat, all cooking was done outside, so no fire had been built inside the tipi. She lay quietly, finally making out Black Hawk sitting and staring at his sleeping son. As far as she could tell Black Hawk was still naked.

Otter Woman smiled at the memory of their reunion. She had ridden out here in the hills to find Black Hawk again, for she had not been with him since the Sun Dance, and she had felt a fire in her loins that only he could quench. She thought of him as a sturdy bull buffalo. He pleased her greatly. She, in turn, tried to please him, and she was sure she had done a good job of it earlier. Still, she had sensed something different about him. The man was always moody and thoughtful, but it seemed now that something more than his usual restlessness over the fate of his people was bothering him. He had never told her about the vision he had had at the Sun Dance, but it had changed him somehow, and she wished it had never happened.

She sat up, throwing the blanket away from her naked body and moving to where Black Hawk sat, running her hands over his bare back, then reaching around his neck from behind and pressing her breasts against his back while she rubbed at his nipples. "What is it that makes you sit awake in the night, my lover?" she asked.

He grasped her wrists and pushed backward, forcing her away from him. "I have much to think about."

Otter Woman pouted, moving to lie back down on the bed of robes where earlier the man had made love to her in wild passion, filling her almost painfully. She had seen something in his eyes then, a strange anger. It almost seemed to be directed at her, yet she knew that it was not. He wanted her, yet by the look in his eyes, she felt as though he saw someone else stretched out naked beneath him. "Is it a woman who disturbs your thoughts?" she asked.

Black Hawk sighed deeply. "You would not understand."

"I understand everything about you, Black Hawk. Something has taken you away in spirit. Is it the vision you had at the Sun Dance?"

Black Hawk could not answer. He knew how possessive Otter Woman could be, even though they did not love each other and were not man and wife. She considered him her bull, someone who could please her whenever she had the need; and he did not mind. She served a purpose, and when she came to him, she scrubbed his clothes and cooked for him and Little Fox. Surely she knew that perhaps one day he might want to marry again, and if he did, it would not be her. If he could tell her that the woman who ate at his insides was another Sioux woman, he would not worry so much about her reaction; but to have it be a *white* woman! He was himself ashamed and embarrassed at his thoughts, yet he knew that the schoolteacher, Miss Gibbons, that feisty, fast-talking, yellow-haired, blue-eyed vision, was the one Night Hunter had told him would help him someday.

When you feel you have found this woman, do not shun her, in spite of how you feel about the wicasa ska, *the man had told him. Only your own heart can tell you what must do, and only your heart will know when you have found this woman . . . You will know, Black Hawk, and you will not be able to turn away from her.*

But he *had* turned away from her. He *had* shunned her. When he saw her that day at Many Birds's puberty ritual, he had been so stunned that it angered him to know that the woman might have some kind of power over him. Was the Great Spirit angry with him for chasing the woman away? And how on earth could a white woman help him in any way?

"You know I cannot tell you of my vision," he answered Otter Woman.

Otter Woman felt a hot jealousy forming in her soul. Something . . . or someone . . . had taken Black Hawk from her. This time when she had come to him, it had been of her own accord, not because he had sent for her like all the times before. This time it seemed he would not have cared if she did not come at all, yet once she offered herself to him, he had taken her gladly, and fiercely; almost as though he thought that through her he could forget someone else. "Who is she?" she asked him. "There is another woman in your heart. I can feel it, Black Hawk."

"It is not what you think. It is not anyone you know."

Otter Woman thought a moment, remembering something Anita's brother, Broken Knife, had told her not so many nights ago. Broken Knife was another man she often visited to bestow sexual favors in return for food and trinkets; but Black Hawk was her favorite. He was built the biggest and strongest, and to grant him his pleasure was an honor. She began to wonder if the woman who was torturing Black Hawk's soul was the white woman Broken Knife had told her about.

Anita was an assistant to the new teacher who had come to the reservation, a woman with golden hair and pretty blue eyes, Broken Knife said. She had not seen this woman yet, but Black Hawk *had* seen her, according to Broken Knife. He said that when Anita visited him recently, she had laughed about how Black Hawk had tried to chase the white woman away from his sister's puberty ritual. The woman had apparently talked right back to him and had shown no fear. She had said she would leave out of respect, but not because Black Hawk frightened her, even though Black Hawk had grabbed her arm and hurt her. According to what Broken Knife said, Anita had told him that the white woman had daringly told Black Hawk they would meet again, that there was something that must be settled between them.

Surely it was not the white schoolteacher who plagued Black Hawk's thoughts! It was not like him to give a moment's consideration to someone like that. She watched him as he leaned over Little Fox and touched his hair for a moment.

"My only son," he said softly. He looked over at Otter Woman. "Perhaps it is wrong for me to continue the fight. Perhaps it will destroy my son's chance for survival in this new way we must live. Perhaps he *should* have some of the white man's schooling."

"What!" Otter Woman could hardly believe her ears. "I have never heard you talk this way before, Black Hawk! What is it that has made you so weak? Is it the white woman? That new schoolteacher? I heard through Broken Knife that she has turned you into a cowering little rabbit."

In a split second he was on her, grasping her arms painfully and pushing her back onto the bed of robes. "No one calls me a rabbit!" he growled. "What do you know of any of it? And how is it you were talking to Broken Knife? I think perhaps while you were talking, he was planting himself between your legs to feed your craving to have a man inside of you!"

She spit at him. "Maybe he was! But it was because *you* had not sent for me like you always have before! I get lonely, Black Hawk, especially for you! That is why I finally came here on my own!"

He remained straddled over her legs and jerked her to a sitting position. "From this moment, you will not talk with others about me or my private visions or feelings or anything I have done or said, or of things you know nothing about!"

Otter Woman's breath came in heavy pants, a mixture of fear and desire. "It *is* her, is it not? The white schoolteacher has somehow touched you. Was she a part of your vision, Black Hawk?"

"It is not for you to know."

"Do not be a fool, Black Hawk! She will poison your mind, and poison Little Fox's mind! She is like all the others, come here to *destroy* us! She has chosen you because you are the strongest, because the People listen to you, follow you. Stay away from that evil one! She will take away all that is Sioux about you! Our ancestors will weep in their graves, and the Great Spirit will punish you if you give any more thought to this woman!"

He eased his grip on her. "Perhaps Wakantanka will punish me if I do *not* speak with this woman."

"Why! It is true, then, isn't it? She was part of your vision!" She gritted her teeth. "I could *kill* her!"

Black Hawk glared at her, then without warning he back-handed her across the face. Otter Woman cried out, and her face spun away from him, but he felt no remorse. "You will never speak of this to another soul, do you hear?" Black Hawk warned her. "You will not speak of it with me, or with your grandmother or any of the many men you allow between your legs! You will say nothing to the white woman or to Broken Knife or Anita or anyone else! Do you understand me, Otter Woman?"

She put a shaking hand to her cheek and nodded her head.

"My son still sleeps, and I have need of you again," Black Hawk told her then.

He pushed her down on the bed of robes, then raised to his knees, parting her legs. He shoved himself inside her, and Otter Woman took him willingly, excited by his anger, glad he still wanted her, all the while thinking how she might get rid of the white woman or scare her into going back to the land of the rising sun where she belonged. In the days of freedom, Sioux women had numerous ways of frightening and torturing captive white women. How she would love to have that light-haired teacher as her slave! She would regret ever coming here! She would not say anything about her again to Black Hawk, but that did not mean she would not find a way to banish the white bitch from the reservation!

Black Hawk surged wildly, grasping Otter Woman's hips and taking his pleasure, fighting the image he saw in that moment. The woman beneath him was not dark and of his own race. She had skin like the white petals of a daisy, hair like yellow grass, eyes blue as the sky. He had never seen the nipples of a white woman. Were they brown? Perhaps they were pink, like sweet berries. Was the hair between her legs as yellow as the hair on her head? Was her skin as soft as it appeared? Did a white woman enjoy a man the way Indian women did?

He wanted to touch her. He wanted to speak with her again, to know why she had been a part of his vision, to know what she meant when she said they must talk again. How did she know that? Why had she not been afraid of him? Why did she already seem to know him that first day he had set eyes on her?

He leaned down and rubbed Otter Woman's sore cheek. "I am sorry," he told her gently. He licked at her neck, but he dreamed of tasting white skin, and his apology was to a woman who was not present to hear him. His life spilled into Otter Woman's barren belly, and she whispered his name in great pleasure. He looked down at her. The woman who looked back at him had blue eyes, and a smile of wonder and pleasure on her full lips. Golden hair spilled about her face and shoulders, and she belonged only to him . . . and he to her.

"Just look, Anita," Evelyn said. She stood beside the desk looking out at the children sitting at the homemade tables that served as desks for the little, one-room school. "In just one month we have gone from no pupils to eight. Most of our progress is thanks to you."

"We would not have the school at all if not for *you.* And they would not have come if they did not trust you. They trust you because they know your heart is good, and because you speak their tongue and do not scold them for speaking it themselves."

"William is learning quickly. He prefers to speak in English, wants very much to learn." Evelyn faced the Indian woman, wishing she could get Black Hawk off her mind. Ever since their run-in a few days ago, she could hardly think about anything else. "Janine mentioned to me once that Black Hawk can speak English when he wants to. Do you know how he learned? Do you think he teaches his son English?"

Anita smiled. She had not been able to help telling everyone she met the story of the confrontation between Black Hawk and Evelyn Gibbons. By now half the reservation was probably talking about it. She wished Evelyn would tell her more about why she had talked to the man the way she did, why she had not seemed afraid of him. "Black Hawk is very wise and cunning," she answered. "He knew at a young age that if he did not understand the white man's language, he could be easily tricked. As a teenager, after he lost his parents in a battle with soldiers who chased them into Canada, he came into the reservation and pretended to surrender. He allowed Catholic missionaries to teach him English, so that later, when more treaties were made, he could understand everything that was being said. It is said that he learned very quickly, that the missionaries were astonished at his intelligence; but he never took to the white man's ways or religion. As soon as he knew all he thought he needed, he left again. Why do you always ask about him, Evy?"

Evelyn felt a blush come to her face. "I just—there is so much mystery about him, that's all."

"Have you spoken with Night Hunter yet?"

"No. I'm not sure—" Evelyn heard a horse ride up. "There is Reverend Phillips for the daily religious lessons." This time it was Anita who blushed. The woman turned to begin erasing some numbers from a chalkboard, and Evelyn knew it was just a way of not having to face the reverend. Phillips came inside, holding a box.

"Good day, ladies. I've brought some little crosses sent by one of our sponsor-churches back East. I thought I would hand them out to each child and try to explain the symbol of the cross . . . that is, Miss Gibbons, if you will help me by interpreting to the ones who do not understand English."

"Of course, Reverend Phillips." Evelyn was glad to change the conversation away from Black Hawk. She had no idea what she was going to do about what seemed a ridiculous situation. She only knew something was left unsettled, and she had to find a way to settle it. Maybe then the dreams would stop visiting her in the night. "Let me see the crosses. Are they necklaces?"

"Yes. I know how the Indians love jewelry, so the children should find these delightful." Phillips walked up close to her, handing her the box, but he did not let go of it right away. "Miss Gibbons, I have been putting off asking you, but there is little time left."

Evelyn looked up at him curiously. "Ask me what?"

The man looked flustered. "Well, I don't much believe in dancing, but out here a person has to take whatever entertainment comes along just to break the lonesomeness of this land. They're having a dance at the fort Saturday night. I wondered if perhaps you would let me take you."

Evelyn could almost feel Anita's disappointment. She needed the woman's friendship and help, wanted no hard feelings; nor did she want to hurt John Phillips's feelings. "I . . . I'm flattered, Reverend." She glanced at Anita, who remained turned away. She looked back at the reverend. "But I'm afraid someone else has already asked me."

"Someone else? Then I *am* too late. Who is taking you?"

"Sergeant Desmond has asked me, and I accepted," she lied. She realized she really *would* have to accept Desmond's invitation, rather than create hard feelings between herself and Anita.

Anita turned around, surprised at Evelyn's answer. "But, Evy—"

Evelyn faced the woman, trying to tell her with her eyes that it was all right. "I gave him my answer yesterday," she told her. She looked back at the reverend. "Perhaps Anita would like to go with you. I am sure she would enjoy it," she told the man.

Phillips turned to Anita, who was staring at both of them with a red face and wide eyes. "Evy! I am sure Reverend Phillips does not need to be told who to take—"

"How about it, Miss Wolf? May I take you to the dance?" Phillips felt he had no choice now but to ask Anita. Still, somehow he did not mind. He had never been sure how to feel about Indian women, what Janine or those back East who sponsored him would think about him seeing one socially; nor had he ever noticed before the look he saw now in Anita's dark eyes. He felt confused. His attraction was to the beautiful Evelyn Gibbons, but he knew deep inside she did not feel the same way for him.

Anita swallowed, feeling hot all over. She loved Evelyn Gibbons for literally sacrificing herself to Sergeant Desmond rather than hurting her by going with the reverend. "I . . . yes, Reverend, I accept your invitation; but are you sure? I mean, I am Sioux . . . and my father and brother are not so well respected." She looked down at the desk.

Phillips smoothed his mustache nervously. "Well, I guess I can't come here and treat you and your people like equals without learning to consider you equal in *every* way, not just in religion and schooling; but also in friendship."

Anita felt light-headed. A dance! With Reverend Phillips! "What about Janine? She would also enjoy the dance."

"My sister is already planning to go. Lieutenant Teller invited her. He will meet her at the fort."

"Oh, I'm glad for her," Evelyn spoke up. "I know she was hoping the lieutenant would ask her."

Phillips looked surprised. "Why on earth would you accept an invitation from the sergeant?" he asked. "I doubt that he is much of a gentleman, Miss Gibbons."

Evelyn smiled. "There were other men with him when he asked me," she answered. "I didn't want to embarrass him by turning him down. Besides, we'll be at the fort surrounded by a lot of people. Maybe I can help teach Desmond a few manners."

Phillips frowned. "I'll be keeping an eye on you." He looked back at Anita. "Be at the church by seven Saturday morning. I'll take you and Janine in the wagon from there. It will take nearly all day to get there. We will all have to spend the night at the fort because of the long ride back. I am told that the colonel in charge is kicking some of the men out of their barracks to accommodate any females who come so that they will have a place to sleep. There will be plenty of food for all, so we should have a good time. You and Miss Gibbons and Janine have all worked very hard, and we have a long, lonely winter ahead of us." He turned to Evelyn. "It gets a lot colder here and the snow a lot deeper than you might realize," he told her. "I know you're used to such things in Wisconsin, but it can get even worse here. There will be days when you'll wish for someone to talk to, days when none of the children can get to school. That's why I'm taking advantage of the dance."

"I'm sure we'll all enjoy ourselves," Evelyn assured him. The reverend's disappointment that she would go with someone else was evident in his eyes, and Evelyn could only pray he would see how much Anita cared for him. She felt sorry for the woman's secret passion for this man who had no inkling of how she felt.

Phillips sighed. "I am sure we will. Is the sergeant coming for you, or will you also go with us?"

"I . . . I'm not sure," Evelyn answered, realizing she would have to find a way to contact Jubal Desmond and tell him she would go with him to the dance after all. "He is supposed to let me know," she lied.

The reverend turned back to Anita. "By the way, ladies, Agent McLaughlin has told me that a circus is coming to the reservation."

"A circus!" Anita's eyes widened. "I have read about such things, but . . . *here?* At Standing Rock?"

"It's being sponsored by the government, some sort of project to show the Sioux a bit of the outside world, exotic animals and acts, that sort of thing. I suppose they feel it might stir their curiosity, to learn more about the white man's world. It should be quite exciting!"

"A circus!" This time it was Evelyn who made the exclamation. "What an unusual idea. Perhaps it *could* help open these people's eyes a little, make them more eager to learn about other things in the world outside the reservation. I think it's a wonderful idea!"

"Well, we'll see about that. It won't be for another six weeks, around mid-September. Right now I am going out to the wagon to get some fresh biscuits Janine baked this morning for the children."

He turned and left, and Anita rushed to Evelyn's side. "Why did you lie to him that way, Evy! You can't stand Sergeant Desmond!"

Evelyn shrugged. "Maybe the man will turn out to be more of a gentleman at a formal dance than I think he is."

"But you already told him no!"

"Then I will have to get a message to him that I have changed my mind."

"I wish you would not have done this. I know why you did it, and it is not necessary."

Evelyn touched the woman's arm. "Yes, it is, Anita. I think it's time you started letting Reverend Phillips know how you feel. You think he wouldn't want you because you're Sioux, but you have to give him the chance to make his own choices."

"It is you he has eyes for."

"And I don't have eyes for him. This is the best way to discourage him and help him see who really loves him."

"But if you go with the sergeant and he insults you or—"

"I can take care of myself, Anita."

"But what if he has already asked someone else by now?"

Evelyn shrugged. "Then I will stay here. It isn't that important to me. I'll think of some excuse to stay behind."

"You could go with the three of us."

Evelyn smiled. "No. I would just be in the way. I want Reverend Phillips to give all his attention to you Saturday night."

Anita's eyes teared. "You are a generous woman, Evy. I—"

The reverend came back inside then, and the conversation ended. Evelyn thought with dread about what it might be like to accept Jubal Desmond's offer. She had no choice now. She would have to put up with him, but it was worth it if it brought Anita and John Phillips together.

Nine

Anita stood beside the reverend. Both of them watched Janine dance with Lieutenant Teller. Anita could tell Janine was bursting with happiness to be there with the lieutenant, and although Janine felt dancing was improper and terribly bold, she had not turned down one dance, welcoming the chance to get closer to Teller. Anita knew the reverend was watching to be sure Janine was treated with respect, but she also knew that his mind was not really on his sister tonight.

"I don't understand it," the man fussed, his gaze turning to Jubal Desmond and Lucille Bridges. Desmond had kept the poor girl dancing to nearly every single tune played, and he held her embarrassingly close. "Lucille is a beautiful girl, of course, but much too young to be dating an army man the sergeant's age. And why would the man ask Miss Gibbons to the dance and then turn around and ask someone else? Not that I would want to see Miss Gibbons with the likes of Desmond all evening, mind you, but it just makes no sense."

"Evy said there was just some kind of mix-up," Anita answered him. "She really didn't mind." She sipped on some punch and wondered if the reverend even remembered he was supposed to be her escort this evening. All he could talk about was the fact that "poor Miss Gibbons" had been left behind alone and what an insult it was for her to discover Sergeant Desmond had apparently asked someone else to the dance.

"She could at least have come anyway. Janine would have enjoyed her company."

And so would you have, Anita thought. She did not blame Evelyn for the fact that the evening had been spoiled. After all, the woman had done her best to make sure the reverend took her to the dance and not Evelyn. How was she to know that Desmond had gone ahead and asked someone else? Lucille certainly was beautiful tonight, but she did not look very happy. She wondered why the girl had accepted the very unlikable Desmond's invitation and why Seth Bridges had apparently agreed to allow his young daughter to be here with a man so much older than she; nothing really mattered as much as the fact that all John Phillips could talk about was the insult to Evelyn Gibbons and the fact that while everyone else was here having a good time, she was back at her cabin alone.

"The prettiest, kindest, most available young woman on this whole reservation, and she is left with no one to bring her to a dance," Phillips muttered, apparently oblivious to how the remark might hurt Anita. "It was ridiculous of her to refuse to come with us. Why, there are any number of men here tonight who would have paid attention to her. They would have been lined up waiting for a dance."

Anita swallowed back an urge to cry. "I am sure Evy thought it might be awkward if she showed up after the confusion over the sergeant's invitation. She told me she had at first turned him down, then changed her mind. By then he had already asked someone else."

"Well, she must have known when *I* asked her that she did not intend to go with Desmond."

The reverend was watching others dance, and Anita took the opportunity to study his profile. He was not a tall man, but he was built well enough, and tonight he looked more handsome than she had ever seen him. Janine had made him a new blue serge suit, and his hair was slicked back and smelled of lilac.

Had he gotten himself all gussied up for her? Or had he been hoping Evelyn Gibbons would come with them after all?

"I believe, Reverend, that she turned you down and said she already had a date because she was afraid the sergeant would be highly insulted if he saw her show up with you after she had told him no. She probably went back to accept and discovered then that it was too late. I am sure she stayed away to avoid any embarrassment or any trouble. I really don't think she minds. There were some things she wanted to work on for school." *Please look at me, Reverend Phillips. Please act as though you care that I am here and that I mean something to you. Please dance with me.* "I am sure she would be less embarrassed if you said nothing more to her about it."

Phillips closed his eyes and sighed. "Yes, I suppose."

When he finally turned and looked at her, Anita waited hopefully. She had worn her best dress, nothing fancy, but a pretty pink-flowered calico that she thought showed off her trim figure in a flattering way. After she had braided her hair and wrapped the braids at the back of her head, she had looked closely at herself in a mirror, pleased with how smooth and perfect her complexion was.

"You look very nice tonight, Anita," Phillips told her.

Her heart fell. He had said the words the way he might say them to anyone, as though just to be kind but with no special meaning. She kept a forced smile on her lips.

"Thank you, Reverend."

"Well, let's have ourselves something to eat. It looks as though they're cutting into that side of beef that's been roasting over there."

He put a hand to Anita's waist and led her over to where some women including Agent McLaughlin's Indian wife, were serving punch. Anita had no appetite, but she would force herself to eat just to be nice. How was she ever going to make Reverend Phillips understand how much she loved him? He probably didn't even care. She could tell his sister Janine, with whom she now lived since Evelyn had moved into her own cabin, but she hadn't had the courage so far, for she was not sure if Janine would be pleased or upset. She only knew that at this moment she had never been more miserable. It would have been better not to come to the dance at all than to be here with the man she loved and have him hardly notice her.

Evelyn sat alone in the schoolhouse, a lantern on the desk turned up so that she could see what she was writing. She had decided that before beginning to teach her Indian pupils about the history of her own people and how they came to America, she would first get them to talk about their own history, to tell her some of the tales handed down to them by their grandfathers and grandmothers over tipi fires in the dead of winter, when there was nothing else to do but sit and tell stories and try to keep warm. She hoped that would stir their interest in history, and show them and their parents and grandparents that their own heritage was just as important as learning about the white man's history.

She wrote down a few things she already knew about North American Indians, wondered if perhaps there were things they didn't even know about themselves, such as the possibility their ancestors might have migrated from Russia, China, and Asia into Alaska and south through Canada, looking for a warmer climate. She would have to be very careful in presenting the theory, as their parents might be offended. After all, most of them believed the Great Spirit created them and planted them right here in America, and who was she to say they were wrong? In her mind Wakantanka could very well be the same God as Jehova. Her father had never liked that theory, but she believed it nonetheless. If it was true, who was she to question where and when God created and placed the first people on earth? The only thing she knew for certain was that in recent history the Sioux had first dwelled in Minnesota and were forced farther west by white settlement and by fleeing eastern Indians. Most eastern tribes were totally gone now, wiped out by white man's diseases and by methodical annihilation. She prayed that would not happen to these plains tribes, who had fought with such heart and bravery against tremendous odds to keep a little bit of land for themselves.

Yes, that was it. She would be sure to mention how brave and skilled the Sioux were. The best way to impress them and make them listen was to compliment them and show respect. She would gradually implant new ideas in their minds, carefully make them think and wonder if perhaps there was more to their being here in this land than they realized.

She quickly scribbled down more thoughts, perfectly content to have been left alone tonight. She would have loved to go to the dance, but not with Jubal Desmond. She had actually been relieved when his messenger told her the sergeant had already asked someone else. She wondered who it could be, as most of the white women she knew at the agency were married. Whoever it was, she was just glad it was not her, although it had been embarrassing to try to explain the situation to Reverend Phillips. It had been even more embarrassing to watch him fuss and fume in front of Anita, making it obvious that if he had known she was still available, he would never have asked Anita. She prayed the man was giving Anita the attention she deserved and would begin to see the love in her eyes. She was determined that if he did not soon realize how Anita felt about him, she would flat-out tell him.

She leaned back in her chair and studied her notes, when suddenly she sensed the door was opening slowly. A chill moved through her when someone moved quietly inside. Because the oil lamp on her desk did not lend its light far enough, she could not see who it was, except that it was a man. No woman was built as large as the tall, shadowy figure that loomed near the doorway, then closed the door and just stood there, saying nothing.

She told herself to remain calm. Whoever it was must have a legitimate reason for visiting her here. She did not want to think about any other reason for his presence. She realized then just how alone she was. The reverend, Janine, Anita, the only whites who lived nearby, were all gone. Were there any Indians around who would help her if she needed it? And who even knew she was here in the schoolhouse instead of home in her own cabin? Why hadn't she made sure to lock the door? She swallowed and took a deep breath to calm herself. "Who is it?" she asked, surprised she could even find her voice.

The figure moved forward, closer to the light. "It is I. Black Hawk."

Evelyn sat stunned, not sure what to think of this unexpected visit in the night, especially from the unpredictable, sometimes volatile Black Hawk, who seldom ever came this close to the settled area of the agency. The last—and only—time she had met the man, he had been very angry with her. She felt herself breaking into a mild sweat, every nerve end alert, her heart pounding with a mixture of fear and fascination. "Hello, Black Hawk."

Was that really her own voice she heard? It sounded so far away. Black Hawk stepped even closer, only a couple of feet in front of her desk now, standing tall and powerful, wearing buckskin britches and vest, his chest and arms bare, his dark skin glowing in the lamplight. His hair was brushed out long, with a circular beaded hairpiece braided into one side with one skinny braid that mixed into the rest of his hair. His handsome face had a stern look to it, his dark eyes drilling into her with unreadable force. Was that anger she saw there? Curiosity? Apology? She swallowed again. "I am sorry for the way I talked to you last week," she said, not sure what he wanted, if it would help to apologize. "You were right. I probably had no right attending a sacred ritual of your people."

"I have come to ask you why you say there is something more to settle between us, why you say we should meet again. That day when I sent you away, why did you look at me as though you knew me?"

Evelyn felt heat moving through her whole body, her cheeks flushing. How could she tell this Indian man she hardly knew that he had been in her dreams? It seemed ridiculous and bold. He would probably laugh at her. Still, it was he who had come to her, and to her surprise he continued to speak to her in English. Coming from a man like Black Hawk, that was an obvious sign of respect for her. She saw an opportunity to get closer to him. She scrambled to think how she could use this moment to her advantage. "I . . . can't explain it. Not yet. You would think I was a crazy white woman."

Was that a hint of a smile she saw at one corner of his handsome mouth?

"*All* white women are crazy," he answered.

She felt offended for a moment, then realized he was teasing her. One thing she had learned about these people was that they had a very wry sense of humor, so subtle that sometimes one could not be sure if they were serious or just joking. Black Hawk was joking with her now. How strange to realize that this feared, rebellious warrior had the same sense of humor as the rest of his people. Still, there was a deep, lingering hurt and hatred in those dark eyes, and she knew it was from his terrible personal loss at Wounded Knee.

"A lot of white *men* think the same way," she answered with her own soft smile. To her relief, she got even more of a grin out of Black Hawk. She breathed a little easier. "I was engaged to be married before I came here," she added. "I broke it off, deciding this was something I had to do first. The man I was supposed to marry certainly thinks I'm crazy, along with several

friends back in Wisconsin. The fact that I left a very comfortable
life and a man who loves me to come here and teach your people
should tell you something about my sincerity, Black Hawk. I am
not like all the others."

He frowned, his eyes moving over her, then around the room,
back to meet her gaze. "Perhaps not." He reached out and picked
up a beginner's reading book. He opened it, studied it a moment.
"You can teach Indian children to know what this writing says?"

"Yes. I think you know how important that will be to them
from here on. They cannot survive, Black Hawk, without learning the white man's language and writing and numbers. I know
you hate to hear that, and in some ways I don't like it, either. I
greatly admire your old way of life. I understand it better than
you think, and I hate to see it have to end. But one must face
reality, and the reality is that you will never be able to live that
way again. I'm very sorry for that, but it was not my doing. I
can only hope to help your people adjust to what must be. I
understand what a shock it is for them, how hard it is for them."

He met her eyes again, and she felt as though he could see
through to her soul. "Can you teach a grown man to read these
marks?"

The question surprised her and filled her heart with hope.
"Certainly, especially if he is as intelligent as you are," she
added, hoping the praise would help win his trust even more.
She saw the instant pride in his eyes.

"You will teach me then," he said, more as a command than
a request. "When we have talked many times, perhaps you will
be honest with me about the things you said when we first met."

Evelyn could hardly believe her ears. Black Hawk wanted to
learn to read? She reminded herself not to get too excited. Maybe
this was some kind of trick. And she decided that the only way
to win with this man was to continue to stand right up to him
and not get overwhelmed with gratitude. She had to remain stern
and brave. She wanted to jump up and tell him how wonderful

it was that he wanted to learn the white man's writing, but somehow she felt that might only chase him away. "Why do you want to learn?" she asked carefully.

He dropped the book on the desk in a show of belligerence. "To keep the white man from cheating my people even more, it is not enough only to understand the language. I must also understand what he puts in writing, in treaties." A sneer came to his mouth then. "Although it does not make so much difference. Your people not only do not keep promises they make with their forked tongues, they do not even keep the promises they put in writing! Still, it is best that we know how to read his language, not just speak it."

"What about Little Fox?" she asked guardedly. "Do you also want him to learn?"

Black Hawk folded his powerful arms. "I will let him learn. But he will not come here. He is all I have left. I seldom let him out of my sight. For now he is at my camp, with Otter Woman, who sometimes visits and sleeps with me and cooks for me. She will take good care of him."

Evelyn felt a surprising wave of jealousy. She had not thought of Black Hawk taking another woman. Why had he made a point of telling her the woman slept with him? Was he wanting to see her reaction? She forced herself to appear unconcerned, but was shocked at her own inward reaction. Why should she care if he had a woman? "How can I teach him if you don't let him come here?" she asked.

"You will come to *us,"* he answered. "Two days each week. When I have decided I can trust you, perhaps then I will let Little Fox come to the school. If I do, and white men come and take him away to one of the faraway schools off the reservation, I will kill you."

A wave of fear pierced Evelyn's chest like a knife. She knew by his eyes that he was serious. Again she had to remind herself she must stand up to this man. It was her only way of keeping his trust and respect. "I would not blame you," she answered. "But I tell you now that if such a thing ever happened, it would not be my doing. I would never allow it." She rose from her chair. "Letting your son learn the white man's language will be a good sign to your people that they should do the same, Black Hawk. You would be helping them, because I think you understand what is necessary to their survival."

"Perhaps. But for now I do not want them to know. You will come to me two days a week, the days you do not teach. Tell your friends whatever excuse you choose, but do not tell them you come to me and Little Fox. I will decide later whether to allow my son to come to this school."

Evelyn was not sure how she was going to manage it, but she was not about to pass up this surprising opportunity. "I will come. Saturdays and Sundays. How will I know where to go?"

"You will ride to Falling Eagle's settlement northwest of here. Do you know where that is?"

"Yes. I visited there with Anita Wolf. Falling Eagle now sends his son and daughter, Fast Arrow and Laughing Girl, to school. Black Hawk, surely you can see from the eight children already attending that no harm has come to them. It would be so much easier—"

"I will not send my son here!" he barked. "Do you want to do it this way or not?"

Evelyn sighed in resignation. "Yes. I already said that I would. What do I do when I get to Falling Eagle's village?"

"Head directly north. You will see twin hills with rocks at the top of each. They look like a woman's breasts and are called Mother's Nest. Ride between them and on down into a canyon that drops below the earth, much like the Badlands. When you get there I will be watching you and will come to you and take you to my camp."

Evelyn ignored his description of the two hills, realizing he was not even aware it might embarrass her. "How long will this ride take? I would not want to ride back after dark."

"It takes perhaps an hour, longer if you walk your horse the entire way."

"In another couple of months the days will grow shorter. I will have less daylight. By then I would want you to start bringing Little Fox here rather than my riding out alone."

He nodded. "We will decide then."

"What about Otter Woman? Maybe she won't like my coming there."

"She will not be there. I will make sure of it." He leaned forward, pressing his hands on the edge of the desk and bringing his face close to hers. "It will be just you and me. Does that frighten you?"

How could she tell him that she was more afraid of the emotions he stirred in her own soul than of him? "No," she answered without a flinch. "You have asked me to come. I trust you to respect my willingness to take my only two days of rest each week to make a long ride to your camp just because I think it is so important for you to learn. I don't believe you are a man of dishonor."

Black Hawk studied her beautiful face. Did this woman realize what she did to his insides? Of course not. She did not know she had been a part of his vision. She did not know that when he made love to Otter Woman, it was this delicate, light-haired woman whom he saw lying beneath him, her lily-white thighs parted in welcome, her pink-and-white breasts hard and peaked, aching for his touch, her soft skin on fire for the feel of his tongue tasting it.

How could she know his thoughts? A woman like this one would never have the same thoughts for an Indian man . . . or would she? What was that he saw in those big blue eyes? A hint of desire? A flash of passion? Was not her chest heaving a little too heavily? Perhaps her heart was pounding harder, not with fear, but with something else. Whatever the meaning of his vision, he would discover it by getting to know this woman better. He only knew he could not ignore her without offending Wakantanka. Perhaps in reaching out for her in his vision, it meant he was to learn from her. He had to try this and see where it would lead him. If this white woman was to share his bed, he would know that, too. Never before had he had any desire for a *wasicu* woman, but a man could not ignore his dreams.

"I will not dishonor you," he promised.

Evelyn studied his face. He was close enough that she could lean forward and press her lips to his own. The thought made her quickly turn away. "Then I will come," she answered, feeling fire surge through her blood. Was she insane, like Steven claimed? Should she tell this man about her dreams? Perhaps he would read more into her revelation than what was there. Perhaps he would think it gave him license to take advantage of her. With all she supposed she knew about the Sioux, how could she fully understand the thoughts of a man like Black Hawk, who was wild and free and took what he wanted without asking questions? Still, the man had a strong sense of honor. She had to trust in that.

She faced him again. "I will come next Saturday then. Watch for me. I prefer not to ride into such country alone."

"I will be waiting."

He had straightened to his full height again. Evelyn wondered at the size of him, since most Sioux were not so tall. His features were also a little softer than most of the other Indian men, with the startling handsomeness usually enjoyed only by those of mixed blood. Perhaps there was some white blood in his background . . . perhaps some poor captive white woman forced into submission . . . or maybe a French trapper who had taken an Indian woman for a wife. "You have chosen wisely, Black Hawk," she told him. "What you are doing will be good for Little Fox's future, and once you tell your people you trust me and that it is a good thing to send their children to school, it will be better for everyone. I do not lie, Black Hawk."

Their eyes held for several silent seconds, each lost in their own dreams and visions, each wondering how this had come to be.

I think someone else's spirit lives within you, she wanted to tell him. *I think you are Wild Horse, come back to me now that I am a woman, still loving my mother through me.* No, she could not tell him these things yet. There would be a right time.

Your skin is white, but your heart is Indian, Black Hawk in turn wanted to say to her. *I do not yet understand how it is you are so close to me in spirit, but some day I will know.* "I believe you," he told her aloud. "I go now."

He turned and left her standing there, bewildered. Evelyn listened to the sound of his horse trotting away, and she wondered for a moment if she had only dreamed these last few minutes. It did not seem possible the notorious Black Hawk had really come here asking her to teach him and his son to read. She moved on shaking legs back to her desk, and then she noticed the beaded hairpiece lying on top of her papers. She had not seen him untie it from his hair. She picked it up, studying it closely, treasuring the gift. She realized how very much it meant, coming from a man like Black Hawk. She pressed it close to her heart.

Lucille continued to watch the crowd for Miss Gibbons, not even sure why. It just seemed that the woman's presence would give her some kind of hope, even though she would probably be too afraid to talk to her even if she *were* here. She suspected that if Miss Gibbons knew the full story of what her and Katy's lives were like with Seth Bridges, she would find some way to get them away from him. The woman was educated and re-sourceful . . . but she was not here. She had been so certain that someone as pretty as the teacher would have been invited to the dance. She had thought perhaps the Reverend Phillips would bring her, but he had brought the Indian woman Anita Wolf.

She supposed she should be having a good time. She had bathed and primped and fixed herself up the prettiest she had ever been. She wore a yellow print dress, the only one that fit her well rather than being too big. Her leather shoes were worn but presentable, and she wore a yellow ribbon in her dark hair. Seth had been surprisingly encouraging, allowing Katy to come along and help at the refreshment table, leaving her alone before they left the farmhouse so she could get ready. He had never done that before.

That was what bothered her. It was not like Seth to be kind or behave like a father ought to behave. And since he enjoyed her in his own bed, why had he set her up with Sergeant Desmond? Why did he suddenly want her to see another man? Did it have something to do with Katy? Was he trying to marry her off so he could have Katy to himself? She would never let that happen.

The little orchestra, which was composed of a couple of fiddles, a guitar, and a piano that had been dragged out from a social room at the fort, struck up a waltz, and before she had a chance to finish the glass of punch the sergeant had brought her, he was back, urging her to set the glass aside and dance with him again. She thought if she could have come to the dance and take turns dancing with all the men, she might have enjoyed it; but Desmond had hoarded her as though he owned her, and she was embarrassed at how close he danced with her.

All evening he had kept her on her feet, pressing her breasts against his chest. Now he urged her toward the edge of the circle of a hundred or so people—soldiers, settlers, Indians—everyone having a good time . . . everyone but her. All evening Desmond had made suggestive remarks, his eyes constantly resting on her breasts, his hands moving over her back as they danced. He had not even asked her yet if she would like to eat. It was dark now, and several people were beginning to retire. She did not like the fact that she could smell liquor on his breath, nor did she like the leering grin on his face. Did his commander know he had been drinking? How had he gotten hold of liquor when it was forbidden on the reservation?

"I've had a good time, honey," Desmond told her, his eyes combing her hungrily. "I knew you were pretty, but you outdid yourself tonight. Ole Seth came through on his pay-off real good."

He led her off into the darkness, and Lucille stiffened. "What do you mean?" She gasped and cringed when the sergeant jerked her close once they were away from the others, her back to him. He began fondling her breasts as he spoke in a low growl.

"I mean this is one time I'll agree that the pay-off on the gambling debt is better than money."

Her throat began to tighten as the reason for the whole night began to become clear to her. "Gambling debt?"

Desmond kissed at her neck. "Didn't Seth tell you? I won you, honey. Seth got in over his head a few nights ago in a card game, put you up for the pot. I won."

Lucille shivered with horror. It was bad enough that she had to submit to Seth Bridges. Did he expect to start selling her off to other men now, like some common whore? She jerked away. "Don't you touch me!"

Desmond grinned. "No protest now, for two reasons." He grasped her wrist painfully. "I know from the way Seth talks you're no virgin, sweetheart, so I'm not takin' anything precious; and if you yell, I'll say you led me on, make you look like a little slut in front of the others. After all, you *did* let me dance awful close to you all night. You think the other men didn't notice that?" He yanked her against him, twisting one arm behind her back. "Besides, Seth said you'd cooperate if I reminded you that if I'm not pleased with my winnings, he'll pay off with your sister instead. I'll admit she's young, but she's ripe enough; and any man would rather have somethin' sweet and tight like that. Which way is it gonna be, honey? It's your decision."

Lucille could hardly get her breath for the sickening reality of what he was telling her. So, this was the reason Seth had been so attentive, so willing to allow her to get prettied up and come to a dance. This was the reason he had set her up with the sergeant, not with any intention of finding someone for her to marry. It was only to pay off a gambling debt, and if she didn't make it worthwhile . . .

Tears stung her eyes and her stomach churned, but she was not about to let Seth or this man—or anyone else—touch Katy. If she screamed for help, she might get it . . . for tonight. But what about once she and Katy went home with Seth? If Miss Gibbons had been here, perhaps there would be a chance that she would step in and not allow her and Katy to go home at all. She didn't trust anyone else to see to that, not even the reverend, who was afraid of Seth. As she did when she was with Seth, she began shutting off all feeling, both physical and emotional. "Where would we go?"

"I've got a place all made up for us, out a ways from the fort. Nobody will know. When we're through, we'll come back and have us a bite to eat. I don't know about you, but I expect to work up quite an appetite."

She could see his sickening grin in the moonlight. "Let's go then," she said.

Desmond thought her voice sounded deeper, harder. He led her away, and from that moment on, Lucille Bridges never said another word, either of protest or pleasure. When he finished with her, he left her lying there naked on a blanket in the grass, curled up and motionless. He walked off to get himself something to eat, satisfied that Seth Bridges's debt to him was paid in full.

Ten

Evelyn rode through Falling Eagle's village, feeling the stares, wondering if Janine and others who had asked believed her when she said she wanted to visit other villages on her own, to get to know as many of the Sioux on a personal basis as she could. Reverend Phillips had been very upset that she would even consider going out alone, and she had had a difficult time persuading him not to come along, something he had at first insisted she allow.

Now she wondered what the Sioux themselves might think once they realized it was Black Hawk she would come through here twice a week to see. She hoped their loyalty to the man would prompt them to trust her more, simply because Black Hawk apparently approved of her. If he decided she was worthy to teach his son, perhaps they would begin sending their own children to school. She wondered what Reverend Phillips and Janine would think of her daring to come and visit alone with the notorious Black Hawk. Would they consider her bold and brave, or terribly sinful and foolish?

Perhaps it was the latter after all. In her own heart she was doing this for reasons more than teaching Black Hawk and his son to read or encouraging other Sioux to send their children to school. She wanted . . . needed to be alone with Black Hawk . . . to gradually tell him the whole truth; and she needed to know where her dreams and her heart were leading her. All night she had lain awake thinking about her mother and Wild Horse. She could still remember how her mother looked at the man, how she looked for years afterward whenever she talked about him. She had loved him very much, and why shouldn't a white woman be able to love an Indian man? Was it such a terrible thing?

She chastised herself for fantasizing over the meaning of her dreams. His reaching out for her was probably a symbol of an Indian asking a white person to help him cross the wide chasm that separated their two worlds. Teaching the man to read was the beginning of the bridge across that chasm.

She arrived at the twin hills Black Hawk had told her about, Mother's Nest, and she rode toward the center of them. As she made her way through the hills, her thoughts turned for a moment to things Anita had told her about the dance. Apparently, Lucille Bridges was not at all happy about being there with Sergeant Desmond, who had danced embarrassingly close to the poor girl. She was even more glad that she had not gone to the dance herself with the man, but at least she could have handled him better than young Lucille.

The situation with the Bridges girls was still something she wanted to look into, but there was just so much time in a day, and now her weekends would be taken teaching Black Hawk and Little Fox. She had thought at first that she would find only loneliness and boredom in this place so far removed from civilization, but in truth she was very busy. One thing occupying her mind was how to find a way to make Reverend Phillips see how Anita felt about him. When she had asked Anita about having a good time at the dance, she had seen the disappointment in the woman's eyes.

"I am just a friend to him," she had answered. "He was very upset that we left you behind, and it was all he talked about. He does not truly see me when he looks at me."

I will make sure he does see you! Evelyn thought. Sometimes men could be so ignorant of a woman's needs and feelings. Steven probably still did not have the slightest understanding of why she had needed to come to Standing Rock. By his thinking, she should have been satisfied to marry and settle on his farm and get fat and have ten babies and never leave.

She came upon a stunning canyon beyond Mother's Nest, a place where it looked as though the earth had simply dropped away, leaving a gaping hole filled with a maze of layered rock formations, the crevices between them formed, she surmised, by rushing waters over thousands of years, or by an ancient glacier. She was glad she had worn her slat bonnet against the penetrating sun. It was early in the day, but already hot. A shadow moved across the ground in front of her. She looked up to see a hawk floating overhead, as though to represent Black Hawk's spirit, for when she followed it, her eyes fell to a distant rise, and, as promised, there was Black Hawk, waiting for her. He waved a lance, and, heart pounding harder with trepidation, she urged her horse down a rocky escarpment and along the canyon floor toward the place where he waited.

She watched Black Hawk also head down an embankment, one so steep she feared he could never make it safely, but his sure-footed Appaloosa and its skilled rider found their way to the bottom with no mishaps. He halted the horse, facing her as she approached. She could not help being impressed by the sight of him. His hair was pulled back into a tail at one side, tied with long, beaded rawhide. Leather armbands accented his powerful biceps, and again, he wore only a vest on his upper torso, except that today his chest was decorated with a beautiful turquoise necklace in the shape of a sunburst. He wore doeskin leggings that were open at the sides, and when she realized they revealed his bare hip to the waist, she quickly looked away. She thought she saw a note of surprise in his eyes, and she supposed he did not really believe she would come alone as promised.

"Before we go farther, you must give me your word you will not tell others where I make my camp."

"Your own people probably already know," she answered.

"Some, but not all. It is not my own people who matter. I do not want your white friends or the soldiers to know."

"I won't tell them. You have my word." Evelyn looked around at a confusing array of scraggly stone formations, already feeling confused. "Besides, I wouldn't know how to begin to find my way around in this place."

Black Hawk studied her quietly for a moment, then turned his horse. "Follow me."

She rode behind him, studying his broad shoulders, wondering what she was getting herself into. She was even self-conscious of how she had dressed. She had fussed half the night deciding, finally putting on a light cotton, pale-blue dress, rather plain, with three-quarter sleeves and a high neckline. She wanted to be properly covered but as cool as possible, and this dress was the lightest material of the ones she owned. She had wanted to look nice for Black Hawk, but now she felt silly for caring.

For several minutes they rode without speaking, the only sound being their horses' hooves echoing against the rocks and the occasional cry of a hawk or a crow. Evelyn felt as though she had ridden into another world, totally removed from the one she had always known. The reservation itself was a far cry from Wisconsin, yet this place was even more remote. It made the reservation seem lively and civilized. Riding into this canyon was like riding into the past, into a time when the Sioux lived free and wild. She could understand why Black Hawk liked it here. Who would bother to come into this confusing mass of twists and turns and hot pathways to find just one man? It was not worth the Army's time, and she wondered why he had made her promise not to tell where he made camp. She could never find it alone no matter how many times he might bring her here.

Finally, to her surprise, they came upon a stream where there was actually some shrubbery and grass and a few trees. She followed Black Hawk through some underbrush, and they came upon a tipi. Little Fox stood in the stream trying to catch fish with his hands. He turned to smile at his father.

"Ate!" he called, using the Sioux term for father.

Black Hawk halted his horse and slid off it, calling a greeting to the boy. He walked over to help Evelyn down from her own horse, wrapping big hands about her waist, and lifted her down as though she were a small doll.

Evelyn tried to ignore the pleasant feel of his hands on her body. "Thank you," she said, quickly turning away from him to take some books out of her saddlebag.

"I will take the saddle from your horse so it can rest and graze before the ride back this afternoon," he told her.

"Yes. That would be nice." Suddenly, she felt awkward and terribly foolish. What on earth was she doing here? If she never returned, no one would know for certain where she had gone. She might never be found. She breathed deeply for courage, telling herself that at least it was cooler here, surprisingly pleasant, considering the hot, dry maze of rocks through which they had just ridden. She walked to the edge of the stream while Black Hawk took care of the horses. She noticed that across the stream the land rose steeply, the bank green and flowered, smattered with trees part way up, before turning into nothing but rock and clay again.

What an oddly beautiful place this is, she thought. No one would expect to find trees and grass in this pit of gray-and-white and yellow rock. She looked over at Little Fox, who was handsome like his father. He stood watching her curiously. "Hello, Little Fox," she said aloud, giving him the hand sign for greetings.

He answered in a hand sign, his eyes moving then to his father, who moved to stand beside Evelyn.

"Come inside the lodge," Black Hawk told her. "It is cooler." He told Little Fox in the Sioux tongue to also come inside. Evelyn followed Black Hawk into the tipi, realizing with relief that

he was right. It was even cooler there than beside the stream.
The bottom of the tipi skins was turned up to allow air to cir-
culate, and inside it was quite roomy. As she looked around and
began untying her bonnet, she drew in her breath at the sight of
many beautiful painted pictures on the inner lining of the tipi.
The artwork showed fine detail: a sunrise over a rocky canyon;
an Indian woman holding a child; Indian children playing; a
warrior on his horse, looking out at distant hills. There were
various other scenes, all in splendid colors, the people and animals portrayed with as much skill as any professional painter.

"Black Hawk! Did *you* paint these scenes?"

He studied them with her. "When a warrior can no longer
hunt or fight his enemies, and when he has no family left but
one little son, he has much time on his hands. Yes, I painted
them. It is the only reason I have for going to the agency, to get
brushes and paint that they order for me. Otherwise I do not
need the agency. I hunt for my own food. Little Fox and I hunt
together now. He has become very skilled with the bow."

Evelyn glanced from Black Hawk to his son, who had also
come inside and now stood in front of his father, grinning. "I
am sure he will be as fine a hunter as his father someday," she
said in the Sioux tongue, watching the boy's eyes light up with
pride.

She wondered if Black Hawk realized what a talent he had
for painting. He could surely make money by selling such paintings if he would put them on canvas that could be framed. She
decided not to mention it for the moment, sure he was not ready
to hear how he could earn money the white man's way. "Your
paintings are very beautiful," she told him as she removed her
hat. *They show you are a man of compassion, with a beautiful
inner soul,* she wanted to add. "I did not know you had the
ability."

Sadness came into his eyes, mixed with a hint of anger. "A
man learns to fill the empty days, or lose his mind," he answered.

He put out one arm. "You will sit over here," he said, indicating the back side of the tipi, across from the entrance. The central fire, which today was just a few glowing embers, was between her and the entrance. "It is the place of honor," he told her.

Evelyn was touched. Black Hawk was a different man here, away from the rest of the reservation, away from commotion and settlement. She knew enough about Sioux culture to realize how honored she was to be offered the position across from the entrance, rather than ushered to the right side, which was usually the place for women. "This area is called *Catku,*" she said as she sat down on a pile of robes and laid her hat aside.

Black Hawk told Little Fox to sit down beside her, and he took his own place on her other side. "You have studied our culture?" he asked.

"Yes. For instance, I know that the walls of this lodge are built to a peak to symbolize the sky. The round shape of a tipi represents the sacred life circle, with no beginning and no end. For special ceremonies, this area, the *Catku,* is where you would build your sacred altar and burn sweet grass to keep away evil spirits."

He frowned in surprise. "And what do you know of the sacred life circle?"

A chill moved through her as she thought again about how she sometimes felt as if the spirit of Wild Horse lived in Black Hawk. They were so much alike. It was as though God was showing her that there really was an endless circle of life. "I know that it is never-ending: birth, life, death, a new birth. The circle of life has no true beginning and no true end."

Their eyes held, each realizing the other was thinking much deeper thoughts than they dared admit. "This is true," he answered, "but now I fear the circle will be broken. It is already broken for many other Indians in the land of the rising sun, whose tribes no longer exist because they vanished when white men took their lands. Their circle of life is no more. I do not want to see that happen to my people. I fear that if they turn fully to the white man's ways, they will lose themselves, and the circle of life for the Sioux will be no more."

"That doesn't have to happen, Black Hawk. There are ways to adjust to this new life without losing all that you are. What you are doing here today is one way of doing that. You made a very wise choice."

He straightened, a proud look on his face. "We shall see. Before we begin, you must tell me why you have learned so much about my people. I have never known another white person, missionary, teacher, trader, none who learned our language and culture and who truly cared about these things. Why would a small white woman from a place in the East care about my people? There are many things you do not tell me."

Evelyn was surprised and touched by his keen insight. "Yes, there are, Black Hawk. Some of them are things I cannot tell you until I know you better. But I *can* tell you that I lived on a Cheyenne reservation down in Indian Territory. My father was a preacher, and my mother insisted that the only way for him to reach the Indians was to learn their ways first, understand their own religion and culture." She looked away from him, disturbed by his compelling, dark eyes. She picked up a reading book and pretended to be looking at it as she continued. "Things happened there that I never forgot, Black Hawk. I learned many things about the Indians, and until my mother died she instilled in me the importance of being tolerant of the beliefs and cultures of others. She often spoke of how she felt there was much yet to do, was always concerned about helping the Indians adjust to the changes in their lives our people brought upon them."

"And why did *she* care?"

Because she fell in love with a Cheyenne man. "I . . . I guess because once she went there with my father, she made many friends among the Cheyenne. She learned to love them and wanted to help them. That love and desire to help carried over to me, I guess. That's why I am here. I feel it's my duty, that God expects me to be here." *I am here because of a dream, Black Hawk, a dream that involves you.* She held up the book for both of them to see. "We really should get started. We don't have a lot of time." She wanted dearly to change the subject. She could not tell him the whole truth . . . not yet.

She began pointing to the letters of the alphabet, printed boldly in the book, with words and pictures that started with each letter beside them. "This is an A," she said. "There are different sounds this letter makes, sometimes long, like in Ape, or short, like in Apple. You will learn which way to pronounce the A by the way—"

Black Hawk touched her wrist. "Ape? What is Ape?"

She smiled softly. "Ape is an animal, a monkcy. See the picture? It's a furry animal that lives mostly in South America and Africa, where there are deep forests called jungles. They use their tails to swing from tree to tree."

Black Hawk and Little Fox both frowned and stared at the picture. "It has a face almost like a man," Little Fox commented.

"Yes." She thought about telling them that some believed men were the descendants of apes, but she decided that would be too much for either of them to consider for the moment.

"I do not like that animal." Black Hawk frowned. "I think they are the spirits of evil men, who have been forbidden to go to the promised land and find peace after death. Instead, they are put into this strange animal and never allowed to be free again."

Evelyn smiled at the idea. "Well, you can see monkeys for yourself in about five weeks. The government is sending a circus to Standing Rock."

"Circus? What is that?"

Evelyn lowered the book to her lap. "A circus is a show, kind of like when your people get together and race horses and have other contests and dress in their fanciest paint and feathers to dance. You know that Buffalo Bill Cody was an entertainer, that your own Sitting Bull traveled with him. They put on Wild West shows to entertain people."

He frowned. "I did not like what he did. I think sometimes it made us look bad." He suddenly smiled. "And sometimes, Sitting Bull told us, he would speak to the crowd in our tongue. He would insult them and call them liars and fools, and they did not even know what he was saying. They would clap and cheer."

Evelyn laughed lightly. "Very clever." She turned to Little Fox. "Well, a circus is a great show for entertainment, much like what Buffalo Bill did. There will be animals from other lands, very unusual animals you have never seen before; and there will be clowns with painted faces, and people will perform wonderful stunts, like swinging from a high trapeze, juggling balls. You really should both come and see for yourselves."

Little Fox's eyes lit up, but Black Hawk frowned again. "I will think about this, but I do not want to look upon the face of one of those apes. I believe it is bad luck to look into the eyes of an animal that might carry a man's lost soul."

Evelyn decided not to press the issue. "Let's just study the letters for now and learn how to sound them." She glanced at one of the paintings again, still overwhelmed by the talent shown. Black Hawk already had a way of entering the white man's world without losing his own, and he did not even know it. She continued with the lesson, pleased at how easily both Black Hawk and his son learned the first five letters of the alphabet. She would have preferred that they come to the school, but as the day progressed, she was glad to have the chance to come here instead. What she thought would be a tiring, uncomfortable experience became refreshingly relaxing, even though she was teaching.

This place was private and peaceful, a beautiful little world of its own. Time passed quickly, and in the early afternoon Black

Hawk cooked rabbit over a fire outside near the bubbling creek. They discussed Sioux culture compared to the white man's.

"We give no thought to time," he told her as he turned the spit. Fat dripped from the rabbit onto the hot coals, making little hissing sounds. "The white man does everything by the clock, getting up, eating, working, going to bed. If the clock says it is time to eat, he eats, even if he is not hungry. If he *is* hungry, but the clock says it is *not* time to eat, he stays hungry. I do not understand this. I also do not understand working for other men, being paid in useless paper that is traded for food. Why not just go out and hunt your own food and not have to work for it? Or why not trade something you already have, like robes or beads or a weapon? We have lived for many lifetimes just by doing our own hunting and trading. We have never needed white man's work or white man's money to survive. Our life was good, so why does the white man think it was so terrible that we must change it? We were happy and free and our bellies were full. It is the white man who is not wise in how to live off the land. He kills animals and cuts down trees as though there is a never-ending supply. Now the buffalo are nearly gone, and hills once forested are bare. The white man is foolish, yet he thinks he is so smart and educated."

Evelyn smiled, then picked up a stick and poked the coals to stir them. "I completely agree with you, Black Hawk. We are smart in book learning, but ignorant in the ways of nature and survival. I believe that some day perhaps we will have to turn to the Indian and ask for his help because we have destroyed all that we need to live on, but I think we can learn from each other. It does not have to be all one way or the other."

He smiled sadly, meeting her eyes. "Most of your people do not think as you do." He watched a piece of her hair drift in a soft breeze. She wore it pulled back at her neck with a pretty hair ornament. She had left it in a long tail, and he was impressed with how thick and wavy and long it was. He could not help picturing it draped over bare shoulders, hiding firm breasts. She was unlike any woman he had ever known, Indian or white: educated but wise, intelligent but caring. He was more sure than ever that she was the woman in his vision, and he knew he must talk to Night Hunter about her.

The three of them ate, then washed their hands in the creek. Evelyn reviewed the morning lesson, pleased to see that both father and son remembered the sounds of the letters they had learned that day, as well as most of the words that went with them. She left them each a reading book to study and promised to return the next day.

"No," Black Hawk spoke up, surprising her.

"Why? Is something wrong, Black Hawk?"

"Nothing is wrong. You taught us well today, enough to study until the next time you come, next Saturday. I was just testing you. I thought you would not even come today. Now I know that you would come again tomorrow as promised, but you should have your own day of rest, and the freedom to practice your own religion. I know that tomorrow is the day white people worship their God in their church. You will want to do the same. Leave us the books and we will study them until you return the next Saturday."

How could she tell him that she would actually rather come here, where it was so peaceful and scenic . . . where she could be close to him? It would seem much too bold. "Thank you, Black Hawk," she answered. "And thank you for the gift you left when you visited me at the school. I will try braiding it into my hair the next time I come."

He smiled, thinking how pretty the colors of the hairpiece he had left her would look in her golden hair. "I will get your horse ready and lead you back," he told her, walking off to where the horses were tied.

Evelyn actually felt a little depressed at having to go. She retied her bonnet, hating the thought of riding back into the heat . . . and into her own world. She had enjoyed teaching Little Fox, who was a warm, intelligent boy, friendly and eager to learn. The love between father and son was touching. It was obvious Little Fox meant everything to Black Hawk. He was all the man had left of his family and his old life.

Black Hawk brought her horse, and their eyes held as he lifted her up to the sidesaddle. She had so much more to tell him, wondered just how much she *should* tell him. Black Hawk moved onto his horse in one swift motion, instructing Little Fox to stay close to the tipi until he returned. He rode away from the little garden spot and back into the hot, dry canyon. Evelyn followed, feeling as though she had only dreamed about the place and the special time she had spent with this rebellious Sioux man who everyone thought was so cunning and dangerous.

As they made their way along the twisting pathway, neither of them noticed a figure quickly duck behind a rock near the place where they rode up the steep bank to the open area that led back to the twin hills. It was Otter Woman, who watched stealthily, her suspicions a reality now. Black Hawk had told her to stay away today and tomorrow, and now she knew why. The white woman! He had brought her to his hidden camp. Why! What was this spell the white teacher woman had over Black Hawk? Had they made love? A raging jealousy burned in her heart. She did not mind being replaced by a younger Sioux woman Black Hawk might want to take for a wife . . . but a *white* woman! She spit on the rock in front of her, wishing it was the teacher woman with the light hair and blue eyes. Otter Woman hated her. She had to find a way to get rid of this white bitch who had probably already taken her place in Black Hawk's bed, before the woman destroyed Black Hawk by turning him to the white man's ways!

Eleven

Jubal Desmond rode up to the dilapidated frame home of Seth Bridges, wondering if the man ever did a lick of work of his own. It seemed that every time he rode by here, the younger girl, Katy, was out hacking away at trying to keep down the grass and weeds, and Lucille was scrubbing clothes and hanging them, or out in the fields picking corn and beans. The house was in disrepair, and the farm as a whole was run-down.

Desmond had never actually stopped here before. His dealings with Seth had always been at the fort or at a secret meeting place with Seth and whiskey traders. This was different. This was a need greater than whiskey or a good card game, a need that could only be satisfied by coming here to see Lucille.

He nodded to Katy as he dismounted. She only frowned and kept whacking away with the scythe. "Someday . . ." he muttered under his breath. He tied his horse. This was his day off, and he was free to go wherever he chose. He hoped no one saw him come here, but if so, he could always say he was just paying a formal thank you visit to Miss Lucille for the good time he'd had two weeks ago.

He did not see Lucille anywhere around as he walked up onto the sagging porch and knocked on the door. He was in uniform, but he had unbuttoned his shirt because of the heat. He could hear Seth grumbling as he came to the door. "Who the hell is it?" he growled.

"It's Sergeant Desmond."

Seth opened the door and peered out at him with bloodshot eyes that still had sleep in them. "C'mon in. What the hell you doin' here at the house?"

Jubal stepped inside and closed the door. "I want to talk to you about Lucille."

Seth scratched his head. He turned and led Jubal into what Jubal figured was supposed to be a parlor, although it was littered with an assortment of furniture covered with another assortment of trash—clothes, newspapers, ashtrays, dirty glasses. "Find yourself a place to sit," Seth told Jubal. "Just shove somethin' aside if you need to. That damn Lucille is always runnin' around tryin' to make the place clean, but I've always told her to stay out of this room. This is *my* room, and I like things comfortable."

"Where is she now?" Jubal asked.

Seth shrugged. "Out sloppin' the hogs, I think." He sat down with a grunt in a broken-down, stuffed chair that was torn and soiled. From the body imprint in the chair, it was obvious to Jubal that this was where Seth Bridges sat when he was not doing anything else, and he figured that was probably most of the day, every day.

Jubal himself turned and shoved aside some clothes and papers from what might have once been an attractive silk loveseat, but which was now faded and ripped. He sat down in it and faced Seth.

"So? What the hell do you want with Lucille, as if I didn't know?" Seth asked him. He reached over and picked up a smoldering cigar.

Jubal grinned. "You were willing to give her over to pay a gambling debt. I'm wondering if you're willing to sell her favors for whiskey—whatever else you'd want. I have a couple of friends I might tell about her. I know they'd be quiet about it, and they'd give a month's pay for a night with her."

Seth rubbed at his bristly chin. "I don't know—"

"Don't go pretending you give a damn about her," Jubal said. "I already know what you do with her—quite the loving father, aren't you?"

Both men chuckled, and Seth leaned back in his chair. "Her pretty little ass got to you, did it? Once a man gets in somethin' like that, it's hard not to want more," Seth said with a grin. "Trouble is, she don't come cheap. For one thing, she ain't gonna like the idea. My only hold on her is threatenin' to turn on her sister. Long as she thinks doin' what I tell her will keep Katy safe, she'll do it. The reason the price is high is because you're takin' away my own pleasure." He puffed on the cigar a minute, then pulled it out of his mouth and leaned forward, resting his elbows on his knees. "Here's how it is, Jubal. You and your men start humpin' on Lucy, and that leaves me with used goods. I can't turn to her sister on account of once I do, I ain't got no more hold over Lucy. She'll run off on me, and I'm out of whiskey and income. I'll let it go for a while, but just you, not your friends. You can have her any time you can come by, long as you keep me in whiskey. I know that goddamn Black Hawk run off them last traders 'cause I seen it with my own eyes, but I know more will come, and I'm countin' on you to let them by."

Jubal straightened. "You *saw* Black Hawk roust out the last ones? Is he the one who destroyed their wagon and all those cases of whiskey?"

Seth nodded.

Jubal rose. "I *knew* it! I *knew* it was Black Hawk!" He paced for a moment. "The sonofabitch knows he can get away with it because you don't dare report it. Even *I* can't, because I'd have to say who told me, and that would get you in trouble. Besides, it would make me look bad—a damn Indian doing what I'm supposed to be doing. *Damn* him!"

"Point is, you've got to see about lettin' more through. I know you've got contacts—know some of the suppliers. Whatever you have to do—do it. I'm runnin' low. After awhile there's somethin' else I'll be wantin' in payment."

Jubal sat back down. "What's that?"

Seth puffed on the cigar again for a moment. "A fresh woman," he answered, keeping the cigar between his teeth. "I'm gettin' tired of Lucy, and once you and your friends start sharin' her, there won't be much left for me. Like I say, I can't take up with Katy yet, or I won't have no control over Lucy. I'm gonna be wantin' somethin' fresh."

Jubal frowned. "Where in hell am I going to find a woman I can bring here who'll willingly go to your bed? The only white women around here are either married or damn missionaries."

"I didn't say she had to be willin', and I didn't say she had to be white. Hell, there's plenty of pretty young Indian women around. Just make sure she's a virgin."

Jubal grinned. "You looking to start another war? There would be hell to pay doing something like that."

Seth shrugged. "Maybe. Maybe not. These Sioux take pride in their young virgins. Any that got soiled by me would be too ashamed to admit it to their relatives. Even if they did, what are any of them gonna do about it? It's the word of a white man against them, and you know what most whites think of Indian women. If I say she came willingly, who's gonna say it ain't so? The Sioux know they can't stir up trouble without sufferin' for it. All in all, nothin' much would be done about it. Maybe the relatives would even be willin' to sell the girl to me for whiskey or food or whatever else they need.

"Even so, it's best I find someone with few relatives, maybe some girl with only a grandmother—no men who care about her."

A cunning look came into Seth's eyes. "Or maybe there is a way to get one particular Sioux man in trouble and get him out of our hair. He puts up a fuss, gets arrested and sent away . . . no more trouble to us."

Jubal frowned. "Black Hawk? How would we—" He hesitated, then smiled.

"I hear tell Black Hawk's got a pretty little sister," Seth told him. "From what I understand from Bill Doogan, she just went through some special ritual three or four weeks ago on account of she's considered a woman now, some damn celebration her people have when a girl has her first time of month. They consider it sacred. I consider it a stupid ceremony."

Jubal shook his head. "I don't know, Seth. Black Hawk's sister. That's pretty risky. You might pay worse than you care to before Black Hawk could be caught and arrested."

Seth shrugged. "I could have me a piece of somethin' tight and pretty, and if she chooses to tell and Black Hawk should come for me, I'd have every right to shoot him down like the skulkin' wolf that he is, and that would be that. Ain't no soldier and no white man's court that would blame me for it. All I have to say is the wild sonofabitch tried to kill me, so I shot him. His people might say he came after me on account of his sister, and I'll just say she slept with me willingly, so Black Hawk was in the wrong. I'm not afraid of that bastard. Fact is, I expect the soldiers and a lot of white folks around here would be glad to be rid of him."

Jubal grinned. "And so would the whiskey runners."

Seth nodded. "You know how I could get my hands on the sister?"

Jubal shook his head. "Many Birds's grandmother keeps her pretty sheltered. She's only thirteen."

"Thirteen's a good enough age. And I've got all the time in the world. There must be a way to get that little girl away from her stingy ole grandma. Maybe you can talk to that stuck-up schoolteacher. Get her to encourage Many Birds to come to school. If she does, the girl will have to ride by here every day to get there."

Jubal shook his head. "It's awfully risky, Seth. I don't think it's a very good idea. Besides, I'm not exactly on Miss High-and-Mighty's good side right now. I don't think she's gotten over the embarrassment of accepting my invitation to that dance and finding out I supposedly already asked somebody else. Your little debt to me cost me a night with the prettiest woman on the reservation."

Seth crushed out his cigar. "You damn well know you had a better time with Lucy than you would have with that straight-laced bitch. Any man gets between her legs will have to tie her down and pry them apart."

Jubal grinned. "Not an unpleasant thought."

Both men laughed deep in their throats, unaware that Lucille had come inside. She stood just out of sight, and had caught only the last remark. What was Jubal Desmond doing here? Her heart pounded with dread, especially at the way he and Seth were laughing. What were they up to now?

"I'll see what I can do," Desmond told Seth. "In the mean-time, when do I get another turn at Lucy?"

"Soon as you bring me a couple bottles of whiskey," Seth answered.

"I just happen to have some with me."

Lucille felt as though the blood was draining from her body. Jubal Desmond had come to do bad things to her again! She turned to run, but just then Katy came through the front door, sweating from cutting the grass. Before she realized Lucille did not want her to say anything, she called out to Seth. "I finished the grass, Seth."

"Katy? Come on in here."

The girl caught the look in her sister's eyes when she came closer, realizing then that something was terribly wrong. She knew better than to defy Seth, so she hesitantly walked into the parlor, eyeing Jubal Desmond warily. "What is it, Seth?"

"Your sister out there someplace?"

Katy swallowed. Before she could answer, Lucille walked into

the parlor, not about to leave Katy alone with Seth and the sergeant. "I'm here." She held her chin proudly, refusing to show
fear or shame. She did not look at the sergeant. She hated him
even more than she hated Seth, had not forgotten how he used
her like a whore the night of the dance.

"The sergeant wants to see you alone, up in our room, Lucy.
You go on up, and you be nice to him. Katy will stay down here
with me till the sergeant leaves."

Lucille knew what he meant. Oblige his order, or let Katy
suffer for it. She turned and walked out, going up the stairs. A
grinning Jubal Desmond nodded to Seth. "You'll have your
whiskey when I'm through." He turned and followed Lucille up
the stairs.

Beverly Evans approached the circus wagon, totally fasci-
nated by its bright colors and by the striped zebra that was tied
behind it. She had never seen such an animal, not even back in
Wisconsin, for her parents had never allowed her to attend any
social functions except church. She had never been to the theater,
to a dance, certainly had never seen a circus, although she had
read about them.

Now here was a wonderful red-and-yellow wagon, with
O'BANYON'S CIRCUS EXTRAVAGANZA painted on its side. A
handsome man with black, slicked-back hair stood up in the
wagon seat, wearing a fancy suit and ruffled shirt, explaining to
settlers who had gathered, and to the Indians through interpret-
ers, that O'Banyon's Circus was coming to Standing Rock and
other reservations. "You have all heard about Buffalo Bill's Wild
West Show," he was telling his audience. "You Indians, your
own Sitting Bull was a part of that show once. That tells you
how important he thought such shows were to the public. Bill
is retired now, but the circus goes on, and the government is
paying you back for Sitting Bull's contributions by bringing cir-

cus to you so that you can see some of the wonderful things that are out there in the white man's world. The government is sending you O'Banyon's Circus! Monkeys! Elephants! Giraffes! Zebras! You will see aerial acts, tumblers, jugglers! There is no trick here. You need not be afraid to bring your children. This is entertainment for all, old and young alike!"

Beverly wiped at sweat on her brow. It was a terribly hot day, but her stern husband refused to allow her to wear anything but long-sleeved dresses that buttoned high on the neck. She hated it here at the Oahe Mission. This land along the Peoria bottom of the Missouri was treeless and flat, the sorriest section of the Standing Rock Reservation. She wished she could have gone on with Evelyn Gibbons and Janine Phillips when they first arrived here together, wished her husband would at least let her visit those women once in awhile. She had not wanted to come here at all, but once married to a missionary, a woman had to follow her man wherever he went.

She watched the handsome announcer, wondering what a glamorous life it must be traveling with a circus. She had already decided that if Greggory would not allow her to go and watch the circus once it arrived, considering it sinful, she would sneak out and go without his permission. When would she ever get another chance like this one? All her life either her parents or her husband had been preaching to her about how to think and behave. She could not recall even being a child, laughing and running and playing. She had never been allowed to do those things, and, for some reason, she had lately begun to long for them.

The fancy man told his audience they would also see "Miss Haley Downs," better known as the "Pretzel Woman." He put out his hand, and a beautiful, slender redheaded woman emerged from the wagon to stand beside him. People gasped and stared. Several clapped. Beverly moved closer in awe. The Pretzel Woman wore a sparse costume of glitter and feathers, with a very short skirt that showed her bare legs. The top was cut low and was held in place only by very thin straps. She knew she should feel ashamed looking at so much skin on another woman, yet the beautiful costume and the paint on the woman's face, as well as her gaudy, feathered hat, intrigued her to the point that she felt almost hypnotized.

"Here is just a taste of the kind of unusual and fascinating acts you will see when you come to the circus!" the man announced.

The Pretzel Woman climbed to the top of the wagon and began moving into a variety of contortions that Beverly could not believe any human body was capable of performing. She went into a full split, then bent over backward and came around under her own legs to look out at the audience as though her body were made of rubber. There came more gasps, some applause, even a few screams, as though some expected the woman to fall apart. Beverly thought it horribly sinful that a woman could expose her body that way, yet she admired the woman for her talent and for the magnificent control she had over her muscles. She gave them quite a show: backbends, handstands, sitting down and pulling her ankles up behind her neck. It was both amazing and revealing. She watched dumbfounded, unaware that she in turn was being watched by the fancy circus man.

Miss Haley Downs finished her act and bowed to cheers and applause before disappearing inside the wagon again. "Three weeks!" the man announced. "In three weeks the full circus will come to Standing Rock for several performances at various locations throughout the reservation. This will be one of them! So come one, come all, compliments of the United States Government!" With that, the man grabbed some hard candy that was wrapped in waxed paper and threw a handful into the crowd. People screamed and laughed and began scrambling to pick it up, and the fancy man climbed down from the wagon. Beverly started to leave when she felt a hand on her arm. "Excuse me, miss."

She turned, feeling almost faint at the realization it was the announcer. Up close, he was even more handsome.

"I couldn't help noticing the longing look on your face." The man bowed slightly. "I am Herbert True, publicity man for O'Banyon's Circus. May I ask your name?"

She swallowed. "Beverly . . . Beverly Evans. I really must go, Mr. True."

He smiled handsomely. "I have a feeling you would like to see the inside of our wagon, maybe meet Miss Downs? *Would* you like that?"

Beverly looked around. Greggory was home preparing a sermon. Herbert True's gentle smile made her feel more relaxed. "I would love to meet her! Are you sure it would be all right?"

"Certainly." The man led her to the back of the wagon and knocked at the door. Haley Downs opened it, startling Beverly by standing there in a thin robe that a person could see through in just the right light. She smiled through painted lips. "I just got my costume off. Who you got with you, Herb?"

"This is Beverly Evans." He looked at Beverly. "Miss? Mrs.?"

"Mrs. My husband is a missionary here."

The man's eyes lit up strangely, and Beverly felt as though he could see right through her. Was he reading the sinful thoughts in her heart? Did he see her childish excitement at seeing such wonders? Did he sense the strange new feelings he stirred in her soul? She felt something awakening deep inside, something she could not even explain yet to herself. It was as though she had been dead and was suddenly coming to life.

"Come inside, Mrs. Evans. Haley, give Mrs. Evans something to drink, some lemonade, perhaps."

Haley smiled knowingly. "Sure, Herb." She put out her hand to Beverly and led her inside.

Herbert True closed the door, smiling. "There's one in every crowd," he muttered.

Evelyn walked her horse through old Night Hunter's village, feeling the stares of others. Although Anita did not know she had met with Black Hawk last Saturday, she did realize she had had dreams about the man. The woman understood why she needed to come and talk to Night Hunter, and she had agreed to stay at school and teach on her own today so that Evelyn could come here. Reverend Phillips thought she had simply decided to take the day to visit another village.

She kept reminding herself she was doing the right thing, but part of her wanted to turn and run. She forced that part to forge ahead. She had to speak to Night Hunter before she went back to Black Hawk's camp tomorrow. Her dreams had been leading her to this place for weeks before even coming to this reservation, and, she supposed, to Black Hawk. Few of her people believed in men like Night Hunter, but for all her Christian upbringing, she had no doubt such men truly did have special spiritual powers. She did not consider it a heathen thought. These people had a very intimate connection to nature, and in her mind nature and God were one and the same. Who was to say that the Great Spirit the Sioux worshiped was not the same God she worshiped. And who was to say that Night Hunter was any different from the old prophets of the Bible?

She stopped to ask an old woman, in the Sioux tongue, where Night Hunter's lodge was located. The woman looked at her as though she were a crazy woman and pointed to a tipi that was larger than the others that were mixed in among small log homes. She ignored the stares of others as she led her horse to the old priest's tipi. Chickens scattered and dogs barked. She tied her horse to a small, scraggly tree nearby, then walked around and shook the rattles that hung over the tipi entrance as an announcement that someone waited outside.

A moment later, old Night Hunter pushed the entrance flap aside and stuck his head out. So close in the sunlight, the man looked even older than Evelyn realized, the deep brown skin of his face carrying a thousand wrinkles. She had seen him once before, from a distance, but had never met him. She expected to see surprise and mixed emotions in his faded brown eyes at the sight of a white woman wanting to come into his tipi, but instead he actually seemed to have been expecting her. "You are the schoolteacher," he said in a gruff voice.

"Yes," Evelyn answered in surprise. "My name is Evelyn Gibbons. How did you know? We have never met." She spoke the words in the Sioux tongue, wanting to impress him.

Night Hunter's eyes drilled into her own as though he was looking at her soul. "I am a man who knows many things. Come."

He ducked inside, and Evelyn followed. The tipi was filled with the sweet smell of burning grasses that had been laid over the hot coals of a fire she suspected was kept going at all times in spite of the heat. To Night Hunter, the fire was sacred, the source of all prayer. It was used for the burning of herbs and grasses to purify the air and the spirit. Because of the hot coals, it was rather stuffy inside the tipi, but not unbearable, since the bottom of the skins were rolled up, as was always done in summer for circulation of air. An old woman sat to the right of the entrance, the area where all women were expected to sit. She supposed the woman was Night Hunter's wife. There was no one else inside.

She waited on the entrance side of the fire, knowing that one did not walk between the fire and the sacred area of the tipi at the rear until and unless invited to do so. Night Hunter moved to sit there, then motioned for her to join him. She thanked him and sat beside him, removing her bonnet. Her heart pounded with dread that the man might laugh at her reason for coming, yet she felt anticipation for what Night Hunter might tell her. Even before she could speak, the old man said the words for her.

"You have come to talk about Black Hawk."

She studied his eyes in shock. "How did you know?"

"Did you not just ask me that question? Did I not tell you that Night Hunter knows many things?" He turned and put more sweetgrass on the fire, then waved some of the smoke toward her. "I have seen you before, not in the physical sense, but in spirit . . . in my own vision. I know the secrets of your heart."

Evelyn frowned. "I do not understand." How strange that only moments before she had been next to terrified of facing this old man, and now she felt completely at ease by the knowledge and gentleness in his dark, discerning eyes.

"I saw a white woman with golden hair. She spoke in my people's tongue and understood our ways. I also saw death. A white man will die, and somehow this white woman will help one of our own who will be blamed for this death. I saw no faces, but I know that you are that woman. I have been expecting you. I knew that if it was you, our spiritual connection would bring you to me." He reached out and pushed his thumb into some of the cooler ashes, then pressed it to her forehead and drew a line across it. "Your heart is good."

A white man will die? What was this man talking about? If she did not believe in his spiritualism, she would not worry about what seemed like a silly statement. And how on earth was she going to help the situation? She breathed deeply of the smell of sweetgrass and Night Hunter's perspiration. Suddenly, it seemed even closer inside the tipi, and she wanted to run, but she could not leave until she got what she had come for. So far the man had only confused her more instead of answering her own concerns. "You said I had come to talk about Black Hawk. How did you know this?"

A twinkle came into his eyes. "You must ask Black Hawk, not me. I will tell you, though, that you had a dream about Black Hawk. Perhaps more than *one* dream. Is this not so?"

He continued to astonish her. "Yes! I dreamed of him before I even came here, before I ever knew who he was." She spoke softly, feeling almost as though she were in a church. "In the dream an Indian man is riding toward me on a spotted horse. He reaches out for me, but the moment our hands touch, he disappears. The dream is very real. I was brought up among Indians. I was very close to a Cheyenne man when I was a little girl. He was killed before my eyes. People who know me think that is the reason for my dreams, and that they really mean nothing. They say they are just memories."

The old man shook his head. "Dreams tell us what is to come, not what has been. When you saw Black Hawk for the first time, you knew he was the man in the vision?"

Anyone else would think her crazy, but she knew this man believed and respected her feelings. "I think he is."

"I *know* he is. Black Hawk can tell you that himself, if you ask him. Do not be afraid to tell him of this dream."

"He would laugh at me."

"No. Black Hawk is a wise man. He will not laugh at you. He knows something that you do not, and so you must talk to him about this, not to me."

"Is Black Hawk the one who will be in trouble?"

"Perhaps. I cannot say until the time comes. You will know. Then the vision will be fulfilled, and when he reaches out for you, he will not disappear." He reached out and patted her hand. "I must know if you are menstruating before I can offer the pipe now."

Evelyn was embarrassed at the question, but she knew that to the Sioux, such things were important, and the question was not considered out of place. A sacred pipe was never removed from its bag in the presence of a menstruating woman.

. "No," she answered, her face flushed,

"Then you will stay now, while I smoke the pipe so that the Spirits will bless you." He picked up a beautifully beaded pipe bag and pulled out his sacred prayer pipe, which was decorated with plaited porcupine quills. White eagle feathers hung from it, the color for peace. Evelyn knew that in wartime, a sacred pipe was decorated with red feathers. She watched Night Hunter attach the bowl to the stem of the pipe, after which he filled the bowl with a native tobacco of redwood.

"Cansasa," she said softly.

Night Hunter nodded with pleasure at her knowledge of the Sioux rituals and language. He held up the pipe, as though to ask her what it was called. "A sacred pipe is called *cannunpa wakan,"* she told him.

He nodded again, the dark eyes that had so frightened her before now glowing with kindness. He held the pipe high above his head, offering it to Wakantanka. He then handed Evelyn a pair of wooden tongs and told her to pick up one of the hot coals with them. She did so, and he held his pipe toward her, putting the end of it in his mouth. She realized he wanted her to light it for him. She held the coal to the bowl, and soon the lovely fragrance of the redwood in its bowl wafted upward from the bowl as Night Hunter pulled air through the stem. He offered the pipe to the four directions, then lowered it in honor of Grandmother Earth. Evelyn knew it was a sign of great honor that the man had asked her to light it, for just to touch a priest's pipe was regarded as sacred, something only men and women of high respect could do. He puffed the pipe once more and blew the smoke at her face, which she realized was a ritual of blessing and purification, not an insult. "May Wakantanka be with you," he told her, "and guide you in the decisions you must make."

Evelyn nodded respectfully. "Thank you for allowing me into your lodge, and for your blessings." She had not gotten the answers she had hoped for. Apparently she would only get them when fate brought whatever it would bring, and by questioning Black Hawk. She rose, and walked around the central fire, then outside, where the sun made her squint. She put her bonnet back on and tied it, feeling happy that Night Hunter had welcomed her and spoken with her as he had. That would help her win the trust and respect of more of the Sioux. But she was not happy with the things he had told her.

A white man would die? Who? And how would Black Hawk be involved? How could she possibly help him? Maybe she never should have come here after all. She climbed up into the old sidesaddle Janine continued to let her use and headed John Phillips's white mare out of the village, as confused as ever, not sure whether to look forward to seeing Black Hawk tomorrow, or to dread it.

From a distant cabin Otter Woman watched the white woman she hated leave Night Hunter's village. Her heart burned with jealousy. Not only was this woman the cause of Black Hawk forbidding her to come and see him; but now the woman had been welcomed into Night Hunter's lodge! Why? What was this magical thing about the woman that made the Sioux accept her, even their most rebellious warrior and their spiritual leader? It wasn't fair, and something had to be done about it. She turned back inside to face her grandmother, who was watching her carefully. "Do not look at me that way!" she snapped.

"I know your heart, child."

"I am not a child. I am a woman who has outlived two husbands. I am the woman who the warrior Black Hawk prefers in his bed. I do not need your advice, old one."

"You know that it is wise to listen to the old ones. I am telling you now, Otter Woman, to stay away from that white teacher. You tell me you saw her go to Night Hunter. He accepted her into his lodge. This has great significance."

"It only means that the white woman, with all her education, has found a way to fool our wisest people. She is somehow tricking them, and I will stop her!"

"And how will you do that, Granddaughter? Please do not do something foolish."

Otter Woman turned away from her. "I will do what I must do," she answered before storming out of the cabin.

The old grandmother shook her head, tears in her eyes. "It is wrong, Granddaughter. It is a bad thing you are thinking of doing."

Twelve

Evelyn rode into the canyon and waited for Black Hawk to meet her again. Her emotions were mixed as she watched him make his way down the same steep bank where he had waited for her the first time. What did the future hold for her and this forbidden Sioux warrior? Did he know she had been to see Night Hunter?

He came closer, watching her with dark, penetrating eyes. It was cooler today, and he wore a buckskin shirt, the lacing undone at his neck, which was graced by a bone hairpipe necklace. His hair was tied to one side with a heavily beaded hairpiece. Another hair ornament, a circular copper barrette-type design, decorated with long beaded strips of rawhide that hung over his shoulder, decorated the other side of his hair. At the ends were tied little pieces of copper that tingled against one another when the wind made the narrow rawhide strips move. His doeskin pants were full-leg, rather than open at the sides, and beaded rawhide fringes decorated the side seams.

"I was not sure you would come again," he told her.

"Why did you doubt it?"

He sighed deeply. "I do not easily trust the *wicasu.*"

His eyes moved over her, and she felt a shiver. Her cautious side told her that perhaps she was too trusting. This man could indeed be dangerous. Many white settlers still feared him, and the soldiers chose to leave him alone. Yet here she was again, riding into a place with him where others would be a long time finding her if she needed help. Rather than being afraid, she found herself wondering if he liked what she had worn today, a lavender dress with puffed sleeves and a fitted bodice that accented her small waist and full bosom. But why on earth did she care if he noticed her shape, or if he thought she was pretty?

"Follow me," he told her. He turned and rode on, and Evelyn obeyed. Was Night Hunter right when he told her she must tell this man about her dreams? Would Black Hawk think her brazen and foolish? How on earth was she going to find just the right opportunity to bring up such a thing, let alone tell him she had ordered oil paints and brushes and special canvas for him, hoping she could convince him to paint pictures for her to try to sell. Everything she needed to tell him or wanted him to do would seem an intrusion on his privacy and his way of life.

Just as she had done the week before, she followed him to where he was camped, the same pretty, grassy spot. Again Little Fox was waiting there for them. To avoid having to talk about herself and her visit to Night Hunter, she got right to the lessons. This time they sat outside beside the creek, enjoying the bright sunshine and cool, fresh air.

Evelyn was surprised and pleased at how much both father and son had remembered from their first lesson, and how intently they apparently had been studying.

"Does grass have an A in it?" Little Fox asked. "It has the same sound as apple."

"Yes, Little Fox," Evelyn answered with a smile of surprise. "What a smart young man you are! Here, I will spell grass for you." She wrote the word on a small chalkboard she had brought with her this time, explaining the sound of the G and the R and the two S's. "Put the sounds together, and they spell grass," she told him.

Little Fox grinned with joy and excitement. "I can remember the S because it looks like a snake," he told Evelyn, "and it has a hissing sound like the snake."

"What a clever way to teach yourself to remember," she complimented. "And I am so pleased at how you have been thinking about these things and studying the sounds of the letters I gave you last week. Today we will do three more new letters: D, E, and F. The D . . ." She hesitated when she felt a touch at the back of her neck. Black Hawk, who sat to her left, fingered the hair ornament he had given her. His touch sent an unexpected fire through her blood.

"You wore the hairpiece," he said softly.

She swallowed. "I told you that I would." She quickly returned to the lessons in an effort to overcome the flutter his touch brought to her heart. She reviewed A, B, and C—going on to the new letters, looking for excuses to extend the lessons beyond the lunch hour and hoping to pick up again after they ate so there would be no time left for talking about other things.

It was two o'clock when Black Hawk suggested she stop and drink some water and eat some Indian fry-bread. "It is good and fresh," he told her. "Otter Woman brought it to me yesterday. I have told her to stay away, but she was worried I might need something. The women at her village do many things for me and Little Fox: wash and mend our clothes, make new ones, bring us bread, make our hair ornaments and jewelry." He handed out a piece of the soft bread.

Their eyes held as Evelyn took it from him, and she felt a new rush of jealousy. Otter Woman had been here! Had he bedded her? The last time they talked, he had casually told her that the woman serviced his every need, as though it was no different from washing his clothes. Was that how men like Black Hawk looked at making love, as just a way of relieving themselves? "Thank you." She dropped her gaze, worried he might read her thoughts, which she knew were foolish. She had no doubt this man had loved Little Fox's mother very much. Something in his eyes told her he was capable of great passion, and that thought only stirred deeper feelings she would rather not have for an Indian man.

"Otter Woman told me something," he said then.

"Oh?" She broke off a piece of the bread and ate it. She wanted not to like it, because Otter Woman had made it, but it was very soft and sweet and coated with sugar. It reminded her of the fresh-made doughnuts her mother used to make. She swallowed and met his eyes. "What did she say? Something about me?"

He studied her intently. "She said that you visited Night Hunter. She thinks you are trying to poison our people to your ways, that you are doing it by trying to win those who they most trust, like me and like Night Hunter, that you only use us to get what you really want."

Evelyn met his eyes squarely. "And do you believe her?"

Black Hawk laid his bread aside. "I do not know."

Evelyn sighed resignedly, realizing she had to tell him the truth. "Black Hawk, I went to see Night Hunter because . . ." She looked down at her lap. "Because I wanted him to help me with something that has troubled me for a long time." She met his eyes again, deciding it was now or never, and whatever his reaction, so be it. "I have no evil intentions toward you or your people. Surely you know that. In fact, I respect your beliefs, your spiritual connections. That is why I went to Night Hunter, because of a strange dream I have had . . . the same dream many times over. It started before I ever even decided to come here."

He bent his legs and crossed them, resting his elbows on his knees. "Tell me about this dream."

She could not continue to meet his gaze. She set her own bread aside and rose, folding her arms and turning toward the creek to watch Little Fox return to his game of catching fish with his hands. "In the dream someone is riding toward me—an Indian man . . . on a spotted horse." She waited a moment, but Black Hawk said nothing. "He comes closer, and he looks very much like an Indian man I once knew as a small girl. He reaches out for me, as though to ask for help, or to take me with him. I'm not sure the reason. I reach back to him, and when our hands touch, he disappears. The dream is very real. It always startles me awake, and I feel very anxious, as though there is something I am supposed to do to help this man, but I'm not sure what it is. When Janine came to my father's church back in Wisconsin and said teachers were needed here, I felt the dream had some connection, so I decided perhaps it meant I should come here." She took a moment to breathe deeply to calm her pounding heart. "I went to Night Hunter because I wanted him to help me interpret the dream. He only confused me more by telling me that a white man would die, and that . . . that someone in your tribe would be connected with the death . . . and that I am to help them."

She waited through another several seconds of silence before he finally spoke. His words startled her, for it was only then she realized he was standing directly behind her. He had moved so quietly she did not even know he had got to his feet.

"Am I the man in the dream?"

She wished she could meet his eyes, but she was too embarrassed. "I—I think that you are. I wasn't sure . . . until that first time I met you. If you want the truth, I feel as if the Indian I knew as a child has returned to me . . . through you." She waited for him to laugh at her, but instead he walked closer to the stream and knelt down to pick up a smooth rock and study it.

"Who was this man?"

His back was to her now, and she wondered if it was just as difficult for him to face her as it was for her to meet his eyes. "His name was Wild Horse. He was Cheyenne. My father was preaching at the Cheyenne reservation in Indian Territory, my mother used to take me to swim at a pond when it was hot. One day Wild Horse came there, and he and my mother . . . became good friends. She learned many things from him about Indian ways. I thought he was the most wonderful, fascinating man I had ever known. He was a friend to both of us, but now that I am grown, I realize he was more than a friend to my mother. I believe that she loved him, and he loved her."

Black Hawk sat down in the grass. "What happened to him?"

It was easier now. He was listening. He was not laughing at her. "He was very much like you, rebellious, sometimes getting into trouble when it wasn't even his fault. One night I heard people talking about soldiers looking for him. I don't even remember why—something about stealing some cattle. I decided that if I went to the pond, maybe I would find him and I could warn him, but I ended up getting lost. I know now that Wild Horse was planning to run away from the agency that night before he could be found and arrested, but instead of saving himself, when he heard I was lost, he stayed and searched for me. He found me where I had fallen down a steep bank and hit my head. The rest of that night I lay in his arms, feeling perfectly safe, and in the morning he carried me up the bank and was going to leave me someplace safe. Soldiers spotted us, and before he could explain . . . they shot him. I was crying, but it was because I was afraid *for* Wild Horse, not afraid *of* him. The soldiers thought he had kidnapped me. Right before my eyes I watched them fill him with bullets. As he was dying, he asked me to never forget him, and I never have. Now I feel his spirit has come back to me."

Black Hawk rose, turning to face her. His dark eyes blazed with something she could not quite determine. Anger? Passion? Surprise? Maybe a mixture of the three. "Through me?" he asked.

She swallowed, her skin feeling prickly all over. "Yes."

His eyes remained unreadable. "And this is why you told me that day we met that we would meet again, that there were things to be settled between us?"

She nodded, suddenly realizing that she was falling in love with this man, a man whose world bore no resemblance to her own, a man forbidden to someone like herself. "I am still not sure what we must do," she said aloud. "Night Hunter believes that I am destined to somehow help your people. Maybe that is why I felt so compelled to find you, convince you to send Little Fox to school. That was the way I thought I was meant to help your people, through you. What did Night Hunter mean when he said that I should ask you why he believes you are the man in my dream?"

A soft breeze blew at the little rawhide tassels of Black Hawk's hair ornament, making them tinkle. She thought how such decorations on a white man would look ridiculous, but on Black Hawk, they only made him more provocative.

"I also had a dream," he told her. "Never in my life would I have thought that I would share a sacred vision with a white woman, but Night Hunter has told me I must do so now. I did not want to tell you, but now that you have told me these things that are close to your heart, and since Night Hunter told you that you must ask me about your dream, I have no choice."

He sighed, and she realized he was as nervous about telling her his dream as she had been to tell him her own.

"It was during the Sun Dance," he continued, "when all feeling and thoughts of this world left me in my pain. I closed my eyes, and I was riding my spotted horse at a hard run, trying to reach a woman with golden hair and wearing white women's clothes. I came close to her, reached out for her, and she to me. The moment our hands touched, she disappeared. When I asked Night Hunter about it, he said that when the time came that this white woman could help me, the vision would be fulfilled, and she would not disappear from my eyes." He stepped closer. "The woman had no face . . . until now. I believe you are the woman. I did not want this to be. That is why the first time I saw you I was very angry, but not truly at you. I was angry that Wakantanka has sent me this vision, that it seems I am destined to turn to a white woman."

Evelyn felt flushed and also awed. To hear of his vision was like a revelation, like opening a doorway to all her confusion. So, she *was* destined to come here! And perhaps Wild Horse did live within this man! It was a chilling experience. Never in her life had she been more sure there was a God, and that that God was the same as the God worshiped by Black Hawk. It was the only explanation for their dreams being so closely linked. She could see by his eyes that he was thinking the same, that he, too, was astounded by what he had learned today.

Evelyn turned away from him, fighting the sudden and powerful urge to step into his arms and let him fold them around her. This was wrong! All wrong! What was she to do? So what if they *had* had the same dream? What did it mean? What were they supposed to do about it? "I think I should leave," she told him. "I think we both need to think about these things, and what it all could mean. I am very confused right now, Black Hawk. To realize we could be so spiritually connected without ever knowing each other is . . . I don't even know how to explain it. In a way it frightens me. I have never had such an experience, and until now I would not have believed such a thing could be." She felt him move close behind her again, sensed that he wanted to touch her, but he did not.

"It is not so hard for me to believe it," he answered. "Your people long ago lost touch with the spirit world, the circle of life, and how it is connected with the earth, the heavens, Wakan-tanka. Our visions have much meaning, Evy, and there is no limit to the power of the spirits. That is what is wrong with your people. They try to understand that which is not *meant* for us to understand. They try to make reason where there *is* no reason. They try to put their God in His proper place. They do not see Him as having no limits of space or time. They try to control their own lives, when we have no control at all. It is the Great

One who leads us, gives us life, takes life away. Trying to control these things, I think, is what leaves your people without vision, and makes them mean and frustrated. *They* want the power, but the Great One will not allow it. Having the same dream is not something to fear, Evy, or to worry about in confusion. It just *is*. It is something we must both accept and wait to discover its meaning."

She finally turned to face him again, awed by his wisdom and simple faith. "I have never looked at it that way."

He smiled softly. "When you do, you will begin to think more like the Sioux. You will not center your mind on little things, but on the universe and all that it holds. I only learned your language and want to learn your letters and numbers because it will help me in the white man's thinking, but to me these things mean nothing. Your people think that knowledge will give them the power to change the world, like a God. I tell you now, I believe that white man's knowledge will one day destroy him. I only want that knowledge so that perhaps I can help *stop* the destruction."

She shook her head. "I wish Reverend Phillips could hear what you just said, him and other preachers and scholars. I never believed—"

They both heard the whirring sound, but too late. Evelyn gasped, unable to finish her sentence. An awful, wrenching pain penetrated her back, just below her left shoulder, and the force of whatever hit her that moment propelled her forward into Black Hawk's arms. She remembered him grabbing hold of her, then everything went black.

Black Hawk clung to her, his eyes wide with shock. He slowly lowered her to the grass, belly-down, and his eyes widened in horror when he saw that an arrow protruded from her back. He studied it, recognized the red-and-black feathers that decorated the arrow as those used by Two Hands, who had been Otter

Woman's second husband. He looked up in the direction from which the arrow must have come, but he saw no one.

"Otter Woman!" he muttered. "I will *kill* her for this!"

Evelyn thought she heard someone scream, and somehow she knew it must be her own voice.

"I had to break the arrow," a man's voice told her. "I am sorry, Evy. I had to push the head out through the front of your chest. It was the only way because of the way it is made. I cannot pull it backward."

Whoever spoke rolled her over onto her back, and she was vaguely aware he had pulled her dress and camisole away from her left side. She gasped when she felt another yank, and moments later there came a horrible burning that was so excruciating that she slipped into blessed unconsciousness. When she awoke again, she opened her eyes to notice that the sky through the top of the tipi in which she lay was dark. A small fire burned at the center of the tipi. She closed her eyes again, trying to think.

What had happened? She had been talking with Black Hawk by the stream, when the pain hit her. Later he had said something about breaking an arrow to get it out. Out of *her?* Someone had shot her with an arrow?

She tried to rise, but excruciating pain tore through her entire left side and left arm, surprising her so that she cried out.

"Do not move," a man's voice said softly.

Someone touched her shoulders gently. She opened her eyes to study his face, his dark skin, dark eyes. "Black Hawk," she whispered. "What . . . happened?"

"You were shot through the back with an arrow. I think it was Otter Woman."

She frowned, wondering why she had ever come to this place. She could be back in Wisconsin, safe, loved, tending to a tidy farmhouse, maybe pregnant with her first child . . . free of this awful pain. "Why would she . . . do this?"

Black Hawk sighed, sitting down beside her and putting his head in his hands. "Because she hates you and is jealous of you. She thinks you have stolen me from her and are poisoning me and the rest of our people. She does not understand."

Evelyn fought the tears that wanted to come. She hated crying, and she certainly did not want to do it in front of Black Hawk and verify what was probably his opinion of white women, that they were weak and easily frightened. Besides, Otter Woman surely wanted her to cry, and she was not about to satisfy that awful woman's wishes. Nor was she about to grant the woman's greatest wish by letting herself die. She had never even met Otter Woman. How could she hate her this much? "I . . . need water," she told Black Hawk.

He quickly left her side, returning with a ladle of water. He lifted her head just enough that she could swallow some. "You lost much blood after I took out the arrow. I burned the wound with a hot metal rod. I learned from the doctors after Wounded Knee that burning wounds on the inside sometimes helps keep away the bad spirits that bring infection. I hurt you, but I had no choice. I am sorry, Evy."

His use of her name in the shortened form strangely touched her. She had never told him to call her Evy. He had just started doing it, as though they had known each other for a very long time. She felt the strength of his arm when he lifted her slightly, but she also sensed he could be very gentle. He carefully lowered her again onto a pile of soft furs. "Does Otter Woman . . . love you?"

Anger and contempt came into his eyes. "Otter Woman loves all men, but she has favorites. I am one. Until today I thought we were at least friends. Now I shall never speak to her again, except to tell her what I think of this. I am not sure I can keep from putting my hands to her throat and squeezing until the life is gone out of her!"

She was going to ask if he loved Otter Woman, though it was obviously an unnecessary question. She felt too sick and was in too much pain at the moment to really care, except that through all her agony, a little part of her was relieved to know there was nothing special between Black Hawk and Otter Woman.

"I must get you back to your own people," he told her. "I am sorry, Evy. This is a terrible thing. You came here out of the goodness of your heart, and because . . ."

She watched his eyes. What was that she saw there? Something new. Admiration? A new respect?

"Because we share a vision," he finished. What was this feeling he had for this white woman? Surely it was not love! He would not soon forget the sight of her breast when he tore away her clothes in order to help her. Such milky whiteness against the dark skin of his hands, her nipple pink as a cherry. This desire for her was wrong and could never lead anywhere but to trouble. He touched her hair. "I was afraid for you. If you should die before the vision is fulfilled, it would be a bad thing."

So, Evelyn thought, *that is all he's worried about, fulfilling a vision.* For a moment she actually thought he was going to tell her he loved her, but then, that was a silly thought, wasn't it? How could there be such feelings between a Sioux man and a white woman, and especially after knowing each other such a short time.

"I must get you back," he told her. "I will take you in the morning. Then I will pay a little visit to Otter Woman!"

She managed to move her right hand enough to touch his wrist. "Please don't hurt her," she said weakly. "She doesn't . . . understand. You must explain to her. Tell her I want to talk . . . to her."

"You cannot trust her."

"I will . . . make her understand."

Black Hawk sighed, pulling back a blanket and studying her wound. "I wrapped the wound with a piece of your own under-skirt." He grinned a little. "Why do white women wear so many clothes? In the summer heat, you would be much more com-fortable in a simple tunic like our women wear."

She managed a smile of her own. "I will have to think about that. My people . . . do have a way of . . . complicating their lives, don't they?"

He studied the wrapping, which went around her shoulder and over her breast. Evelyn was only dimly aware that he must have had to bare her breast to treat her, yet, strangely, she was not embarrassed or afraid. Perhaps it was only because she was in too much pain for it to matter right now.

"You will have a scar. I am sorry," he said, apologizing for the third time.

"It isn't . . . your fault."

Their eyes held. "Such beautiful skin you have. It is sad that it should be scarred."

She felt herself blushing then. How long had his eyes lingered on her nakedness? Had he touched her there? She had been unconscious for a while. He could have done anything. She moved her other hand beneath the blanket to be sure the rest of her clothes were intact, then chastised herself for having such thoughts about this man who she knew would never harm her or take advantage of her. They shared something too deep and sacred for that.

"Stop . . . blaming yourself, Black Hawk. I'll heal . . . and I will come back."

"No. You should not have to come all the way here. I will begin sending Little Fox to school."

Her eyes widened in surprise. "You will? But what about your . . . own lessons?"

"I do not know yet. Perhaps I will come, too—one day a week. I must think about it."

She looked around the tipi at the beautiful paintings inside. "I like coming here," she admitted. "I really don't mind. It's . . . beautiful here . . . peaceful." *I like being alone with you, Black Hawk.* No, she could not tell him that yet. She thought about her mother and Wild Horse, how they used to meet at the pond. Those thoughts led to others: Wild Horse rescuing her, bringing her back . . . the soldiers! She drew in her breath and met Black Hawk's eyes. "You . . . can't take me back . . . Black Hawk!"

He frowned. "What do you mean?"

"They might not understand . . . what happened. You could get in trouble. Maybe get hurt!"

"I did nothing but help you."

She closed her eyes, the memory of watching Wild Horse shot down still vivid in her mind after all these years. "You must be careful. Take me directly to Reverend Phillips . . . not the agency . . . or the fort."

He nodded. "I will make a up a travois when the sun rises and take you to the white preacher."

Little Fox came to sit at her other side. "Will she live, Father?"

Black Hawk put the back of his hand to the side of her face, and Evelyn felt a surprising comfort in the touch. His hand was big and powerful. She knew he could probably kill her with one blow if he chose, but she felt safe and protected; and she knew that if she asked him to kill Otter Woman for what she had done, he would probably do it. He would kill anyone, man or woman, who tried to hurt her.

"She will live," he told his son. "There is a vision yet to be fulfilled."

"Sergeant Desmond, wake up your men and start searching the villages!" Lieutenant Teller ordered.

Desmond left to gather some men, and Teller turned to Reverend Phillips, who had made a dangerous ride in the dark to agency headquarters to report that Evelyn Gibbons had never returned from riding out to visit the various villages.

"I knew I never should have let her go doing something like that alone!" Phillips lamented. "She is too trusting!"

"When it comes to the Sioux, Reverend, I don't trust them any farther than I can throw them," the lieutenant told him. "I'll have Sergeant Desmond search every single village thoroughly. In fact, I've sent a rider up to the fort to bring back a few more men so we can double the search. You're lucky we happened to be camped here at the agency for a meeting with Agent McLaughlin or we wouldn't have men already on hand for a search. You say you think she headed out to the Northwest?"

"I believe so. She was very vague about where she was going, just said she had decided to spend every Saturday visiting various families and trying to convince them to send their children to school. That's so important to her that she doesn't even think about her own safety." Phillips felt sick inside at what might have happened to poor Evelyn . . . beautiful Evelyn. Why didn't she look at him the way he wished she would?

Sergeant Desmond reported back to the lieutenant. "We'll be ready to move in ten minutes, Lieutenant. Any special orders once we find her?"

"Take her to the reverend's place behind the church and send a man to report to me that you have found her."

"What if she's been hurt? Do I arrest any Indian that might have done it?"

"Use your own judgment, Sergeant. If it's a situation where you and the men would be in danger and it could cause a possible uprising, report to me first. It's possible her horse could have taken a spill or some other accident that didn't even involve any Indians."

Desmond snickered. "Not likely. We'll find her, Lieutenant, and we'll take care of whatever the situation is."

"I'll ride back and wait at the church," the reverend told the lieutenant. "With any luck, she'll be there. Either way, my sister and Anita Wolf will be worried. I have to get back and tell them what is being done." He climbed into the seat of the rickety wagon he had driven to the agency. "Thank you, Lieutenant."

As Phillips drove off, Sergeant Desmond watched after him, his mind whirling with all the possibilities of what could have happened to the pretty Evelyn Gibbons. He grinned at the thought that some drunken Sioux man might have attacked and raped her.

It would serve the bitch right, he thought. *And give me good reason to kill me an Indian.* Wouldn't it be perfectly ironic if that man were Black Hawk? He grinned at the delicious thought.

Thirteen

Vague remembrances danced through Evelyn's foggy mind. Pain . . . Black Hawk's gentle voice . . . his soothing touch. She thought she remembered drinking a little water, remembered crying out when someone lifted her and carried her out into the sunlight. It was strange, this terrible trap between semiconsciousness and reality. She knew she was on a travois, felt the pain of every bump and jolt, felt the sun beating down on her. She knew it must be Black Hawk pulling the travois, yet everything that happened seemed more like a dream. Sometime after that first time she awoke and talked to Black Hawk . . . was that just hours ago? She could not be sure. She only knew that sometime after that she had slipped into this world of the living dead, where she was conscious of what went on around her, yet could not seem to voice her words or be sure where she was or what time of day it was. The pain was so deep that she could not even turn her head to *try* to ascertain her surroundings.

The travois hit another rut, and she groaned.

"Father!" a boy's voice called out. "That last bump hurt her."

Quickly, the travois stopped moving, and moments later she looked into Black Hawk's dark eyes. "I am sorry for your pain," he told her. "There is no other way to get you out of here to a place where one of your own doctors can help you."

"Where . . . are we?"

"We are out of Eagle Canyon now. Little Fox is riding beside you. I am taking you to your people."

He left, and his words lingered in her mind. *Your people*. That was how he thought of her: separate, different, another race, just like she thought of the Sioux . . . all but Black Hawk. She remembered his soft voice, how he'd held her, how she had grown to love him as just a man; but perhaps it was just a dream that she loved, for it was only dreams that had led her to him. Now she lay near death, a fitting omen that there could never be anything intimate between her and Black Hawk.

What was Evelyn Gibbons, with her college degree and a comfortable life in Wisconsin, doing here . . . laid out on a travois in so much pain that she could barely speak? What was she doing here with an arrow wound inflicted by an Indian woman she had never met but who hated her enough to want to kill her? Why had she cared about those dreams and what they might mean?

She sensed that many horses were coming now, could feel their thundering hooves against the earth.

"Halt, or we'll shoot!" someone shouted. The voice sounded familiar. Sergeant Desmond? Visions floated in a confused maze, and she saw Wild Horse, bullet holes ripping into him, blood pouring from his body. Wild Horse! Black Hawk! Soldiers! Sergeant Desmond was not a man to listen to reason. She opened her mouth to cry out, to explain, but the words would not come, except in a small whisper that could not be heard above the shouting that was taking place now. Dust swirled around her.

"I have done nothing wrong!" she heard Black Hawk saying. "This woman needs help. I am taking her to the church."

"What the hell happened to her!" Desmond demanded. "And what is she doing with *you!*"

"She came to teach me and my son. Someone shot her with an arrow."

"What!"

Evelyn heard a thud, followed by a chilling grunt and the sound of someone hitting the ground.

"Ate!" Little Fox cried out the Sioux word for father. "Leave my father alone!"

"Shut up, you little vermin, or you'll get the same!" Desmond yelled. "And stay on that horse if you know what's good for you!"

There came a pause. "Let him speak, Sergeant," someone else said.

"I'm in charge here! All of you know Black Hawk makes trouble wherever he goes."

Evelyn heard a kicking sound, followed by a grunt. "You goddamn savage!" Desmond shouted even louder. "What the hell is going on here! Miss Gibbons would never ride out alone to meet with the likes of you! And *who* shot her? *You?"*

Evelyn could tell Black Hawk had been hurt by the pain she detected in his voice. She wished she could see, wished she could scream at the sergeant not to hurt him, that he was completely innocent of any wrongdoing.

"If I had done it, why would I bring her here . . . for help?" Black Hawk questioned. "Someone else shot her while we . . . were talking at my camp. I do not know who it might be. There are many of my people who do not trust the white teacher and want to scare her away."

Evelyn knew that in spite of how angry he must be at Otter Woman, Black Hawk had decided to protect her. He might want to kill her himself, but he would still never turn one of his own over to soldiers.

"You're a goddamn liar, and you're going to sit behind bars at the fort until we get this straightened out!" Desmond commanded. "When we get the story straight from Miss Gibbons, *then* we'll decide what to do with you. You'd just better hope the lady doesn't die!"

"You are a fool!" Black Hawk responded. "Can you not see

I was bringing her here for help? And if I had done something wrong, why would I have brought my son with me and put him in danger? What will happen to my son?"

"We'll take him to your sister and your grandmother. You just shed that knife of yours and any other weapons you're carrying."

"Is all this really necessary, Sergeant?" another man asked. "He *was* bringing her to get help."

"Shut up, Foster! Get down off your horse and come tie his wrists! Clark, you see that the boy gets to his grandmother's village. Henley, you and I will take Miss Gibbons to the reverend's place. The rest of you be sure that Black Hawk is locked up good and tight at the fort until we can talk to Miss Gibbons and Agent McLaughlin and get this straightened out! And send the medic over to the reverend's to have a look at Miss Gibbons."

There were several "Yes, sir's," and through it all Evelyn tried with all her strength to speak loudly enough for someone to pay attention; but no one seemed to notice or care.

"I have done nothing wrong!" she heard Black Hawk protest again. She prayed he would not put up too much of a fight, sure that the sergeant would love any excuse to beat the man, or maybe even shoot him. How awful for Black Hawk to be imprisoned! This whole experience could only turn him against the whites and soldiers again. This would erase what little progress she had made with him in her two short visits. Night Hunter had predicted she was supposed to help him, yet here she lay not even able to speak up to defend him. Surely this was not the meaning of the vision . . . and wasn't a white man supposed to die?

Her mind reeled with visions and reality. "Help him back up on his horse!" someone demanded.

"Ate! Ate!" Little Fox continued to shout. Evelyn could tell he was crying.

"Go with the soldiers to Many Birds and Dancing Woman,"

Black Hawk called back in the Sioux tongue. "Do not be afraid, Little Fox. I will come back for you. Trust no one but Many Birds and Miss Gibbons. Tell Night Hunter what has happened! Tell him—"

There came the sound of another blow.

Black Hawk! Evelyn wanted to shout the name. What were they doing to him? He was innocent of any wrongdoing! This was all her fault. "Throw him over his horse!" Desmond was ordering. She could hear Little Fox crying. Why had she even come here? Why had she been so adamant that these people needed to go to school? Why had she so daringly gone out to meet Black Hawk alone without explaining to someone so there would be no misunderstandings if something like this happened? She had done a foolish thing, and not only would the reverend and the soldiers think less of her, but Agent McLaughlin and the reverend and the rest of them would probably be very upset, perhaps even ask her to leave the reservation. She could lose the grant that had been gifted to her to use for living here and for necessary supplies. She could be sent home, and then what? More and more she felt she belonged here, and she could not let herself die, nor could she go home without knowing the fulfillment of her vision . . . a vision she shared with Black Hawk.

"God only knows what that wild sonofabitch did to that woman while she lay hurt and unconscious," she heard Desmond say. His voice was closer now. She felt someone bend down near her. "Miss Gibbons? Can you hear me?"

She opened her eyes to see Jubal Desmond staring down at her. "Black Hawk . . . innocent," she whispered.

"What?" The man scowled, callously pulling back the blankets that covered her and exposing the bandages wrapped around her left shoulder and breast. She prayed her breast was completely covered, hated the man for pulling her dress open even more than it already was in a pretense of seeing if she had other wounds. "Hell, he could have raped her," he commented. How many were with him, watching her? "The state she's in, she wouldn't have known the difference."

"With a man like Black Hawk?" Someone actually laughed. "She would have known." There came more laughter, and Desmond covered her up again.

"We'd better get her to the reverend. It's a good hour from here," Desmond said.

Evelyn wanted to call out to him, to demand that he listen to the truth. Wasn't he even going to ask? He could bend close so she could whisper that he should let Black Hawk go. Desmond was only showing he was even more ignorant and intolerant than she had first suspected. Oh, how she hated him!

There followed several days of fever and sickness, during which Evelyn sometimes did not even know where she was or if she was even still alive. Once she saw her mother reaching out for her, telling her to be true to herself and to not give up the fight. Faces. Wild Horse, Reverend Phillips, Anita, Sergeant Desmond, Night Hunter . . . Black Hawk. She imagined resting in Black Hawk's arms, and she felt comforted.

Finally, the moment came when she opened her eyes to full consciousness. She was lying in her own bedroom, in the little cabin she had come to call home. For the first time in . . . how long? She had no idea what day it was, had to think for a few minutes to realize how she had come to be here. She only knew that she was more aware of her surroundings again, felt more like herself. She was alive, and she didn't feel sick. She moved slowly, realizing she could rest on her right arm and push herself up. There was still pain in her left shoulder and side, but now it was bearable. With much effort she scooted herself to a sitting position, took a moment to look around the room, think about all that had happened.

"Black Hawk," she whispered. "What have they done with

you?" She touched her shoulder, realized it was still bandaged. She unbuttoned her nightgown and looked down at herself, but could see only the bandages. She remembered with anger the sergeant yanking her blankets away and jerking her dress aside. What had he seen? Why did it upset her that he might have seen something he shouldn't, yet knowing that Black Hawk had seen and touched much more did not bother her at all.

She took a deep breath, leaning against her pillows and pushing some of her hair behind her ear. She was hungry. She knew that was a good sign that she would be all right. She realized she must look terrible, but that was not important now. What *was* important was to help Black Hawk. Was he still incarcerated? Had anyone listened to his story? Had Otter Woman been arrested? She had to be careful what she said. If Black Hawk had not implicated Otter Woman, he had his reasons. She was not going to go against his wishes.

She heard someone moving about in the main room of her little two-room cabin. "Anita? Reverend?" she called out. "Is anyone out there?"

Janine quickly came through the curtain. "Evy! Oh, you look so much better!" She rushed to her side, bending over her and grasping her hand. "How do you feel? Are you really back with us? Your eyes are so much brighter. We thought we were going to lose you, Evy. What were you doing out there with Black Hawk? What happened? Black Hawk is sitting in jail, and the Sioux are getting restless. We fear there will be trouble if—"

"Stop, Janine!" Evelyn lightly squeezed her hand. "Please . . . one thing at a time. Get your brother . . . please."

"Yes. Right away! Oh, he'll be so glad to see how much better you are! Do you want some tea? Something to eat?"

Evelyn smiled at the gentle Janine, realizing she had probably been nursing her faithfully. "Yes. That would be nice. How long have I been . . . lying here like this?"

Janine straightened, dabbing at tears of joy. "It's been five days since the soldiers found you with Black Hawk. You were delirious for part of that time with a high fever. The Army doctor didn't quite know what to do other than to keep treating your wound with carbolic acid and have us bathe you in cool water. He said there was nothing to do but wait. He even had to lance your wound once. For a while we thought . . ." She sniffed. "I can see now that you're going to be all right."

Evelyn wondered what kind of scars she would have—an arrow wound, burned out by Black Hawk, lanced by the Army doctor, who probably didn't know what he was doing. "They must release Black Hawk . . . right away, Janine. He did nothing wrong."

Janine looked almost disappointed. "Evelyn, he said you had come to his camp alone to teach him and Little Fox. That was a very dangerous thing to do, and it's something some people won't understand. If it's true, we have to find a way to make this look good when we report it to Mission Service."

Evelyn frowned. "Just tell them that I was so dedicated to my work that I risked my life trying to convert . . . one of the most difficult men on the reservation."

Janine wiped at her eyes again. "Is that the whole truth?"

Evelyn closed her eyes. *No. I dreamed about Black Hawk. I am in love with him, in love with a Sioux warrior.* "What difference does it make?" she asked aloud. "No one is going to understand the truth. Just please report this however you have to . . . in order for me to stay here. Many things have been left unfinished, Janine, and more children keep coming to school. Our work has just begun. I don't want this . . . to change any of that."

Janine nodded. "I will get John." As she left the room, Evelyn felt a sudden urge to cry. What was everyone thinking? It was obvious the horror she would see on their faces if she said she was in love with an Indian man. Why had God brought her here? Where was all of this taking her? She let out one gulping sob, then fought the tears, breathing deeply to control them minutes later when she heard Reverend Phillips coming inside the cabin. He smiled with relief when he saw her sitting up.

"Janine, go ahead and fix her that tea," he told his sister.

Janine looked at Evelyn sadly, then left to do his bidding. Evelyn pulled the covers up to her neck, self-conscious that Phillips was in her bedroom. The man pulled up a chair beside the bed. "Miss Gibbons, what happened?" In spite of how well the man now knew her, he continued to address her formally, although there was a strong hint of emotion and familiarity in the way he spoke her name today. "We've been so worried," he added. "I have been praying night and day for your recovery. Thank God you look so much better today, and you're coherent. Now maybe we can get to the truth of the matter, before trouble breaks out."

Evelyn touched her hair, embarrassed at how she must look, but there was no time for bathing and dressing. "You must ride to the agency and tell McLaughlin to go to Fort Yates and order Black Hawk to be released. He did nothing wrong, John."

The man frowned in curiosity. "But how—"

"Black Hawk came to see me at the school the night of the dance. He doesn't trust us enough as a group yet to allow Little Fox to come to the school, but he . . . trusted me alone. He asked if I would come to his camp and teach him and Little Fox to read and write. He wanted to learn himself just for protection against future treaties. He wants Little Fox to learn for the same reasons, to protect himself in the white man's world. Because I understand the Sioux ways and their language, I guess he trusted me to teach his son without trying to destroy his Sioux beliefs and customs."

Phillips shook his head. "I don't understand. Why you? All these months we have been here, and Black Hawk would never come in and talk to any of us. And why in God's name did you agree to go out there alone, to meet with such an unpredictable, dangerous man?"

"He is not dangerous, Reverend. He is extremely intelligent, and he is just cautious . . . and distrustful. He has good reason, considering what happened to his family at Wounded Knee . . . and what has happened to many of the Sioux children who were taken away to schools outside the reservation. Now with his arrest . . ."

"Miss Gibbons, you went to a place none of us ever could have found and met alone with a Sioux Indian man who could have . . ." He closed his eyes. "I just don't understand. Why didn't you insist he come to the school instead? He could have accompanied his son, to see that nothing would happen to him."

Evelyn sighed. How could she tell him the whole truth, tell him about her dreams? "Reverend, if you want to make this look acceptable, just tell others it was my dedication to my work that made me do a foolish thing. I did what he asked, because I thought it was my only chance to get close to the very person who could influence the rest of the Sioux. If I showed him I could be trusted, perhaps then . . . he would start trusting more himself, bring Little Fox to school. I think I could have convinced him of it, but now . . . after this . . ." Her eyes teared. "Reverend, you have got to have him released just as fast as possible! Let him go to his son . . . go back to his own camp. Black Hawk shouldn't be imprisoned! It will kill him."

The reverend rose, running a hand through his hair. "How did you get hurt?"

"I was standing with Black Hawk near a stream when an arrow hit me from behind. I don't know who might have done it," she lied. "For all I know, they might have been shooting at Black Hawk for some reason . . . maybe it was someone who was angry that he was letting a white woman teach him; but I was most likely the target. We both know nearly every Sioux man and woman out there would probably like all of us to leave;

but I am not going to let that stop me from what I came here to do, and I am *not* going to let Black Hawk sit in prison. You have to go to McLaughlin. Tell him that Black Hawk saved my life. He took out the arrow and burned out the wound. Can't anyone see that if he had meant to hurt me, he wouldn't have been bringing me back on his own? He would *never* hurt me . . . and he wasn't running off with me." She breathed deeply, already feeling tired. "What have they done with him, Reverend? Has *he* been hurt? I remember the day the soldiers found us . . . they were beating Black Hawk."

Phillips sighed, eyeing her closely. "He was hurt pretty bad, but he'll be all right. Sergeant Desmond got a good reprimanding for beating him when he was defenseless and had his hands tied behind his back."

"The *sergeant* is the one who should be jailed! If there is any trouble around here it will be his fault, not any of the Indians'. The man looks for excuses to start something."

The reverend rubbed at the back of his neck in frustration. "What is really going on, Evelyn? Is there anything you aren't telling me?"

She held his gaze boldly. "No. I was just doing what I came here to do. If I die doing it, then so be it. I am determined . . . and I saw my chance to win over the most important man on this reservation. Someone tried to hurt me, Reverend, but it wasn't Black Hawk. He saved my life."

Phillips folded his arms. "Rumor has it you visited old Night Hunter. Why?"

She felt her cheeks flushing, but she forced a look of innocence. "I only wanted to ask him about Black Hawk . . . if he thought I could trust him. He told me I should not be afraid of him, that Black Hawk is a man of his word."

"And why didn't you tell me and Janine what you were doing? Why did you lie and say you were visiting other families?"

She blinked back tears, hating having to deceive these good

people. "I was afraid you wouldn't understand . . . and now I see I was right. You never would have let me go alone, but if I hadn't, I would not have won Black Hawk's trust. Now I fear, because of all that has happened, I've lost it again. God only knows when he'll show his face around here again . . . once he is freed."

"That just shows you you went about this the wrong way, but I don't hold it against you, and neither will the others once they understand your dedication." He came closer and patted her arm. "I'll take care of this."

She met his eyes. "Please tell Black Hawk that I'll be all right, and that I'm sorry if my coming to his camp got him in trouble. I never meant for any of it to happen."

"It isn't your fault. It's Black Hawk's, for insisting you come to him; and it's the fault of whoever put that arrow in you. I cannot imagine anyone wanting to do such a vile thing." He held her gaze for a moment. "Miss Gibbons, don't get carried away by your dedication and your emotions. Remember your place."

Her place? Did he suspect how she really felt about Black Hawk? Was it such a terrible thing for a white woman to love an Indian man? Her mother had gone through so much heartache over the same thing . . . and the Indian man had lost his life.

"My place is here, Reverend . . . teaching the Sioux, helping them through this terrible and frightening time of transition. They fear they are a dying race . . . and they have lost hope and pride. They drink whiskey to erase the hurt, and the whiskey is killing them. You know me well enough by now . . . to know that I don't care what others think of anything I do. You tell them what you have to, but I will continue doing what *I* have to do . . . and if it means my going out alone to meet with someone in order to win their trust, then I will do it again."

He shook his head. "You're a single-minded woman, and as dedicated as any missionary. I admire your courage, Miss Gibbons. I will go and talk to Agent McLaughlin right away."

"Please let me know as quickly as possible when Black Hawk has been released," she asked.

Their eyes held, and she realized he suspected her true feelings for the man and was not sure what to think. "I'll do that," he answered. He turned and left, and Janine came inside the room with a tray that held a pot of hot water and a cup for tea.

"We'll have you up and about in no time," she told Evelyn. "I'll bet you would like a bath and to have your hair washed. Anita and I can help you." She set the tray on a stand beside the bed.

"Janine."

The woman looked at Evelyn. "Yes?"

"Did you know that Anita is in love with your brother?"

Janine lost her smile. "What!"

"She is a good, sweet, intelligent, educated young woman, Janine. Your brother should know how much he is loved."

Janine straightened, a look of incredulity on her face. "John could never love an Indian woman, Evy. It just isn't right."

Evelyn closed her eyes for a moment in exasperation. "If you believe God loves these people, Janine . . . then why would it be wrong for a man of another race to love them? A lot of white men have married Indian women."

"But not . . . not men like John . . . not men of God. Whatever made you say such a thing? I think the fever has affected your mind." The woman put on a smile and poured some tea. "Please don't bring up such foolishness again, Evy."

But I love an Indian man. How could anything ever come of that love? No one understood it, and now she had lost what progress she might have made with Black Hawk. There was only one ray of hope left for her confusion and her aching heart: the vision . . . the dream yet to be realized.

Fourteen

Black Hawk sat quietly on his cot, forcing himself to concentrate on the outside world, the cool creek water and the green grass where he camped; the joy of holding his son in his arms, teaching him to hunt. He wondered if Wakantanka had forgotten him, for in this stinking, small dark hole, with no sunlight and no access to the outside world, how could his God hear his prayers?

For six days now he had sat sweltering in this miserable, dark cubicle of a jail. Being built of brick only turned it into an oven in the hot late-August sun, and there was only one small, barred window high in the back for air. There was nothing inside but a cot with one blanket and a pot in the corner for personal needs.

The heat and smell were so bad that sometimes he felt weak and nauseated. He wondered how much longer he could go on without literally getting physically sick and dying. He understood even better now why so many of his kind had died of disease and broken hearts in the white man's prisons in the place far to the south, where he had heard it was always hot and where the air was also heavy with moisture; where insects ate a man to death.

His misery was made worse by the beating he had taken from Sergeant Desmond and his men, cuts and bruises left untended. A blow to the head from the butt end of a rifle had left him dizzy the first three days he was here. His hatred for soldiers and whites in general had grown deeper. Why had he been put here when he had done nothing wrong? He had to get out, get to Little Fox. He had to see the sun, smell fresh air, bathe himself. No one had told him anything about Evelyn Gibbons—if she had improved, if she had died. Why had he been here so long? Was she unable to tell them the truth? Maybe they had not believed her.

He closed his eyes, wishing he could get the beautiful school-teacher out of his mind . . . and his heart. The things she had told him confused him. Was he meant to love her? He most certainly cared deeply for her, and to know she had had her own vision involving him only verified they were spiritually con-nected—but it was so wrong. He could not allow himself to love a white woman. He was in trouble already just from a mild friendship with her. And she in turn would surely never allow anything deeper than friendship between them. She was white, educated, from a world totally foreign to his own.

He stretched out on the cot, his body bathed in perspiration, the air so stifling he felt like he would gag. He needed to talk to Night Hunter again, tell him of this revelation, these new, forbidden feelings. After what had happened, he was certainly better off never to see the white woman again, but then his vision could not be fulfilled.

He heard someone at the thick, wooden door then, slipping aside the iron bar that kept it bolted shut. He slowly sat up, waiting, hoping that this was the day he would get his freedom. All senses came alert when Sergeant Desmond himself stepped inside. He could not see the man well because of the bright sunlight at his back, but by now he knew the shape of the man, knew his scent. He hated him as he had never hated anyone else in his life. There had been no cause for Desmond to have him beaten the day he was arrested, and the gleam of joy he'd seen in the man's eyes when he was thrown into this sickening hole of a jail would burn in his memory for a long time to come. Why was he here now? To gloat? To tell him he was going to prison in a faraway place, or maybe be hanged? To have him beaten again? He would kill him before he let the man lay a hand on him again, even if it meant his own death.

"Well, Black Hawk, much against my better judgment, you are a free man today. I think Agent McLaughlin and the Army are missing a good chance to be rid of you, but they say you're to be released."

Black Hawk could hardly believe his ears. He slowly stood up, wearing only a loincloth. Because of the miserable heat inside the jail, he had shed the buckskin pants and shirt he had been wearing when he was brought here. He turned to pick them up from the cot, his eyes gradually adjusting to the light that was shed inside when the door was opened. He faced Desmond again, cautiously stepping closer. "The woman lives? She told you the truth?"

Desmond's pale-blue eyes moved over him scathingly. "She claims you saved her life. My question, and everybody else's, is what in hell was she doing alone with you in the first place? I've got a feeling that white bitch has a burning for Indian men. You been humpin' on that woman?"

Black Hawk checked an urge to beat the man within an inch of his life. He could so easily do it. But more than anything he wanted to get out of this place. He didn't dare touch the sergeant, and the man damn well knew it. "You have the mind of a child . . . an *evil* child. Miss Gibbons is a good woman, who was teaching my son to read and write, using her spare time to do it. Do not speak against her and insult her, or one day you might feel an arrow going into *your* back!" he sneered.

Desmond's hands moved into fists. "You threatening me, Black Hawk?"

"I am telling you that you will not spread lies about Miss

Gibbons! If you do, then you had better start always looking behind you!"

"*You're* the liar! You say you don't know who shot Miss Gibbons. I think you *do* know! Why would you cover for them, when they might try to hurt her again?"

"It will not happen again. I will make sure of it."

"And how do you propose to do that?"

"It is not your concern. Give me my horse and my knife and I will leave this place."

"I'm supposed to take you to the lieutenant first. Agent McLaughlin and Reverend Phillips are waiting with him to talk to you before we let you go."

Black Hawk knew what they would say. They would warn him to cause no more trouble, even though he had done nothing wrong in the first place. He would listen to their rhetoric, and then he would leave this place and get Little Fox and never come back! "Then take me to them now," he told Desmond. The longer he looked at the sergeant, the more difficult it was not to kill him. How many times had he been haunted by Wounded Knee? How many times did he wake up in a cold sweat after dreaming about his wife and baby son lying dead, Sergeant Jubal Desmond sitting nearby astride his horse, a bloody sword in his hand? Why was it all right for this man to murder a defenseless woman and a little boy, but it was *not* all right for the husband and father to get his revenge?

"I'll take you to headquarters," Desmond told him. "You'll get your knife back *after* that. You don't really think I'd hand you that big blade while I'm standing here alone with you, do you?"

Black Hawk moved closer, towering over him. "Are you *afraid* of me, sergeant?"

Desmond drew in his breath, raising his chin. "I never said that. I just don't trust any of you savages. You'd just as soon split a man's gut as eat."

Black Hawk leaned closer, his dark eyes boring into the man. "If I could find a way, I would cut out your heart while you were still alive, and I would feed it *and* you to the wolves!"

Desmond's eyes moved into narrow slits. "You're looking to lose your chance of getting out of here, you stinking savage!"

Black Hawk just grinned. "I have not touched you. There will be a better time." He enjoyed the worried look in Desmond's eyes. Let him wonder. Let him lose sleep. "I am ready to go," he announced.

Desmond pulled his army revolver from its holster, cocking it and pressing it against Black Hawk's belly. "One wrong move, you bastard, and it's all I'll need for an excuse to blow your guts out! Don't forget what happened to Crazy Horse and Sitting Bull. Little misunderstandings, a little resistance, and you're dead!"

Black Hawk's lips moved into a sneer. "I am not afraid of a little man like you. Perhaps one day your scalp will decorate my war lance!" He looked down at the gun. "Go ahead and pull the trigger, little man. My people will know that I was unarmed and was murdered. You will start an uprising, and before it is over, every soldier at Standing Rock will be dead, including you. There are six thousand Sioux on this reservation, and only a few hundred soldiers. Remember that."

Desmond's jaw flexed in anger. "And you and the rest of them had better remember what happened at Wounded Knee."

Fire came into Black Hawk's eyes. "I remember it all very well," he answered, his voice a low growl. He enjoyed the fear he saw in Desmond's eyes.

"Get moving," the sergeant ordered.

Black Hawk walked past the man and into the bright sunlight, covering his eyes for a moment until they could adjust. He breathed deeply of the fresh air. He was free again, at least as free as a man could be when he was forced to stay on a certain piece of land and forbidden to go beyond it. He couldn't wait

to see his son again . . . and Otter Woman. She would be very
sorry for what she had done!

"Hello, Evy." Anita Wolf stepped closer to Evelyn, who was
sitting up in bed reading some old newspapers that had been
shipped to Reverend Phillips from Omaha. "It is good to see
you looking so well."

Evelyn laid the papers aside. "I think the infection affected
me much more than the wound itself. Now that that has cleared
up, I'm feeling very good. I intend to get out of this bed tomorrow and be human again, although it will probably be a while
before I can fully use my left arm."

Anita pulled up a chair. "You should not get up too soon.
Give yourself a few more days to heal well. Can you raise your
arm yet?"

Evelyn thought how pretty Anita looked today. She wore a
nicely fitted, green cotton dress, and her dark hair was braided
and twisted neatly on top of her head. Her creamy, dark complexion was flawless, her smile bright. Considering how the reverend had treated her at the dance three weeks ago, she was
surprised the woman was still friendly to her, since John Phillips
had done nothing but lament that Evelyn was not there. "A little," she replied. "I have been exercising it as much as I can.
The only thing I haven't been brave enough to do is look at
myself and see what kind of scar has been left."

Anita's eyes saddened. "You are so beautiful. It is too bad
that there will be any kind of scar, but at least it is in a place
that no one will see."

Evelyn felt embarrassed at realizing just how many people
had seen the scar . . . and more. Probably the reverend, certainly
the Army doctor . . . and Black Hawk. The thought of his hands
on her, his eyes seeing things that were private, brought warm
feelings of passion, feelings that were surely forbidden. "No

one but my husband, if I ever find a man willing to put up with me," she answered with a bashful smile.

Anita blushed, and Evelyn suspected she was thinking about the reverend.

"How are things at the school, Anita?"

"Fine. Janine and I are doing the teaching. My people think you are very brave to have gone out alone to teach Black Hawk and Little Fox. They respect you for it, but they are upset with the soldiers and Agent McLaughlin for having Black Hawk arrested when he did nothing wrong. I thought you should know . . . they have finally freed Black Hawk."

Evelyn closed her eyes for a moment, breathing a silent prayer of thanksgiving. "Oh, I'm so glad. I just worry this has set everything back. I can't go out to him now, and he'll never come here."

"I think in time he *will* come. You have opened his eyes to new things." She studied Evelyn questioningly. "You went to him . . . because of your dreams, didn't you?" she asked cautiously.

Evelyn knew there was no sense hiding anything more from Anita, who was almost as discerning as Black Hawk and old Night Hunter. "Yes." Her eyes suddenly teared. "If you want the truth, Anita . . . I have very deep feelings for Black Hawk, and I don't know what to do about it."

Anita nodded in understanding. "So like my feelings for Reverend Phillips. I fear it is wrong, so I am afraid to tell him."

Evelyn moved to sit up a little straighter. "I know it sounds terribly prejudiced, Anita, but it's almost worse for me. It is not so uncommon for a white man to marry an Indian woman, but for a white woman to love an Indian man . . . it's so unacceptable to society. I just don't know what to do."

Anita smiled softly. "You told me that your mother said to always follow your heart. I think you should do whatever the spirits guide you to do."

"It isn't me that I care about. It's Black Hawk. I don't want to get him into any more trouble." She studied Anita's dark eyes. "You mustn't say anything to anyone else about this."

Anita shook her head. "I will say nothing. I am just sorry and embarrassed that someone from my people did this terrible thing to you. There are rumors that it might have been Otter Woman. Everyone knows she is jealous and possessive. She favors Black Hawk, gives herself to him whenever he has the need."

A burning jealousy surged in Evelyn's soul. She did not like to feel hatred toward anyone, but she could not help feeling it for Otter Woman. She could only pray Black Hawk would not bring harm to the woman. Not that she minded so much for Otter Woman, but she did not want Black Hawk to get into any more trouble. "There is no way to prove who did it," she answered. "I am sure there are any number of your people who would like to see me dead—me and Janine and the reverend . . . the soldiers . . . *all* of us. I don't blame them, and I am not going to let this keep me from going back out there and doing what I must do."

"It is good you do not let them stop you or frighten you away. When they see you have not given up, they will have even more respect for you. I think more will send their children to the school."

Before Anita could go on, Reverend Phillips announced his presence outside the doorway curtain. "Good afternoon, Miss Gibbons. May I come inside?"

Evelyn glanced at Anita. She saw the woman was immediately flustered. "Thank you for understanding about Black Hawk," she told Anita in a near whisper. "I have to be able to tell some-one, and you are the only one who would understand my predicament." She glanced at the doorway. "Come in, Reverend."

The man moved inside, holding a bouquet of wildflowers in his hand. "Well, isn't it amazing what forty-eight hours can do! When I left for the fort, you looked pretty sorry, I must say.

Today you look almost like your old self." He handed out the flowers. "These are for you, along with prayers for a very speedy recovery. And I thought you would like to know that Black Hawk has been set free."

The man hardly seemed to notice Anita was in the room, and Evelyn could see the disappointment in the woman's eyes. She wished he had brought the flowers for Anita, not for her. "Thank you, Reverend. Did you see Black Hawk? Is he all right?"

The man frowned, finally turning to Anita and nodding to her. "You look lovely today, Anita."

"Thank you, Reverend," she answered shyly.

The man turned back to Evelyn. "He was still bruised from the beating the soldiers gave him, but overall he was in fine shape. He was warned by Agent McLaughlin to stay out of trouble and to keep away from you, after which he got on his horse and rode like a demon. I am sure the first thing he will do is go and get his son. I would not be surprised if none of us saw him again between now and next spring. It's too bad. I know you were making progress with him, but perhaps you will understand now that there are some of these people who you just have to stay away from. To try too hard to go after them will only cause trouble, Evelyn. Just do your teaching and let them come to you."

"Excuse me, Reverend," Anita said, rising from her chair. "I must get back to help Janine. I only wanted to see how Evy was doing today." She smiled and patted Evelyn's arm. "The children are anxious for you to come back to school. I told them perhaps in four or five more days."

"It will be sooner than that," Evelyn promised. She waited for Anita to leave, then looked at the reverend, who had sat down in Anita's chair. "You can be a very callous man, Reverend Phillips."

The man lost his smile, his eyes widening in surprise. "What?"

"You talk about the Sioux in front of Anita as though she were not one of them, as though she had no feelings."

The man's face reddened. "Well, I—I . . ."

"I have seen you do it several times, and it hurts her, Reverend. Don't you know by now how she feels about you?"

"About me?" His dark eyes betrayed his surprise and confusion.

"You are a good man, Reverend, dedicated, devoted, intelligent. But when it comes to women, you have a blind spot. Anita Wolf is in love with you. You should be bringing *her* flowers, not me." Why was it suddenly so easy to say it? "She is Sioux, Reverend, but she is a woman first, a very lovely, educated, respectable woman who happens to worship the ground you walk on. *I* think you are a fine man, but I will never look at you the way Anita does. If you are truly wanting to marry and start a family, I am not the woman for that. Talk to Anita. Get to know her, and stop looking at her as someone unworthy just because she has darker skin than we do."

A look of hurt pride came into his eyes, and he rose from the chair. "It is not your place to tell me who I should love, Miss Gibbons."

"I'm sorry, Reverend, but I care very much about Anita, and I can't stand to see you behave almost as though she doesn't exist. I also care about you, and I know you are at a point in your life where you are tired of being alone. You want a wife, a home, children. Anita can give you those things."

As the reverend rose, Evelyn could see he was struggling against his embarrassment. "I am glad you're better," he told her, "and I thought you should know Black Hawk is free again. While we are on the subject of who we should and should not love, I hope you do not have the feelings for Black Hawk that I suspect you have. He would never allow himself to become involved with a white woman, and I hope you realize how it looks for a white woman to be involved with an Indian man. I am not speaking for myself, Miss Gibbons, but for the soldiers and settlers who would look upon such a thing as a gross sin."

Evelyn felt a flush of anger and disappointment warm her face. "And how would *you* look at it, Reverend? You are a man of God, vowed to love all people equally."

"Are you saying you love Black Hawk?"

"I am only saying that when it comes to loving all human beings, we cannot draw a line and say we love them only so far. We either love and accept all people fully, or we don't. I believe that God sees no color, no race, and if you are a true man of God, neither should you."

He grasped the lapels of his suit jacket and straightened it nervously. "You are quite an outspoken woman, Miss Gibbons. I saw that the first day you arrived here. I know you are dedicated and brave, and that you are doing your best; and you already know that I care very much for you, which is why I must warn you to be careful how you talk and whom you go off to see alone. You are risking your job . . . and your reputation."

"You know that I am right, Reverend. I can only pray that I will continue to have the support of you and Janine. I was sent here to teach the Sioux, and I will do whatever I have to do to bring them into our fold and help them learn to live a new way. As far as my personal life, neither Mission Service nor the government has any business telling me how I must behave or whom *I* should love."

Phillips pushed the chair aside, his face flushed. "You are the most frustrating woman—"

"You *do* care deeply about the Sioux, Reverend. I can see it in your eyes, and in the fact that you have spent four years here already."

He met her gaze. "Of course I care."

"Then stop looking at them as though they were some strange race from another world. They are human beings, with feelings and families, a lost people groping to find themselves again.

And Anita is just a woman, as educated and refined as any white woman, certainly more beautiful than most. Open your eyes and see her for who she really is, Reverend, a young woman with so much to offer."

John Phillips just stared at her a moment. "You have overstepped your bounds, Miss Gibbons. I am glad you are recovering, and I appreciate all you are doing here. I hope they find whoever did this terrible thing to you so that we do not have to worry about your being in danger. I know your intentions are good, but I would appreciate it if you would not mention this again, nor attempt to tell me how I should conduct my ministry. You are only a teacher, and I will remind you that you are here at the permission of Mission Services, who encouraged the government to grant the money to support you. You must conduct yourself in a proper manner befitting your post here. I know how much this job means to you, which is the only reason I warn you to be careful how you behave . . . and to whom you show affection. I think you have let your concern for these people carry away your emotions to a place more personal than is proper. Do not lose your perspective, Miss Gibbons."

Evelyn knew she had offended him deeply, so deeply that she wondered if she could ever again enjoy the close friendship they had known until now. "I mean harm nor hurt to anyone, Reverend. I do what I do out of love, just like you do."

He nodded. "We just have two different ways of looking at things, I suppose." He sighed. "I can see you are right about one thing. I admit I have been infatuated by your beauty and your dedication, but I see now that we could never get along. You are too independent for the average man, perhaps for any man." He shook his head. "What a waste."

As he turned and left, a heavy feeling pressed on Evelyn's heart. Maybe he was right. She would never find a man to put up with her, and she and Black Hawk were certainly too different to think there could ever be anything between them. At the moment she didn't care about her dreams or his vision. She could not imagine how any of it could ever come to be. Black Hawk would flee to his camp and seldom return—and certainly not to her. She had left poor Steven back in Wisconsin. He was probably already engaged to someone else. Now she had lost one of her best friends, would probably lose Janine once the reverend told her what she had said; and eventually she would probably lose Anita's friendship, for she had surely spoiled any chance Anita had of winning the reverend's heart. Her big mouth and her good intentions only kept getting her in trouble.

A deep loneliness engulfed her, and she found herself wishing she could curl up into Black Hawk's arms. When she curled into her pillow instead, the flowers Reverend Phillips had brought her fell to the floor.

Otter Woman awoke to a pounding at her cabin door. She quickly rose, wearing a thin, sleeveless flannel gown.

"What is it, child?" her grandmother asked, sitting up on a pile of robes in one corner of the room, where she preferred to sleep instead of in a bed.

When someone pounded again, Otter Woman's chest tightened with fear. She already knew that Black Hawk had been released from jail. "Stay there, Grandmother," she said quietly, then turned up an oil lamp and went to the door. "Who is it?"

"You know who it is," came Black Hawk's deep voice. "Let me in, or I will break down this door!"

"I did what I thought was best for you, Black Hawk," Otter Woman said firmly. "If they had kept you in jail any longer, or if the white bitch had died, I would have come forward. I would not have let you suffer."

"But you did not mind if *she* suffered!"

The door suddenly burst open, and Otter Woman screamed as Black Hawk lunged for her. She ran to a corner, but there was no getting away from him. He grabbed her arms and slammed her against the wall.

"Do not kill me! Do not kill me!" Otter Woman wailed.

"You stay away from my granddaughter!" the old woman screeched. She rose from her bed and began clawing at Black Hawk, but he seemed to notice her flailing at him no more than if she were a mosquito. He yanked Otter Woman away from the wall, and, still grasping her wrists, he flung her across the room against yet another wall. He forced her left hand over to her right so that he could hold both her wrists in one powerful hand. He turned to the wizened old lady.

"You stay away, ancient one!" he ordered. "You know that your granddaughter did a bad thing! She interfered with a vision that must be fulfilled!"

Otter Woman's grandmother stepped back, putting a hand to her chest. "What is this you have done, Otter Woman?"

Black Hawk turned his fiery gaze back to Otter Woman, who stood panting, her hair hanging partially over her face. "You said nothing to me of a vision."

"I *did* tell you! You did not want to hear it! The white woman is a part of it, and to interfere or try to harm her will bring you great shame! *I* will decide who I will and will not see, not you! You could have *killed* her! You *tried* to kill her, because of your jealousy! I tell you now, Otter Woman, that you will never again be welcome in my camp or in my bed!"

Otter Woman grimaced at his painful hold on her wrists. "I am sorry, Black Hawk. I would not have let you stay in that jail one day longer; and I am sorry that I have somehow interfered with a holy vision."

"Sorry? You should be grateful that I did not tell the authorities who tried to kill the white woman!"

"I am! I *am* grateful, Black Hawk! Please do not hurt me!"

He shoved her against the wall again. "I will not hurt you . . . *this* time! But if you ever again bring harm to the white woman, or even go near her, you will suffer for it! She could also have told the agency who tried to kill her, but she did *not*. She *protected* you! Remember that, the next time you think about harming her!"

"I will, Black Hawk. I will remember! Please don't turn me away." Otter Woman began to cry. "Please let me come to you."

He looked her over scathingly. "You will find many other men to satisfy your needs!" With his right hand he reached out and grabbed hold of her hair. He let go of her wrists then, and Otter Woman screamed when he used both hands to bunch up her hair and jerk her forward, pushing her to the floor, facedown. She wriggled and screeched and cursed, trying to reach backward to claw at him, but all to no avail. She begged him not to do what she knew he meant to do. Others in the village could hear the commotion, but they did not interfere. They understood that it was necessary. This was a battle between a man and a woman, enough reason to stay out of it; but since the man was Black Hawk, who had been sorely wronged by Otter Woman, there was even more reason to let the man do what he must do. Otter Woman was a loose woman, a troublemaker. She must be punished.

Amid screams and struggling, Black Hawk kept hold of Otter Woman's hair in his left hand, and with his right hand he yanked his knife from its sheath. With one quick whack he lopped off her hair close to the head so that all that was left were short, scraggly stubs.

"No! No! No!" the woman screamed, putting her hands to her head and fingering what was left of her once-beautiful dark mane.

Black Hawk threw down the handful of hair and shoved his knife back in place. "Be glad it was not your throat that I cut!" he growled. He stormed out, and Otter Woman drew up her legs, shivering in wrenching sobs.

"I warned you," her grandmother told her, tears coming to her own eyes. "I told you to stay away from that white woman."

Otter Woman curled into a ball of shame and horror and felt her hair again. "I wish the arrow had found her *heart!*" she sobbed.

Fifteen

Evelyn sat beside Anita inside the circus tent, enjoying the looks on the faces of the Sioux as elephants and camels were paraded before them. The spectacle was amazing enough for the surrounding settlers and traders who had come to watch, but the Indians were awestruck, some even fearful. Many stayed away altogether, sure evil spirits lived in the strange animals.

On the way inside they had passed cages containing monkeys and tigers. Most of the Indians shied away from the monkeys, afraid of them because they so resembled humans in their faces and hands. Their reaction brought Black Hawk to mind. Evelyn had hoped perhaps he would bring Little Fox to the circus, but Anita told her he had not been heard from since he had been freed . . . except for one stop.

"My brother says Black Hawk went to see Otter Woman," Anita had told her. "He was very angry with her, and he cut off all her hair." Word traveled fast among the Sioux, and Evelyn knew that by now probably every tribe on the reservation knew it was Otter Woman who had hurt her, but no one would admit it to the soldiers, and no arrests had been made. Lieutenant Teller had visited her and offered to post a guard for her, but she had insisted she was not afraid and wanted no special favors.

Still, she could not help a secret worry that Otter Woman would try to hurt her again. She was determined not to let the woman keep her out of the villages and make her afraid to visit Sioux families. In fact, now that she was better, she had decided she would return to Black Hawk's camp, no matter what anyone thought of it, and in spite of the danger. So much had been left unfinished between them. She was not even sure she could find his camp, but if she talked to Night Hunter, she was sure the old man could get the message to Black Hawk to look for her at a specified time and day. She could take Anita with her as far as one of the villages, so the reverend would not suspect what she was really doing.

Reverend Phillips had remained rather cool to her, but Janine and Anita were as friendly as ever. Apparently, the reverend had said nothing to either of them about his conversation with her or the fact that he was upset with her. Anita probably did not know she had mentioned to the man that Anita loved him; and Janine had apparently dismissed the idea as impossible. If the woman had been treating Anita differently, Anita had said nothing about it. She hoped she had planted a seed of love for Anita in Reverend Phillips's mind and heart, and that he would seriously consider the things she had told him.

She tried to concentrate on the wonderful show about to take place before her, glad she was well enough to come. She had been up and around for eleven days now, had even taught school the past few days. She used a sling for her left arm because it was still too sore to move too much, but she could use it when necessary and was forcing herself to do exercises to gain back her strength.

It felt good to be almost back to normal, and she would not have missed the circus for the world. The circus tent had been set up on an incline so that the one and only ring where acts would take place was at the lowest level, and the audience could sit at a gradual rise up a hill and see everything that was going on. So many curious Sioux wanted to see the show that they had to be divided into groups. Three shows a day would take place today and tomorrow, since only about four hundred people at a time could get inside the viewing area. Outside the tent were the caged animals, as well as clowns and many brightly painted wagons.

The circus announcer stepped up onto a platform, holding a megaphone to announce the first act. From where she sat, Evelyn thought the man looked quite handsome. He wore a red jacket and knee-high black leather boots; and his dark hair was neatly slicked back. "Ladies and Gentlemen!" he announced. "I am Herbert True, manager of the spectacular O'Banyon's Circus Extravaganza! Today several acts of bravery and astounding skill will take place before your very eyes, right here in our circus ring! First, a most daring event!"

Five huge boxes had been pulled by horses into the arena, then the horses unhitched so that the boxes could be shoved against openings in a cage set up in the arena. Men jumped up on the tops of the boxes, then slid open doorways to let five huge tigers into the cage. As they growled and paced nervously inside, people gasped and stared at the beautiful but ferocious-looking animals.

"Now you know why there is a cage in our arena!" Herbert True shouted through the megaphone. "These exotic animals are called tigers, and they are from India, a land far, far away and across the Pacific Ocean. You will see that even the wildest beasts can be tamed, if a man is brave enough to do it! We have that man! Ladies and gentlemen, meet Adolph Dierdorf, the bravest man who ever walked this land!"

The announcer put out his arm, and a man came running through the tent to the arena wearing revealing tights and an open shirt. Evelyn smiled at what an odd lot these circus people were. She realized most of the Sioux understood little of what the announcer had said, but they didn't need to. It was obvious what was happening, and when Adolph Dierdorf entered the ring with the tigers, they watched wide-eyed in near silence as the man put the tigers through their act. Evelyn was herself distracted when she looked down to her left to see Seth Bridges and his two adopted daughters. She was glad Bridges had thought to bring the girls to the circus, but she couldn't help wondering if he was only putting on a show for others, pretending to be a good father. She felt mixed emotions for not having had the time to try to visit the girls and talk to their father again; even though she did not know just what she could do about the situation. She had caused enough trouble lately and was not sure she should take the chance of stirring up more.

The tiger show was followed by a variety of other acts, all appropriately accompanied by a circus band: jugglers, a balancing act, a trapeze act that brought gasps and wondrous "ooohh's" from the crowd, and the Pretzel Woman, a female contortionist, whose body movements were both astonishing and embarrassing. The few white women present covered their eyes, but Evelyn hardly noticed. Her entertainment was in watching the faces of the audience, especially those of the little Indian children.

O'Banyon's Circus Extravaganza finally ended, and Herbert True announced that the next show would start in two hours. An excited Anita left Evelyn to go and find the tiger cages outside, and Evelyn decided to try to talk to Lucille and Katy Bridges. She noticed that Sergeant Desmond had appeared from somewhere and was talking to Seth Bridges as the crowd dispersed. Lucille and Katy had run ahead to look again at some of the wagons and animals outside the tent. Evelyn hurried after them, catching up with them at a cage of monkeys.

"Monkeys are quite fascinating, aren't they?" she spoke up.

Both girls turned to look at her. Katy smiled, but Lucille seemed instantly alarmed. Her gaze moved past Evelyn, as though to check and see if anybody might be watching them before she finally greeted her. "Hello, Miss Gibbons."

"If the two of you could attend school, we could study other countries and the unusual animals that live there," Evelyn told them, not sure how else to start the conversation. "Has your father said anything about allowing you to come to school?"

"He won't let us," Katy said with a scowl. "Seth isn't really our father. We don't call him that. He just wants us to do his work, and he—"

Lucille grabbed her sister's arm. "Be quiet, Katy. Seth is coming."

Evelyn saw fear come into both the girls' eyes. It irritated her that they should have to live in such terror. Her hunch was right. There was something terribly wrong at the Bridges household, and somehow she had to get to the bottom of it without getting the girls into trouble with Seth. Before Seth reached them, she spoke quickly to Lucille.

"If you girls need help, please come to me. I have been wanting to talk to you. If Seth Bridges is hurting you or threatening you somehow, or making you work too hard, I can try to do something about it."

"You stay away from us and from our house," Lucille told her. She quickly grabbed Katy and pushed her away, walking over to greet Seth and the sergeant, who was still with the man. She longed to tell Miss Gibbons the truth, realized she had just missed her chance, but she knew how cruel Seth could be . . . how cruel Sergeant Desmond could be. She could not risk something bad happening to poor Miss Gibbons, who she'd heard had already nearly lost her life for coming here and trying to teach the Indians. Besides, to tell the woman the truth would mean having to tell her all the ugliness of what Seth had been doing with her, and what he now allowed the sergeant to do. She was ashamed, mortified. How could she tell a pretty, proper lady like Evelyn Gibbons something like that? The woman would think she was bad, that she liked men. She probably wouldn't want to help her if she knew the truth.

Evelyn in turn was already putting that truth together. She watched the sergeant put a hand on Lucille's waist, noticed how he looked at her hungrily. The four of them approached her, Seth glaring with a look that made her feel sick inside.

"Well, Miss Gibbons!" the sergeant said with a sneering smile. "I see you're up and about. You're the talk at the fort, you know. There aren't many soldiers who have suffered an arrow wound, then you come along, an innocent, pretty little school-teacher, and in a matter of weeks you come close to starting another Indian war! I thought us soldiers were the ones the Indians hated." He laughed. "So, who do you think put that arrow in you?"

Evelyn rubbed at her arm, wincing slightly from lingering pain in the muscles at the left side of her chest and back. "I have no idea, Sergeant. A lot of the Sioux resent my being here. It could have been any number of men."

The man shrugged. "Or a woman. Everybody knows that slut, Otter Woman, was Black Hawk's favorite under the blankets. She's a vicious, jealous woman, Miss Gibbons, and you going out to see Black Hawk alone . . ." His eyes moved over her as though she were a saloon girl. "Well, she might have thought maybe you were taking her man away from her. I hear tell Black Hawk cut off all her hair. Why do you think he did that?"

Evelyn struggled to keep her composure. The man was delib-erately baiting her, insulting her. Seth Bridges stood there with a smirk on his face, enjoying the suggestive remarks. "I am sure I don't know," she answered. "I only saw Black Hawk twice, Sergeant, to teach him and his little boy. He never talked about Otter Woman, and to this day I have never even met the woman. Perhaps Black Hawk was angry with her for some other reason. I don't know anything about his personal affairs, but one thing you now know for certain is that Black Hawk is not the one who hurt me. You had no reason and no right to attack him the way you did."

"He resisted arrest."

"With his hands tied behind his back?" Desmond reddened and Evelyn glared into his narrow eyes. "It takes a brave man to beat an unarmed man who is also tied, Sergeant, especially when you're backed by several other men. I am impressed by your bravery."

Desmond smiled, but a hateful glint sparkled in his eyes. "Well, I'm glad to see you're all better and back to your old cocky self, Miss Gibbons." He leaned closer. "You watch yourself, lady. You need us on your side. Some day you might holler for help, and nobody will come running." He straightened, putting an arm around Lucille, who hung her head. "Me, I prefer white girls. My own kind." He chuckled again. "Oh, by the way," he added, before Evelyn could reply, "if you're so hell-bent on getting Black Hawk and his kid to school, why don't you try doing it through his sister? You get on Many Birds's good side, and Black Hawk will think highly of it. It's better than putting yourself in danger by going out to meet the man alone. Use your good sense, woman." He tipped his hat. "Goodday to you, ma'am."

The man walked off with Lucille, and Seth glowered at Evelyn. "I warned you once, lady, to stay away from my girls, or I'll see you get kicked off this reservation altogether! With what I hear has been goin' on, I expect that wouldn't be too hard to do." He grabbed Katy's hand. "Let's go!" he said angrily. "And don't let me catch you talkin' to this woman again!"

The man left, tugging Katy along. The girl glanced back at Evelyn, tears in her eyes, and Evelyn wanted to run and grab her away from the man. What was going on at the Bridges household? She did not need to guess what was going on between the sergeant and Lucille, nor did she need anyone to tell her that it was not a willing act on Lucille's part. She hated this helpless feeling, and she decided she must try talking to Reverend Phillips about it, and perhaps to Agent McLaughlin. Something had to be done.

She turned away, surprised the sergeant had suggested she try to get Black Hawk's sister to school. She had already thought of that but hadn't the time to meet the girl yet. Desmond was right in one respect. If Many Birds came to school, perhaps Black Hawk would at least send Little Fox, knowing the boy's aunt would be there to watch him. If the man was afraid to send Little Fox now because of a new distrust of the soldiers and the agency, Many Birds might be the to link to winning back his confidence. What confused her was the fact that it was Sergeant Desmond who had suggested it. Why on earth would he care?

Her thoughts were interrupted when someone called her name. She turned to see Beverly Evans standing at the corner of a colorful wagon where taffy candy was being given away in small, wrapped pieces free to the Indians. "Beverly! How nice to see you."

She walked to where the woman stood, surprised to see that Beverly's hair was worn hanging long and clipped at the back of her neck with a fancy barrette. She had not even seen the woman since leaving her and her husband at the Oahe Mission when first arriving at Standing Rock, but she remembered how prim and proper the Reverend Greggory Evans's wife was, how stern and demanding Evans himself was. She was surprised the man would even come to a circus, much less allow his wife to have her hair hang loose, and to wear a lovely yellow, short-sleeved dress that was cut low at the bodice. Far from the quiet, reserved, and unsmiling Beverly Evans with whom she had traveled here by train, this woman was glowing.

"Evelyn!" she greeted, grasping her hands. "How good to see you!"

To Evelyn's surprise the woman embraced her.

"You're as beautiful as ever. I'm so glad you're up and around. I heard what happened, but I was having some problems of my own at the time, and I couldn't get away to see you."

"Problems?" Evelyn pulled away. "What is wrong, Beverly? You look very happy, and so beautiful! What a lovely dress, and you look so different with your hair down."

"Herbert thinks so, too. Oh, Evelyn, I feel like a new woman since I've met Herbert."

Evelyn frowned in surprise. "Herbert?"

"Did you see the circus announcer, the handsome man in those wonderful high boots and that dashing red coat? That's Herbert True. He manages the circus. When they leave Standing Rock, I am going with him, Evelyn." Her eyes suddenly teared. "Please be happy for me. I've been so unhappy all my life, until now."

Evelyn struggled to keep her composure. A little over two months ago this woman had been as submissive and proper as any minister's wife could be. Now she was leaving her husband, to run off with the circus? "Beverly! Have you given serious thought to what you are doing? What does your husband have to say about it? Are you *divorcing* him?"

Beverly pulled her aside. "I've given Greggory a letter telling him I have never loved him and have never been happy and that I want a divorce. I don't even care if he claims adultery on my part. I'm so happy with Herbert, Evelyn. All my life it was either my parents or my husband telling me how I must behave, whether I was allowed to laugh, telling me I couldn't sing or dance. Greggory has treated me like just a piece of dust under his thumb—even worse, since it turned out I would never be able to give him children. Herbert doesn't care about those things. He makes me laugh, and we dance together. His life is so exciting, traveling all over the country with unusual people and exotic animals. I don't care what anyone thinks, Evelyn. I am going away with Herbert. I just wish . . ." She wiped at a tear that slipped out of her eye. "I wish just one person would be happy *for* me. I hoped it would be you. I could tell when we talked on that train trip out here that you were different from other women, more accepting, understanding of a woman's need to be independent and joyous. Oh, Evelyn, is it true you went out alone to visit that wild renegade, Black Hawk? I smiled when

I heard that. It didn't surprise me one bit, but I was so worried when I heard someone tried to kill you. Still, you're single and independent and you're doing something daring and different. I think you're wonderful, and it's so important to me that you be happy for me."

For a moment, Evelyn was at a loss for words. She led Beverly to a bench the circus had set out, and both women sat down. Evelyn thought for a moment how her own mother had gone through a similar experience—forced to live a certain way, told how to behave. Wild Horse had awakened new passions and a yearning for freedom that had come close to destroying her own parents' marriage, but they had worked it out. After Wild Horse's death, her mother had managed to talk things out with her father.

"Beverly, maybe you should try to talk to your husband, tell him your feelings, your needs."

"It would do no good. I know him too well, and since meeting Herbert, I have no desire to keep my marriage going."

Evelyn sighed, in shock at what she was seeing and hearing. "If this makes you so utterly happy, then I am happy for you. But . . . Beverly, I left a fiancé, not a husband. And what do you know about this Herbert True?"

The woman's blue eyes sparkled. "I know that he is single, and he has a zest for life; that he is the most handsome man I have ever met, and that he makes me happy. That is all I need to know . . . except that I also know that he loves me."

Evelyn hated to spoil the woman's joy, but she felt only alarm. She took hold of her hands. "Beverly, the man is a showman, an *actor*. He is a man of the world. How do you know he doesn't toy with innocent women everyplace he goes?"

Beverly's smile faded. "He wouldn't. I can tell. Please, Evelyn. I need a friend, one person who understands how I feel. If Greggory had come after me, tried to stop me, I might have considered changing my mind. But he never came, Evelyn, never said one word. To him I was just a display to others that he was a family man. He married me to show others the proper way to go in life. A man must marry and have a family. A woman must bear children and be submissive to her husband. I meant nothing more to him than that, and once it was discovered I wouldn't be able to give him children, he turned even less passionate and attentive, more critical of every move I made, everything I wore." Her eyes misted again. "He doesn't love me, Evelyn, and now that he considers that I have transgressed and have been an un- faithful wife, he would never take me back; but I don't care. I have Herbert, and once I am divorced from Greggory, Herbert and I will be married, and if Greggory never forgives me, I know that God will, for I believe God never meant for me to be with Greggory. He meant for me to be with Herbert True."

Evelyn wondered if that was an idea Mr. True had planted in the woman's head. A man like that was surely a smooth talker. She couldn't believe such a worldly soul would suddenly want to marry and settle with a plain and inexperienced woman like Beverly Evans, but it was obvious Beverly was not going to be convinced the man was anything but a saint. Who was she to spoil what little happiness this woman had ever known? "I will pray for you, Beverly, that all will go smoothly and that God will bless this new love you have found. I am just so surprised, I am rather at a loss for words. Of course I am happy for you. However this all turns out, I would never condemn you for what you have done. My mother always told me to follow my heart, but sometimes the heart can lead us to dangerous places, so I must also always be careful. That is what I am telling you now. Be careful, Beverly, but be happy."

The woman sniffed and suddenly hugged her. "You're younger than I, and have never even been married, yet I knew I could talk to you about this. I have wanted to visit with you since arriving at Oahe, but Greggory wouldn't let me. He thinks you are much too modern in your thinking, too bold in the way you dress and in your ideas; but all the time I have admired you."

Evelyn pulled away. "Beverly, most of the time I feel like I am stumbling in the dark. I am having my own problems with the heart, and sometimes I just want to run back home and marry Steven."

Beverly watched her sympathetically, quickly dabbing at her eyes with a handkerchief she retrieved from where it was tucked into the sash of her dress. "It's Black Hawk, isn't it? You have special feelings for him."

Evelyn looked away. "He's a Sioux Indian, Beverly."

"He's just a man."

"Not in the eyes of most of our own kind. They see him as Sioux first, and you know what people think of a white woman who would dare to have feelings for an Indian."

Beverly sighed deeply. "I will be the first to admit that it's a rather startling and difficult thing for me to imagine; and yet now that I have met Herbert, I understand that love can transcend all things, all difficulties and obstacles; and I understand that a woman should be free to love whoever awakens her passion and fulfills her needs. I would no more tell you it's wrong to care about Black Hawk than I would want you to tell me it's wrong to love Herbert True."

But Herbert True is using you, Beverly. When he is through with you he will throw you away like yesterday's trash. Evelyn could not bring herself to say the words out loud, and she prayed with all her heart that she was wrong. After all, she had never met Herbert True. She had only watched the man put on his act for an audience. "Thank you for understanding," she told Beverly. "You must write me and tell me where you have gone, how things worked out. And let me know where I in turn can write to you."

"I will. And just as you will be praying for me, I will pray for you. I—" The woman's eyes brightened. "Herbert!"

"Well, dear, *here* you are. I wondered where you have been."

Beverly rose, her cheeks reddening with pleasure. "Herbert, this is a dear friend, Miss Evelyn Gibbons. She is a schoolteacher here on the reservation. We traveled here together."

Evelyn rose to greet the handsome Mr. True. She did not miss the meaning in his eyes when they moved over her appreciatively. He grasped her hand and bent down to kiss the back of it. "How do you do, Miss Gibbons. I am pleased to make your acquaintance."

Beverly moved beside him and put an arm through his. "I have told Evelyn our plans. She's happy for us."

The man smiled, patting Beverly's hand. "How kind of you, Miss Gibbons," he told Evelyn, his eyes roving her body again.

Evelyn sensed he was wishing he had met her before meeting Beverly, and in spite of his handsome exterior, she sensed the cool, calculating man who dwelled within. She hoped her suspicions were unwarranted, that she was being too critical of a traveling showman. She felt a distinct urge to grab Beverly and beg her not to run off with this man, that he would break her heart, but the look on Beverly's face told her that the woman would never listen to one word of it, and it would break her heart just as much to feel she had lost another friend.

"I have to go and find Anita," she said aloud. She touched Beverly's arm. "Please remember that I am here, Beverly. If you ever need me, or just need a friend, I will always be that for you."

Beverly reached out with one arm and hugged her once more. "Thank you, but I have Herbert. I will probably never see this place again once we leave." She let go but kept her arm wrapped around Herbert's. "Unlike you, I never wanted to come here, Evelyn. I have hated every minute of it."

Evelyn glanced up at Herbert, saw the glint of victory in his dark eyes. "Be good to her, Mr. True. She is a sweet, good-hearted woman, and she has done a very difficult thing, leaving her husband for another man. She will need your love and your strength."

He nodded. "And she will get both." He tipped his top hat. "Come and visit our trailer any time you wish, Miss Gibbons. It's the blue one down the row there, with the yellow trim. We can give you a taste of circus life."

"I believe I have seen all I need to see," she answered, holding his gaze challengingly. She moved her gaze to Beverly. "God be with you, Beverly. Write me."

"I promised I would. We're going up to Fort Yates day after tomorrow, then one more show at the northern edge of the agency. From there we go to Cheyenne. It's so exciting!"

Evelyn glanced at Herbert True. "I am sure it is."

"Well, shall we be off, darling? I have many things to tend to."

Evelyn knew the man was only anxious to get away from her discerning eyes.

"Yes, my darling," Beverly squeezed Evelyn's hand once more and left with her new love, and Evelyn felt sick at the sight. Herbert True had totally hypnotized poor Beverly, taking her on a flight of fancy, filling her with wonderful dreams.

"God help you, Beverly," she murmured. She headed toward the tiger cages to find Anita, but just as she rounded one of the wagons, a woman stepped into her pathway, an Indian woman with dark eyes that were filled with hate. She wore a red bandana around her short, cropped hair. Evelyn drew in her breath, backing away slightly. No Indian woman wore her hair like that, and since she knew Black Hawk had cut off Otter Woman's hair, she realized this had to be her . . . the woman who had tried to kill her!

"Otter Woman," she said, wondering how she had managed to find her voice.

"So, finally we meet," Otter Woman sneered.

Sixteen

Evelyn felt light-headed at the sight of the dark, menacing-looking woman standing before her. Here was the woman responsible for all her pain and suffering, the woman who would have killed her if the good Lord had not diverted the pathway of the arrow. She took a deep breath, unwilling to cower before her, as she was sure Otter Woman wanted her to do.

"Yes, at last we meet," she answered. "I am glad to finally see you face-to-face. Now you can see that I am not some horrible monster to be feared, Otter Woman. I am just a schoolteacher who wants to help your people learn how to survive this new way of life."

Otter Woman's eyebrows knitted in a frown. Evelyn could tell she was surprised at the reply. This woman had probably expected some kind of tirade out of her, perhaps even scratching and screaming and accusations.

"You lie," Otter Woman accused, speaking in English. "You only *pretend* to help us,"

Evelyn could see how beautiful the woman had once been. She still had a subtle beauty, but there was nothing delicate or gentle about her. It was a rugged, wild, earthy beauty, and it was obvious, even under her loose-fitting tunic, that her voluptuous body was well curved in all the right places. Evelyn could not help another surge of unwanted jealousy. Otter Woman was a little heavy, but the weight lay more in muscle than fat. She was not a woman Evelyn cared to contend with physically. The only area in which she might be able to beat this woman was in mental cunning.

"You're wrong, Otter Woman. And if I was trying to trick Black Hawk and others in some way, don't you think I would have told the soldiers who tried to kill me? I could have had you out of my way, but I said nothing."

Otter Woman folded her arms, studying this white woman with whom so many of her people were impressed. There was genuine concern in the woman's eyes. She did not want to like her. She was too beautiful, standing there with her golden hair tied at one shoulder with a pretty pink ribbon that matched her pink dress. This white woman wanted to steal Black Hawk's heart, maybe his soul. "Why did you not tell them?" she asked, a hint of guilt in her eyes.

"Because I did not want to make trouble for you. I don't want to make trouble for *any* of your people . . . and because I understand why you did what you did. I am not your enemy, Otter Woman. I would much prefer to be your friend."

The woman sniffed. "Because of you, Black Hawk no longer speaks to me or asks me to come to him."

"No, Otter Woman. It is because of *you* and what you did that Black Hawk has cast you out. Though you brought this upon yourself, I am still truly sorry for what Black Hawk did to you. If I had known, I would have begged him to bring you no harm, because hurting you would only make you hate me more, and I don't want that."

"Is there a problem here?"

Evelyn looked past Otter Woman to see Lieutenant Teller approaching with Janine on his arm. She knew that the entire army and the agency personnel probably suspected it was Otter Woman who had tried to kill her, and she had done everything in her power to keep them from arresting her. She glanced at Otter Woman, saw fear and defense come into her eyes at the approach of a "bluecoat." She put on a smile for Teller. "None at all, Lieutenant. I was just getting acquainted with Otter Woman."

Janine's eyes widened as she and the lieutenant came closer. "Evy, you shouldn't—"

"We're having a very nice conversation," Evelyn interrupted, trying to warn the woman with her eyes not to say anything more. "Otter Woman was just telling me she would like me to come and visit her grandmother." She turned her gaze to Otter Woman. "Weren't you, Otter Woman?"

Otter Woman refused to even look at the lieutenant. "Yes," she said meekly, aware that Evelyn Gibbons was trying to protect her. Was she truly sincere in her concern, or was she trying to trick her? Why did this woman continue to protect her?

Teller scrutinized the situation with discerning blue eyes, stroking his mustache thoughtfully. "You sure everything is all right here?" he repeated.

Evelyn nodded. "I'm sure. How did you and Janine like the circus?"

Janine stood gawking at Otter Woman. The lieutenant answered for them. "It was wonderful," he said, his eyes still showing concern. He put an arm around Janine. "And by the way, Janine and I are going to be married in October. I've had to send for the rings—they're hard to come by out here. But the engagement is still official."

Evelyn smiled, reaching out with her right arm to embrace Janine, finally drawing her attention away from Otter Woman. "Janine, I'm so happy for you!"

Janine finally smiled and turned her attention to Evelyn. "Yes. We were coming to tell you when we saw you talking with Otter Woman." She glanced again at Otter Woman, who had moved farther away from them. "Evy, you—"

"Everything is fine," Evelyn assured her. "And I'm so happy for you!"

"We still have to tell John. Don't say anything if you see him.

Jacob is being transferred to Fort Leonard in November, so I will have to give up the missionary service then. I just feel bad for John. We have always worked together. He'll be so alone." She kept hold of Evelyn's hand. "I wish he, too, could find a companion. He's a lonely man, Evy."

Evelyn caught the meaning of the words. The woman wanted to see her brother with her, not with Anita Wolf; but this was not the time or place to argue about it. She had many things to discuss with the reverend, and number one on the list was Anita, no matter how angry it made him whenever she brought up the issue. "He will find someone, Janine. In the meantime, he is a grown man and doesn't need you to keep mothering him. You are going to be the wife of Lieutenant Jacob Teller. John will be happy for you."

Janine smiled, looking up at the lieutenant and thinking herself the luckiest woman who ever walked. She had always considered herself too plain to be attractive to any man. She knew Teller was not the most handsome man who ever walked, but in her eyes he was a knight in shining armor. It would be difficult to leave John and the reservation, but her place would be to follow her husband wherever he was sent. "We're going to the church now to talk to John," she told Evelyn. "I wish he would have come to the circus, but he is studying for his sermon on Sunday."

"Your brother works much too hard. I will have a talk with him myself about that," Evelyn answered her. "You really should see if you can't talk him into coming to the next show."

The lieutenant and Janine both stood there hesitantly. "You sure it's all right to leave you here alone with . . ." Teller cleared his throat. "Miss Gibbons, we have strong suspicions—"

Otter Woman stepped even farther away from them.

"You're wrong, Lieutenant, I assure you. I am having quite a pleasant conversation with Otter Woman. You two go ahead and ride to the church. It will take you at least a half hour." Evelyn decided to say nothing about what she had learned from Beverly Evans. She did not want to spoil the moment for Janine. She would talk to John Phillips about it tomorrow.

Teller frowned, but nodded in resignation. "You be careful, Miss Gibbons. Don't forget that *someone*— " He glanced over at Otter Woman, then back to Evelyn. "Tried to kill you," he finished. "It could happen again."

"I don't think that it will," Evelyn answered. "They can see that it didn't work the first time. Since it could have brought considerable trouble to the Sioux, I think whoever tried to hurt me has probably already been properly chastised by his own people."

Teller nodded. "I hope you're right." He left with Janine, and Evelyn turned to Otter Woman, who stood several feet away now, watching her sullenly.

"You are not a very wise woman," Otter Woman told her.

Evelyn stepped closer. "Perhaps not. But I think *you* are wise, Otter Woman, wise enough to understand you must never again try to hurt me. Not only would it be trouble for you, but for all your people. You should know as well as anyone that when one Sioux commits a crime, often all of them suffer for it. Besides, you could have gotten Black Hawk killed. The soldiers beat him badly when they found me with him. It would not have taken much to give them cause to shoot him, the mood they were in that day. If he had brought me back dead, they just might *have* shot him."

Otter Woman turned away. "I thought I was protecting him . . . from you."

"You only made more trouble for him." Evelyn studied the woman's cropped hair. In spite of what Otter Woman had done to her, she was sorry for the way Black Hawk had spoiled what beauty she had left, and for the shame it must bring her. She knew she should take pleasure in the sight, but she could not. "Otter Woman, you have no reason to hate me. Black Hawk did not attack you in defense of me. He did it because of a vision that is very important to him. You almost destroyed the chance for him to discover what the spirits mean for him to do. You know how important visions are to your people, especially to a warrior like Black Hawk. It isn't me he cares about; it's the fact that he thinks I have something to do with his future. And if you want to know the truth, I have had dreams of my own. That is what brought me here, that and a love and concern for the Sioux. I grew up among Indians. My mother and father taught at a reservation in Indian Territory for years. I am not your enemy. Please understand that."

The woman met her gaze, and Evelyn was sure she saw tears in her eyes. She studied her intently for a moment before speaking again. "What is this vision? Do you belong to Black Hawk?"

Evelyn shook her head. "No one can belong to another human being, Otter Woman. As far as Black Hawk's vision, I can't tell you what it is or what it means. That is only for Black Hawk to do, if he chooses. Nor do I understand my own dreams, but those dreams are the reason I went to see Night Hunter. That should tell you how much I trust and respect your own people. How many whites would go to Night Hunter and ask for his advice, believe in his wisdom?"

Otter Woman sniffed, holding her chin proudly. "I do not understand you. You are not like the other white women who have come before you who behaved as though just to touch us is a terrible thing. Great fear always showed in their eyes. Even the men, the preachers like John Phillips, look down on us. They do not even *try* to understand our ways. Their minds are set that we are bad, that nothing we believe is right. They think they must change every part of us—our spirits, our hearts, our clothes, our hair, our way of life. They do not want us to be Indian in any way."

"I understand that, and I believe it is wrong. I have already been in some trouble for the way I think and the way I believe the Sioux should be taught. Do you think either Black Hawk or Night Hunter would listen to one thing I had to say if they did not believe I was sincere? If they did not see into my soul and know that I am not like all the others?"

Otter Woman's lips moved into a pout, and her dark eyes moved over her, as though to sum up her strength and her worth. "Perhaps not. But then perhaps you are just more clever than the others."

"That is for you to decide. I can only tell you the truth and hope that you believe me. In fact, to prove to the soldiers and others that you were not the one who tried to kill me, why don't you come to my cabin tomorrow morning, and we will ride out together. I want to talk to Black Hawk's sister. You can take me to her village. A few days after that, perhaps we can meet at Mother's Nest, and you can guide me into Eagle Canyon to Black Hawk's camp. I could never find my way alone, and I need to talk to him. You know where to find him. Will you take me?"

Otter Woman looked at her as though she were crazy. "You want *me* to take you into Eagle Canyon alone?"

"Yes. I am afraid if I don't talk to Black Hawk soon, I might lose all chance of still convincing him to send Little Fox to school. If I can talk Many Birds into coming, and can then tell Black Hawk she will be there, maybe he will still send him."

"He will not send the boy. He is very bitter." Otter Woman put a hand to her hair self-consciously. "And he told me I must never go near you or come to his camp again."

"That was because he thought you would try to hurt me again. If you lead me to his camp, he will see that you have changed your mind about me. He will forgive you, and you won't have to be afraid of him. He won't bring you any harm if I explain that I asked you to take me there."

Otter Woman bit her lower lip in thought. "Perhaps I will take you to his camp; and I will think about taking you to see Many Birds."

The woman whirled and walked away without another word. Evelyn wondered what had possessed her to put herself in her care, to travel alone with her into Eagle Canyon. There was not one person on the entire reservation who would not think she was a complete fool for taking such a chance, but it was her only hope of winning Otter Woman's trust and confidence.

"This is outrageous!" John Phillips paced the forward section of the church, while Evelyn sat up front in one of the hand-carved pews, hating to give the man the bad news.

"I saw her two days ago," she said, referring to Beverly Evans. "By now the circus has gone on up to Fort Yates. A couple of days after that they head for Cheyenne. I didn't know whether it was my place to mention anything at all. I supposed Reverend Evans had already said something to you."

"I have heard nothing from the man." He faced her. "Does he intend to let her go? Just like that? In God's name, why doesn't he go after his wife?"

"I suppose because he thinks she has committed an unforgivable sin."

Phillips frowned. "Well, I didn't mean that he should take her back. That is a personal matter for them. But to be married to someone . . . . I mean, surely he loved the woman. Surely he sees the folly of her ways and is concerned with how badly she could be hurt by this . . . this *devil* Herbert True! If he is any kind of man, he will try to stop her, bring her to her senses! Didn't *you* try to?"

Evelyn sighed. "In my own way; but you didn't see her, Reverend. She was simply glowing, totally oblivious to any warnings. She didn't want to hear anything I had to say, or believe that Herbert True is anything but a prince. I could see that there was no use trying to talk her out of it, and then Mr. True was there, and I couldn't say anything in front of him. I could tell on the way out here, Reverend, that Beverly was a very unhappy woman. All her life she's been——"

"Who are you to judge? Who are you, twenty years old and never married, an independent, forward-thinking woman who cares little for rules and the high morals of men like Greggory Evans, to say it was right for his wife to run off with an obvious cad . . . a womanizer!"

Evelyn felt her cheeks growing hot, as rage burned within. "I judge no one, Reverend, and I *do* care for rules and morals! I never said it was right for Beverly to do this. I wanted desperately to stop her, but she was not about to listen. If you had been there, you could not have stopped her any more than I could!" She rose from her seat. "And do not speak to me of morals and caring! If you truly cared about others, you wouldn't think it was so terrible that I tried to help Black Hawk and his son! You wouldn't be so quick to judge people like me, and like Beverly. You wouldn't be so callous toward Anita Wolf! And what about Lucille and Katy Bridges! What have you done for those poor girls?"

He frowned, fingering the lapels of his neat brown suitcoat. "What do you mean?"

Evelyn closed her eyes to gain control. "Reverend, can't you see what is going on under your nose? Those girls are being terribly mistreated. Seth Bridges treats them like little slaves. I don't think Lucille cares one little bit for Sergeant Desmond, but you said they were together at the dance, and I saw them together at the circus. Lucille looked very unhappy, and the sergeant was being much too familiar with her. She's too young for a man like that, and for Seth to allow it to go on only shows what a poor father he is."

"I am aware there are problems there, but I believe Seth Bridges is a very dangerous man, one *you* certainly should stay away from. I have tried talking to him myself, and was greeted with a shotgun. The fact remains that those girls were legally adopted by Seth, and there are no laws that give us permission to go in and drag them out of there. I have petitioned to both the agency and the Army, and neither one wants to get involved in a civil matter. Believe me, I am certain that the more you interfere, the more problems you will create for those girls. You will only make Seth angry, and he'll take that anger out on Lucille and Katy."

The reverend sighed, running a hand through his hair. "I wish you wouldn't think I have no concern in that matter, Miss Gibbons . . . or for Anita. I am not as unfeeling as you think. I am, after all, a man who believes that because God loves all of us, who are we not to love everyone in return? I am a *Christian,* for goodness sake! You have totally misunderstood my feelings and motives. It's just that . . . I have to be very careful. I was sent here by Mission Services, and they expect me to behave a certain way. I can't get involved in civil matters, and I am not sure how they would feel about me getting personally involved with an Indian woman."

"Are you saying you *do* care about Anita?"

He reddened at the question. "I'm not saying anything right now. I just want you to understand why a man in my position has to be cautious in his decisions." He put his hands on his hips, his gaze moving over her with a rather sad look in his eyes. "You must know I have been very attracted to you." He looked away then, his face red. "It embarrasses me to admit it, but with all this talk about Anita . . ." He sighed. "It is obvious to me that you and I are as different as night and day in our philosophy toward life, that it would be useless to pursue my feelings because it could never work between us. And I know you have special feelings for Black Hawk." He turned to meet her eyes again. "That will lead to disaster, Miss Gibbons."

Evelyn held his gaze. "Reverend, there are things you don't know. When the time is right, I will explain them to you. I know that my interest in Black Hawk is unusual and puts my reputation and job at great risk. I am not saying I . . . have special feelings for the man. At the moment I simply feel he is the key to helping a lot of these Sioux change, and I will do anything required to win their trust and get their children to school. Others can think what they like. I have never cared much one way or another. People are going to think what they want no matter what I do, and I am too busy to be concerned about their petty jealousies and judgments."

Phillips shook his head. "I don't know if you're terribly foolish, or very wise, Miss Gibbons. I do know you are very brave. I will give you that."

She smiled softly. "Thank you, Reverend. I—"

The door to the church burst open, and Dancing Eagle, who had driven Evelyn to the reservation in his wagon that first day she got off the train, walked much more quickly than usual on his old legs, hurrying to the front of the church, his eyes showing near terror. "Big trouble, Reverend," he said.

Evelyn's heart tightened, and the reverend frowned in concern. "What is it, Dancing Eagle?"

"Sickness, all over the reservation. The Army doctor says he thinks it is cholera! He thinks it came from the circus people, or maybe the animals and all the flies they brought. Many are already very sick. One has died!"

"Dear God," Evelyn whispered.

"Most of the sick have been taken to the agency, and Agent McLaughlin has sent for doctors from other forts to come and help. He says if things get worse, they will need the school and the church for the sick ones."

"Yes, that's fine," the reverend answered. He looked at Evelyn. "Go and get Janine and Anita. We'll take the wagon to the agency and see what we can do to help."

"Yes, right away!" Evelyn hurried out, a lump rising in her throat at the thought of what this could mean. White man's diseases had obliterated some tribes, desecrated many of the Plains tribes by the thousands. This could be a disaster for the agency, for the Sioux. She worried about Black Hawk. What if he or Little Fox or both got sick out there where no one even knew how to find them?

She hurried to Janine's cabin and pounded on the door. "Janine! Hurry! We need to go to the agency. Some kind of sickness—"

Janine opened the door, terror in her own eyes. "I know," she said quietly. "Anita has it, too. She's terribly sick, Evy. I don't dare leave her."

Evelyn rushed past her into the house to where Anita lay on her cot, bathed in perspiration and looking too pale. Evelyn knelt beside her. "Have faith, Anita. We will get you through this. I need you, remember? Who will help me teach?"

The girl managed a weak smile, but Evelyn could see she was already wanting to give up the fight. Just then the reverend came running up onto the porch of the cabin and inside the still-open door. "Miss Gibbons, we have to hurry." Deep concern moved into his eyes when he saw Evelyn bent over Anita.

"Anita already has the sickness," Evelyn told the man. "I think I should stay here with her. Janine and I can be here for any who come to the church and school for help." She was surprised but pleased to see sudden tears in Phillips's eyes when he saw Anita looking so horribly close to death. The man just nodded in reply, and he kept his eyes on Anita's loving gaze.

"I'll be back as soon as I can," he said, apparently directing the words at Anita in reassurance that he cared. "I'm sorry, Anita."

He turned and left, and as soon as his wagon clattered away, Anita smiled more, in spite of the horrible cramping and vomiting she had experienced over the last two hours. Everything hurt, but for the moment it didn't matter. For the first time she had seen concern, maybe even love, in Reverend Phillips's eyes.

Seventeen

Seth Bridges met the riverboat at Deer Point, a small peninsula where the Missouri and White rivers met, and where he had been told in the letter from Luke Smith in Omaha he should be in the afternoon on this date. He was actually glad for the cholera epidemic. It diverted the attention of the agency and Army both, and he figured that as long as he stayed away from contact with any Indians on this trip, he shouldn't have to worry about catching the horrid disease from any of them.

Besides, he had no choice but to take this chance. If he waited, he would miss his river connection. He had brought a load of corn, as directed, which he would use as a cover. Anyone who stopped him would be told that he was delivering corn to a steamboat for shipment to a buyer in Omaha, in trade for grain and oats for his animals. In reality, Luke Smith and Marty Able would meet him at the river, and the sacks of grain would be stuffed with bottles of whiskey to be handed out however he could get them to the Sioux.

Whiskey smugglers had been filtering onto the reservation unimpeded since the cholera had kept soldiers confined to Fort Yates. There could not be a better time to do his own dealing, and he was not going to let the cholera scare keep him from his own chance to make some good money and get hold of some whiskey for himself before it was hard to come by again.

Luke and Marty refused to come onto the reservation because of the cholera, so they had made these arrangements for him to meet them at the river. He would hide the whiskey at his farm, and he would be well paid for it. Off-reservation merchants were willing to give just about anything to keep the Indians drunk, which made it easier for them to buy up Indian land, especially along the rivers, land they knew would be the most valuable some day for farming and for port cities.

Seth watched the steamboat, called *Jessie Lee,* float to the bank and the men jump off to pull it closer with ropes. He waved at Luke and Marty as more men lowered a loading ramp, then came to the wagon to begin unloading the corn. Others came carrying huge gunny sacks, sacks Seth knew were filled with more than just grain.

"You sure there won't be any trouble?" Luke asked as Seth came on board.

"Not with the cholera goin' around. Besides, you know I've got connections. Sergeant Desmond is screwin' my daughter now. He knows I'll cut him off if he tries to stop me."

Both Luke and Marty laughed. "Holdin' the girl's ass over his head, are you?" Marty remarked. "I'll have to see about that once the cholera scare is over. You've talked before about that oldest daughter of yours. You ought to bring her along next time."

"I'll think on it," Seth answered. "Right now it's best they don't know anything about this."

Luke shouted some orders to the men loading the grain and whiskey. He turned to Seth. "Maybe we'll get lucky and the whole damn Sioux nation will die of the cholera. Then we can all come in here and get this land without any argument and without havin' to sneak around like this."

All three men laughed at the remark, and Seth slugged down a gulp of whiskey from a bottle he had opened. "Just so's I always have a supply of whiskey for myself," he answered. "If we ever do get hold of this land, maybe I'll open a tavern and whorehouse, use my two girls to start with."

"There's an idea," Marty said with a grin.

All three men watched the workers trade corn for feed until the last bag was finally loaded onto Seth's wagon. Luke took a wad of bills out of his pants pocket "I'm to pay you something extra besides the whiskey and grain."

"That's the agreement," Seth answered with a grin. "Them fancy merchants down in Omaha can afford it. Just so's it's in small bills and such. People would suspect if I went handin' out big amounts of money at the tradin' post."

Luke laughed lightly, counting out two hundred dollars in coins and various bills. "You make sure that whiskey gets where it's supposed to go, and don't go drinkin' it all yourself," he warned with a chuckle. "There will be some land agents coming here as soon as the cholera epidemic seems to be over. Don't dish out all the whiskey till you hear they're coming. The men we work for want the Sioux to be good and drunk while they're here. The agency can't stop the buyers from talking to the Indians. They have a legal right."

"I get the message." Seth licked his lips at the sight of the money. Two hundred dollars! He stuffed it into a drawstring bag be had brought along. "See you next month," he told Luke. "I'll have a load of squash for you." He walked down the loading ramp and climbed up into the wagon seat, then drank some more whiskey before slapping the reins on the rumps of his sorry-looking horses. He departed, hauling his load of "grain." All he had to do now was get word to Big Belly that he had whiskey to trade for blankets, clothing, food, and other government rations the Indians were willing to trade for the firewater. In turn, he could take those supplies on his next trip to the riverboat and sell them, and they in turn would be shipped to merchants in Omaha to sell to the public. He would make a double profit, at the expense of the government. All he had to do was keep from being caught, and as long as Sergeant Desmond enjoyed sharing

We've got your authors!

If you seek out the latest historical romances by today's bestselling authors, our new reader's service, KENSINGTON CHOICE, is the club for you.

KENSINGTON CHOICE is the only club where you can find authors like Janelle Taylor, Shannon Drake, Rosanne Bittner, Sylvie Sommerfield, Penelope Neri and Phoebe Conn all in one place...

...and the only service that will deliver their romances direct to your home as soon as they are published—even before they reach the bookstores.

KENSINGTON CHOICE is also the only service that will give you a substantial guaranteed discount off the publisher's prices on every one of those romances.

That's right: Every month, the Editors at Zebra and Pinnacle select four of the newest novels by our bestselling authors and rush them straight to you, even *before they reach the bookstores*. The publisher's prices for these romances range from $4.99 to $5.99—but they are always yours for the guaranteed low price of just *$3.95!*

That means you'll always save over $1.00...often as much as *$2.00*...off the publisher's prices on every new novel you get from KENSINGTON CHOICE!

All books are sent on a 10-day free examination basis, and there is no minimum number of books to buy. (A postage and handling charge of $1.50 is added to each shipment.)

As your introduction to the convenience and value of this new service, we invite you to accept

4 BOOKS FREE

The 4 books, worth up to $23.96, are our welcoming gift. You pay only $1 to help cover postage and handling.

To start your subscription to KENSINGTON CHOICE and receive your introductory package of 4 FREE romances, detach and mail the postpaid card at right *today*.

We have 4 FREE BOOKS for you as your introduction to KENSINGTON CHOICE

To get your FREE BOOKS, worth up to $23.96, mail card below.

FREE BOOK CERTIFICATE

As my introduction to your new KENSINGTON CHOICE reader's service, please send me 4 FREE historical romances (worth up to $23.96), billing me just $1 to help cover postage and handling. As a KENSINGTON CHOICE subscriber, I will then receive 4 brand-new romances to preview each month for 10 days FREE. I can return any books I decide not to keep and owe nothing. The publisher's prices for the KENSINGTON CHOICE romances range from $4.99 to $5.99, but as a subscriber I will be entitled to get them for just $3.95 per book. There is no minimum number of books to buy, and I can cancel my subscription at any time. A $1.50 postage and handling charge is added to each shipment.

Name _____

Address _____ Apt. # _____

City _____ State _____ Zip _____

Telephone (___) _____

Signature _____

(If under 18, parent or guardian must sign)

Subscription subject to acceptance

KC 0994

We have
4
FREE
Historical
Romances
for you!

Details inside!

KENSINGTON CHOICE
Reader's Service
120 Brighton Road
P.O.Box 5214
Clifton, NJ 07015-5214

Lucille's bed, that was not likely to happen. Besides, the sergeant had his own neck to protect.

My dear father, Evelyn wrote, *In my last letter to you I told you of the wonderful progress we were making. All that has changed now. Cholera has visited the reservation with its evil greeting, and many have already died. So far I am fine, only very tired from working night and day with Reverend Phillips and Janine, nursing the sick. One Army doctor cannot possibly keep up with an entire reservation, and it is left to the rest of us to do what we can.*

I fear all progress I have made winning the trust of these people has been erased, for the Indians feel we have brought this terrible plague upon them by bringing a circus from the white man's world to the reservation. Some think we planned for this to happen! Now I am afraid the few families who had agreed to send children to school will never send them back.

All night we see fires everywhere, a tipi burning here, clothing there, all belongings of the dead, being burned to help prevent the spread of the disease. Since the sickness seems to be confined to the areas between the Cheyenne and White rivers, we are quarantined from the rest of the reservation and from Fort Yates. The soldiers in turn will not leave the fort to perform their regular duties because they refuse to come to this part of the reservation, and therefore whiskey smugglers, who love the money that is paid to them by outsiders more than they fear the cholera, are enjoying complete freedom. I have seen frightened Indians drinking rotten alcohol, thinking it will help ease their fears and make them feel happy. Some even believe that if they stay drunk, they won't get sick.

Please pray for our situation here, and pray for me and the loss of someone who had become a dear friend, Anita Wolf. She died four days ago.

The statement brought tears to Evelyn's eyes, and she had to stop writing for a moment. She still could not believe the beautiful, giving Anita had died. Why did God take sweet people like her, and let people like Sergeant Desmond live? Poor Reverend Phillips had lost his composure when speaking over Anita's grave. He had waited too long, realized too late that he had foolishly ignored the love Anita had to offer him; realized too late that he could have loved her.

Also dead was Otter Woman. Evelyn had never seen her again after their talk the day of the circus. Big Belly had also succumbed to the disease, and his two children now lived with his brother, Dancing Cloud. Falling Eagle's ten-year-old son, Fast Arrow, was also dead. No longer would he sit in the little school playing with the counting beads. Bill Doogan's Sioux wife had died, as had Red Foot Woman, whose many children were now under the care of her young sister, Yellow Sky, and their shared husband, White Eagle.

So many gone . . . forty so far. Many more lay in misery with the terrible cramps, diarrhea, and vomiting. Some had lived through it and were recovering, but only the strongest. Evelyn fretted over the fact that she would have to start winning the trust of these people all over again once the disease had abated; and since she had been so busy, there had not been a chance to do anything more about Lucille and Katy Bridges, who were not allowed to step foot beyond their property line because of the cholera.

Anita was such a sweet person, she continued. *She was a full-blood Sioux woman, and had been educated at Genoa Indian School and was very bright. She helped me teach the little ones, and was one of those who cherished and sometimes practiced her Sioux religion and customs, but understood that things have changed and the Sioux must adjust, as she had done, although most of her own people ostracized her for it.*

Unlike most of the Indians in Indian Territory, Father, the

Sioux continue to cling to the old ways and remain quite stead-
fast in refusing to even consider the white man's religion and
education. As you and Mother did years ago, I have tried to
make them understand that they do not need to forget old beliefs
or their own language and dress and customs. My theories and
methods of teaching do not stand well with Agent McLaughlin
or with Mission Services, but you of all people understand the
problems I face. I do not need to spell them out.

It is all so sad, Father, and although I know you grew tired
of such remote places and the long struggle, I wish that you
could come here and help. We are short one mission couple now.
You would never believe the reason. Reverend Greggory Evans's
wife ran off with the manager of a circus! She has not been
heard from for over two weeks now, and Reverend Evans, who
came here to help tend to the sick, came down with the cholera
himself and died. Now the Oahe Mission needs another
preacher, someone who can also teach. Mission Services has
promised to send someone, but volunteers are appreciated.

Evelyn put down her pen. Did Beverly Evans know or care
that her husband was dead? The sad part was that Greggory
Evans had not once mentioned her name when he came to help.
He had seemed totally unaffected by his wife's departure, and
even in the throes of death he did not ask for her. It was as
though she had never existed for him. By now Beverly was at
Cheyenne, perhaps on her way someplace even farther away.
There had been no letter, no way to contact her to let her know
she was a widow now, free to marry someone else without getting a divorce . . . if, indeed, Herbert True intended to marry her
at all.

She decided not to tell her father about her own injury. He
would be worried enough about the cholera epidemic. She was
mostly healed now, and Otter Woman was no longer a threat.
She rose from her desk, everything aching from weariness. Over
the past two weeks she had slept an average of three hours a

night. Reverend Phillips had insisted she go to her cabin and get some rest, but even when she did lie down, sleep would not come. There had been too much loss. She had seen too much horror and misery, and she was worried about Black Hawk and Little Fox. She had at least managed to bathe and change her clothes, although she wore her plainest, oldest dresses now because of the heat and the hard work of cleaning up human filth. A fire was kept burning night and day in front of the schoolhouse, where bedclothes and the garments of those who had died were quickly burned.

She looked into the mirror at a pale, haggard face, deep circles under her eyes. She wore her hair twisted into a bun, the simplest way when there was work to do. She prayed the disease was finally beating itself out. Every day there were fewer who got sick, and those who had lived through the entire ordeal were apparently out of danger. The overpowering heat of summer had finally abated, and late September had brought pleasant days and cool nights.

She splashed water on her face and toweled it off, deciding to eat something before finishing her letter and going back to the school to help Janine and John. She still felt the sting of Anita's loss, would miss her terribly; and she wondered how she was going to get children back to school without Anita's help.

She was headed for the bread box when she heard a horse ride up close to the cabin. Before she could get to a window to see who it was, someone pounded on her door. She quickly opened it to see Black Hawk standing there, holding Little Fox in his arms. His eyes betrayed his terror.

"I did not know where else to take him," he said, agony in his voice.

"Dear God!" Evelyn stepped aside, her joy at seeing Black Hawk again, alive and well, spoiled by the fact that Little Fox had apparently contracted the sickness. "Bring him in and lay him on my bed." She directed Black Hawk to her bedroom, where she pulled back the bedcovers. The man gently laid his son on the cotton sheets, and Little Fox groaned. Evelyn could see he was much thinner, knew he was probably terribly dehydrated. Death usually came when the patient was almost drained of body fluids. "We have to get some water into him."

"He will only spit it up," Black Hawk told her.

"We have to try. The only hope of salvation is keeping water or hot broth in them and working to keep the fever down." Evelyn hurried out and returned with a cup of still-warm water. "This has been boiled. We have learned that boiling water kills whatever germs might be lurking in it. When there is a lot of sickness like this, it especially helps to boil the water. Hold him up a little and I'll try to get some into him."

Black Hawk obeyed. This was a white man's disease, and only the white man seemed to know what to do about it. His hatred for what the *wicasa ska* had brought to his people was for the moment overshadowed by his agony over the possible loss of his only remaining son. A semiconscious Little Fox managed to swallow some of the water, and to Black Hawk's relief, it stayed down.

"Now we wait a little while and give him some more. I'll get some cooler water from the well and we'll use it to bathe him and keep the fever down. It's only the drinking water that has to be boiled."

Evelyn hurried out again, and Black Hawk looked around the tidy room. Lace curtains hung at the window, and the bed looked homemade, the posts cut from the trunks of pine trees. He touched the bedding, noticing how Little Fox had sunk into it, and he knew it was probably stuffed with feathers. How white people slept on such soft beds, he could not understand. Everything in the room showed that a white woman lived here: the brightly colored quilts on the bed, a picture of the white man's Jesus on the wall, a trunk in one corner painted with yellow flowers, a wooden contraption on another wall that had doors on it, where he supposed Evelyn Gibbons kept her pretty dresses. Beside it was a mirror, under which sat a stand with a bowl and pitcher.

Evelyn came back inside with a small bucket of water and a rag. She set the bucket on a stand near the bed and dipped the rag into it, then wrung it out and laid it on Little Fox's forehead. "How long has he been sick?"

"Three days. We visited my sister and grandmother before that, and it was only then that I knew there was sickness in our village. When we got back, I took Little Fox with me to hunt. I spotted Seth Bridges driving a wagonload of corn to the river, so I followed him, sure he was going to meet whiskey traders. I watched them unload his corn onto a riverboat, but before I could see what they loaded onto the wagon, Little Fox suddenly turned away and doubled over in pain and vomited. In only minutes he had a high fever, and I knew he had the terrible sickness. I took him first to my grandmother's village, but he only got worse, so I took him to Night Hunter. He told me this is something only the white doctors know how to care for. I do not trust the Army doctor, so I brought him to you."

Evelyn looked across the bed, meeting his gaze. It had all happened so fast. One minute she was worrying and wondering about this man, and now here he was, in her own cabin. There had not even been time to say hello or to ask about his arrest. She had not seen him since that day. "You still trust me, after what happened, even when your own son could die from a disease my people brought to you?"

"My arrest was not your fault. It was Otter Woman's. And you did not yourself bring the disease. It was the circus. I told you those animals carried evil spirits. My people believe that the animals with human faces brought the sickness."

"The monkeys?"

"I never saw them. I would not come. There would be too many white people there, too many soldiers. But Many Birds told me about the monkeys and how our people were very afraid of them. It is just as I told you it would be. They are an evil animal."

Evelyn decided there was no sense trying to make him understand that sickness did not come from evil spirits. It came from germs. Some day when Little Fox was better, she would explain. She watched him take the rag from the boy's forehead and begin gently washing his face and neck with it. He spoke softly to him, words of love and encouragement. Evelyn wished that whites who did not even think of the Sioux as human could see this moment, a father soothing his son lovingly, tears in his eyes.

She studied Black Hawk's powerful arms as he bathed the boy, realizing she had been so concerned for Little Fox when he first arrived that she had not really taken a good look at the man. It struck her that he was more handsome than she had remembered. Today he wore the lightweight doeskin leggings that were open at the sides, and a buckskin shirt. A turquoise bracelet on his wrist only made his skin seem darker, and his hair was pulled back into a simple tail at the back of his neck, tied with a strip of rawhide that had little turquoise beads on the ends. His throat and chest were bare of jewelry, and his face was unpainted.

"How do *you* feel, Black Hawk?"

"I am well." He met her gaze, his eyes moving over her then. "You are too thin. Have you had the sickness?"

She smiled self-consciously. "No. I have just been working very hard helping those who *are* sick. I guess this all happened a little too soon after I recovered from the arrow wound. I don't really have all my own strength back yet."

Their eyes held for several silent seconds, and Evelyn wondered if he had missed her and thought about her as much as she had him; if he felt the same deep pull at his insides at seeing her again that she felt when she was near him.

He finally spoke. "I never got the chance to say that I am

sorry. If I had known that asking you to come there would mean so much pain and suffering—"

"I would do it again, Black Hawk. I was afraid I would never see you again. I am the one who is sorry, for the way the soldiers treated you."

Hatred came into his eyes, so deep that it almost frightened her. "That is not your fault. The one called Sergeant Desmond looks for any excuse to give me trouble. He is afraid of me because of Wounded Knee."

Evelyn took the rag from him and wet it again so it would be cooler. She handed it back to him. "Wounded Knee? Was the sergeant there?"

Black Hawk reached around to the back of Little Fox's neck and held the rag there for a moment. "He was there. When I found my wife, shot in the head, and my little son, Small Bear, stabbed in the heart, I also found the sergeant sitting on his horse nearby, holding a bloody sword. He just stared at me at first, then turned his horse and quickly rode away before I could reach for him. I had no weapons, but I would have killed him with my bare hands!" He moved the rag back to Little Fox's face. "I will never forget that day, and the sergeant knows it. He is afraid that one day I will sneak up on him and cut out his heart!"

Evelyn shivered. She had no doubt that if Black Hawk thought he could get away with it, he would do just that. The only thing holding him back was Little Fox. He was all the boy had. He would never do anything that would mean leaving his son alone.

"I am so sorry, Black Hawk."

He kept his eyes on Little Fox. "A blizzard came later that day. When I went back to find Turtle Woman and Small Bear, their bodies were frozen and covered with snow." His voice broke, and he took a deep breath to keep his composure. "The Army dug one big hole and loaded bodies onto wagons like rotten logs, then dumped them into the hole and covered them. We could not even give them a proper Indian burial. I would have buried my wife and son together, on a scaffold up high, where they could easily walk the road to the heavens. I would have buried with them all the things they need for the journey: new moccasins, blankets, food. Now I do not know if their spirits were able to climb out of that terrible hole and find their way to the land where there are many buffalo and the grass is always green and there is no pain."

Evelyn blinked back tears. "Black Hawk, I believe we worship the same God, and my God finds lost souls and takes them to Him. It doesn't matter where they are buried or how they died. He finds them and sets their spirits free. I have no doubt that Turtle Woman and Small Bear are playing happily together somewhere in a land just like what you described. My own mother is probably with them."

He looked up from Little Fox with a frown of surprise. "You believe that white people go to the same place as my people?"

It was the first time in many days that Evelyn felt an urge to laugh, but she only smiled reassuringly. "I believe that all good people go to the same place. My God does not see the color of a person's skin. He sees only the soul, Black Hawk, the goodness of their hearts."

He nodded, then laid the rag across Little Fox's forehead and straightened, taking a deep breath. "I was afraid when I came here that I would find you, too, had died of this terrible thing. I was glad when they released me to learn from Agent McLaughlin that you had survived the arrow wound. Then when I heard about this sickness . . ." His dark eyes studied her almost lovingly, making her blush.

"I'll be fine, Black Hawk. I just need a little more rest."

He glanced down at his son. "Now my son is in your bed. Do you want me to move him?"

"No. He seems to be resting well. I can borrow a cot and put it in the outer room to sleep on. Most of the sick I am helping care for are in the school and at the church, but Little Fox is special. We'll leave him right here."

His eyes teared again. "Tell me he will not die. He is all I have."

"I can't make such a promise, Black Hawk. Only God makes those decisions. I can only pray."

He sighed. "I leave him in your care. I am going into the hills to pray in my own way, and to make a blood sacrifice."

A chill moved down her spine. She knew what he meant. He would cut himself and shed blood in an offering to Wakantanka, in hopes the sacrifice would convince his God to spare Little Fox's life. She wanted to beg him not to do it, shout at him that it was a heathen, barbaric act, but she knew it was all the hope a man like Black Hawk had. She understood how strongly he believed in such things, and this was not the time to argue with him about the difference in their religious practices. One had to move slowly with Black Hawk, teach him a little at a time. It was enough that she had planted the idea that they worshipped the same God. "When will you come back?" she asked.

Black Hawk studied her blue eyes, surprised she had not objected to what he wanted to do. Most white women would have been shocked, would have told him it was wrong. He thought what a small thing she was. He could easily hurt her, but he would rather hold her, feel himself inside her, give her pleasure and take his own in return. He wanted to love her fully, in every sense, spiritually, emotionally, physically. "I will return when the spirits tell me I have shed enough blood."

Evelyn swallowed, feeling the weight of her responsibility. "I will do what I can, Black Hawk."

"I know that you will. That is why I brought him here." His dark eyes held her in their hypnotic spell a moment longer before he turned and left the room. A moment later the outer door closed, and she heard him ride away.

Evelyn looked at Little Fox, so pale and wasted. "God help me," she whispered. "Don't let him die."

She thought about his remark concerning Seth Bridges. *Was it whiskey the man had traded the corn for?* She wished she could prove it! She could have the man arrested and get his daughters out from under their horrible living conditions.

She began bathing Little Fox again. There was no time now to worry about Seth Bridges and his possible involvement with selling whiskey to Indians. Black Hawk's precious son was in her bed, and Black Hawk was counting on her to take care of him. He had to live, for if he did not, Black Hawk would feel he himself had nothing to live for, and she would lose him forever.

For three days Little Fox lay near death, but inexplicably, on the third night, his fever broke and the vomiting stopped. Late on the fourth day the boy was able to sit up and eat bread and soup.

"Your father's connection with the spirits must be very powerful," Evelyn told him. "Look how strong you are getting."

"Father's prayers are strong because Wakantanka knows he is brave and has not forgotten the Sioux way." The boy's voice was still weak. "His inner circle of life has not been broken."

Evelyn smiled. It was obvious Black Hawk had spoken often with his son about the importance of keeping to Sioux customs.

"Father said that when I am better, we will go and see Night Hunter and we will celebrate *inikaqapi* to become stronger again."

"The sweat lodge?"

"Yes. It will be the first time for me. Some would say I am too young, but Father has already taught me much." The boy breathed deeply for strength. "Allowing me to take part in *ini-*

kaqapi shows that he believes I am close to being a man. Do you know the seven rites of the Sioux?"

Evelyn sat down on the edge of his bed. "Well, there is the sweat lodge and the vision quest."

"My father has had many visions. He has made the Sun Dance sacrifice three times." Little Fox spoke with great pride.

"Yes, I have heard," Evelyn answered, thinking about the one vision that still had not been realized. She touched Little Fox's hair, smoothing it back from his face, aching at the circles around his eyes and the way his cheekbones protruded from loss of weight. "The Sun Dance is another rite," she added.

Little Fox nodded. "See if you can name them all," he said softly, too weak to speak in a normal voice. "That is three. If you can name them all, I will give you a present for helping me get well."

Evelyn thought how easy this sweet, intelligent child would be to love. "All right. Let's see . . . another is, I think, something about keeping around a dead relative's spirit for a while . . . *Wanaqi* . . . *Wanaqi yuhapi,* I think it's called."

Little Fox's grin widened. "You are right! If a family wants to keep the spirit of a loved around, they must give away everything they own in sacrifice. There are many steps that must be taken to preserve a ghost spirit." He sat up a little straighter. "Now you must name three more rituals."

Evelyn could not help wondering if it was her prayers that had let the boy live . . . or if it was because of Black Hawk's bloody sacrifice. Sioux customs were not something to be taken lightly. There was much merit to many of them, and she thought it very foolish for most whites to laugh them off.

"Well, there is the *Hunka* ritual, in which two unrelated people decide to create a bond between them that is stronger than kinship. After a special ceremony, they are forever obliged to die for each other if necessary."

"It is also sometimes called *Hunkalowanpi.* After the ritual, the older person is called *Hunka ate* by the younger one, meaning father. The younger one is just called *Hunka*. I think that you and my father should take part in the *Hunkalowanpi.*"

"You do, do you? I don't think your people would appreciate your father wanting to bond with a white woman."

"Why not? My father says you have an Indian heart. My father loves you."

Evelyn lost her smile, taken back by the unexpected statement. Surely the boy would not say such a thing so casually if Black Hawk had not told him of such feelings. She felt suddenly too warm, even though the weather had cooled, and her whole body tingled. "I . . . you mean . . . as a friend. Yes, we are good friends, Little Fox."

"I think he loves you more than like a friend. He thinks about you all the time. He says you are a part of his vision and that the spirits want you to be his woman."

Evelyn got up from the bed, suddenly completely flustered. How was she going to face Black Hawk after hearing such a statement? "Well, I . . . we will just have to see about that, Little Fox."

The boy shrugged. "What are the last two rituals?"

His remark had left her so shaken that she could not think. Little Fox apparently did not think much about what he had just said. It was something he simply took for granted and supposed she should, too. "I—I can't remember," she told him.

"They are the puberty ritual, *Isnati awicalowan,* like what my aunt, Many Birds, had. The other is *Tapa wankayeyapi,* the throwing of the ball. A ball made of buffalo hide is painted to represent the earth and held by a young girl, who then throws it to many people who are gathered around her in the four directions. As each person catches the ball, they throw it back to her. The ball is the same as Wakantanka, and the people around the girl represent people who are trying to get close to the spirits so they can stay in the Indian world and out of the white man's world. The ball is knowledge, and those trying to catch it are doing so because they want to free themselves from the darkness of ignorance. Now I cannot give you the gift. You did not name all the rituals."

"What?" Evelyn had hardly heard the boy. Her thoughts were reeling with what he had said about Black Hawk loving her. "Oh! I would have remembered if you had given me time to think about it."

The boy smiled. "I know. I will give you the gift anyway. It is something that belonged to my mother. I cannot give it to you until Father returns. He will have to go back to our camp to get it. Will you come with us?"

Being alone with Black Hawk had new meaning now . . . new dangers. "I will think about it, Little Fox. If the reverend and his sister no longer need my help, I will come."

"After you were hurt, I was afraid you would never come back. I want to learn more from the books you gave us. I studied them often."

"That's very good, Little Fox," Evelyn told him rather absently. She turned and urged him to scoot back down in the bed and try to sleep. "You are very weak yet. You need a lot of rest."

"You should rest, too, so that you can go back with us when we leave here."

"We will see about that." Evelyn tucked a light blanket around him. "You sleep awhile and I will make you more of the beef soup you like so much."

"I am grateful."

Evelyn could not resist the urge to lean down and kiss his cheek. He was a child who was easy to become attached to. His smile and openness had already won her heart, but so had his father won a place there, and that was not as easy to accept. She left the room and walked outside to the small front porch of the cabin, looking out to the hills. Black Hawk would come back anytime now. How was she going to be able to look him in the eyes, after what Little Fox had told her? She knew she should be offended hearing that an Indian man loved her, but she only felt a wonderful joy, and more—a deep and surely sinful longing to be held lovingly in Black Hawk's arms.

Eighteen

It was late afternoon when John Phillips came to the church to tell Evelyn that a spotted horse with an Indian blanket on its back was tied in front of her cabin, along with a spare horse and packhorse. Evelyn pushed a strand of hair behind her ear and rose from a small girl's bedside. Because Little Fox was so much better, she had come to the church after lunch to help the reverend and Janine with their patients.

"That means Black Hawk is back," she told the reverend. "It's been a whole week." She started past him when he grasped hold of her arm.

"Miss Gibbons, be careful."

Evelyn studied the man's haggard-looking face. He had worked as hard as she and Janine helping the sick, and he still mourned the loss of Anita. "Reverend, surely you know by now that I have nothing to fear from Black Hawk. He would not have left Little Fox in my care if he did not have a great respect for me."

Phillips sighed. "I still don't fully trust him. If he takes the boy away today, you should stay away from him after that." He let go of her. "After he leaves, just stay home and get some sleep. I think the worst is over, and there haven't been any newly reported cases for three days now. This has been hard on you, after suffering that arrow wound."

"I'll be fine." Evelyn turned to leave, then hesitated. "Reverend, I think Little Fox should rest a few more days before his father takes him back to their camp. It's a long ride. If you see Black Hawk's horse around the cabin overnight, don't be alarmed. I will ask him to camp outside and wait at least until tomorrow. I am not at all afraid to have him around."

She left, too tired to stay and argue the issue. She was more concerned with how she was going to face Black Hawk after what Little Fox had told her. Would the boy tell Black Hawk he had told her he loved her? She supposed she should behave as though things were just as they always had been and let Black Hawk be the one to say something first, but ever since hearing him tell about Wounded Knee, her heart had gone out to him, and the deep feelings she had for him had only grown more intense. He had shown a vulnerable side, a compassion and deep emotions she knew outsiders never saw in him.

She reached her cabin, recognizing Black Hawk's Appaloosa. She touched the horse's rump, which was warm and damp. That meant Black Hawk had not been here long. Before going inside, she took a moment to study the animal, a handsome gelding with a hawk painted on its right rump. She walked around it to see a sun painted on the other rump. The rawhide reins were decorated with beads, and a brightly colored blanket rested on its back under a very small doeskin saddle—actually more of a seat than a saddle—that appeared to be lightly stuffed, she supposed with grass. A beautifully beaded and painted deerskin parfleche, for personal supplies, was tied against the rawhide straps that held the saddle in place.

The horse looked powerful, its form beautiful and yet graceful, much like its owner. It seemed eerie to think how much this animal resembled the horse in her dreams. She patted its neck and went inside the cabin, where she heard voices from the bedroom. She put a hand to her chest, breathing deeply to try to still her pounding heart, feeling like a silly young girl in love, reminding herself she was twenty years old, educated, reasonably wise, and that she must be careful not to let pity and unrealistic dreams rule her heart. Perhaps her dreams didn't mean any of the things she thought they meant, and perhaps Little Fox had misinterpreted some of the things his father had told him about his feelings for her.

She knew she still looked haggard. Her bun was in an untidy disarray, her dress had a couple of stains on the skirt from where she had spilled soup on it while feeding a sick child. She needed a bath, and she had not put any creams or color on her face for days. She told herself it didn't matter. She should not care how she looked to an Indian man. She straightened her shoulders and marched into the bedroom to see Black Hawk sitting beside the bed. "Well, at last you—"

All of her confidence left her when Black Hawk looked up at her. He was a little thinner, and there were deep circles under his own eyes. Both of his arms showed long, scabbed lines from what had obviously been deep cuts.

"My father is very weak," Little Fox told her. "He fasted for five days and shed blood in prayer for me. Now I am almost well."

Evelyn held Black Hawk's gaze the whole time the boy spoke. "Yes. He has much power." She felt light-headed at the sight of him, wanting to scream at him for cutting himself that way. "Please go out there and lie down on my cot, Black Hawk. I will fix you some hot broth and some bread."

He nodded, tears in his eyes. "My son will live. It is not just because of my prayers. It is because of you."

She shook her head. "No. It is because I prayed, too. God chose to let him live. Please, come and lie down."

He took a deep breath and grasped the back of the chair, rising slowly, and from the sight of him, Evelyn was surprised he was able to ride a horse back to the cabin. He took a couple of hesitant steps away from the chair.

"My God, Black Hawk, you can hardly walk! You should not have done this to yourself!" She moved beside him, putting an arm around his waist. He rested an arm around her shoulders and let her help him into the main room, where he lowered himself to a sitting position on her cot.

"I will be fine in a day or so," he told her.

Evelyn knelt to inspect his arms. "And what if these cuts get infected? It probably won't do much good now that they're scabbed over, but I will try to clean them with carbolic acid. It will sting, but it's certainly better than losing your arms, or dying." She could not help the sudden tears that came into her eyes. "It is not necessary to mutilate yourself in order for prayers to be answered, Black Hawk. You must stop doing these things. I understand your beliefs, but I believe our Gods are the same, and my God would never ask you to shed blood and starve yourself to get a prayer answered. He loves you too much. *Ask, and ye shall receive.* That is what my God teaches. He asks only that you believe in Him and trust Him, nothing more. These rituals of shedding blood in prayer . . . perhaps someone generations back, some holy person, misunderstood something that was shown him in a dream. Perhaps your God does not want you to do these things to yourself."

He watched her for several silent seconds before answering. "I will think on these things. I only know that when I brought my son here, he was near death; and after five days of fasting and shedding of blood, I have come back to see he is well."

She sighed in frustration, rising to walk over to a coal-burning cook stove the agency had procured for her. "Please think about what I have told you." She quickly wiped at tears and told herself she must not care so much. "I have some hot beef stew here from lunchtime. It's still warm. I'll reheat it. You can eat some of the meat and potatoes if you think your stomach can take the solids. Otherwise, just drink the broth. A couple of pieces of bread should help." She reached over with wooden tongs and took a couple of chunks of coal from a bucket, then opened a fire door at the front of the stove and threw them in on top of a few coals still glowing. "I baked some bread late last night, so it is nice and fresh."

She turned to see him watching her carefully. His dark eyes moved over her, and she was not sure if he was thinking she was beautiful, or that she looked terrible. It was more likely the latter, and maybe that was good. "I'll clean up your arms while the stew is heating." She walked to a cupboard and took out a brown bottle, then cut some gauze from a large roll that was in the same cupboard. She walked over to where he still sat and knelt in front of him again. "I know I look a mess. I spilled soup on my dress today while I was feeding a sick child." She doused the gauze with carbolic acid and took hold of his right wrist, thinking how thick and strong it was. She gently washed the cuts on that arm, noticing his hand move into a fist because of the sting.

"Why do you care that your dress is soiled?" he asked her. "In my eyes you are always beautiful."

Evelyn felt a tingle move through every part of her body. "Well, your eyes are not seeing too well today," she tried to joke. "Let me have your other arm." She took hold of his left arm and began washing that one, then froze when with his right hand he touched her hair.

"It is so much lovelier when it is worn long," he told her.

She began to tremble, and she quickly rose and moved away from him. "It is more practical this way when I have so much work to do and the weather is still so warm," she answered. Why had he done that? Why had he touched her that way, so lovingly? It was wrong, wasn't it? Reverend Phillips had told her to be careful. Perhaps he had been more correct than she realized. It seemed only right to allow both Black Hawk and Little Fox one more day's rest, but now . . . to let Black Hawk sleep anywhere near her cabin all night . . .

She walked over to put back the carbolic acid, then walked to the stove to stir the stew. "This will be ready soon. You and

Little Fox can stay here and rest today and tonight, then leave in the morning. You need some food and a few hours sleep to get your strength back. If you want to sleep inside, I will go and sleep at the church."

"No. You will sleep right here. I will sleep outside, as I have done many times in my life. You should stay in your own dwelling."

"That's fine, if that is what you prefer." Evelyn was suddenly self-conscious of every move she made, feeling watched by his dark eyes, eyes that made it seem he could see right through her.

"I want you to know," he told her, "that if I had not been told you had recovered and would live, I would not have gone back to my camp when they let me out of the fort prison. I would have come here. All the time I was locked away, I worried about you. I prayed for you, but I was afraid my prayers would not be heard in that dark place."

"I am just sorry they put you there. They had no right." Evelyn turned to face him. "And you should not have cut off Otter Woman's hair."

He sat a little straighter. "She had to be punished."

"I talked with her."

His eyes widened in surprise. "When?"

"The day the circus was here. I attempted to make friends with her, to make her see that I was not her enemy. I think I managed to convince her. She was going to guide me to your camp, but . . ." She closed her eyes at the memories of agony and suffering over the past three weeks. "She died of the cholera before we could ever see each other again."

"My sister told me of Otter Woman's death. I think it was her punishment from Wakantanka for interfering with a vision."

There it was again. The vision. Everything always came back to that. She was beginning to feel foolish for thinking her exact dream had to be fulfilled. Maybe she should just go home, before her heart ran away with her. She felt lost in that dream world whenever Black Hawk was near her.

"Tell me, Evy," he said, using her name as casually as a best friend, "you said Otter Woman was going to bring you to my camp. You were going to come and teach again? You were not afraid?"

She took some wooden bowls from a cupboard. All her kitchenware was donated by the agency. In fact, nearly *everything* in the cabin other than her personal belongings had been donated by the agency or Mission Services, and sometimes she felt guilty for conducting herself so much against the way they wanted things done. She walked to the table and set out the bowls, then picked up a knife that lay beside a fresh loaf of bread in the center of the table. She cut two slices, then met Black Hawk's gaze. "I was not afraid. You had saved my life. And once Otter Woman understood that to hurt me would mean interfering with a holy vision, I knew she would not try it again." She pulled out a chair. "Come and sit down, Black Hawk. I will dish you up some stew." She took his bowl to the stove and dipped some stew into it. "You must eat slowly."

"I have fasted before. I know what to do." When Evelyn turned around, he was standing at the table. "This to me is a strange way of eating, but I have done it before, when I came to live with missionaries." He sat down, and Evelyn could tell it was taking a great deal of effort for him to keep his balance. She set the stew in front of him, then walked to the bedroom to tell Little Fox she would bring him something to eat, but the boy had fallen back to sleep. She smiled, turning back to dish up her own stew. "Your son is sleeping."

Black Hawk nodded. He said little then as he ate. Evelyn stole glances at him, studying the way the muscles of his upper arms moved, noticing how clean and shiny his hair was. It looked soft, as though just washed. Had he bathed just for her? His hair was tied to one side with a colorfully beaded piece of rawhide. She thought his face exotic, with its high cheekbones, dark skin, full lips, wide-set eyes so dark they were almost black—eyes that could one minute be full of compassion and the next, full of hatred. He had a high forehead and a straight nose that seemed the perfect size for the rest of his face, a square jawline and—

She quickly glanced down at her stew. He had caught her staring at him, which was the last thing she wanted. "I'm worried you went too long without food," she said, needing an excuse for studying him. "I don't want you to eat too much too quickly."

He pushed the bowl away, and she noticed it was only half empty.

"I know when to stop." He bit into the bread.

"Would you like butter?"

He shook his head while he chewed. This time when she met his eyes, their gaze locked for several silent seconds. Black Hawk swallowed his bread. "Tell me again about your mother, and the Indian called Wild Horse. They loved each other?"

Evelyn knew her embarrassment must be evident. She looked back down at her stew. "Yes. I am not sure what might have happened if Wild Horse had not been killed. I only know that his death forced my mother to admit to my father that she had been very unhappy. They resolved a lot of their differences after that."

"And what were these differences?"

Evelyn aimlessly stirred the stew in her bowl. "My father was very strict in his beliefs. There was little joy in our household. My mother wanted him to be more open, more compassionate. She wanted to be able to dance and to laugh." She thought for a moment about Beverly Evans, and she prayed the woman had found the happiness she sought. "She also wanted my father to try to understand the Indian way. She felt that was the key to reaching them and winning their trust before trying to change them."

He smiled softly. "Much like you."

She could not help a smile of her own. "My father has told me all my life that I am just like my mother. 'Too independent for your own good,' he is always saying."

"You are a woman who follows her heart."

Evelyn's smile faded at the words, so insightful. She found it amazing that this supposedly wild, untrustworthy Indian renegade could be so easy to talk to. "It's strange that you would say that. My mother had always taught me to follow my heart, but to be careful." She felt her cheeks growing hotter. "She said that sometimes the heart can lead a person into danger." She wished she could look away from him, but it would do no good. He surely knew exactly what she was thinking, and she could see by his own eyes that he was thinking the same. To love each other could be dangerous for both of them.

"Your mother is dead now," he finally spoke up softly. "Perhaps her spirit lives on, in you. And perhaps, as you suggested yourself, Wild Horse lives in me. Would that not mean that the two spirits who could not be together in life should now finally be together, through us? Could that be the meaning of your dream, and my vision? Perhaps if we came together ourselves, the vision would be fulfilled. Then when our hands touch in the dream, neither of us would disappear."

Evelyn could hardly breathe. *If we came together ourselves.* What did he mean? *Physically?* She was afraid to ask. It was impossible to consider what she feared he was considering. She looked away, rising and picking up her bowl. "If you are finished, I would like to clean up. It will be dark soon, and I would like to take a bath. Will you please go on outside? There is a shed between here and the school where you can put up your horse. You'll find some oats in there for him to eat. There is also an extra stall that is clean. You can sleep there if you wish."

She set her bowl on a counter near her pan for washing dishes and waited for his reply, then gasped when his strong arms came around to brace themselves against the counter on either side of her, caging her there. She froze in place, not out of fear, but because she knew if she turned around she would fall into his arms. He bent near her, speaking close to her ear. "You feel as I do, Evy. You should not fight it." He put one hand gently against her belly, and she felt faint at the touch. "Keep your door bolted tonight."

With that he left, as silently as he had walked up behind her. All she heard was the screen door closing. Evelyn turned and stared at it, fully understanding the meaning of his words. If he tried the door later in the night and found it unlocked, it would mean she was inviting him to come inside. All common sense told her she could not let that happen. She hurried over and closed the inner door, hesitating a moment with her hand on the bolt before sliding it into the ring that held it fast.

The morning awoke gray and still. Evelyn quickly dressed and heated the cook stove to boil water for tea. She set a black fry pan on another burner, deciding Black Hawk would probably want to leave today. He should eat something heartier before the long ride back to his camp. Part of her hated the thought of his leaving, but another part of her was relieved he would be gone. That meant she did not have to wrestle with the nearly painful desires the man stirred deep inside her, or with her own conscience over what was right and wrong.

You feel as I do, Evy. You should not fight it. Yes, she *should* fight it! It could lead nowhere, except to a terribly guilty conscience, losing every friend she had, and getting kicked off the reservation. Such a thing as freely acting on one's desires came as easily to a man like Black Hawk as breathing, but although she often went against common practices in many other matters, giving herself to a man was something else. She had not slept well at all. She had lain awake wondering what it was like to be with a man that way, especially a man like Black Hawk. Part of her longed to be a full woman, but in spite of her liberal thinking, she could not abide the thought of sharing her body with anyone but a Christian man to whom she was legally married.

She glanced at the bolted front door. Had she really heard someone trying to open it last night? Of course she had. Black Hawk had come for her. It was not a dream. How had he felt when he found the door bolted? Angry? Disappointed? Humored? "He must go home today," she muttered. She marched into the bedroom to check on Little Fox, alarmed to discover the boy felt hot. He stirred awake at the touch of her hand on his forehead. "Little Fox, how do you feel?"

He blinked and sat up a little. "My head hurts a little, and I am very warm."

Evelyn frowned. "I will fix you and your father something to eat, but I don't think you're ready to leave yet. You're having a little setback, but don't worry about it. It happens sometimes. You stay in bed another day." *Now what do I do?* she wondered. She had counted on Black Hawk leaving today.

She reached under the bed to remove the chamber pot that was kept there, a rather fancy, lead-glazed earthenware pot that her mother had once kept in her bedroom. She carried it to the door, setting it down a moment to unbolt and open the door, then went outside to the privy out back, which she used herself before emptying the pot. She carried the pot to a nearby well shared with the church and school, raised a bucket from the well, and poured water from the bucket into the pot to rinse it. She brought it back to the cabin, setting it outside and leaving off the lid so that it could dry out in the sun, then walked back to the well to get a full bucket of water for washing and cooking. She poured some into a basin back at the cabin and washed her hands, then carried the bucket into the bedroom to pour some into the wash basin she had left beside the bed.

"There is a clean cloth beside the pan here," she told Little

Fox. "Wet it and wash your face and neck and arms. It will cool you down."

The boy nodded. "I am sorry. My father and I should leave. I make a lot of work for you."

Evelyn set down the bucket. "I don't mind, Little Fox. I just want you to get completely well. You're a good and uncomplaining boy. I am going to fry some pork this morning and make you a nice breakfast, along with some hot tea. I'll . . ." She hesitated when the boy looked past her.

"Ate!"

Evelyn turned to see Black Hawk standing in the bedroom doorway. Again she was astonished at how quiet he could be for such a big man. She felt a tingle at the sight of him standing there in buckskins. Today he wore the beautiful turquoise stone outside his shirt, and his hair was brushed out long and untied. She caught the curiosity in his eyes . . . and yes, humor. It irritated her. He had tried the door and probably laughed to himself when he found it locked, thinking what a frightened little mouse she was after all—so courageous in other ways, such a coward when it came to her own heart.

"I am afraid your son has taken a little turn for the worse," she told him, hoping he would not bring up the subject of the locked door. "You will both have to stay another day or two."

Quickly, Black Hawk was at his son's side, gently touching his face. "What is this? You have fever again!" He looked at Evelyn in alarm.

"Don't get upset, Black Hawk. It's just temporary. I've seen it happen before in other patients who survived the worst. I'm sure he'll be fine after a few more days' rest."

Black Hawk straightened, fear in his eyes, and Evelyn realized that probably the only thing that frightened him was the possibility of losing his son.

"I promise, Black Hawk, he'll be fine. Come into the other

room and have something to eat. You still don't have all your own strength back."

I was strong enough last night to come to your door, he thought. *I was strong enough to make love to you, if you would have let me.* He leaned down and touched his cheek to Little Fox's. "We will wait another day," he said in the Sioux tongue, "longer, if we must. Perhaps I should have Night Hunter come and pray over you."

"No, *Ate,*" the boy replied. "Evy takes good care of me."

Evelyn was surprised that the boy, too, had begun using her shortened name casually, as though they were close friends. Black Hawk looked up at her, his gaze moving over her appreciatively. Now she wondered if she had tried too hard to look prettier this morning than she should have. Would he get the wrong idea? She wore a clean dress, soft green in color, with white eyelet lace bordering the short sleeves and the slightly scooped neckline. She had bathed and washed her hair last night, and today she wore it loose, with a green ribbon tied through it. She had brushed it to a shine, and had put a little color on her cheeks.

Now she wished she had not done any of it. She felt as though there were two Evelyn Gibbonses, the one who wanted Black Hawk to leave and never touch her, and the one who wanted to be pretty for him, the one who absently wanted to tempt him. "I'll go finish breakfast," she said, quickly leaving the room.

The curtain over the bedroom doorway was open, and Black Hawk watched her move about in the outer room, studied her slender waist, tried to picture how the rest of her looked beneath her full-skirted dress and the many layers of slips white women wore under those dresses. He liked the fullness of her breasts, the way the cut of her dress displayed them. He was stirred by her hair, not just its golden color, but how thick and long and full of lovely waves it was, not stick-straight like Indian women's hair. He should not be admiring her full lips, her blue eyes, the milky whiteness of the skin at her neck and shoulders, her slender hands. He should not love a white woman, nor should he have come and tried to open her door last night . . . but he had done just that, feeling a deep disappointment that it was bolted. He had planned on leaving today. Now he would have to suffer through another night, maybe two, before he could get away from her and not have to set eyes on the beautiful Evelyn Gibbons, the princess who reached out to him in his vision.

He walked into the next room, his appetite revived by the smell of frying meat. He wondered if perhaps he could always live this way, as long as it was with this woman. It was the only way he could have her. How could he ask her to come to his camp and live like an Indian woman? She had a mission, to help his people, and he must not stop her from doing that. He felt torn between his own needs and desires and what he knew was best for her and for his people.

"Do you know the man named Seth Bridges?" he asked her. He noticed she jumped slightly, knew his presence made her nervous and jumpy. He suspected it was not because she feared him, but because she was herself torn. Had she considered leaving the door unbolted last night? Had she heard him come and try to open it?

Evelyn set the frying pan away from the direct heat, surprised at Black Hawk's question. "Yes, I know who he is. I think he is a reprehensible, filthy, lazy, irresponsible man who ought to be shot for the way he treats his adopted daughters!"

Black Hawk grinned. "You have told him this?"

"In so many words."

Black Hawk wanted to laugh. Part of what he loved about this woman was her courage. He could just imagine her standing up to a threatening Seth Bridges and giving him a piece of her mind. Still, his hatred for Seth overshadowed the humor of the moment. "As I told you when I brought Little Fox to you, I know that Seth Bridges helps bring whiskey onto the reservation. I have caught him at it before. If I tell the agency this, they will not believe me. If I tell the Army, they will arrest me and accuse me of attacking white men. I have attacked and destroyed whiskey wagons before. The traders cannot report it because they would have to admit what they are doing. I in turn can say nothing. If the Army should catch me attacking the smugglers, I am the one who would be punished, not them. That is why I cannot go to them myself, but if you and Reverend Phillips go to James McLaughlin, tell him someone has told you they have seen Seth Bridges hauling whiskey, perhaps they will go to his farm and see if they can find it. You do not have to tell them who said this. Just convince them to go there."

Evelyn stepped closer, feeling excited at the prospect. "I had already thought of that, after what you told me. If Seth Bridges could be caught running whiskey, he could be arrested, and his daughters would have to be taken out of his home. It might be a way to get them away from there. Are you sure of what you saw, Black Hawk?"

"It is as I told you. I have seen him before with whiskey runners. He helps guide them onto the reservation. I cannot prove he traded for whiskey that day at the river. Before I could see what they gave him, Little Fox suddenly fell ill, so I had to leave, but I believe Seth Bridges got a load of whiskey for his corn. He will sell it to men like Big Belly and Broken Knife, who will give him clothing and blankets and food that he can take back to the ship another time and sell to them; but you will never get Big Belly and the others to admit where they get the firewater. Someone has to catch Seth Bridges with the whiskey on his land, in his house or outbuildings."

It infuriated Evelyn to think that men like Seth Bridges could get away with what they did. "I will tell the right people, Black Hawk. I would like nothing more than to see Seth Bridges put in jail. I want to get his daughters away from him, but I am having trouble finding a way to do it. I know there are terrible things going on there, but I can't prove it, and they are too afraid of Seth to talk." She grasped his hands. "Oh, Black Hawk, I hope you're right! This could be my answer!"

Their gazes locked, and he squeezed her hands gently. "Before the day is over, I will go to my grandmother's village. I will stay there for two nights and then come for Little Fox. He trusts in your care, and so do I. It is best that I do not sleep close by again."

She understood what he was telling her, and she quickly let go of his hands, only then realizing *she* had grasped them in the first place. "Yes, well, you do what you feel you must do. I will finish your breakfast." She turned back to the stove, so flustered she could hardly see the meat in the pan. She prepared some food for him, then took a tray in to Little Fox, too embarrassed to sit at the table with Black Hawk. He had not mentioned the bolted door, but she suspected it was right there in his mind all the time . . . just as it was for her. She shared her meal in the bedroom with Little Fox, and before she finished, Black Hawk came inside to tell his son where he was going. He glanced at her then. "Tell McLaughlin about Seth Bridges meeting the riverboat. I also believe that the white soldier, Sergeant Jubal Desmond, is involved. I think he knows sometimes when the traders are coming through, and he looks the other way and lets them. He is like many white men. He loves money more than honor. If someone pays him enough, he will not stop the smugglers. You tell those in charge to watch him. I think Seth Bridges and the sergeant secretly work together."

Evelyn did not doubt the possibility, especially knowing that Seth was allowing the sergeant to see Lucille.

Black Hawk walked over and again leaned down to touch Little Hawk's cheek. "I will be back in two days for my son," he told her.

Without another word the man left. Evelyn heard his horse trot away, and part of her wanted to run after him and beg him to stay. She helped Little Fox finish eating, then tucked him in and told him to try to sleep. "I have to go and talk to Reverend Phillips."

"You will tell him about that white man named Seth?" he asked.

"Yes, I will tell him."

"Father hates the white men who bring the firewater to our people. He says it makes them lazy and useless. It takes away their pride."

"Your father is a very wise man, Little Fox." Evelyn picked up the tray. "You rest now." She carried the tray to the washbasin but decided not to clean up the breakfast pans and dishes just now. The news about Seth Bridges was too important, especially if Jubal Desmond could also be implicated! If the sergeant was arrested or discharged, he couldn't bother poor Lucille Bridges any longer. It infuriated her to think that any army man could be involved in the whiskey running. Once Desmond and Bridges were caught, she could tell Lieutenant Teller and Colonel Gere who had found them out. This only proved that Black Hawk was not the untrustworthy renegade they regarded him as being. He was doing a job the *Army* should have been doing!

She hurried out to find John Phillips. All they needed to do was convince James McLaughlin to have Seth Bridges's farm raided. If they found whiskey, they could frighten the man into telling them who helped him. Bridges was living free on government land. He could be threatened with losing everything he owned if he didn't tell the truth!

Evelyn was so determined in her mission that she did not even notice that she was being watched from a distance. Black Hawk patted his horse's neck as he watched her walk briskly toward the church. He knew no one would listen to him, but they would listen to Miss Evelyn Gibbons, because she would *make* them listen!

He smiled. *You are a brave woman, Evy,* he thought, *brave and beautiful; but you are not brave enough to leave your door unbolted, or to welcome the man you love into your arms.*

He turned his horse and rode off. He would try again . . . another night, when she was not expecting him.

Nineteen

Seth heard several horses ride up to the house, and with energy unusual for the man, he jumped up from his sagging chair and hurried to a window to see who had come in such numbers. He peered through lace curtains so dirty and sun-damaged that the one he grabbed hold of tore in his hand, but he paid little attention. Outside were six army men, one of them Lieutenant Teller. Jubal Desmond was with him.

"Jesus!" he muttered, "what the hell do they want?"

He knew that Desmond had probably been given orders and had to follow them. He heard Teller order his men to dismount, then the words, "Search the place thoroughly, but put things back and don't break anything, men. This is probably just a hoax or a misunderstanding."

"Search the place?" Seth muttered. The whiskey! He ran to the kitchen, on the way yelling for Lucille, who was already in the room. She looked up at him from her task peeling potatoes.

"What's wrong?"

"Soldiers!" He held a fist in front of her face. "If you say one word about me dealin' with the sergeant on whiskey, or about me sellin' you to him, you won't see the light of day for a long time to come! You understand me, girl? Whatever they ask you, you don't know *nothin'*! You go find your sister and warn her, too!" He hurried over to a cupboard where he kept his whiskey—but only two bottles at a time. He grabbed them both.

"Lift up that loose floorboard before you go find Katy!" he ordered Lucille.

Already soldiers were pounding at the front door. Seth quickly hid the whiskey under the floorboard, then stood up and stomped on it to push it more tightly back in place. Lucille turned to go and find Katy, and Seth grabbed her arm so tightly that it hurt.

"You remember what I told you!" he warned.

Lucille glared back at him, thinking for a moment how easily she could get Seth Bridges in trouble. "I'll remember," she said calmly.

"Get out to the barn and make sure I didn't leave a feed sack open with a whiskey bottle showin'!"

Seth let go of her, and Lucille went out the back door, reminding herself that even if she told on Seth, he still might not even be arrested; and if he *was* arrested, it might only be for a little while. After all, he was a white man, and the crime was against the Indians. Who was going to punish him severely for that? He would get out of jail and he would most certainly come for her, wherever she was, or maybe he would come after Katy. He would have every legal right to take them back, and his fury would know no bounds.

She ran to the barn, where Katy was cleaning out a stall. She glanced at the feed bags. Katy didn't even know these feed bags—and more that were stored in the corn crib—contained bottles of whiskey. She only knew about the whiskey kept in the house. One feed bag was open, so Lucille quickly tied it shut again. "Come up to the house, Katy."

The girl looked up from her raking. "Why? Seth told me I had to—"

"There are soldiers here. I'm not sure what they want, but Seth says to keep quiet, no matter what they ask you. We'd better do like he says."

Katy set the rake aside. "Maybe now he'll get in bad trouble for selling you to Sergeant Desmond and for having whiskey in the house."

"You keep quiet about both those things. Come on." Lucille took her sister's arm and led her toward the house, an idea forming as she walked . . . one that could keep Seth Bridges out of her bed at night. He was always holding Katy over her head, using her sister to threaten her. Now she knew something with which she could use to threaten Seth Bridges. Did she dare try it and risk his wrath? He didn't dare punish her by raping Katy, because he knew that if he did that, he would no longer have a hold on her. She would have no reason left to cooperate with him.

She smiled softly as she herded Katy toward the house. "Remember what I said," she told her.

Inside the house, Seth had gone to the front door, greeting the lieutenant and his men with a smile. "Well, Lieutenant Teller! What brings you here? I know I owe Colonel Gere a load of corn, but with the cholera and all, I've been afraid to let the girls go out and pick and afraid to bring them to the fort. If I don't get in the rest of the corn soon—"

"This isn't about corn, Mr. Bridges, and the cholera scare seems to be over. There have been no new cases for nearly a week now."

"Well, even so, I ain't sure I ought to let you men inside the house. What's the problem?"

Teller glanced past the man at the mess inside what looked to be the parlor. He moved his gaze to Bridges again, noticing the man needed a shave. His uncombed gray hair was sticking out in several places, and his overalls were soiled, as was the faded shirt he wore under them. He could smell alcohol on the man's breath. "Mr. Bridges, we have reason to believe you are harboring whiskey on your premises, perhaps as much as a wagonload of it, whiskey that you are selling to the Indians. We are here to search your house and outbuildings."

Seth's smile faded. He glanced only briefly at Desmond, then back to Teller. "Who the hell told you a lie like that?"

"I am not supposed to reveal the source. Please let us pass peacefully. Don't make us use force."

Seth shrugged and stepped aside. "I don't know who told you I'm a whiskey runner, but they're a goddamn liar! You won't find nothin' here."

The soldiers came inside, and Teller began directing them to begin the search. Desmond came through last, and he quickly shoved a note into Seth's hand when the others were not looking. Seth eyed the rest of them, realizing they were involved in their task, then read the note. *Keep your mouth shut, and remember, we hardly know each other. I've taken your daughter out a couple of times, that's all. We'll talk later.* Seth shoved the note into his pocket.

"Mr. Bridges!" Teller shouted in typical commander voice. "Come here, please!"

A scowling Seth walked into the parlor. Teller was standing beside his favorite, sagging chair, holding a half full bottle of whiskey in his hand. "Where did you get this?"

Seth rubbed at his lips. In his rush, he had forgotten about the one bottle he'd been drinking from. "Well, sir, I do manage to get a bottle or two once in awhile, just for my own purposes. I know it's against reservation rules, but hell, it's just one bottle, and I don't never associate with the damn Indians. I sure as hell don't sell them whiskey. If I did, I'd have to have a lot more than one little bottle now, wouldn't I?"

"And where did you get this?"

Seth ran a hand through his hair. "Hell, Lieutenant, can't one white man on this whole damn reservation have himself a private little bottle of whiskey without havin' to say where it come from? I ain't no damn dealer. Besides, I don't ask names. When I run into a peddler, I just buy me a bottle and leave."

Lucille and Katy peeked around the corner. The lieutenant

caught sight of them. Both girls looked tired and unwashed. Like Evelyn Gibbons and Janine and Reverend Phillips and the rest of them, he would enjoy catching Seth Bridges doing something illegal so that he could have the man arrested and get his daughters out of the house. "Keep up the search, men!" he ordered. "Hit every room!"

Teller walked closer to Seth, posing threateningly. "Mr. Bridges, things will go easier on you if you just tell us the truth! Our source says you met a riverboat a week ago, took them a load of corn. You just told me you haven't been picking your corn or delivering it anywhere because of the cholera epidemic. Why did you lie to me, Mr. Bridges, and what did you get in return for that corn?"

Seth swallowed, scrambling to think. Who had seen him? Who would report him? Desmond didn't even know about his last deal, didn't know his bags of feed were stuffed with whiskey bottles. Besides, Desmond would never tell on him. He could get in too much trouble himself. If it was some other Army man, he would have stopped him right away and searched his wagon. He scratched his head in wonder and sighed, putting on a look of resignation and apology.

"Look, Lieutenant Teller, I lied because I figured Colonel Gere would be angry if he knew I took some corn to that riverboat, what with everybody supposed to be under quarantine and all. I needed the money, and I needed feed for my animals. That's all I got for the corn. Some sacks of feed, a little money. Hell, you know a man can't just let his corn rot in the fields. When there's some ready to be picked, it's got to be picked, so me and the girls here, we picked a wagonload and I took it to the river to see if I could sell it. Now I'll admit that while I was there, I talked the riverboat captain into sellin' me a bottle of whiskey. He didn't want to do it, on account of I live on an Indian reservation, but he finally let me have one bottle." He put on a show of indignation. "Just one bottle!" he said, shaking his finger.

"You gonna arrest me for that? I've got aches and pains, Lieu-tenant, and the whiskey helps ease them. They're the reason I have the girls do so much of my work for me. I don't like makin' them work so hard, but this old body just don't cooperate so much anymore. The whiskey makes me feel better. You gonna arrest a man for havin' one bottle of whiskey around for me-dicinal purposes?"

Teller glared at him, hating the man for having such a ready answer. Unless he could find more whiskey, there was nothing he could do but believe the old bastard and let him go. He glanced at Lucille and Katy. "That true, girls? Is that the only bottle of whiskey around here? You know anything about Seth here dealing in whiskey?"

"No," Katy answered honestly. "He gets whiskey sometimes, but I never saw him sell any to Indians. It's just for him."

Lucille gave her a nudge, afraid in her innocent honesty she would say too much. She glanced at Seth, caught the warning in his ugly eyes. "We've never seen more than one or two bottles of whiskey around at a time. Seth just drinks it for aches and pains, sir." She confirmed Seth's story to the lieutenant.

Teller sighed, glancing from Lucille to Seth. He walked past them then and shouted up the stairs. "Anything up there?"

"No, sir," someone yelled down to him.

"Check the mattresses! Make sure they haven't been slit open to hide something!"

Lucille and Seth glared at each other. Lucille's plan becoming more concrete as she saw the worry in Seth's eyes that he would be found out. The search went on for several more minutes. It included cupboards and closets, and produced nothing. Teller ordered a couple of his men to check the barn and corn crib, then shouted for Sergeant Desmond to come over to where he stood. Desmond quickly obeyed, giving Seth a warning look. "Yes, sir," he answered.

Teller looked from Seth to the sergeant. "Our source, Sergeant

Desmond, implied that you have also been involved in whiskey running, in the form of allowing whiskey traders to pass through certain checkpoints. We are also told it is possible you are in collaboration with Mr. Bridges here in dealing with whiskey smugglers."

Desmond reddened with guilt, but he pretended his color rose from being offended. "That's an out-and-out lie! Who is telling you these things, Sir! I have a right to know!"

"How well do you know Mr. Bridges, Sergeant?"

Desmond's hands moved into fists. "Only as well as everybody else knows him, sir. You know he sells corn at the fort, sometimes plays poker with some of the men. You also know that I have seen his daughter a couple of times. You yourself saw me with Lucille at the dance, and I took her to the circus. Am I to be punished for being attracted to the man's daughter? If that is so, sir, then every man at the fort should be punished! Lucille is a very lovely young woman."

Teller glanced at Lucille. He did not miss the contempt in her eyes as she stared at Desmond. No woman who had just been complimented would look at a man that way. "That true, Lucille? Is Sergeant Desmond just a casual acquaintance? Is there anything serious between you and him, or any problems? Do you know anything about Seth here having other dealings with the sergeant?"

Lucille's confidence in having something on both Seth and Desmond grew stronger. She folded her arms and faced the lieutenant. "I know of nothing going on between my father and the sergeant, Lieutenant. Yes, I did go with Sergeant Desmond to the dance, and to the circus. That's all there is to it. There is no reason for the sergeant to get in trouble over that."

Katy looked up at her sister. She knew Desmond had been visiting, doing bad things to Lucille, but she also knew that if Lucille said they should not tell, then she had better not. She loved Lucille for the sacrifices she made to protect her, but she was not sure how much longer she could go on letting her do it and not sure what she could do to stop it.

The lieutenant scowled in disappointment. "All of you wait right here!" He walked through the kitchen, where two of his men were still rummaging through cupboards and looking inside every cavity and cranny. The lieutenant then went outside and headed for the barn.

Jubal, Seth, and the two girls all glared at one another, each wanting to keep the secret for different reasons. Lucille's reason was foremost pure shame at having anyone know what Jubal Desmond had been doing to her, and secondly because she was afraid of what the consequences would be if she told. Keeping quiet could be an advantage for her, and the thought gave her courage. A smirk came across her face as she faced Seth, and she held her chin a little higher. Neither Jubal nor Seth could say anything at the moment because of the presence of other soldiers.

After several minutes Teller came back inside, sighing as he faced Jubal and Seth. "There is nothing out there but some sacks of feed. I guess I owe you both an apology."

"I told you I didn't have no big stash of liquor," Seth told the man. "You had no right comin' in here and searchin' my personal possessions and scarin' my girls like you did! I ought to—"

"You ought to treat your daughters a little better, Mr. Bridges, and clean this place up! You ought to do a better job of running this farm! I will remind you that you're living on government property! If you want to continue the privilege, you'd better do a little more work around here and show you're taking care of the place; and no more whiskey, not even for personal use! It's forbidden. That's the *law*, Mr. Bridges, and if I had found even one extra bottle, I would have you taken to jail!" He turned and shouted for one of his men to dump out the remaining whiskey in the bottle they had found.

"You can't—"

"Yes, I can, Mr. Bridges! And considering the mess this place is already in, I don't think my men did much damage." He moved his gaze to Desmond. "Sergeant, my apologies, although I do think Lucille here is a bit young for a thirty-two-year-old man. If you don't want to be investigated again, I suggest you stay away from Mr. Bridges and his family, and I think you could be doing a better job of routing out the peddlers." He turned and tipped his hat to the girls. "Good day, ladies." He walked past Seth and out the front door, ordering his men to follow.

After they were all out of the house, Jubal glanced once more at Seth. "We have something to settle!"

"I never said anything! Why in hell would I do that and get myself in trouble!"

Jubal glanced at the girls. "You two been talking to the wrong people?"

"Hell, they ain't that stupid!" Seth put in for them. "They know what I'd do to them if they did somethin' like that. Besides, they've been right here with me since the cholera thing. The lieutenant said somebody *saw* me at the riverboat. The girls wasn't even with me. It had to be somebody else."

Their eyes turned to slivers of hatred when they both thought the same thing at the same time. "Black Hawk," Seth sneered. "Either that, or somehow that damn bitch of a schoolteacher has somethin' to do with this. She'd pull any trick to get her hands on the girls, goddamn troublemaker!"

"I'll see what I can find out. You just make sure Lucille keeps quiet about my coming here. I've got to get out there before they suspect we've both been lying."

Desmond quickly left, and Seth turned to Lucille. "It's damn good they didn't go snoopin' inside them feed bags."

"Why?" Katy asked innocently.

Seth leaned closer, leering at her. "Because that's where the whiskey's hid, you stupid brat!" He poked a finger into one of her developing breasts. "And you'll keep quiet about it, or it won't be Lucille sharin' my bed!"

Katy jerked back, her eyes tearing from shame.

"You leave her alone," Lucille instructed the man, her voice low and cold.

Seth straightened, eyeing her carefully. "You did good," he told her, deciding it might be best to appease her for the moment. "You and your sister both. I'd have beat the hell out of you both if you had said anything. You just remember, if you talk and I'm arrested or the sergeant gets in trouble, I'll by God come back, and I'll make you both pay!" He marched into the parlor to watch out the window and make sure all the soldiers left before he hollered for Lucille to get him one of the bottles of whiskey hidden under the kitchen floorboard.

Lucille obeyed, grinning to herself as she did so. "We'll see who pays," she muttered.

Evelyn paced in front of her cabin. It was nearly dark, and Reverend Phillips had just returned from the agency with word about the raid on Seth Bridges's farm. She had insisted on talking outside so that Little Fox could not hear their conversation. What the reverend had told her left her angry and frustrated.

"Black Hawk would not lie," she told Phillips. She stopped and faced the man. "He would not *lie!*" she repeated.

"He did not actually *see* any whiskey loaded into the wagon, Miss Gibbons. He only guessed."

"Not that day, but he *has* seen Seth Bridges dealing with whiskey traders before this, and maybe Sergeant Desmond also! He knew no one would believe him directly. That's why he asked me to tell you and have you tell the colonel without revealing your source."

"And now I feel like a fool!" Phillips answered angrily. "The colonel pressed me to tell him who told us this in the first place. I felt it was my responsibility to do so."

Evelyn's eyes widened. "You *told* him it was Black Hawk?"

"I did. He was very upset to know that. The whole army knows Black Hawk hates Sergeant Desmond. The colonel said that if he had known, he would never have ordered the search of Seth Bridges's house."

"Why would Black Hawk have implicated Bridges in addition to the sergeant? There is no history between Black Hawk and Bridges. He had no personal reason for doing that."

The reverend ran a hand through his hair in exasperation. "I don't know the reason for that. I only know that the colonel told me that a few months ago Desmond and his men found a camp along the reservation's border where there were the remains of a destroyed wagon and hundreds of smashed whiskey bottles. Desmond claims Black Hawk all but admitted to him later that he had attacked a camp of whiskey peddlers. Maybe Seth Bridges was with them. The point is, routing out whiskey peddlers is a job for the soldiers, not the Indians. If Black Hawk wants a job like that, let him join the Indian police. To just do it on his own will only get him in trouble. If a man gets killed, he'll be accused of murder and hanged, no matter how right he was to do what he did. You had better warn him when he comes back for Little Fox."

Evelyn felt the frustration of knowing she was right and being unable to do anything about it. "Maybe when Sergeant Desmond found that destroyed whiskey wagon, he was more upset that his plans to let it through had been foiled than with the fact that an Indian had done what *he* was supposed to be doing. I still think the sergeant is involved in allowing whiskey onto the reservation, just as Black Hawk says he is."

Phillips sighed, putting his hands on his hips. "We could go on like this the rest of the night, and it wouldn't solve anything. The point is, they never found any proof of any wrongdoing.

You have got to stick to your teaching, Miss Gibbons, and stay out of Army and agency affairs. You also have to stop interfering with Seth Bridges. The man can't be trusted." He stepped closer. "Most of all, you have to stop being involved with Black Hawk. When he comes for Little Fox, let him take the boy and go. You're putting yourself in a bad situation, linking yourself with a renegade. I worry it will cost you your job, maybe more than that. It could cost you your reputation, Miss Gibbons, this infatuation with civilizing a renegade Indian who probably has only one thing in mind when he is around you. Someday—"

"Stop it!" Evelyn's eyes teared. "I have done nothing wrong. I am trying to do what's *right,* what I came here for! Aren't we all here to help the Sioux? To guide them toward learning new ways so that they can assimilate into white society? I know of only one way to do that, and if the agency and the Mission Services don't like my methods and I lose their support, then I will find another way to go on! As far as Black Hawk, he is not an ignorant, uncivilized renegade. He speaks very good English and is quite intelligent, and, I might add, very talented. I have seen some of the things he has painted, and they are exquisite enough to sell. If he has been raiding whiskey smugglers, it is because he knows what liquor does to his people and he wants to keep it off the reservation. He has every right to do that! If he seems the renegade, it is because he is still hurting from Wounded Knee. He saw his wife shot in the head and his baby son stabbed through the heart! How is he *supposed* to feel toward the Army after a thing like that? I don't have one ounce of fear of the man, Reverend, and I don't care one whit for what others think of my trying to help the Sioux through Black Hawk, a man they honor and whose judgment they trust. I will continue seeing him and teaching him and Little Fox as long as they will allow it!"

Phillips studied the beautiful woman standing before him intently, wishing she would carry the same look in her eyes for him that she did for Black Hawk. "You love him, don't you?"

Evelyn blushed deeply, turning away. "I don't know." She leaned her head back and sighed deeply. "I might as well tell you that part of the reason I came out here . . . part of the reason I was determined to get to know Black Hawk better, was because of recurring dreams I had back in Wisconsin." She explained her dreams to him in the same detailed fashion she had explained them to the others. "The first time I saw Black Hawk . . ." She folded her arms across her chest and stared at a wild rosebush. "Somehow I knew he was the man in the dream. I think I am supposed to stay here, that there is something unfinished, Reverend. I don't know what it is. I only know that Black Hawk told me he had the same dream, of riding toward a white woman, reaching out to her. It is the dreams that have brought us together, and we both need to know why. You know how important dreams and visions are to the Sioux. For two people who had never met to have the same dream . . . it's ironic and chilling. It has drawn us together in a special way."

Phillips grunted in disgust. "Dreams! You had better face *reality,* Miss Gibbons. Maybe Black Hawk never even had such a dream. Maybe he's just saying that to win you over. Maybe he just wants a white woman in his bed!"

Evelyn turned to face him in wide-eyed surprise that he was capable of such a remark. "And maybe you are angry because I am not in *your* bed!"

Phillips stiffened as though someone had just hit him. His face turned a deep red. "Maybe I am."

Evelyn closed her eyes. "You threw away your chance at a very sweet, devoted love when you would not listen to me about Anita." She opened her eyes and held his gaze boldly. "You are a fine man, Reverend Phillips, and I know that when you speak to me in anger and insults, it is only because you are concerned. I will forget what you said a moment ago, and I hope that if I did admit I was in love with Black Hawk and wanted to spend my life with him, you would accept that and understand that love knows no boundaries. You will yourself make a wonderful husband for someone someday, except that you will have to learn to be more tolerant and compassionate, which you should have been with Anita!" She saw the hurt in his eyes, and she sighed, angry with herself for arguing. "I admire and respect you in many ways, but if you want a wife, Reverend, you will have to look elsewhere. Please don't hold that against me or let it destroy our friendship. Out here we need each other."

Phillips rubbed at the back of his neck. "My God," he muttered. "I am sorry for what I said. I am also sorry that we can't . . ." He looked toward the church. "Once Janine marries the lieutenant, she will leave when he's transferred to Kansas. I guess that's been on my mind. I am going to be very lonely."

"Reverend, with Greggory Evans dead and his wife . . . gone, I am sure Mission Services will be sending someone else soon. They may also send someone to replace Janine. Things will work out."

He smiled rather sadly. "I truly am sorry. As far as this thing about the whiskey peddlers, I did my best. They simply found no proof."

She nodded. "Our best is all any of us can do, Reverend."

The man glanced at her cabin. "When is he coming for Little Fox?"

"I don't know. Black Hawk is very unpredictable. He just shows up unannounced. It's been two days since he left, so I suppose it could be any time."

He turned back to her, his eyes moving over her. "Be careful. And keep your door bolted."

Evelyn almost smiled at the words, remembering Black Hawk telling her that same thing. "Yes, Reverend."

The man turned and left, and with a heavy heart at knowing things had not turned out as she had hoped, Evelyn walked into her cabin, deciding that since there was nothing she could do for now about Seth Bridges or the whiskey smuggling, she must begin thinking about how she was going to win back the trust of the elder Sioux and encourage them to begin sending their children back to school now that the epidemic seemed to be waning. She would not have Anita's help this time. Keeping Little Fox here and getting Many Birds to also come to school would be more important than ever in getting others to come.

Winter would soon arrive. She could not keep going out to Black Hawk to teach his son. Could she convince him to stay closer to the school, or perhaps leave Little Fox with her for the winter? He was all Black Hawk had. It would be very hard for him to leave his son behind. She sighed, going to check on Little Fox, who was studying a reading book she had given him. "Time to go to sleep," she told him. She touched his forehead, glad to feel it was still cool. "I think you're going to get completely well very quickly now."

The boy smiled. "My father will come soon."

"Yes, he will." Would the boy even *want* to stay here with her? He was so devoted to his father. She took away the book and tucked him in, then left to sit down wearily on the smaller cot in the main room. The news about the failed raid at Seth's farm had left her feeling weary and discouraged. She got up again and undressed and washed, then put on a soft cotton nightgown. She did not have the energy tonight to go and draw water and carry it in and then heat it to wash the dishes from supper. She would not even feel like washing them if the water were already prepared. She decided to leave them for morning.

She walked back to the cot on bare feet and sank into it, pulling a light blanket over herself, grateful for how the weather had finally cooled. When she closed her eyes, for a few minutes her mind raced with the reverend's words, some of them hurtful. A little part of her wanted to give up and go home to Wisconsin, but her stubborn side would not let her.

After a few minutes weariness overcame her confused thoughts, and she was asleep, never realizing she had forgotten to bolt the door.

Twenty

The dream returned, as vivid as the first night it had visited her. This time Evelyn could hear drumming and singing somewhere in the distance. As the vision of the Indian man on a spotted horse moved toward her, he and the horse were bright and easy to see, but all around them was solid blackness. The mount appeared to be coming at a hard gallop, mane flying, chest muscles moving in beautiful rhythm with each thundering step, nostrils flared. The handsome man who rode him leaned into the wind, his own dark eyes on fire. So fast they came, yet it was taking them so long to reach her.

The drumming and singing became louder, and she felt her heart beating faster. Closer they came, the man reaching out for her. She grasped his hand, and in the dream Evelyn was so startled that she literally gasped in her sleep and sat straight up, putting a hand to her chest. Her heart truly was pounding, and she felt too warm.

Still foggy from just awakening, she did not even think before removing her gown. She scrambled to get it off, breathing deeply, reminding herself she had just been dreaming. She used the gown to fan herself for a moment, wondering how she could be so hot when outside the night was cool. She put her legs over the edge of the cot, shaking her hair back and then setting aside the gown so she could run her fingers through her hair to get it entirely away from her face. It was only then that she realized someone was standing at the head of the cot, near the doorway to the bedroom where Little Fox slept. The one lantern she had left lit was nearly ready to go out, but it shed just enough light that she caught the intruder's movement.

She grabbed up her nightgown and leapt off the cot with a startled gasp, clutching the garment to her bosom. She ran to the door, but before she could reach it, a powerful arm came around her. Quickly, she was pinned against a man's hard body. Another hand came over her mouth before she could scream.

"It is I, Black Hawk," he said softly near her ear.

She stiffened, mortified yet strangely stirred by the feel of him touching her naked body.

"Promise you will not scream," he said softly.

She nodded, and he slowly took his hand away from her mouth, but remained close behind her.

"What are you doing here in the night like this!" she said in a whispered squeak, shivering with a strange mixture of terror and desire. "Get out!"

He moved both arms around her, massaging her belly with one strong though gentle hand, while he continued to hold her own arms fast with his other arm pressed across her naked breasts. "The door was not locked," he said, nuzzling at her neck.

Why couldn't she scream? Why didn't she try harder to get away? All she felt was a wonderful warmth, a glorious feeling of being treasured and protected. Before she could try to reason with her feelings, the hand he had pressed to her belly moved down to a place no man had ever touched or seen. His fingers crept into the cavity between her legs, exploring, toying, awakening a part of her that had slept until now. "Please don't do this, Black Hawk," she groaned. "I only forgot . . . I didn't mean . . ."

"You had the dream again." It was a statement rather than a question.

"Black Hawk—"

"I had the same dream." He spoke in a low whisper. "I knew it was a sign that the time is right."

She wondered if her chest would explode from the literal ache there, as her heart beat wildly from fear and excitement. "Right for what?"

He moved his hand from private places and used it to tear the gown from her tightly closed fists while he continued to keep her arms pinned in a grip so strong there was nothing she could do to get out of it. "I think you know."

He rubbed himself against her bare bottom, and it was only then she realized he was also naked. His shaft was hard and hot pressing against her back.

"No, Black Hawk!" she whimpered. "Don't do this. I've never—"

"Who else would you want to be your first man? Your *only* man?" He licked at her cheek, her neck, moved his other hand back down to secret places. "You know it is right, Evy. You knew this was meant to be before you even came to the reservation."

She should fight him, scream, but the wild, passionate woman buried deep inside secretly wanted this man, had wondered what it would be like to be his woman.

"I have made up a bed on the floor and bolted the door."

Evelyn knew she should be angry that he had actually been here for several minutes, maybe longer! He had undressed, made up the bed, apparently had watched her sleep without ever making a sound that brought her awake. He had come here with the express purpose of uniting with her, taking it for granted that it would happen. How dare he! She should turn and slap him, kick him, scream bloody murder and accuse him of a most heinous crime . . . shouldn't she?

Was she still partially in a dream? Why did she only rest her head against his shoulder when he picked her up in powerful arms? Why did she let him lay her down on the several blankets he had laid out on the floor? Where had he gotten them? From her trunk while she slept? Why did she lie so limp and unprotesting when he moved on top of her, his shining black hair shrouding her face?

He smelled so good when he leaned down to touch his cheek to her own. The lantern shed just enough light that she could see his eyes, eyes that blazed with desire. He licked at her lips, and she surprised herself when she opened her mouth and leaned up to kiss him almost savagely. She felt him hesitate a little, realized perhaps he had never actually kissed. Rubbing cheeks was the Indian's usual way of showing affection, but quickly he caught on, and in the next moment he groaned, returning her kiss with great fervor.

What had happened to her good sense? Her honor? Her ability to resist the wrong and do what was right? Perhaps it was just that she was not fully awake. Perhaps all of this was just an extension of her dream. She would wake up soon and realize she had not really done these things, wouldn't she? His strong hands moved up the sides of her body, to her breasts, massaging them gently. His mouth left her own, trailed over her throat, down to her breasts, breasts he had seen the day she'd taken the arrow, the day he saved her life when he removed it and burned out the wound.

What would he think of the puffy white scar beneath her left breast? Her answer came when he kissed it lovingly, then pushed the breast upward, lightly flicking his tongue against the nipple until she whimpered his name, aching for him to taste both breasts. Utter ecstasy ripped through her like lightning when he took time with each nipple, kissing, licking, lightly pulling one, then the other, into his soft, warm lips, then tasting them with more vigor, groaning as he savored each one as though hungry for her.

Evelyn Gibbons had never known such intensity of feeling. His lips trailed on down, over her flat belly, then to the soft curves of her thighs, licking around places she never dreamed she would let any man explore this way. She was astounded at her own boldness, and the magical ways he had with her body.

He briefly tasted the magic spot he had learned brought a woman to utter surrender, and he knew now that it was the same for a white woman. This woman had never been touched so intimately by any man, yet she trembled now with desire, and she made no effort to stop him. He wished the lamp was brighter so that he could better see her milky skin, the blond hairs that hid this special place that would belong only to him now. He wanted to see how pink it was, wanted to see all of her better, her full, firm breasts, her ripe lips, her blue eyes, glazed with desire only for him.

Evelyn wondered where she would find her next breath. Whatever he was doing to her, she felt utterly helpless. Her whole body was on fire. His touch was magic, and instead of protests, all that came out of her lips were gasps of ecstasy. She drew in her breath and slowly let it out in a long, whimpering sigh. When a wonderful pulsating feeling engulfed her, rippling through her insides and making her feel wild and free and wanton, she grasped his hair, gasping his name, and he moved back up over her body with licks and kisses.

Strangely, she was not afraid of what she knew must come next. She only knew that whatever this man had done to her, he had made her want to feel him inside her. He whispered sweet words in the Sioux tongue, moving between her legs and then sitting up slightly, spreading his own knees to push her legs apart. By the dim light of the lamp she could see that part of man that, on grown men, had been a mystery to her . . . until now. He was swollen like a stallion, and, momentarily, desire was overcome by fear of the unknown. Before she could act on that fear, he pushed himself into her in one quick thrust.

Evelyn thought at first she might faint from the pain. He held himself there for a moment, their eyes locked, determination in his eyes, startled pain in her own. He was up on his knees now, grasping her thighs, looking down at her like the conquering warrior. "It will not hurt after this," he promised.

Evelyn was nearly in shock from the tearing, burning sensation between her legs. She wanted to cry, but she refused.

"Relax, my sweet one," he told her as he began gently moving in rhythmic thrusts. *"Hechetu alo."*

It is good, he had said. Evelyn was beyond reasoning whether or not he was right. She watched his dark eyes, trusted that he was not lying. Did his words that it "would not hurt after this" mean they would do this again? She did not want to think about the consequences of this act, their different worlds, the fact that they surely could never live as a husband and wife. She only wanted this moment.

Black Hawk threw back his head and groaned, holding himself deep inside her then as he shuddered with his own release. She felt his life flowing into her, and after a moment of stillness, he leaned close, whispering in her ear. "We will do it again," he told her. "Black Hawk loves you, Evy. You are his woman now. You belong only to him."

From then on the night moved in a magical, mystic swirl of lovemaking, exotic touches, exploration, and awakenings. Evelyn felt hypnotized by Black Hawk's dark eyes, helpless under his touch. He brought out a wantonness she never realized dwelled in her soul. She could not imagine allowing Steven to do to her what Black Hawk was now doing, nor would she want it to be any other man, no matter how socially wrong some might think this was. She loved this man as much as any woman could love, and he loved her in return. Yes, she did belong to him, heart, soul, spirit, body. There was no going back, and she must not be fearful of the future. Surely God meant for this to be, or He would not have led her here so full of hopes and plans. He would not have brought the dreams that compelled her to come here.

This was the answer, lying here in Black Hawk's arms, feeling his power, taking pleasure in feeling him inside her and giving him pleasure in return. There was nothing reserved or hesitant about his lovemaking. This came as naturally to him as breathing. In his thinking, a man acted on his feelings without concern for rules or protocol. He did not live by white people's standards, but by a kind of free thinking that taught joy and celebration, sharing love in the fullest sense.

It was deep in the night before they finally fell asleep, naked bodies entwined, needing to touch, wishing the night would never end.

Dawn broke, cool and pleasant. Evelyn stirred awake, lying still and listening to birds singing, taking a moment to try to remember why she was on the floor instead of on her cot. As she came fully awake, the memories startled her into a sitting position. She looked down at herself, realizing she was still naked. The bedding on the floor was in scattered disarray, and the place beside her was empty. "Black Hawk!" she whispered.

She quickly stood up, wrapping a blanket around herself. For that brief moment between sleep and wakefulness, she had thought perhaps it all had been a dream, but her aching body and her burning insides told her otherwise. Her flannel gown still lay near the front door where Black Hawk had ripped it from her hands. All through the night she had been so sure what she was doing was right. Never had she known such a beautiful experience. But this morning . . . why was he gone? Had he just wanted to prove something? Was he laughing at her now, basking in his victory over the educated white woman?

Surely not. He had been so gentle, so sincere. *Black Hawk loves you, Evy. You are his woman now. You belong only to him.* What had she done? What had *he* done to make her so bold and wild and sinful? Did he represent the devil? What on earth were they to do now?

She walked over to peek into the bedroom. Little Fox lay sleeping peacefully. She hoped he had not awakened last night and heard, maybe even seen, what she and his father were doing! What would the boy think of her? She decided to quickly wash before he awoke. Hastily, she brushed through her hair and twisted it into a bun, pinning it tight. Why did she feel that today she must dress more primly and properly than she would usually bother to do? Would others know what she had done just by looking at her? If she wore something very humble and plain, scrubbed her face and put no color on it, kept her hair hidden in the bun, would she look more innocent?

She did just that, picking out a plain gray dress with a touch of white lace at the high neckline and at the ends of the long sleeves. Thank goodness it was cool today. When she washed, she noticed blood on her thighs. She hoped it wouldn't keep flowing and show on her clothing. She pulled on two pairs of drawers, stuffing a clean menstrual cloth inside them to help prevent any staining. She laced on her camisole, pulled on several slips, then the dress. It seemed to take forever to button the long row of buttons up the front. She hurriedly picked up all the blankets from the floor, carrying them into the bedroom and stuffing them under the bed. She would have to wash them as soon as possible, but there was no time to worry about that now. She walked back to the outer room, made up the cot, looked around to be sure everything looked in order. None of Black Hawk's things were there.

Little Fox awoke, and she went through her routine of emptying the chamber pot and then making breakfast. Still no Black Hawk. His horse was not tied at the shed, where he had slept that first time he brought Little Fox to her. Reverend Phillips came to check on her, apologizing for their argument the day before. She felt much too hot as they talked and shared coffee. Did he know? Had he seen Black Hawk come to her cabin last night? Did she look different now?

"Are you ill, Miss Gibbons?" Philips asked. "You look flushed."

"I'm fine." Evelyn turned away to pour herself more coffee, unable to meet the man's eyes.

"Good heavens, I hope you aren't coming down with the cholera!"

"No, really, I'm fine. I'm just tired from all we've been through the last couple of weeks. Once Black Hawk comes for his son and leaves, I think I will take several days to rest before starting up the school again."

"That is a very good idea. I hope he comes today. I just hope he doesn't make trouble when he finds out we couldn't do anything about the sergeant or Seth Bridges."

"I'll make sure he understands that he must not try going after whiskey peddlers himself, and I will assure him we will be doing everything we can to keep an eye on Seth Bridges and Jubal Desmond."

"Well, you can also assure him that the Army will be working harder to keep out the smugglers. Colonel Gere and Agent McLaughlin will see to that."

The reverend finally bade his farewell, and Evelyn was never more glad to see him leave. She breathed a sigh of relief. He apparently did not know about Black Hawk visiting her in the night, nor had he guessed anything by her appearance this morning. *You look flushed.* Yes, flushed with love and this wonderful new awakening to womanhood! How sad that it all had to be spoiled by the realization that a permanent union between herself and Black Hawk was next to impossible. She tried to determine what she should say, how she should behave when Black Hawk returned. Thank goodness he *had* left. What if the reverend had come and found the man here so early in the morning?

Oh, how she wished her mother were still alive. How she needed to talk to someone who would understand what had just happened to her, would understand how a white woman could love an Indian man, someone who accepted her and loved her no matter what she did with her life. She almost felt like crying for the want of the woman, the need to ask her advice. But there was no one to turn to. She had to solve this dilemma on her own.

Her heart rushed faster then when she heard a horse trotting toward the cabin. She hurried to a window and looked out. "Black Hawk!" she whispered.

Evelyn stepped outside. For all her usual confidence, she was amazed at how the man watching her silently now could unravel her. She wanted to hate him for the predicament in which he had put her . . . yet she had done nothing to stop him last night. It was she who had come here in the first place, looking for this man who had haunted her dreams. She wanted to run to him now, embrace him; yet she also wanted to run *away* from him.

"Where did you go?" she finally managed to ask.

He looked toward the church, then back at her. "I slept on the ground, out of sight of the church. I did not think you would want others to wake up and see my horse or come here and find us together."

She nodded. "I appreciate that. We have much to talk about, much to decide, before others are allowed to know we—" She turned and went inside, feeling light-headed at the memory of what she had let this man do to her last night. Was she really the woman who had done those things? Wasn't it someone else?

In a moment Black Hawk was there, moving his arms around her from behind, nuzzling her neck. "We do have much to talk about, my sweet one." He rubbed a hand firmly over her belly, and she drew in her breath, chastising herself for being unable to resist his touch. "You are my woman now, my wife in the Sioux way. Yet I know that a woman like you cannot come and live in a tipi and do nothing more. I in turn am not sure I can come here and live. I could not—"

"Black Hawk, you have no choice." She turned in his arms, resting her head against his chest and thinking how good he smelled. He wore a clean blue calico shirt and soft leggings. "Last night was the most . . . I never knew I could feel that way. I love you, Black Hawk. I don't care what one person on this reservation thinks about it. I want you to stay here. We can be married the Christian way. Somehow it will work." Her eyes misted as she leaned back to look up at him. "We can make it work, Black Hawk. Look!"

She left him and walked to the foot of the cot, where she had set the box of canvases and paints that had finally arrived a few days earlier. She carried them to the table and opened the box. "I ordered these wood-backed canvases and paints for you through my father back in Wisconsin. I want you to use them to paint pictures you can sell. I have no doubt whatsoever that you could make a living with your painting. We'll get in touch with dealers in St. Louis, maybe Chicago. My father will help. You could make a living the white man's way, but you would be doing something you love, capturing the land and the animals and all the beauty out here on canvas, sending it to buyers who can enjoy the pictures and appreciate this land as it is seen through the eyes of one of its true natives."

He looked doubtful, but he reached into the box, fingering the canvas.

"Don't you see? It's a way for us to be together but for you to remain right here where you love it so much. I can continue to teach, and—"

"What happened with Seth Bridges and the sergeant?" he interrupted. "You have said nothing about it. I think it is because you do not want me to know."

She closed her eyes and sighed. "They found nothing, no proof that Seth Bridges did anything wrong. They found only one half-empty bottle of whiskey in the house, nothing in the barn or other buildings." She turned away. "Sergeant Desmond, of course, denied having any connections with whiskey smugglers, and said his only connection with Seth Bridges was that he had seen his daughter socially a couple of times. Both of them were, of course, very angry and indignant."

Black Hawk grasped her arms and turned her to face him. "The sergeant will be even more angry with me. He will know I am the one who accused him. Until I can prove what he is doing and stop him and Seth Bridges, I cannot come here and live. The sergeant would be watching my every move. He would make sure I find much trouble, and he would make trouble for you also."

"I don't care. We can survive it, Black Hawk."

He watched her lovingly; and the way his eyes raked over her gave her shivers of desire.

"There is a vision yet to be fulfilled," he reminded her. "Night Hunter said that a white man would die, and it will be much trouble for me. We do not know yet what this means."

Evelyn pulled away from him, folding her arms nervously. "I watched Wild Horse shot down in front of my eyes." She faced him, a tear slipping down her cheek. "I don't want the same thing to happen to you, Black Hawk. Please stay away from Sergeant Desmond and Seth Bridges. Let it go."

He shook his head. "I cannot allow either of them to do things that destroy my people's pride. I want nothing more than to kill the sergeant. I know in my heart he is the one who killed Turtle Woman and Small Bear. It is only because Little Fox needs me that I do not hunt that man down and cut out his heart, but I can at least show others that he is doing wrong. Somehow I will find a way to prove it!"

Evelyn put a hand to her forehead. "Then why did you come here last night?" she asked, her voice breaking on the words. "It wasn't . . . fair to me. If you knew we couldn't be together—"

"I did not say that. I only said there is still something unfinished. Somehow we will be together, Evy, but not yet."

"Then when? You said you would not live here. My work is here, Black Hawk. I can't and I won't leave it. If loving you means losing support from Mission Services, then I will petition the government to take up that support. There is a need here, and they know it. I won't let my love for you keep me from teaching, and I won't let *you* keep me from it. If you truly care about your people, you will want me to continue. You won't ask me to quit."

He smiled sadly. "No. I would not ask that. You are a woman who does what is right in her heart, even when it means going against those you love most. That is part of why I love you."

Their eyes held. There were the words, finally. He had not just used her last night, only to scoff at her today. He loved her. He considered her his wife now. "You said you didn't think you could come here and live, so how can we be together?"

He sighed softly, reaching out and touching her cheek with the back of his hand. "I must think about all of this. I only meant I could not live completely like a white man, watching the clock, seldom laughing, never feeling truly free. I must think on these things, and when the vision is fulfilled, I will decide."

Evelyn felt an angry resentment at the words. "You should have done all this thinking before you came into this cabin last night!" She turned away. "You say I am your wife now. By white man's thinking I am something else, at least until we are legally married." She threw back her head. "I want you here with me, Black Hawk."

He walked up and touched her shoulders. "Not yet. There is still much to be settled. It is too soon to tell the reverend and Agent McLaughlin that we wish to be married the Christian way. They will not accept it. Perhaps they would send you away, and then we could not be together, because I am not allowed to leave this land, nor would I. It is my life's blood."

"Then go!" She whirled. "Go away from here. I can't bear to be around you and not be able to be together as husband and wife. I cannot have just a night with you now and again and nothing more. I only ask . . . I ask you to take the canvas with you and to think about what I said about how you could earn money the white man's way. And I also ask that you leave Little Fox here with me. He needs schooling, Black Hawk, and now that Anita has died and I have no help, I cannot leave here to come out to you to teach him. If you would stay, I could also continue teaching you."

Black Hawk looked toward the curtained-off bedroom, feeling a great loneliness. He wished he knew what it was the spirits wanted from him. And how could he bear the emptiness of going back to his camp alone? Still, he knew she was right. The lessons must continue, and this woman who stood before him was the only white person he trusted. "I will speak with Little Fox. If he agrees, I will leave him."

She stepped closer. "And you will go." She shook her head. "Please don't do this, Black Hawk. Don't go looking for trouble, and don't leave me. I belong to you now. If you knew we could not be together, then why did you come and steal my soul last night?"

"Because it was necessary. It was what you wanted and needed, and it was the same for me. I could not go one more day without possessing you, and I felt no protest from you. If you had asked me to stop, I would have."

She stiffened. "Then I am asking you now. I cannot live two lives! Go and see your son. Decide if he will stay or go. Either way, you must go back to your own camp. Do your praying. Go and talk to Night Hunter. Do whatever it is you think you need to do before you come back to me. Go and get yourself shot, if you think you must!" She shivered, new tears coming, the memory of seeing Wild Horse's body riddled with bullets remaining ever fresh in her mind. "Just don't wring such passion and need from me until you can come here and be fully mine and are willing to stay . . . and until you can accept the fact that there is nothing you can do about Sergeant Desmond or Seth Bridges. That is *Army* business, Black Hawk! I refuse to relive the kind of agony my mother suffered when Wild Horse was killed!"

Black Hawk studied her stoic reserve, the determined glare in her eyes, then stepped closer, leaning down and touching her cheek with his own. "It is too late for you not to suffer if something should happen to me."

He left her then, and Evelyn stood rigid while he walked into the bedroom to talk to Little Fox. She loved him. She hated him. She wanted him to stay, yet she knew he must go . . . for now. She heard Little Fox protesting, heard Black Hawk continue to talk to him softly, urgently, telling him he could trust her and promising he would see that Many Birds began coming to school.

After several minutes Black Hawk reappeared. "My son will stay," he told her.

She met his eyes, knowing how much it hurt him to leave the boy.

"I have told him it is best."

She nodded. She wanted to scream at him for doing this to her. Her body still ached from their night of lovemaking. His eyes moved over her again, and she felt naked, trembling at the realization of what she had allowed this man to do to her in the darkness of night.

Black Hawk walked over and picked up the box of canvases and paints. "I will tie this to my horse."

A faint ray of hope that things could change erased some of her anxiety. He would paint, as she had asked. If she could sell some of those paintings, she could show him just how valuable they were, show him that sometimes white man's money could be earned by creating a thing of beauty and doing what a man loved to do.

Don't go, Black Hawk. I never thought that I could fall so deeply in love with a man such as you, but I have, and I need you. She turned away. "Go, then."

She waited, heard the screen door open and close. Moments later she heard a horse trotting away. She covered her face with her hand and sat down in a chair, unable to control the tears of torn emotions.

Twenty-one

Seth scowled with curiosity at who might be at his door after dark. Whoever it was, they pounded on the door again. "Hold on!" Seth barked, hoping the agency had not found another reason to send soldiers to the house. It would be difficult explaining the bruises on Lucille's face. "Who is it!"

"It's me—Jubal. Let me in, damn it, before somebody sees me. My horse is hid in your barn!"

Seth quickly opened the door, and the sergeant hustled himself inside. "I found out it *was* Black Hawk who set the agency on us," he said angrily, without a hello.

Seth closed the door and followed the irritated Jubal into the parlor.

"I think that sonofabitch might be sweet on the schoolteacher, and her on him!" Desmond continued. He walked over and picked up a whiskey bottle on the floor near Seth's chair. "Can you believe that?" He swallowed some of the amber liquid.

"Only thing I believe is there ain't an Indian man alive who wouldn't like to stick a white woman, and there ain't a white woman alive that ain't secretly hot for most any man who'll give her a smile; and there's plenty of these prim and proper missionary ladies who fantasize about big bucks like Black Hawk. Sure, I'd believe it. How'd you find out?"

"I didn't, not all of it anyway. I just *figured* it out. Lieutenant Teller told me—"Just then Jubal noticed Lucille lying curled up on a cot in a corner of the room. A sniffling Katy sat beside her on the edge of the cot. Even by the rather dim lantern light he could see Lucille's face was badly bruised. One eye was swollen and black. She glared back at him sullenly, and Jubal turned around and looked at Seth. "What the hell happened?"

Seth's hands went into fists. "The bitch tried to threaten me— said she'd go to the agency and tell them where I've got the whiskey hid if I touched her again or bothered Katy. I had to remind her who has the last word around here. She's damn lucky I didn't finish her punishment by haulin' Katy upstairs, but she's got me there, and the little slut knows it. We come to an agreement. I don't touch Katy, she don't go runnin' to the agency. She figured just because she knew where the whiskey is, she had somethin' on me. I had to remind her that ain't how it works." Seth glowered at Katy, knowing how intimidating it had been for her to watch him beat her sister. "Katy there knows better than to even think about tellin' any tall stories herself. She knows I'd find a way to get out of trouble, and I'd come back for her and her sister both, only then I'd *kill* her sister." He stepped a little closer to both girls. "You don't want Lucille's death to be your fault, do you, Katy?"

The girl just continued her quiet crying, saying nothing. Seth turned back to the sergeant. "Don't concern yourself with them two. How do you know Black Hawk might be seein' the school-teacher?"

Desmond met his eyes with anger. "If those girls get me in trouble—"

"They won't."

"Even so, I'm through coming here. It's not worth the risk. I found out it was Black Hawk who told someone he saw you meet a riverboat with your wagon and suspected you got whiskey in return for your corn. It was Reverend Phillips who finally admitted that was where the information came from. The way I see it, the only person Black Hawk trusts around here is Miss Evelyn Gibbons. I think he told her and she told the reverend.

Black Hawk wouldn't want to go to the agency or to the lieutenant himself. He might get in trouble, letting them know he's
sneaking around looking for whiskey smugglers. That's why nobody would say anything at first about who started this whole
thing. The reverend and the schoolteacher were protecting Black
Hawk."

Seth grabbed the whiskey bottle out of the sergeant's hand
and took a swallow himself. "That red bastard! I'll find a way
to kill that sonofabitch someday!"

"I'll probably do it first. I want him dead, too, for more reasons than him making trouble over whiskey traders."

Seth rubbed at his lips, wincing a little at pain in his hand,
which was sore from beating Lucille. "Just because Black
Hawk told Miss Gibbons about the whiskey don't mean he's
stickin' her."

Jubal removed his hat and ran a hand through his thinning
brown hair. "I found out she's been taking care of his kid. The
little nit got the cholera, and Black Hawk brought him to Miss
Gibbons. Why would he take him to her and not to the church,
or to Night Hunter? I can't say for sure there is something going
on there. It's just a feeling I got in my gut." He sighed. "How I
would love to catch those two in the act! I could get Black Hawk
hanged and send that cocky, big-mouth schoolteacher packing!
She goes on about being so proper, sticking her nose in other
people's business! Somebody ought to stick their nose a little
more into *her* business."

Seth took another swallow of whiskey, then rubbed at puffy,
bloodshot eyes. "What do we do now?"

"We?" Jubal jerked the whiskey from his hand. "There *is* no
'we.' From now on, you and I have no contact. I intend to move
up in rank and get myself a position of command someday, not
rot in an army jail! I won't be getting any promotions if I'm
discovered helping with the flow of whiskey onto this reservation! It also won't help if the Army finds out I'm coming here

and paying you for Lucy's favors. I'm not coming back, Seth, and, by God, you'd better keep those girls in line! If you or them gets me in trouble, I'll come after you, Seth Bridges! If you end up getting yourself in hot water, you'd better not say anything about me!"

Seth stepped back a little. "What about the whiskey? Can I still count on you to help get it through?"

"Not for a while. Things are too dangerous right now. If I were you, I'd lay low myself."

"It's good money."

"Money you can't spend if you're sitting in jail. If you want to keep selling Lucille's services, that's your business, but if I were you, I'd stay away from the whiskey dealings for a while. And be careful how you dole out what whiskey you've got. Don't ever let your Indian customers know where you keep it hidden, or they'll sneak over here some night and take it all. Winter is coming, so ration what you've got." Jubal glanced over at the girls. "You two had better listen to Seth and do like he says; otherwise, you won't answer just to him. You'll answer to me, too! I know men who buy women for whorehouses! I'll arrange for them to carry you both off, and you'll wish you were back here with Seth!"

Lucille wished she had a gun so she could shoot them both. She had thought she had a good idea, threatening Seth with going to the agency about the whiskey. Her plan had backfired when he began beating her and threatening to take Katy upstairs and "make a woman of her." It was the worst beating he had ever given her. He had kept Katy locked in a closet while he did it, and poor Katy was terrified now, properly frightened into abiding by Seth Bridges's wishes. Lucille was not sure how she was going to get through another winter with Seth, but at least the sergeant was not going to come around anymore.

Was it true about Miss Gibbons and the Indian called Black Hawk? She refused to believe the pretty schoolteacher could do anything wrong or sinful. Maybe she loved Black Hawk. What was so terrible about that? She couldn't even imagine what it might be like to truly love a man and want to be with him that way. She was sure she would never know that kind of love, for what man would want her now? Even Seth didn't want her anymore. He seldom came to her bed, said he was "tired" of her. The words terrified her, for she feared his desire for a new woman in his bed would make him turn to Katy. What she knew about the whiskey was the only way she had left of protecting her sister.

She gave Sergeant Desmond her most defiant look, but his words made her feel sick to her stomach. He was probably not lying about handing her and Katy both off to men who bought and sold women like cattle. She could not imagine anything more horrible than having to lie with many different men, and she had already decided that once she got herself and Katy away from Seth, there would never be another man in her life. All she had to do was figure out how she was going to run away, where she would get the money to do it.

"If you see me at the agency or the fort," Jubal was telling Seth, "you just nod a hello. We hardly know each other. Remember that. I did see your daughter a couple of times but decided she was too young for me. That's the only connection we have, except that you sometimes come to the fort to play a little poker with me and some of the other men. I want no more dealings with you."

Seth set down his whiskey bottle. "You just try to find a way to get rid of Black Hawk. *He's* our only problem. I want that bastard dead!"

Jubal sneered. "Not as much as I do!" He grabbed his hat and glanced over at Katy and Lucille again. "You girls keep your mouths shut like you did earlier today, or you'll suffer the consequences!"

He stormed out, and Seth turned to Lucille. "Good advice,"

he growled. He took up the whiskey bottle and plunked down into the soiled, stuffed chair. "Goddamn Black Hawk," he muttered. "That redskin is costin' me money! If the sergeant don't find a way to kill that sonofabitch someday, *I'll* do it!"

Black Hawk wanted to stay away, knew he must for the time being; yet here he stood, watching the tiny cabin where his son and the woman he loved lay sleeping. Perhaps it *was* possible for Evelyn and him to be together with no trouble. Did he dare hope for such a thing? What about the vision, and Night Hunter's prediction that a white man would die? What if the vision did not mean what he thought it did . . . that he and Evy would one day be together, free and happy? What if it meant one of them would die?

She had been angry when he left two days ago. Maybe he should leave it that way and just go, but the woman kept drawing him back like a buck to a doe. Turtle Woman had never made him feel so helpless. She had not had this power to make him act unwisely. If he went to the door now, would it be bolted again . . . or unlocked? He had said his good-byes. He should stay away now until the vision was fulfilled. He had done what was necessary, had claimed the white woman as his own because to wait was worse torture than the Sun Dance sacrifice. He had hurt her in ways only a white woman could be hurt. She did not fully understand that it was all right to act on their great passion and then be apart again. She probably feared he had somehow tricked her, had taken his pleasure and now was done with her. If he left, perhaps she would never allow him to take her into his arms again.

He thought she understood, but now he was not sure. He must see her once more, show her his sincerity, promise her that somehow they would find a way to be together always. He would tell her that he would try what she had suggested; let her try to sell the paintings. He had no use for white man's money, but under this new way of living, it was apparently a necessary thing.

He left his horse tied in back of the shed between the church and the school and walked on silent, moccasined feet to her cabin. He could not go back without seeing her once more. He had spent the last two days at his sister and grandmother's, convincing Many Birds to begin coming to school. Before he retreated to his hidden camp, he must see Evelyn Gibbons one more time, feel himself inside her once more, show her how much he loved her.

He stuck to the shadows whenever possible. There was a bright moon tonight, which made it very difficult to keep himself hidden at all times. He crept up onto the porch. It was important to her that others did not know yet that she was in love with an Indian man, not until he was ready to marry her the Christian way. Would she even let him inside? He needed to hold her again, to reassure her, and himself, that somehow they would always be together.

He reached the door, tried the latch. Pain stabbed at his heart when he discovered it was locked. He told himself that of course it should be bolted, for her own protection. She thought he was gone and would not be coming back anytime soon. He tapped lightly on the door, then hesitated when he felt something jab him in the back.

"Hold it right there, Black Hawk" came the familiar, hated voice of Jubal Desmond. "What the hell do you think you're doing? Gonna break in there and rape the poor teacher lady? Pretty, isn't she?"

Black Hawk swallowed, scrambling to think of a logical answer for his presence. "I came for my son. I have changed my mind about letting him stay here. I am taking him back to my camp."

"At twelve o'clock at night?"

Suddenly the door opened, and Evelyn stood there in a robe,

holding up a lamp to see who was outside the door. "Black Hawk!"

All of Jubal's suspicions were verified when he saw how Evelyn Gibbons and Black Hawk looked at each other.

"I came for my son," he told her.

"He came here for more than that," Jubal added. "He came to get a piece of white woman. Question is, would that white woman protest, or would she have let him in willingly?"

Evelyn was confused at first. Jubal Desmond had a rifle jabbed into Black Hawk's side, clearly eager for the flimsiest excuse to pull the trigger. Memories of another innocent man dying before her eyes stabbed at her heart. How could she bear it if something happened to Black Hawk now? She faced Desmond boldly, realizing Black Hawk's life could depend on what she said at this moment.

"I would have let him in willingly," she answered. "Black Hawk said he came for Little Fox. Why would I deny him his son?"

"And why would he come for him this time of night?" Jubal sneered.

Evelyn glanced up at Black Hawk, studying his wild eyes, understanding the danger of the moment. One wrong move . . . She knew why he had come, and it was not for Little Fox. She thought he had already gone back to his camp. Apparently he had decided to come to her once more, and as foolish and unwise as it would have been of her to let him inside, she would have; but now there was Sergeant Desmond to contend with. She looked back at Jubal, pulling her robe closer around her neck.

"I have no idea," she answered him. "When a man's son is involved, who are we to predict these things?" She looked up at Black Hawk, understanding she had to go along with what he'd told the sergeant about his reason for being here. "I will go and wake Little Fox."

"Wait just a damn minute!" Jubal growled. He jabbed the rifle harder into Black Hawk's ribs. "Get inside!"

Evelyn could see the hatred growing in Black Hawk's eyes. She knew how much he wanted to kill this man, and prayed that he would not do something foolish. She stepped aside and let them in, then hurried to a table and turned up the lamp. Jubal kicked shut the door, then moved around to face Black Hawk, keeping the rifle steady.

"I want the truth!" he said. "Black Hawk left his horse hidden." His gaze moved back and forth from Black Hawk to Evelyn. "I've had some free time these last couple of days, and I decided to use it to keep a watch on this place at night; and just like I expected, Black Hawk here came sneaking to your porch like a thief in the night. If he came for Little Fox, he'd have his horse with him, Little Fox's, too. Why don't the two of you quit lying to me and tell me what's *really* going on?"

Evelyn breathed deeply, beginning to hate this man as much as Black Hawk did. "All right," she answered. "I happen to be in love with Black Hawk, and he with me. We are going to be married, a Christian ceremony. We haven't decided yet just when." She looked up at Black Hawk, but he kept his eyes on the sergeant.

Jubal's mouth fell open for a moment, then he grinned. "Married?" He moved his gaze to Evelyn. "You're in love with a filthy Indian, and you're going to *marry* him?" His eyes raked over her scathingly. "You pious little slut! Has the big buck already got between your legs, Miss High and Mighty?"

Quickly, Black Hawk grabbed the end of the rifle and pushed it upward. Evelyn heard a click, and her blood ran cold. Apparently, by God's grace, the rifle had misfired, and there was no actual shot. In a fraction of a second Black Hawk yanked the weapon out of the sergeant's hands and slammed it crosswise against the man's throat, shoving him against a wall. He continued to push, choking Desmond in a furious grip that left Desmond helplessly pinned.

"Father! Father!" Little Fox had heard the commotion and came running out of the bedroom.

"Black Hawk, don't!" Evelyn begged. She watched Desmond's eyes bulge and his face grow purple as Black Hawk continued to press the rifle, choking off the man's air. Evelyn grabbed at Black Hawk's arms, but he was too powerful, trying to pull them away was like tugging at concrete posts. "Black Hawk, you must let the vision be played out by others. You can't be the one to make it happen. If you do this, you destroy the vision! I'm supposed to be able to help you, but I can't if you deliberately kill him! Please, Black Hawk! If you do this, we can never be together! Never!"

Reference to the vision seemed to bring him back to his senses. Breathing heavily with murderous intent, he slowly released Jubal, backing away and letting him slide to the floor, gasping for breath. Black Hawk grasped the rifle by the barrel and slammed it against the wall, cracking it in half, then threw both pieces down in front of Jubal. He yanked out his hunting knife, kneeling and grabbing hold of Jubal's hair. He jerked the man's head back, with Jubal still holding his throat and gasping for breath, and Jubal looked up at him, his eyes wide and showing his terror. Black Hawk laid his knife against the man's cheek. "You will not insult Miss Gibbons again, or there will be nothing more I can do to keep from slicing you open from between your legs up to your throat!" he added. He let go of the man's hair and stood up, keeping his knife ready. "The day is coming, Jubal Desmond, when Wakantanka will see that I know my revenge!"

Evelyn stood back, thinking how, at this moment, Black Hawk looked every bit the terrifying warrior whom so many of her own people had feared over the years. He came from a people who were taught to fear no one, for whom revenge was as natural as breathing, and solving that revenge with a tomahawk or a knife seemed perfectly proper. How could anyone expect to change such a culture overnight?

Jubal managed to get to his knees, then finally to his feet. "You'll . . . pay for this . . . Black Hawk!" he said, his voice gruff from the choking he had endured. He moved his eyes to Evelyn. "So will . . . you!"

"You will say nothing to no one!" Black Hawk demanded. "If you do, I will find a way to *kill* you! You know that I will do it!"

A shaking Jubal Desmond continued to rub at his throat. "The Army would hunt you down and hang you as fast as they could do it. Where would that . . . leave your *son,* Black Hawk! You're all he's got!"

"Not anymore," Evelyn put in. "I am already growing to love the boy."

Little Fox moved closer to his father. He glared at the sergeant with eyes as full of hate as his father's were.

"Love?" Desmond ran a hand through his hair and stooped down to pick up his hat from where it had fallen on the floor. "Maybe you do think . . . you love this Indian and his nit," he said, the pain of finding his voice evident in his eyes. "But I guarantee, lady, men like Black Hawk don't know the meaning of the word . . . especially when it comes to white people." He moved icy-blue eyes to look at Black Hawk. "Maybe I *will* keep quiet . . . for now. I think you understand how this would go for the woman here if folks found out about this. I won't say anything if you promise to keep your nose out of Army business! And quit trying to make trouble for Seth Bridges. I don't know that much about the man's personal business and I don't appreciate being accused of . . . being in cahoots with him. All I did was take his daughter dancin' and to church a couple of times."

"I suspect you've done more than that, Jubal Desmond!" Evelyn spoke up.

He glared at her, embarrassed that she had seen Black Hawk

get the best of him in front of her. "You've got one hell of an imagination, lady. Fact is, I don't intend to see Lucille Bridges at all anymore. It's not worth the trouble if her father is mixed up in running whiskey. I don't want . . . any part of that."

"You are a liar!" Black Hawk told him. "With my own eyes I have seen you lead men away from an area where whiskey peddlers come through! You *knew* they were coming!"

Jubal's upper lip curled in anger. "And you don't dare say a thing about it without getting yourself in trouble! It goes both ways, Black Hawk! I keep my mouth shut about you and . . . the little woman here . . . and you keep quiet about the whiskey and quit hunting down the smugglers. You make your choice, now that you've decided to take yourself a white woman. You show her which is more important to you— your people or the woman you're supposed to love. If you want to protect her from being ridiculed and insulted and probably kicked off this reservation and sent back to where she came from, then stay out of the whiskey business!"

The sergeant breathed deeply, still visibly shaken. It was obvious to Evelyn that he honestly thought for a brief moment that Black Hawk would kill him. She had been stunned and shaken herself by Black Hawk's speed and strength, and thought she was going to see murder committed before her eyes. Now she admired him even more. For Black Hawk to restrain himself from killing Jubal Desmond in the heat of such passionate anger, knowing what he knew about the man, showed the intelligence and wisdom of this man she loved. She watched Jubal, shivered at the look he gave her then.

"You're a very foolish woman. You're playing with fire . . . looking to get burned. You're risking your good name . . . your job . . . your friendships—everything—for a goddamn rebel Indian who'll never amount to a hill of beans!" He picked up the pieces of his rifle and stared at it a moment, wondering how he was going to explain this to the lieutenant. He stumbled to the door then and left.

Evelyn breathed a sigh of relief, and Black Hawk turned to hug Little Fox. "It will be all right," he told the boy.

"I thought you had gone back to camp, Father. Why are you here?"

"I needed to talk to Evy. We will talk outside. You go back to bed. Perhaps tomorrow you can start your lessons. Many Birds has agreed to come to school, so you will not be so lonely."

"I am glad, Father, but I am not so lonely. Evy is good to me. We are special friends. Is it true you will marry her?"

Black Hawk glanced at Evelyn, whose back was turned. "Yes, but not for a while. There is much to be settled first."

"Are you in trouble, Father?"

Black Hawk sighed. "Not right now, but if people know about my loving Evy, there could be trouble for both of us. Do you understand?"

"Yes, Father, but it is not right."

"No, it is not. Many things are not as they should be. Ever since the white man came to our land, much has changed for us. Nothing is the same, and we must learn a new way. That is why I want you to take the lessons."

When Little Fox turned and went into the bedroom, Black Hawk walked to where Evelyn stood. He touched her shoulders, and she turned and rested her head against his chest. "I thought one of you would be killed. I thought for a moment perhaps tonight was an answer to the vision, the worst answer." She hugged him tightly. "Oh, Black Hawk, all I could see was Wild Horse being shot down in front of me! I knew in that one quick moment that I don't ever want to go on with life without you."

He ran a hand over her lustrous hair, which hung nearly to her waist. He relished its softness, and the feel of her breasts beneath the soft robe. "Nor I without you," he answered. "But we both know this is not the right time to inform others of our love. I spoke with Night Hunter. I told him I had made you mine."

She looked up at him. "What did he say?"

"He said we should tell no one yet. He will know when the vision has been fulfilled. The spirits will bless us then, and we will be together forever."

She closed her eyes, laying her head against his chest again. "Why did you come here? I thought you had gone back to your camp."

"I went to see my sister. When I left there . . . I missed you. I ached for you. I wanted to see you once more."

Evelyn knew what he meant by the statement, and her own awakened womanly desires made her glad he had come back once more, no matter what the risk. She wanted him again that way as much as he wanted her. The chance that she could have lost him tonight only made her feel more desperate to have him again, to prove to herself that this beautiful man still belonged to her. She felt like the frightened four-year-old child who saw Wild Horse shot down and stood there crying, wanting to run to him and hug him but afraid of all the blood. Now she clung to Black Hawk. "You must be so careful, Black Hawk."

"Not just me, but also you." He grasped her arms and leaned down to kiss her once more. "I like this kissing," he whispered. He nuzzled at her neck. "I want to be with you once more before I go, but my son still lies awake. You can come to the shed over by the church. That is where I am. I will go out and search all around the cabin for the sergeant and make sure he is gone, then I will signal you."

She knew she should be angry that he was taking it for granted she would come to him, and yet she knew she would do just that.

"I should have known he was close by when I first arrived," he told her, letting go of her, "but I am so full of the want of you that my senses were not alert. I will not let that happen again." He touched her face. "Wait until you hear the sound of an owl. That will mean all is clear."

She nodded. "I hate having to share our love this way," she whispered.

"It is only for a while. The time will come when we know the vision has been fulfilled." He turned and left, looking around cautiously before going out and closing the door. Evelyn waited, hating Sergeant Desmond, doubting that he would really keep quiet. After nearly getting in trouble over the whiskey problem, and now the confrontation with Black Hawk, the man would be more determined than ever to find a way to get rid of him; and the only way to do that would be to kill him. She worried what he might think to do to see that that happened.

She picked up two extra blankets and pulled on a pair of slippers, wondering if she had gone mad. She was preparing to sneak out of her own house to go to a shed and secretly make love to a renegade Indian! She carried a lantern over to check on Little Fox, who was still awake. "I am going out soon to talk more with your father," she told him. "I won't be far away."

The boy grinned. "I know."

Evelyn felt embarrassed, realizing there was no fooling the youngster, who had already told her his father loved her. She carried the lamp back to the table and snuffed it out, then waited at the door. Finally, she heard the hoot of an owl, and she silently went out, clinging to the blankets. She strained to see her way to the shed, and as soon as she walked inside, Black Hawk swept her up into his arms. She put her arms around his neck and rested her head on his shoulder.

"I have a place ready," he told her quietly. He laid her into straw that was covered with blankets.

"I brought more blankets," she whispered.

He set them aside, hovering over her in the darkness, and as their eyes adjusted, they could see each other by the light of the bright moon that shined through a small window nearby. "Someday we will do this in the light of day," he said softly as he untied and opened her robe, "and I will look upon my beautiful Evy and see the true colors of her skin, her breasts."

Evelyn wondered at the spell this man could so easily cast over her. She leaned up and met his mouth, again feeling wild and free, this time unafraid of what was to come, aching for it, needing to feel him inside her. They kissed savagely, and he then pulled her to a sitting position and roughly helped her tear off her robe and nightgown. He grasped hold of her drawers and yanked them down and over her ankles, and she opened herself to him, not even wanting to bother with preliminaries. This was Black Hawk, her precious Black Hawk, who moments earlier she feared might die right in front of her eyes. She prayed that was not the meaning of the vision.

As he buried his hardness inside her, she gasped with the glory of it. He was all power and beauty and gracefulness. He leaned close, grasping her bottom and moving in rocking rhythm, and she met his movements with eagerness, leaning her head back and arching up to him in total abandon. There was still some pain, but now it was a welcome, exotic pain that took her to another realm, away from reality, away from her fears, to a place shared only by the two of them. She ran her hands over his powerful arms and shoulders, and he sat up grasping her hips in his strong hands and pulling her to him. He threw back his head, moving faster. She wanted to scream with the glorious ecstasy of the act, but she knew she dared not make any noise. She could only groan softly, and her nails dug into his arms when finally his life spilled into her.

He held himself there for a moment, then leaned down and began softly kissing her face, her eyes. "We will do it again," he whispered. He remained inside her, resting his elbows on either side of her shoulders. "I am sorry, my beautiful Evy, that loving me will make life so hard for you. Perhaps I should go and never come back."

She reached up and touched his cheek. "Don't say that."

"Little Fox must stay with you, learn a new way. It hurts my heart to leave him." He leaned down and touched her cheek. "I know I should stay, but it is hard for me to change my life and live this new way. In my eyes and in my heart you are my wife now, yet I cannot be a true husband to you except in this way. I want to take care of you, protect you, provide for you, but this new life will not allow me to do those things in the Sioux way. I must think about this, go off and pray alone, wait for the vision to be fulfilled, and pray that Wakantanka will help me know what I should do, how I can always be with this white woman who has stolen my heart."

She traced her fingers over his lips. "And you have stolen mine, Black Hawk," she whispered. "But we must be very careful now. If anything happened to you, I would want to die."

He breathed deeply, and it seemed to her he was trembling. "Nothing will happen to me, for I know in my heart we are supposed to be together always. Perhaps this is the new way of keeping the circle of life. When I lost Turtle Woman and our baby son, and knew that life would never be the same for me, I was sure the circle was broken. You have changed all of that, and have shown me that perhaps I can learn this new way and not lose my soul, my connection to the spirits and the Indian way." He touched her cheek again, and Evelyn was surprised to realize there were tears on his own cheeks. "It is so hard, Evy. Your people do not understand what it is like for a warrior to be imprisoned on a small piece of land and told he can never again . . ."

When he could not finish, she touched his hair and kissed his cheek. "It will be all right, Black Hawk. I will help you and your people through this terrible time, and you will discover you do not need to lose all that is precious to you. I love you so, just the way you are."

"I do not want you to be hurt," he groaned.

"No one can go through life without being hurt, Black Hawk. I am not afraid."

He lay down beside her, wrapping strong arms around her. "I just want to hold you for a while before I am inside you again. I want to think about what it will be like being able to sleep with you every night, to hold and protect you."

She kissed his chest, feeling safe and loved, imagining what it must have been like in the days of total freedom for a Sioux woman to lie in her warrior's arms and know she was protected from enemy tribes, from wild animals . . . from soldiers. Jubal Desmond was the epitome of the kind of men who had brought so much misery to Black Hawk's people. Suddenly she had a keener understanding of the emotional pain Black Hawk and others like him suffered. It was the reason so many of the Indians turned to whiskey.

"Sometimes it all makes me feel so weary," Black Hawk told her, as though to read her thoughts.

Evelyn did not know how to reply. There were no words she could offer that would comfort the one deepest agony she could not fully share with him, for she had never suffered what he had suffered. She could only be there for him, love him totally . . . and she was determined to do that, no matter what people like Reverend Phillips or Jubal Desmond thought of it. She would stand against the world, if need be, for she loved this man more than life itself.

Twenty-two

Seth stood watching out the window. *She should be comin'
along anytime now,* he thought. He drank down some whiskey
and turned toward the parlor entrance to holler for Katy, who
was helping Lucille make breakfast. "Get in here quick!" he
ordered.

Moments later Katy appeared, standing hesitantly on the other
side of the room. "What do you want, Seth?"

"Come on over here by the window."

Katy swallowed, never sure of Seth's mood. "Why?" She
watched Seth's eyes narrow with instant anger, and she thought
how extra ugly he was in the mornings, unshaven, his clothes
wrinkled from sleeping in them, his eyes still full of grit. He
used whiskey to wash out his mouth, and she could hardly stand
to be close to him when he spoke. His thinning gray hair stuck
out every which way. The only thing to be glad about this morning was that last night he had drunk so much he had fallen asleep
in his big chair, and neither she nor Lucille had been disturbed
all night.

"Because I *said* to, that's why!" he barked. "I ain't gonna
hurt you. Just come over here!"

Katy approached slowly, and when she got close enough, Seth
reached out and grabbed her arm, yanking her in front of the
window beside him. "When I give you an order, girl, don't lolly-
gag around!"

Katy winced with pain when he gave her arm an extra pinch.

She looked out the window, folding her arms protectively in front of her. "What do you want, Seth?"

"You ever notice that pretty Indian girl that rides by here just about the same time every day?"

Katy shrugged. "A couple of times. Me and Lucy are usually doing chores in the mornings. We don't have time to notice people going by."

"Well, *take* the time! She's just about your age, and she rides a red horse with black tail and mane." He licked his lips. "Straddles that horse just like a man, even though she's only wearin' a tunic and blanket. Her name is Many Birds."

Katy frowned. "How do you know all that?"

"Because I make it a point to know what I *need* to know, and because I've been watchin' her, every mornin'. I want you to make friends with her."

Katy frowned in surprise. "Why should I do that? She's an Indian girl. You always tell us to stay away from the Indians."

"You ask too goddamn many questions for your own good! Now shut your smart mouth and do like I say!"

Katy looked up at him. "You going to hurt her?"

Seth took another drink of whiskey. "Hell, no. Do you think I'd risk her relatives comin' after me? Hell, her own brother is that damn Black Hawk. I just want you to make friends so's to show that Black Hawk I ain't got nothin' against his people," he lied, knowing Katy always needed a good reason for things. She was harder to control than Lucy. "If we're gonna stay on here, we gotta get along with the Sioux, maybe start tradin' with them."

Katy pouted. "You said before that you hated Black Hawk. You said you'd like to kill him."

Seth controlled an urge to slap her. "A man can change his mind, can't he? Best way to get Black Hawk to quit makin' trouble for me is to convince him I ain't as bad as he thinks. You make friends with his sister, and it might help. She'll be comin' along anytime now, on her way to school. You go out and pretend you're doin' something in the yard, make her acquaintance."

Katy watched out the window. "What if she doesn't speak English?"

Seth's irritation at her questions made him grip the whiskey bottle tighter. "She's Black Hawk's sister. Of *course* she speaks English! He most likely made sure of that as she was growin' up. He thinks it's important his people know our language. Besides, you bein' about the same age, you ought to be able to communicate somehow even if you don't speak the same words." He saw someone coming then. "There! That's her! Go on out there now and look busy."

Katy scowled. "I don't want to, Seth. I don't know her."

He grasped hold of her hair, pulling it painfully and forcing her head back. "Then *get* to know her, girl!" He released her, giving her a shove. "You do like I say, or it's Lucy who'll suffer for it! You want that?"

Katy glared at him, wanting to shout back at him but knowing better. She refused to let the tears come. "No," she said quietly.

"Then do like I say and go on out there before she gets too close. Just take your time. Just say hello or somethin'. Hell, wouldn't you *like* to have a friend? You girls are always beefin' about wantin' to go to school and meet other kids your age. Go on out there now. You might find out you really like each other."

Katy glanced at the hallway, where Lucille stood quietly watching both of them. She met her sister's gaze, and they shared the same thought. What was Seth up to now?

"Get goin', or I'll take a strap to Lucy!" Seth roared.

Katy turned and ran, grabbing her flimsy, worn wool coat before going out. Seth looked at Lucille. "What are you lookin' at? Get back in there and finish my breakfast!"

"What are you aiming to do, Seth? You better not hurt that Indian girl, or you'll make big trouble."

"I ain't gonna hurt nobody, and you keep your nose out of it. What's wrong with your sister makin' a friend?"

Lucille gave him a knowing look but said nothing. When she returned to the kitchen, Seth watched out the window as Many Birds rode closer. She was just about the prettiest thing he'd ever seen, except for the schoolteacher. In his estimation, he figured it shouldn't be too hard getting her into his bed eventually. All he had to do was coax her inside, get her to drink some whiskey. All Indians liked whiskey. They got hooked on it real fast, and once they were drunk, a man could talk them into just about anything.

"You'll never feel it, sweet thing," he muttered.

As the Indian girl came even closer, Seth watched Katy walk to the gate, say something to her. Many Birds halted her horse, said something in return. She smiled. What a pretty smile!

"Damn cold weather," he mumbled, upset that the late-October mornings compelled Many Birds to wear winter leggings that covered her pretty legs. "That's it, girl," he said to himself then, referring to Katy's attempt at friendship. "Slow and easy." He'd have to take his time on this, make sure he had the girl's full trust, let her and Katy become good friends so that eventually she came inside the house with Katy. Even then he would be cordial, show his good side, let the girl come to trust him. The only way this would work was if she was known to visit several times, willingly. Once she came into the house a few times, no white man was going to believe he'd forced that pretty Indian girl when she was known to frequent his premises of her own free will. Once it was done, she would probably never say anything anyway. She'd be too ashamed to tell her people what had happened, with a white man, no less.

He licked his lips and took another swallow of whiskey, then turned to see Lucille was watching him again. God, he hated that knowing look in her eyes! If she gave him trouble over this, he would have to knock that cocky look right off her face!

"Breakfast is ready," she told him sullenly. "You'd better call Katy and let that Indian girl go on to school."

She turned and walked back into the kitchen, and Seth set his bottle aside and walked to the door. Yes, a hello was enough for starters. He opened the door and called to Katy to come and eat, then smiled and waved at Many Birds. The lovely young girl waved in return. She still sat on her horse, unaware of how the sight of her made Seth's mouth water. She rode on then, heading south toward the school. Katy came inside, and Seth patted her shoulder. "You did good, Katy-girl."

She shook off his hand. "She's nice, Seth. Leave her be."

"I've got no bad intentions for her. I've just decided you and Lucy might as well have a friend. Makes me look better. I don't want them soldiers comin' around again, and I want Black Hawk to see me and my girls can be right cordial. You gonna go out and talk to her when she rides back from school?"

Katy turned toward the kitchen. "Maybe," she said quietly.

"Good. Life can be right good for you and your sister around here if you just do like I say. Besides that, you'll have a friend to talk to and play with. I just don't want either of you goin' off with her. You make sure she always comes here. I want her brother to know she trusts us. Then he won't give me no more trouble. Understand?"

Katie and Lucille looked at each other silently, both still suspicious. Katy decided that for now, if making friends with Many Birds would keep Seth from hurting Lucille, then she would do as he asked. Besides, she already liked her, and ever since Lucille had threatened to tell on him about the whiskey, he had been different. Other than the beating he gave Lucille, he had not been quite so demanding, and he had left Lucille alone at night. They could only hope that the soldiers' raid had put enough of a scare in him that maybe he would be more careful from now on.

Thank God for Miss Gibbons, Lucille thought. It was the

schoolteacher who had prompted the raid, and she was glad for it. Seth would have to be careful from now on.

Evelyn adjusted her shawl before writing several spelling words on the blackboard. She was full of hope for the future of the school. Now that Little Fox lived with her and came every day, and his aunt, Many Birds, also attended, a few more Sioux had begun sending their children again. John and Linda Adams, who now lived with their uncle, Dancing Cloud, since their father, Big Belly, died of the cholera, had been allowed to return, as had He-Who-Hunts, William Eagle, whose mother, Red Foot Woman, had also died. Falling Eagle still had not allowed his son, Fast Arrow, to return, but Many Hands's sons, Tall Buffalo, Prairie Runner, and Flying Horse were all back, as were four new students: ten-year-olds David Bigfeather and Marie Fox, and Howard and Jack Longtooth, twelve and nine. Counting Small Fox and Many Birds, that brought her total students to twelve, nine boys and three girls.

She turned and watched them all copy what she had written on the board, her heart swelling with joy at the sight of so many children coming to learn. Her only problem now was getting more girls to come. Most Sioux parents did not feel that learning was important for girls. Their role was to learn to clean and skin animals, to cook and sew, do beadwork and make moccasins. Schooling was of no use to the females, who usually married young and needed to stay home and care for their babies. The only reason the boys were allowed to come was for the same purpose Black Hawk had learned and wanted his son to learn, so that the white man could not fool them with written words.

The biggest teaching problem was to make them all sit still and listen. They were so restless, hating having to sit inside, away from fresh air and sunshine. Their spirits longed to run free, to chase the wind, learn to hunt and make war. It was not their nature to sit inside all day working only with their minds, and she was not sure all of the boys would make it through several weeks of schooling. She had to pack in the lessons as rapidly as possible, for winter was coming, and she had already been told that here in South Dakota the temperatures could be so cold and the snow so deep that there would be days when no one ventured forth from their homes. School would most likely have to wait until early spring. Already the weather was much colder, and she'd had to make a fire in the heating stove this morning; but it had warmed toward afternoon to more comfortable temperatures.

She watched Little Fox, who in spite of his own restlessness was surprisingly diligent in his schoolwork, so smart . . . like his father. Every bone in her body ached for Black Hawk. It had been nearly two weeks since her two precious nights with him, two nights of exotic touches and bold lovemaking that had left her breathless, and so hungry for more, longing to express her love for her Indian warrior in the fullest sense. She still could hardly believe what she had done, lying with him on the floor of her cabin, and again in the shed. Not quite five months ago she never would have given thought to such wild abandon with any man, certainly not with Steven.

There could be no Steven now. She had never wanted him the way she wanted Black Hawk, had never felt such passion, such an aching desire so intense that she could hardly sleep. More than ever she wished she could talk to her mother. There was no one to help her with the guilt of what she had done, but that guilt was eased by knowing how deeply she loved Black Hawk, be it right or wrong. She didn't even want to imagine what her father would think of her actions. She was certain he would not be so much against her marrying Black Hawk, when and if that day ever came; but he would not be pleased that in the eyes of the Sioux, she was already his wife. She liked the feel of it, told herself that in God's eyes they were just as married as if they had stood before a preacher. What difference did a little piece of paper make? Could the absence of it make a person love another less? Did having it make people love each other more? The love was there, no matter whether a marriage ceremony had taken place, and she was convinced God had meant for her to find Black Hawk, to love him and to accept his love in return.

She was so busy now with school and with recruiting new students in her spare time that there had been no chance to go to Black Hawk's camp and meet with him there. She would have to wait for him to come back, and she had no way of knowing when that would be. How would they both know when the time was right to tell the whole world about their love? When would the vision be truly fulfilled?

Black Hawk at least understood why having to stay here and teach was so important to her, and she in turn understood why he needed to go back to his own camp. There was much for both of them to think about. In the meantime, if Black Hawk did not come to her soon, she knew she would have to find a way to go to him, not just because of her own need to see him again, but because Little Hawk missed his father. That would at least give her reason to go to him . . .

Janine was gone now, married and off to Fort Leonard with her new husband. All teaching duties fell on her, and she was anxious for help to arrive. She reviewed the words with the students, asking them one by one to pick a particular word, spell it, and tell her what it meant. That finished the lessons for the day, and she sent them all home with instructions to leave behind their slate boards but to take home their reading books. Tomorrow was the Sabbath, so they did not have to come back until the day after. "Be sure to bring the books back with you," she reminded them, hardly able to get the words out before they had all scrambled to charge out of the little one-room school.

"I want to go and practice shooting the bow my father made for me," Little Fox told her. Every day he worked with the small bow and arrows Black Hawk had sent him through Many Birds. Reverend Phillips had set up a target made out of bales of hay, and Little Fox was becoming quite adept with his new weapon, still the little Indian at heart. Evelyn watched him run off, realizing she loved him like her own. He was eager to please, obedient, bright, a joy to have around. It could not have been easy for him to be away from his father, but he was doing what he knew his father wanted him to do, and that was good enough for him.

She began studying each slate left on the wooden tables in front of the crates still used for chairs. Each child had written his or her name in the corner of the slates. She smiled at the way Many Birds had of signing: several birds drawn in the right corner. The clatter of a buggy interrupted her thoughts, and she turned curiously toward the entrance door of the little school. Thunder rumbled in the distance as she looked down to brush chalk from the skirt of the plain gray dress she had worn today. Someone had come visiting in a buggy. Had help from Mission Services arrived?

She wrapped her shawl tighter and folded her arms, frowning at the thought of a chilling November rainstorm approaching. She hated rain this time of year, wondered if it would turn to snow overnight. She looked out a window at the front of the school to see a woman dressed in black setting baggage at the front of the building. She was helped by old Dancing Eagle, who often drove outside visitors about the reservation for the agency. At first she did not recognize the woman, for she wore a wide-brimmed black hat, with a veil over her face. She was apparently in mourning. It seemed strange that Mission Services would send someone who had obviously just lost a loved one. And why bring her directly to the school instead of to Reverend Phillips at the church? She walked to the door and opened it, and the woman straightened, facing her. "Hello, Evy."

"Beverly!" Evelyn was astounded at how thin the woman was,

at the deep circles under her eyes. Both women just stood there looking at each other for a moment. It did not take Evelyn long to realize what had happened to Beverly Evans. Just as she had feared, Beverly's handsome circus man had turned her out like excess baggage.

"I didn't know where else to go," Beverly said quietly. She turned and thanked Dancing Eagle, telling him he could take the buggy back to the agency. "May I come in?"

Evelyn stepped aside. "Yes. Bring your things. A storm is coming." She reached down and picked up a carpetbag and hat box, carrying them inside.

Beverly followed, bringing one small and one larger suitcase. "I couldn't bring myself to go to Reverend Phillips first," she told Evelyn. "I needed to talk to a woman. I need a friend, Evy." She set the bags on the floor and closed the door. "Not someone who is going to say 'I told you so.' I need a friend more than I need to breathe." Her voice broke, and Evelyn walked closer, reaching out and taking her hands.

"Come and sit down, Beverly. Tell me what happened."

"As if . . . you can't guess," the woman replied, taking a handkerchief from a pocket of her dress and blowing her nose.

Evelyn led her to the crude crates, noticing the dress she wore looked expensive. Its black taffeta and the many organdy and taffeta slips under the skirt rustled noisily as Beverly sat down. This was not the way the Beverly Evans who first came here would dress, nor would that woman wear such a fine hat, with her dark hair underneath pulled back at the sides and worn loose in back. "Why here, Beverly? Why didn't you just go back to Illinois, back home?"

The woman shook her head. "I have no home. My family there is just as stern and unforgiving as Greggory was. I really didn't know what to do." She wiped at her eyes. "Herbert kept me with him as far as Denver. I had every reason to believe he intended to marry me when we got there." She sniffed and turned away. "What a fool I've been! He took me on a shopping spree, bought me beautiful dresses, wined and dined me, got me . . . into his bed." She swallowed, staring at her lap. "I had shared that much with him several times by then. He had a way of . . . touching me . . . saying just the things I needed to hear; and he was so utterly handsome." She sniffed back tears again, shaking her head in wonder. "One morning he handed me a wad of money, told me to use it to go wherever I wanted to go and make a good life for myself, said he wasn't the marrying type and that the circus was no place for a gentle woman like me. He announced that when the circus left town, he was not taking me along. Just like that . . . no emotion, no regrets. He paid me off like a . . . like a harlot! God knows I behaved like one!"

She broke into sobs, and Evelyn put an arm around her shoulders. The story frightened her. What if Black Hawk just wanted to prove an Indian could have his way with a white woman? No, not Black Hawk. He was too honest, too straightforward . . . but then, he hated most whites, enjoyed getting the better of them and making them out to be fools.

She shook away the thought, telling herself she could not compare Black Hawk to a man like Herbert True. Black Hawk was incapable of such treachery. Only a white man could talk out of both sides of his mouth like that. "Beverly, this is not your fault. It all came from being forced to hold in your passion and joy all your life. You found someone who could free those things inside you that needed to be let go. I worried this would happen. Men like Herbert True care only for themselves. You're much too good for him."

The woman's whole body jerked in a deep sob. "I didn't know where to go. I bought this black dress . . . to mourn the innocence I lost. I didn't want to wear a pretty color or look pretty. I didn't care about anything . . . if I lived or died. I loved him so, Evy!" She cried harder for several minutes. All Evelyn knew to do was keep an arm around her. It seemed strange, Beverly being older than she, that she should be the one to do the comforting, to try to give soothing advice. She needed so badly to talk to someone about her own predicament. Who was she to judge or give advice to this woman, when she had herself shared her passion with a Sioux Indian man? Was she also in love with the wrong man? What would Beverly—indeed, what would everyone in Mission Services do or say if they knew?

"I hated it here," Beverly sobbed. "I didn't want to come back, but where else could I go? I came here with a train of wagons bringing supplies to Fort Yates. They left me off at the agency, and Dancing Eagle brought me here. I thought perhaps . . . Oh, little did I know I would truly need this dress for mourning a dead husband! When I reached the agency, they told me about Greggory dying from cholera. I should have been here with him, Evy! Now he's dead, and Mission Services will surely ostracize me as a terrible sinner, running off on my husband like that. I am not sure how much everyone knows about what happened. My guilt over all of this is enough that I would end my life if not for the fact that I . . . I think I am with child."

Evelyn's eyes widened in surprise. "Beverly! Are you sure?"

She looked at Evelyn with a tear-stained face. "Pretty sure. I only came back here thinking perhaps Greggory would take me back so I could have a father for the child and could say it was his. I don't want my baby to be called a bastard, Evy. I want this baby, no matter how much I hate the father now. All these years of marriage to Greggory, I thought I was the one who couldn't have children. Now I know something was wrong with Greggory, not me. I want this child. Someone to love . . . to love me back. I want to raise it to be joyful and free, but I can't raise it alone. What am I to do, Evy?"

Evelyn rose and paced, thinking. "I really don't think Mission Services knows, Beverly. Your husband never told them. In fact, he did not talk about you at all when he was here helping with the cholera victims. I know Reverend Phillips has said nothing.

You could stay on here, let everyone back East think the baby is Greggory's. We need the help, Beverly. Anita Wolf died from cholera, and Janine is gone now. She married Lieutenant Teller, and he was transferred to Fort Leonard. The agency has asked for Mission Services to send out new people for the Oahe Mission, and I know for a fact that Reverend Phillips asked Agent McLaughlin to simply state that your husband had died and you had come here rather than be alone at Oahe."

"He did that? Why?"

Evelyn faced her. "I asked him to. I . . . had a feeling you might be back. I saw no reason to tell Mission Services the truth and risk having your good name blackened back home. I thought, if you came back, there would be no loss. If you didn't, eventually they would have to be told."

"Evy! I don't know what to say . . . how to thank you . . ." More tears came then, and Evelyn walked over to kneel in front of her.

"Beverly, stay here, help me with the school. You can stay in Janine's cabin. We'll go talk to Reverend Phillips together. I'm sure you don't want to face him alone. I think he'll be understanding about it. We'll all be here for you when the baby comes. The child will grow up thinking Greggory Evans was his father, a respectable man who gave his life in mission services, someone he can be proud of. Did you ever tell Herbert True you were carrying his child?"

Beverly shook her head. "I was going to . . . the same morning he handed me the money and bid his farewell." She swallowed and breathed deeply to control more tears that wanted to come. "I saw no sense in telling him then."

"Good. Then he will never know and never try to come for the child." Evelyn grasped her hands and squeezed them. "I'm so sorry, Beverly. You must not blame yourself or feel that you're bad. Blame the parents who raised you to so stifle your emotions that the moment you had a chance to release them, you got

carried away. Blame Greggory, for being so cold and unfeeling."
She bowed her head. "Blame me, for not stopping you when I
knew I should try." She met Beverly's gaze again. "You were so
happy, I didn't have the heart, and I don't think you would have
listened to me anyway, just like I don't always listen to the advice
of others." She wanted to tell her about Black Hawk, but now
was not the time. Maybe at least Beverly would understand.
"Let's go and talk to Reverend Phillips."

Beverly shook her head. "I'm too ashamed."

"Don't be, Beverly. You were crying out for help, and there
was no one to hear you, not even your own husband. Herbert
True took advantage of that. I'll help you explain to the reverend."

Beverly finally nodded, and thunder boomed louder. A light
drizzle began to fall, the chill in the air giving hint to the winter
that was just around the corner.

"The rain is so fitting for the way I feel," Beverly told Evelyn
sadly.

Their eyes held, and then the two of them embraced. Evelyn
did not know how to tell her that she felt the same way, afraid
for the future. In spite of the circumstances, she was glad Beverly
was back. It would be comforting to have a woman around,
someone in whom she could confide once Beverly felt stronger.

"I'll never raise my baby the way I was raised," Beverly told
her as she pulled away.

Evelyn thought about her own mother, how she had strived
to allow her daughter to be free with her emotions. She had
had a happy life, but that freedom of emotions had led her to
give herself and all her passion to a man she might never be
able to keep.

The thunder rolled louder, the sky growing very dark. "Let's
get over to the church before it pours," she told Beverly. "Everything will be all right, Beverly." She put an arm around her
and led her to the door.

"Thank you for coming with me," Beverly told her.

As they headed out into a stinging wind that was already spitting rain and sleet, Evelyn thought about Black Hawk, alone at Eagle Canyon. When would he come for her again? When would they know the answer to the vision that was yet unfulfilled? It looked as though a long, lonely winter lay ahead.

Twenty-three

Evelyn let go of Little Fox's hand long enough to button her woolen coat higher at the neck to ward off a chilling north wind. She took the boy's hand again. Both of them stood in line with hundreds of other Sioux who had gathered at the agency. This was the week that rations were handed out by the government. Each day Indians from a different section of the reservation lined up to get their share. Evelyn could understand the humiliation and anger they felt at this degrading procedure.

Such a proud people they were, once totally self-sufficient. Now they were reduced to standing in line for hand-outs like beggars. The government was trying to teach them to farm, but farming simply did not come naturally to these Plains warriors who were accustomed to hunting for their food, and who despised digging into Mother Earth and bringing Her pain. It went totally against their spiritual beliefs, but most whites could not understand that. They only thought them lazy and belligerent.

In spite of the shame waiting in line meant for him, she had decided that Little Fox might as well get his fair share of blankets and clothing, as well as whatever food he had coming. She had no doubt the meat would be tainted and mostly inedible, but there would be grains and canned food, although many of the Indians refused to eat some of the unfamiliar foods they were given. In the five months she had been here, she knew of at least seven deliberate cases of starvation, stubborn men and women who had allowed themselves to starve to death rather than eat the white man's food.

She looked back at the long line behind her, at the stony, unsmiling faces, such a contrast to a people who once celebrated a good buffalo hunt with dancing and story-telling and feasting. The women would laugh together then as they helped each other clean the hides and smoke the meat, while the warriors who had risked their lives on the hunt would lounge about with full bellies and tell stories of war and argue over who had killed the most buffalo. This was a people who normally enjoyed celebrating just about everything, whose sense of humor was sweet and subtle; but there was no laughter among this crowd, not even much talking.

They were dressed in a mixture of Indian and white clothing. Some women wore tunics, others faded, white women's dresses, most of which did not fit right. It was all clothing discarded by whites and shipped to the Indians. Some men wore deerskin leggings and moccasins, fringed shirts and jackets, others wore calico shirts and woolen jackets. A few wore white man's wool pants and leather boots. She had allowed Little Fox to continue wearing the deerskin clothing Black Hawk had left for him, but she had purchased a few pair of cotton long johns for him from Bill Doogan's trading post, as well as a pair of leather shoes, which he hated. He much preferred his moccasins, but Evelyn knew that the day was coming when all Indians would have to learn to wear white man's clothing. Eventually, the deerskin clothing would wear out, and there was not enough wild game left in the area for six thousand Indians to continue killing deer for meat and clothing. The buffalo, once almost all they needed for every stitch of clothing, every utensil, footwear, bags, housing, was now nearly extinct. The raw material necessary for their survival the old way had disappeared.

"My father does not come to the agency for supplies," Little Fox told her. "I have never done this."

Evelyn looked down at his dark eyes, full of innocence and pride. "I know, Little Fox. Your father is very proud, and so far he has been able to find his own food. I don't like this any more than the rest of your people do, but the government owes you these things, and you might as well take them. Winter is coming." She squeezed his hand. "Maybe it will be different for your generation. You will be educated, but will still keep your old customs and beliefs. You *can* live in both worlds, Little Fox. That is what I have to convince your father of."

They reached the long tables where goods were distributed. Soldiers milled about, watching the procedure closely, and James McLaughlin paced behind the tables, keeping an eye on everything. Agency personnel sat scattered behind the tables, stern looks on their faces. It irritated Evelyn that they could not hand out the supplies with at least a friendly smile. "Name?" The first man they came to studied a long list of names.

"Little Fox," she answered. "Son of Black Hawk."

The man looked up at her as though surprised. "Black Hawk never comes for his supplies."

"I am aware of that. He is not here today, but he has left his son for schooling. I brought the boy here to get what he fairly has coming."

The man scowled, his eyes moving over her with a look that told her he thought she was crazy to be here. "Where's the boy's father? We're handing out supplies to Indians, not white women."

Evelyn stiffened. "I am looking after the boy while he goes to school. I am not here to get anything for myself."

"Why would Black Hawk let a white schoolteacher look after his kid?"

Evelyn could not help wondering if Sergeant Desmond had been telling others about her and Black Hawk. "That is none of your business," she answered. "The point is Little Fox has no one here to see that he gets his fair share, so I have elected myself."

The man looked down at his ledger. "Does he have a white name?"

"No."

He scanned the ledger. "He should be assigned a white name. You'd better talk to McLaughlin about it. Makes it easier to keep records if they have regular names."

Evelyn bristled. "Why? The alphabet is the same no matter what they go by. Just look under 'L' for Little Fox. You *can* read, can't you? I imagine that is why you are the one checking off names."

The man, who wore a wool suit and sported a full, curled mustache, glanced up at her again, dark animosity in his eyes. "You have quite a mouth on you, lady. You're that schoolteacher, aren't you?"

"Yes. I am Evelyn Gibbons. I don't remember seeing you around the agency."

He looked back down at the ledger, turning to the "L's." "Vincent Jacoby. I'm usually cooped up in a back office keeping records updated, which is why you've never happened to see me. I've had to do a lot of rearranging and deleting since the cholera epidemic. Some of these people come through twice, try to get the rations of a dead relative."

"Can you blame them? What they get probably isn't near enough, nor is it what was actually promised by treaty."

"A treaty most of them refuse to recognize or sign. They're lucky to be getting what they're getting, after Custer and then Wounded Knee. They don't have sense enough to admit they've lost their land, keep yelling that the Black Hills still belong to them. By all rights, we don't have to give them a damn thing."

Evelyn squeezed Little Fox's hand reassuringly. "Well, Mr. Jacoby, I am glad to know how understanding and generous men like you can be," she answered with bitter sarcasm. "Have you found the boy's name yet, or do you need help? As I said, it begins with 'L'."

Jacoby breathed deeply to check his irritation, then checked off a name. "Get going," he said with a note of anger.

Evelyn only smiled. She led Little Fox down the long line of tables, picking up shirts and pants she thought would fit him, then taking two blankets. She opened one of them and put the clothes inside. "We will carry the food in the other blanket," she told him.

"You make sure only the kid and his father get the food," another agency man called out to her. "This stuff isn't for the whites. The government and Mission Services provides for you teachers."

Evelyn forced herself to ignore the ignorant and insulting remark. She gathered up the blanket of clothes and gave it to Little Fox to carry. "Is it too heavy?"

"I can do it," he said with a grin. He hoisted the bundle over his back, and walked with her to the area of food distribution. Evelyn spread out the other blanket and walked back and forth with Little Fox, carrying a sack of flour, dried beans, sugar, coffee, and canned goods to the blanket, as well as a package of smoked meat. The other meat being offered looked rancid, but she kept her temper in check. Somewhere there were white people eating the good meat meant for the Indians, meat that the government had paid for but had been traded off en route for meat of lesser quality. Someone had made a profit at the government's expense. She intended to start a letter-writing campaign, both to the President, Congress, and to Mission Services. Something had to be done about the corruption among the suppliers to reservations and many of the agents themselves.

"Go and get our horses, Little Fox. We'll load all of this on your horse and ride home on Reverend Phillips's old white nag."

Little Fox grinned. "She is old, true, but she has a good spirit."

Evelyn watched him run off to get the horses, and it was then she saw the familiar spotted horse. Black Hawk had come! She stood still as he rode closer, leading a second horse laden with supplies. Little Fox spotted his father and ran to him. Quickly, Black Hawk grabbed up his son and embraced him. They talked for a moment, and Little Fox pointed in her direction. Black Hawk looked her way, and even from a distance, Evelyn could feel the passion. She watched him ride over to where her and Little Fox's horses were tied. He let the boy down, and Little Fox untied the animals and led them in her direction. Black Hawk followed, and as he came closer, neither of them could take their eyes off each other. Evelyn felt fire creeping through her blood.

"I knew it was rations day," he told her. "My grandmother is getting too old to walk all the way to the agency, as many have to do now. I brought her and Many Birds on my two extra horses." He looked toward the line, then back at her, and she saw the sorrow in his eyes.

"I don't like it any more than you do, Black Hawk."

He remained on his horse, looking past her, then at a line of soldiers that stood watching, rifles ready, as though they thought the unarmed, ragged line of Indians was going to suddenly attack. "I do not like being here at the agency around so many soldiers," he said. "I only came because you and Little Fox were not at your cabin or at the school. I decided you must have come here."

"I thought Little Fox might as well get his share of what he had coming. I hope I haven't offended you." He looked grand today, wearing winter moccasins and deerskin leggings decorated down the outside with diamond-shaped beadwork. His outer coat was also deerskin, the hair still on it for warmth. His own long black hair was worn loose, except for a braid at one side with a leather string of beads wound into it. The cold wind blew his hair about his handsome face, and she saw the agony in his eyes, knew how much he hated rations day, hated that his people had to do this.

"You only do what must be done. It takes courage for a white woman to stand in that line." His eyes moved over her, and in spite of the cold day, Evelyn felt warm. "I will wait for my grandmother. She is not well."

"Oh, I'm sorry, Black Hawk. Many Birds didn't say anything about it."

"She has been coming to school as promised?"

"Yes. She's doing very well. So is Little Fox. You should come yourself, Black Hawk. I never got to continue your lessons."

He glanced at the soldiers again. "We will talk about it tomorrow. It is your Sabbath, is it not?"

"Yes."

"I have decided to stay with my grandmother for the winter. Come there tomorrow. Tell your preacher friend that you are going to visit some of the others, as you have often done in the past. We will talk then."

She nodded. "I have missed you, Black Hawk." In the two weeks since Beverly Evans had returned, she had worried and wondered, afraid this man had no intention of coming back. But now she could see the love and desire in his eyes.

"As I have missed you," he told her. "I want to embrace you, but we cannot do it here. It is not good that the soldiers even see us talking. I will see you tomorrow. I have something to show you, a surprise."

She smiled. "You mean you aren't going to tell me what it is?"

He smiled a little himself then. "Tomorrow." He reached out for Little Fox, and the boy grabbed hold of his father's hands and let him hoist him up onto his horse. "If the soldiers ask, you only spoke with me because Little Fox was with you. I am taking him with me back to my grandmother's village. I wish to spend some time with my son. You take your horses and the supplies back to your cabin. I go to wait for Many Birds and old Grandmother. I will ride with them back to their village."

Their eyes held a moment longer before he turned his horse and rode farther away. Evelyn watched after him, longing to go along, but he was right: they dared not show affection here, or be seen riding off together. She tied the supplies onto Little Fox's horse, then managed to mount the sidesaddle on her own horse. The last thing she wanted to do was ride away when Black Hawk was so close. She ached for him, needed to feel his arms around her. He said he had missed her, and wanted to embrace her. It warmed her heart to be reassured that he was nothing like Herbert True. There was not a dishonest or evil bone in his body. He was so misunderstood by others.

She picked up the reins to Little Fox's horse and led it along as she headed south to her own cabin, several miles away; and she realized how attached she had grown to Little Fox. It would be very lonely without him there tonight. She had already begun to think of him as her own.

Evelyn wondered at the giggling that was going on among the few Sioux women who happened to be working or cooking outside when she rode into the village where Black Hawk's grandmother lived. The cold weather kept most inside their tipis and cabins, but a few peeked out as she trotted her old white mare toward Dancing Woman's tipi, which she knew from previous visits was the one painted with a moon and stars on one side, a sun and mountains on the other. She kept the hood of her fur coat pulled over her head against the cold wind, but she could still hear some of the remarks the Indian women made.

"You are a lucky woman!" one of them shouted.

"It is the schoolteacher," someone else told another, as though her coming today was somehow a different and more exciting event than her other visits. Some just watched her quietly, but most of them grinned. Never in her other visits had there been this sense of frivolity or the feeling she was the center of their humor.

"Black Hawk is waiting for you," another woman told her with a grin.

Evelyn felt her face flushing. What had Black Hawk told them about her? Somehow she thought these people were unaware of the deep love she and Black Hawk shared.

She smiled and nodded to some of those who spoke to her, then dismounted, ducking her head against stinging sleet. She realized Reverend Phillips had been partially right earlier this morning when he told her she should not come here today because it would be a very cold trip. She felt chilled to the bone, and she was anxious to get inside, where she supposed old Dancing Woman and Many Birds, as well as Black Hawk and Little Fox, all sat around a warm fire; but when she started to tie her horse to a nearby post, Little Fox came running from a different direction and took the reins for her.

"I will take care of your horse," he told her with a grin. "I will let it graze out in the fields where my father's horses graze." He grasped his short wool jacket tighter around himself and ran off before she could ask where he had come from, why he wasn't in the tipi with Many Birds. With a shiver she jiggled the cow bell that hung over the tipi entrance to signal her arrival, and in the next moment Black Hawk himself threw back the buffalo-hide entrance flap. He grinned with delight, stepping aside to let her in. He closed and tied the flap, then turned to sweep her into his arms.

"It has been too long," he told her, moving his mouth to smother her in a kiss before she could say a word.

Evelyn felt herself melting against him, not even thinking his grandmother and Many Birds might be watching until he let go of her to lead her to a bed made of robes and blankets to the right of the warm fire burning at the center of the tipi. Evelyn looked around, saw no one.

"My sister and grandmother are with someone else for the day," Black Hawk answered her unasked question.

Evelyn started to ask why, then realized what he had planned. Now she understood the giggles and smiles from the other women. The whole village must know his intentions! "Black Hawk, everyone knows—"

He moved a foot behind one of her ankles and kicked lightly, making her lose her balance. He held her as she went down, pressed her into the robes. "They know that Black Hawk loves the schoolteacher. They know you have the heart of an Indian, so they do not mind. They understand that by Sioux custom, we are married, and I wish to make love to my wife."

Before she could answer, his mouth met hers again, parting her lips, searching with his tongue. She had not even had a chance to get a good look at him, and she only then realized he wore no shirt, in spite of the cold. He left her mouth, and his lips trailed over her throat.

"You said you had something to show me," she told him, feeling breathless.

"In time," he answered. "Take off your coat, woman, and I will help you undress."

"I . . . someone could come . . ."

"No one will come until I go out and tell them it is all right. They know they are to leave us alone."

Evelyn was sure she heard drumming and singing, and she felt almost in a trance while she helped him remove her clothes, both of them hurrying now, needing to touch again, be one again. She had missed him so, had not considered they might be able to be alone. Paintings of various scenes of hunting and making war swirled around her as he laid her naked body back into the robes and she studied the bright paintings on the inner tipi walls, paintings she was sure Black Hawk had done himself. She was vaguely aware that he threw his breechcloth aside, and she opened herself willingly, so much on fire for him that she could already feel the hot moistness deep in private places that meant she was ready for her man. He did not even have to touch her in any special way this time, and neither of them wanted to take time for preliminaries. They had been too long apart and were too hungry for each other.

Quickly, he was inside her, his hard, hot shaft moving in quick thrusts. Both groaned with the ecstasy of being one again, sharing bodies in this beautiful act of love. This time there was no pain at all for her, only a trembling, glorious fulfillment. She was so achingly in need that just the act of being united brought on the wonderful, almost agonizing climax that made her arch up to him in naked splendor, wanting to give and take at the same time. She cried out his name, dug her nails into his powerful arms, and in the next moment his own life spilled into her in throbbing force until finally they both lay spent. He breathed deeply, kissing at her neck then and pulling a blanket over them. "Do not move," he told her, both of them damp with the perspiration of heated lovemaking. "We have much to talk about, but first we will make love again, more slowly this time."

Evelyn did not argue. She only lay quietly while he moved down to gently taste her breasts, pulling teasingly at her nipples, circling each one with his tongue until the fire began to build again deep in her belly. Whatever he had to say, and whatever his surprise was, it would have to wait.

Beverly Evans, wearing a plain but neat dark-gray dress, helped pick up hymnals. This Sunday, as they did once a month, the families of white farmers who lived just beyond the eastern border of the Standing Rock Reservation had come to church, swelling the otherwise sparse congregation to completely fill the little church. A few more Indians were beginning to filter

in, but only those who understood English, their long faces
showing their tired resignation to a new way of life.

Beverly stacked the hymnals on a table at the front corner of
the church, near the piano, which had been sent to Reverend
Phillips by Mission Services two months earlier but had sat silent, since no one knew how to play it. That was now Beverly's
duty, and she gladly obliged the reverend and his congregation
with her musical talents, feeling grateful to have a place to stay.
She cherished Evelyn Gibbons's friendship. She and Evelyn had
had some long talks, and she understood how Evelyn felt about
Black Hawk, although she kept it to herself, knowing Evelyn
was not ready for everyone to know the extent to which her
relationship with Black Hawk had gone.

Beverly had decided she was in no position to judge. Her
heart still ached over the pain Herbert True had brought her, and
her only joy was knowing that in a few months she would have
a baby to love and to love her in return, a baby who would be
raised to be joyful and free.

"She's with Black Hawk, isn't she?"

Reverend Phillips interrupted Beverly's thoughts as she
stacked the last hymnal. She turned to face the man, trying to
read his eyes. Anger? Hurt? Condemnation? She wasn't sure.
"Yes."

He sighed. "She could have at least come to church services
first."

"She wouldn't have had time to ride all the way to Black
Hawk's grandmother's village if she had done that."

Phillips folded his arms. "You're close to her already, Mrs.
Evans. Can't you warn her? After what you've been through,
surely you understand the folly of falling in love with the
wrong man."

Beverly felt her cheeks growing hotter. "We can't always be
wise in the ways of love, Reverend. I was forced into my marriage to Greggory. I never loved him. Now I know that loving

Herbert was just a way out for me. I needed someone who would let me laugh, let me be a woman in the fullest sense. I'm sorry if I might have hurt Greggory and you and Mission Services. I never meant to hurt anyone, but I'm really not sorry I went away with Herbert, because I learned a lot about myself and about passion and freedom of expression. Perhaps what I did was wrong in the eyes of others, but not in my eyes; I truly loved Herbert, and in the eyes of God, the heart is all that matters. That is how it is with Evy and Black Hawk, except that Black Hawk is a much more sincere man than Herbert True. He is not a liar. Black Hawk is completely honest about his feelings."

Phillips turned away. "I thought at first I could . . . care for Miss Gibbons." He snickered with a hint of sarcasm. "But we are as different as night and day. We disagree on most things, but I respect her motives as far as her method of teaching and reaching these Indians. She has done a good job of winning their confidence. In some ways she seems so wise for her age, and then again so foolish . . . like when she talks about seeing Black Hawk in some kind of a vision, some dream— And it just isn't right for a white woman to care about an Indian man."

"Why not, Reverend? He is first a man, nothing more, nothing less. God teaches us to love everyone the same. To say she shouldn't be with him is to say the Sioux are beneath us, not worthy. That kind of thinking is unChristian. Doesn't God love us all the same? Isn't that what we teach? Who are we to love someone less than God loves them?"

He faced her, frowning, but the frown slowly changed to a soft smile. "Spoken like a true preacher's wife."

She smiled. "I was the daughter of a preacher and the wife of one. Just because I had a bad experience on both counts and then ran off with a near stranger doesn't mean I don't have faith, Reverend, or that I don't believe in God's love. I simply feel God means for us to be happy in that faith, to celebrate life and love. The bad things that happen to us come from things we do to ourselves, not because God is punishing us for something. I believe God loves us the same, no matter what mistakes we make. He understands."

His eyebrows arched in approval. "My, my. Maybe I should let *you* preach next week's sermon."

She laughed lightly. "No, thank you. You do a fine job all by yourself." Her smile faded. "Thank you, Reverend Phillips, for accepting me, allowing me to live in Janine's cabin, to play the piano for church and help Evelyn teach."

"Well, you might be sharing that cabin before long. Mission Services plans to send us more help as soon as they can."

Their eyes held, a sudden, new light beginning to shine for both of them, although neither quite recognized it yet for what it was. Beverly felt suddenly warm all over, and she looked away to absently straighten the stacks of hymnals. "You have no one to cook for you, Reverend, since Janine left. I have some fresh bread at the cabin, some pie and leftover stew." She faced him again. "Would you like to share lunch with me, Reverend Phillips?"

Phillips could not help moving his gaze over her lovely form. Beverly Evans was a very pretty woman when she smiled, and he was somewhat astounded at the impressive words of faith she had just spoken, especially after what she had been through. He could not help thinking how Greggory Evans had wasted his wife's talents. He should have made her a partner in his ministry, not just kept her hidden at home with strict orders to be silent and no duties except to cook and clean for him. He had gone to visit with them just once at the Oahe Mission, and it was obvious to him even then that Beverly Evans was nothing more to the man than a pretty ornament on his arm on Sundays, something to show that he was a faithful, married man. He wondered sometimes at the strange turns life took for some people. Maybe there was a reason for what had happened to Beverly, for Greggory Evans's death, but then such things were not for him to understand.

"Yes, I would like that," he answered. "I would like that very much."

Twenty-four

Evelyn lay nestled in Black Hawk's shoulder, moving her gaze to study the paintings inside the tipi. "You painted those horses, didn't you?" she asked Black Hawk.

"For my sister. She dreams of owning many horses."

"How did she get her name of Many Birds, if she so loves horses?"

Black Hawk smiled softly. "At birth she was first called Rising Sun. When she was ten, she found a spot out in the hills where birds would come to her and let them feed them. Because of that, she feels she shares the spirit of the birds, and from then on she was called Many Birds."

Evelyn thought it quite nice to be able to change one's name as he or she grew and changed. "Perhaps *I* should have an Indian name. What do you think would be a good name for me?"

He leaned over her, tracing a finger over her lips. "I have already thought much about this. You have brought new light to me and my people. You are like a princess, and that is what I would call you, *Wenonah,* Princess."

"Wenonah." She smiled. "I like it." Their eyes held in mutual love. Evelyn wondered at the power he had over her. She was so sure of herself and independent in most ways, but when Black Hawk touched her, or put her under this spell with those dark eyes of his, she was weak and totally at his command.

He rolled onto his back and pulled her on top of him. "We

will make love once more, *Wenonah,* before you must go. This time you will be the master."

"What do you—"

Black Hawk grasped her thighs and pushed her back slightly. "Raise up and make love to me, *Wenonah.*"

It was only then she understood what he was asking. "Black Hawk, I can't . . . I mean, proper ladies don't do such things!"

He only grinned. "You have not been a proper lady since you came here, but you have been a proper and most satisfying wife. What happened to your free spirit Evelyn Gibbons Hawk?"

She felt the fire again moving under her skin at the thought of such a bold and daring way of making love. "Hawk?"

"That will be your name when we are married the Christian way. I will take the name James Hawk. James was the name of the missionary man who taught me to speak English. He was the only good white man I ever knew."

The statement warmed her heart, gave her hope. He was already talking about a Christian wedding, had already decided he would take a white man's name. What better sign that this man truly loved her than to concede to something he once would never have considered?

"Black Hawk," she whispered, her eyes tearing. She closed her eyes and raised up, felt him easing himself into her.

"My *Wenonah.*"

She grasped his hands for support and began moving rhythmically, shivering at the glory of it, her breath leaving her at the wonder of the way he filled her to near-maddening ecstasy. She felt wild and wicked, alive and free. She leaned down, bracing her hands on either side of him so that his own hands were free to massage and tease her breasts. For several minutes she kept up the glorious union, until he rolled her onto her back and continued the act with exotic thrusts that made her cry out with a release of passion and high emotion. Everything swirled about her as she fell under his rapturous spell. When he finished with her, she felt wondrously ravished, blissful, so sweetly satisfied. She wondered how many women ever got to experience this kind of ecstasy.

She felt no guilt, for she was already this man's wife by Indian custom, and who was to say that was any different from her own custom? She loved him, and soon she would be Mrs. James Hawk. Somehow they would find a way to survive together. Their children would be taught Indian customs and skills, and also be educated and brought up in the Christian religion.

Nothing stood in their way now . . . except the yet-unfulfilled vision. She forced herself not to think about it. She was too happy to worry about a silly dream, or to give thought to Night Hunter's prediction that a white man would die and would somehow bring great troubles to Black Hawk. Maybe he was wrong. He *had* to be wrong. She was too happy now. She reached up and touched Black Hawk's hair. "When will we marry the Christian way?" she asked.

He leaned down and kissed her lightly, then moved away from her. "As soon as we know the meaning of Night Hunter's dream we will be free to tell your people of our love. There is something else."

"Something else?"

He looked over at her and grinned. "My surprise. We will wash and dress first."

He had a way of telling her to do something without being demanding. She moved to where he kept water hot in a kettle beside the fire. It annoyed her that so many of her own people thought these people were unclean. Black Hawk prided himself on cleanliness, his hair was always soft, his teeth scrubbed with baking soda, a habit he had learned as a boy when he lived with the missionaries. He had not agreed with many things they made him do, but he enjoyed the feel of clean teeth and took pride in an immaculate body. She wondered how insulted a lot of whites would be if they knew that the Sioux thought of *them* as sometimes smelling offensive. Black Hawk had often mentioned white men did not seem to care about washing, and that they were too hairy.

As they washed and dressed, already Evelyn was feeling the heaviness of knowing she must leave him again, dreading the loneliness she felt now when they were apart.

"I will ride most of the way back with you for your protection," Black Hawk told her, as though to read her thoughts.

"I'll be fine. I came out here alone."

"It will be getting dark. I will go with you."

Another command, spoken so gently yet firmly. Black Hawk left for a moment to throw out the water they had used, then returned, setting the pan aside and walking to the left side of the tipi. He picked up a beautifully beaded parfleche and brought it over to where she sat waiting. "This is a gift to you from Little Fox. He told me he promised you a gift when you named the seven Sioux rituals."

Evelyn took the parfleche, studying it almost reverently. "Oh, he shouldn't. I didn't name the last two."

Black Hawk grinned. "He said you knew them, but you forgot for just a moment because he had told you that I loved you and your thoughts became confused."

She met his eyes, enjoying his handsome grin, the square set of his jaw, the white, even teeth, the beautiful dark eyes. "I could hardly believe my ears. I think I loved you before I even came out here and met you."

His smile faded as he touched the bag himself. "This bag belonged to Little Fox's mother, so you know how special you have become to him. There is something inside that also belonged to Turtle Woman. It is a gift from me."

Evelyn untied the rawhide strings of the parfleche and opened it, reaching inside to pull out a bleached doeskin dress. She gently unfolded it, nearly gasping at the spectacular beadwork in a sunburst design of many colors on the breast. There was more beadwork on the skirt, she noticed with delight. The fringes on the sleeves, down the sides, and at the hem each had tiny pieces of tin tied to them so that the slightest movement made a lovely tinkling sound. She had no doubt the dress had taken weeks to make. In her own world, such an original Indian garment would be worth hundreds of dollars. The garment was so beautiful, Evelyn hardly knew what to say. "Black Hawk, I don't deserve—"

"It was Turtle Woman's wedding dress," he interrupted. "I wish for you to wear it when we are married the Christian way. She would want you to have it, and it will show your white friends that part of you is Indian. It will show my own people how fully I have accepted you. This is a sign of my love for you."

Evelyn's eyes teared. "Black Hawk, it's so beautiful." For a moment she felt a rush of jealousy, imagining what Turtle Woman's wedding night must have been like, wondering how lovely she must have been, yet her heart ached for how the woman had died, the hellish memories Black Hawk had to live with. She met his eyes. "Someday I will give you more sons, Black Hawk."

He nodded. "They will belong to both worlds. Perhaps that is the only way to keep the circle complete. Life can never be as it once was for us, and it hurts my heart to know this; but I also know that it cannot be changed. We must go on, learn to live this new way. You can help me do this, and our children will keep the circle of life turning so that the circle is never broken."

A tear slipped down her cheek. How long would it be before they knew the meaning of Night Hunter's predictions; before they knew the full meaning of their own dreams? How much longer could she bear to wait before she could live with this man openly? "I don't know what to say. It's the most beautiful gift anyone has ever given me. I will treasure it always, and I will be proud to wear it when we marry." She felt overwhelmed by the touching gift. "You said there was something else besides the vision that had to come before we marry. What did you mean?"

"That is my surprise," he said with a grin.

Evelyn carefully laid the dress aside as he leapt up and walked over to take something from under a blanket. She had thought the dress was his surprise, but instead, he turned toward her holding a wood-framed canvas in each hand. "What do you think?"

She stared at one picture of rolling green hills, with deeper green pine trees nestled in each depression. The pines were mixed with aspen trees, their leaves bright green, their white trunks bright from sun that shone on them. In the distance was the dark outline of mountains, with gray clouds hanging overhead, telling of a rainstorm to come. Wild horses ran across the hills.

He looked down at that particular picture. "I can no longer ride west to the higher hills and the mountains, where you find the trees with white trunks and where you see this kind of beauty, but my memory of that country is vivid. I dream about it often, long to go wherever I please, to the cool mountains in summer."

He turned his attention to the other picture, of an Indian man riding a golden horse with white mane and tail. The horse was in a galloping pose, preparing to leap across a stream, a wolf running beside him. The ground was covered with snow, as were the pine trees in the background. The Indian man wore full, beaded and fringed dress, a hat made from the head and fur of a wolf. He carried a lance decorated with feathers, and a hawk sat on his outstretched arm. He was the very image of a true warrior. "This is how I see myself, if I were free to live the old way," he told her, "riding to war against my enemies, going on the hunt to bring food to my family."

When Evelyn sat there saying nothing, he frowned. "Do you not like them?"

Evelyn blinked, astounded at the accuracy of the paintings. "Oh, Black Hawk, I more than like them. They are spectacular! Do you realize what talent you have?"

He smiled again, bringing the picture of the Indian man to eye level. "You told me that your people would buy paintings like this. I want you to see if truly they can be sold. You said sometimes a man can earn money the white man's way by doing something that he loves. I love to paint. It helps me live the things I can no longer do, helps calm the anger in my soul. I know that you cannot live fully the Indian way, so I must take care of you in the way you are accustomed. If I can sell my paintings, it is a way for me to do that. I would give you all the money. I have no use for it. I will still hunt for our meat and am satisfied with the clothes my sister and grandmother make for me from skins and from the cloth they get on rations day. With the money you can buy yourself the things a white woman needs. I will just paint the pictures. You can sell them."

She lifted the picture of the mountains and studied it closer, finding not one flaw. "Black Hawk, I have no doubt that you can most certainly receive money for these." She met his eyes. "I'll send them off to my father right away. He can find out about places in Milwaukee, or perhaps Chicago, that would take them to sell."

He nodded, smiling. "If they bring money, it will be a good sign that we have found a way to be together and still live in both worlds."

She blinked against more tears that wanted to come. "I can see that you love me very much."

He frowned. "Did you doubt it?"

"There were times . . ." She set the painting aside and threw her arms around his neck. Black Hawk let go of the other painting and embraced her, standing up and pulling her up with him.

He kissed her hungrily, gratefully. "Do not ever doubt my love, *Wenonah.*"

"I feel so much more sure about our future together, Black Hawk. And the dress . . . it's so beautiful. Are you *sure* you want me to wear Turtle Woman's dress when we marry?"

He studied her eyes. "She would be honored, and happy to know how much you care for Little Fox, and he for you. She would be glad to know you have taken my broken heart of sorrow and have filled it with joy again." Reluctantly, he pulled away. "We must go. I will wrap the paintings in blankets and tie them to a spare horse."

Her heart aching to stay with him, Evelyn walked over and carefully folded the dress, putting it back into the parfleche. "I must thank Little Fox for his beautiful gift."

"He will come with us. I wish for him to continue staying with you and going to school. He could stay here and go with Many Birds, but you will become closer if he lives with you."

"I love having him with me. When he is gone, I miss him and feel very lonely now."

Black Hawk pulled on his deerskin coat, tying it at the front with rawhide strings. Their eyes held for a moment in mutual pain at having to part. Evelyn was surprised to realize he had tears in his eyes. "I will go and get Little Fox," he finally told her. As he turned and went out, a stiff wind blew against the tipi. Evelyn just then realized that in spite of the chill inside, she had not noticed it until now. She had lain safe and warm in Black Hawk's arms.

"I wanted to take you home this way," Black Hawk told Evelyn. He led her along the Grand River, where the land was more heavily wooded. "It is not a place you should ride alone, because none of my people are camped here, but it is prettier. I like it here because it is so peaceful. Farther east there is another Sioux village."

"Why don't more of the Sioux camp right here along the river, where they're close to better grass and water?" Evelyn rode beside him, and Little Fox followed with the packhorse.

"They would, if the agency would let them. The agency tells them where they can place their tipis. They say we must preserve this area for a while, until the land farther north and west has been well grazed. Even on land that is still supposed to belong to us, we are told where we can live."

Evelyn sensed the bitterness in the words. "I'm sorry, Black Hawk."

An owl hooted nearby, and Black Hawk looked past her at a rising moon, although the sun was still not set. "I must get you back before dark. We will head north now." He turned his horse, but before they could head away from the trees, two men came charging out of a thicker stand of trees ahead of them. They hooted and whistled as they rode closer, quickly cutting off Black Hawk's pathway. One of them pulled a rifle from its boot on his saddle.

"Hold up there, Black Hawk!" he called.

Evelyn's heart pounded with fear. The one with the rifle was middle-aged and sported a dark beard. His clothing was soiled and wrinkled. His companion was much younger, a clean-shaven man wearing much neater clothing. However, his eyes showed a hatred and cunning that spoiled his otherwise handsome appearance.

Black Hawk drew his horse to a halt. "Stay behind me," he ordered Evelyn and Little Fox.

"Who are they?" Evelyn asked.

"Black Hawk can tell you who we are," the older one sneered. "Can't you, you troublemaking sonofabitch! I could shoot you right off that horse now and not get in one bit of trouble for it," he added, glaring at Black Hawk.

"You would have to explain your presence to the agency," Black Hawk answered. "And do not forget there is a white woman present. The agency might not believe me or my son, but they would believe her if she tells them you killed me for no reason."

Both men leaned over slightly to get a better look at Evelyn. "Even with that hood over your head and that coat on, you look like a nice piece of woman, lady," the younger one told her. He looked at Black Hawk. "How about it, Black Hawk? Want to trade her for some whiskey?"

"You know what I think of you and your whiskey," Black Hawk said calmly. "Do not make trouble here, or it is you who will suffer for it. Now you have let yourself be seen by a white woman who has much authority."

"A woman with authority?" The older one laughed. "All I know is you and some of your young bucks raided our camp a few months back, and you destroyed hundreds of dollars worth of whiskey! That didn't set too good with the men who sent us, and I've got a hunch that even if you was able to catch us and turn us in, you'd be in as much trouble as we would, just for takin' the law into your own hands—you, a stinkin' *Indian!*"

Evelyn watched Black Hawk stiffen, and she was terrified of what could happen here. He had no weapon with him but a hunting knife. "If you were worried about being seen or caught, why did you ride out here to bother us?" she asked. "Let us be on our way. We've done you no harm. You're the ones who let your presence be known!"

The younger one rode closer. "We seen Black Hawk here with a white woman, thought maybe you needed help." His eyes moved over her. "How come you're with the big buck here, lady? Or *are* you a lady? Maybe you aren't even *worth* a couple of bottles of whiskey."

Evelyn bristled. Against Black Hawk's wishes she rode her horse up beside him, praying Little Fox would stay back if there was trouble. "I am Evelyn Gibbons, a schoolteacher here on the reservation. I was visiting one of the villages to recruit more children, and Black Hawk is accompanying me back to my quarters. His son is coming back with me to attend school. Now get out of our way!"

The young man snickered, glancing over at his companion. "Feisty little thing."

The older man joined in the light laughter. "Lady, we thought we'd check and see if you needed help," he said, sitting straighter and leveling his rifle, "but the more I get a look at you, the more I see you don't need any help. Fact is, I *like* what I see. Now I've got a real hatred for Black Hawk here, and the way I see it, I could kill him and the kid both, and we could take you off with us on the flatboat we've got docked down past the trees there, haul you along the Grand to the Mississippi, where there's a bigger steamboat waitin' for us. Ain't a man on that riverboat who'd care if you was willin' or not. We'd all have a good time with you, then dump you off in Omaha, and nobody here would ever know what happened to you."

Evelyn struggled to keep her composure and show no fear. "You don't really think you could get away with such a thing! Who are you?"

"They are whiskey traders," Black Hawk answered for her, keeping his eyes on the older one. "The hairy one is Luke Smith. The young one who cannot keep his manpart small is Marty Able. I have caught them bringing whiskey onto the reservation other times, and once I stopped them. Seth Bridges was with them that day, and Jubal Desmond is the one who was supposed to be patrolling the area where I found them. That is why I told you Bridges and Desmond help men like this, but it could not be proved."

Evelyn glared at both men. "Well, it can certainly be proved now! I know your names, and I know how you got into the reservation! Where is the whiskey? On your flatboat?"

Luke just kept grinning. "You won't find any whiskey there. It's already been took care of. Anybody finds us now, we're clean as a whistle. We was fixin' to go back when we seen you comin' along with the troublemaker here. We figured out here, with nobody around, maybe we can get us a woman to go back with us. Ole Seth was supposed to trade us off one of his daughters, but he never came through."

Evelyn shivered at the words. So, Seth Bridges *was* abusing his daughters, just as she suspected. Had he also "traded off" poor Lucille to Sergeant Desmond for something? Maybe for whiskey? She would never believe Lucille willingly went to that dance with the man, or to the circus. Something was terribly wrong!

"Black Hawk can hand you over with no trouble, or we can do this the hard way, if that's what it takes," Marty said. He leaned forward, resting his elbow on the pommel of his saddle. "What will it be, Black Hawk?"

Evelyn gasped when Black Hawk suddenly ducked and charged his horse forward, at the same time letting out a chilling war whoop. Luke's rifle fired, but the bullet whizzed over Black Hawk's head and into the trees. In that instant, Black Hawk thundered his horse into Luke's, leaping from his own horse and knocking Luke from his mount. Both men landed on their hind-quarters, and Luke's rifle went skidding across the ground several feet away from him.

"Father!" Little Fox cried.

Evelyn backed her horse, grabbing the reins to Little Fox's horse and forcing him to also move farther back. "Stay where you are, Little Fox!" she warned, a sick dread inside at what could happen to Black Hawk, who wrestled on the ground with Luke.

Luke got Black Hawk onto his back and began pummeling him, but Black Hawk managed to kick up with his knee, catching the man in the crotch and then hoisting him with his leg so that he literally flipped over Black Hawk's head and landed on his back. In an instant Black Hawk was on him, knife pulled. Evelyn noticed Marty watching the fight closely, his hand on the handle of his revolver. She took advantage of his diverted attention and leapt down from her horse, running over and grabbing up Luke's rifle. She aimed it at Marty.

"Don't touch that gun, or I swear I'll shoot!" she ordered.

The man hesitated, obviously debating if she meant it, then moved his hand away. Evelyn glanced at Black Hawk, who was straddled over Luke, his left fist holding the man's hair tightly. Luke's head was jerked awkwardly sideways, and the man was groaning with the terrible pain it caused in his neck.

"Let me go!" he begged.

Black Hawk laid his knife on Marty's cheek, slithering its tip along the surface of Luke's skin, just enough to draw blood. He traced it over Luke's jaw and on down his neck to the fur collar of the man's coat. Luke cried out in terror, begging Black Hawk not to slit his throat.

"You are the scum of white men!" Black Hawk seethed. "You *deserve* to die. I only wish I could do it *slowly,* in the ways my people have of making a man suffer!"

"Black Hawk, don't!" Evelyn screamed. "You'll destroy everything if you kill him! Remember the vision! A white man cannot die at your own hands!" She noticed a slight movement then, realized instantly that Marty Able was going for his gun again while she was not watching. Her reaction a spontaneous act of panic. She fired the rifle, and even though she had not actually aimed it, Marty screamed out when a bullet ripped through his left shoulder. He nearly fell from his horse.

Evelyn could hardly believe what she had done, but for the moment there was no time to think about it. "I *warned* you!" she screamed. "If you try to hurt Black Hawk or his son, I'll *kill* you!"

The gunshot startled both Black Hawk and Luke. Black Hawk turned in terror, thinking Evelyn was the one shot at by Marty. He kept a painful hold on Luke's hair, and when he saw Evelyn standing there with a smoking rifle, he was filled with relief, and a great pride. The gunshot seemed to bring him back to his senses. After he stood up, jerking Luke up by the hair of the head, he moved behind the man and stuck the tip of the knife against his Adam's apple.

"You and your friend will leave now, and you will not come back," he snarled. "If I see you again, I will cut you from ear to ear! That is a promise, no matter what might happen to me!" He brought the knife to the side of Luke's head, slitting off part of his earlobe.

Luke grabbed his ear and screamed like a wild man, blood running through his fingers and down the back of his hand into his coat sleeve. "You stinking Indian!" he hollered. "My ear! My ear!"

"Be glad it was not your throat!" Black Hawk told him. "Go! Both of you!"

Evelyn shivered at the bloody sight.

"I want my rifle!" Luke demanded.

"I am keeping it to show the authorities!" Evelyn answered the man. "Get going before Black Hawk changes his mind!"

By now Luke was crying. "Goddamn . . . sonofabitch!" he wept. "You ain't heard the end of this, Black Hawk!"

Black Hawk just grinned as the man struggled to get back on his horse. "Who will you tell?" he asked. "The agency? They will know what you are doing here, and you will be arrested."

"You bitch!" Marty growled at Evelyn, terrible pain showing in his icy-blue eyes. The whole left side of his jacket was blood-stained, and a stiff wind made him shake.

"Let's go!" Luke told the man. "Let's get back to the steamboat and get the hell out of here!" He was still holding his ear with his right hand, but he managed to keep the reins in his left. He turned his horse and rode back into the trees. Marty glared at Evelyn a moment longer, then joined his partner.

For several minutes Black Hawk and Evelyn kept watching

the direction in which they had ridden. They could hear Luke's continued screaming and Marty's cussing.

"Get the horses onto the flatboat!" Luke was ordering. "Get our gear!"

"How can I, with my shoulder like this, damn you!" Marty answered.

Luke shouted something about bleeding to death, and Marty said "So am I!" Then there was nothing but curses that began to fade, signifying that they were on the flatboat and headed away from their campsite, probably east to the Mississippi.

Evelyn finally lowered the rifle with shaking hands. "My God, I've shot a man!" she groaned.

Black Hawk walked a few feet away, struggling with his anger and the frustration of not being able to kill the men who had threatened him and the woman he loved. There was a time . . . He pushed back his coat and rammed his knife back into its sheath, then turned to Evelyn, his eyes still blazing.

"You did what you had to do." He looked her over, thinking how big the rifle looked compared to her small stature. It would be amusing if not for the gravity of the moment. "You are a warrior Evelyn Hawk. I did not know you had such courage. My people will only respect and trust you more when I tell them what you have done this day. You saved my life."

Little Fox ran up to the man, putting his arms around his waist. "I thought they would kill you, Father!"

Black Hawk rubbed lightly at the boy's back, his eyes still on Evelyn, who had seen firsthand the true warrior that lived within this man she loved, the warrior he would still be, if not for the changes forced upon him. Part of her was almost afraid of him, but that was the part that had grown up in a different world. For the way he was raised, he had actually shown great restraint. She knew most white women would have been appalled by what he had done to Luke Smith's ear, would call it savage; but she knew that not killing the man had taken great courage, and his strength and bravery only made her love and want him more.

"You put your own life at great risk to save me from something *worse* than death," she told him. "When his gun fired, I thought . . . all I could think of was Wild Horse . . . seeing him shot down." Her eyes teared, and she came closer to embrace both Black Hawk and Little Fox.

"We must leave here, get you home," Black Hawk told her. "Then I must get back to my own camp. If the agency finds out what I did today—"

"They *will* find out, because I will tell them!" Evelyn said, looking up at him. "Why should we wait and take the risk that they will hand them some story themselves to make you look bad? It's best to tell the truth, Black Hawk, and I am going straight to the agency when I get back! If the Army was doing their job right, such awful men wouldn't even get onto the reservation! And I intend to tell them they admitted they were with Seth Bridges when you destroyed their whiskey supply!"

He shook his head. "It will do no good. They have already searched that man's home and found nothing. Telling them about all of this will only let them know that I am the one who attacked the whiskey traders a few months ago, something they have been wanting to prove."

"Fine! You did the right thing, something the *Army* is supposed to be doing! They have no right punishing you for it. If we are going to be married, Black Hawk, I intend for James McLaughlin and Reverend Phillips and Colonel Gere and the rest to understand the kind of man you really are!"

"It will only mean trouble for me."

"Not when *I'm* finished with them!"

He sighed, watching the trees where Luke and Marty had disappeared. He had no doubt Sergeant Jubal Desmond knew about those two. Maybe they would even tell him what had happened. If Desmond could get him in trouble over it, he would.

Now he was not so sure that he could live at Evelyn's cabin, so near the agency, when they married. But it was the only way Evelyn could live, and it hurt his heart to think perhaps his plans to do it all her way could not be realized. "We must go."

He pulled away, and Evelyn sensed his doubts. "Black Hawk, we can make it work. I promise you."

He looked at her sadly, then turned away and in one swift movement jumped onto the back of his saddleless horse. "We must go," he repeated, raising his voice against an increasing wind.

Her own heart feeling heavy, Evelyn walked over and stepped into the stirrup of her sidesaddle, climbing onto her own horse. "Black Hawk, please listen to me—" she shouted into the wind. "We have much to think about."

She held his eyes. "And you have given me Turtle Woman's wedding dress. I intend to wear it . . . *soon*. I will talk to the agency and to the colonel, Black Hawk, and I will come to your camp and tell you what they say. We will be together!"

He studied her lovingly. "Just remember that a white man did not die here today. Something worse is going to happen, and because of what happened here, I will be blamed. I feel it in my soul. We cannot marry before all of this trouble is settled."

She wanted to argue more, scream at him, but she knew it was no use. As he headed out in front of her, she glanced back at Little Fox, who had remounted his own horse. He showed the same anger and fear in his dark eyes as his father. "Nothing is going to happen to him, Little Fox," she told the boy. "I promise." She turned her horse to follow Black Hawk, refusing to let her own doubts get the better of her. Nothing and no one was going to keep her from the man she loved. She would make sure of it, even if it meant fleeing to Canada with him.

Twenty-five

Colonel Gere frowned in irritation at being called from a busy schedule to listen to some kind of complaint from the schoolteacher, Evelyn Gibbons. It seemed the woman had done nothing but cause trouble since she'd arrived. It was her fault that Lieutenant Teller and the men with him had been embarrassed at finding nothing when they raided Seth Bridges's home and property. She had falsely accused Sergeant Desmond of being involved in the whiskey smuggling, and to top it all off, she had taken the word of Black Hawk that Bridges and Desmond were involved, let alone the fact that she had accused his own troops of not doing their job.

Now here she was again, registering yet another complaint at the agency offices. At least this time she was doing it herself, rather than sending the poor Reverend Phillips to do it for her. He'd been told by his messenger that she was alone, and he did not doubt that Phillips was growing tired of her infatuation with Black Hawk and her fantasies about someone among his own troops being involved in smuggling whiskey.

He reminded himself to remain the gentleman as he removed his hat and went inside Agent McLaughlin's office. After all, demented or not, Evelyn Gibbons was certainly refined and educated, not to mention the prettiest woman he'd ever set eyes on. She just needed to get her thinking straight about the Sioux and stop defending them to the point of embarrassment. When he went inside the office, he found her seated in a hardwood chair near James McLaughlin's desk. She wore a deep blue velvet dress with long sleeves and high neckline. White cotton lace decorated the border of the neck and the ends of the sleeves. The dress made the blue eyes that looked up at him seem even bluer. She wore her honey-blond hair in a very demure bun at the nape of her neck. He wondered if she was trying to look especially prim and proper just to make herself more believable. Rumor had it the woman was more deeply involved with Black Hawk than just as his son's teacher. He could not imagine that an educated white woman, one raised in a Christian home, could possibly have romantic thoughts for an Indian man.

He nodded to her. "Miss Gibbons. I hope this interruption in my busy day is for something worthwhile." He looked at McLaughlin, whose own doubt showed in his eyes.

"Have a seat, Colonel."

The man obliged, and McLaughlin shuffled some papers on his desk. "Miss Gibbons here tells me she was attacked by whiskey smugglers yesterday. She was so upset by it that she left today's lessons to Mrs. Evans and came directly here to tell us about it."

"Something must be done," Evelyn said, sitting straight and confident in the chair. "I have said it before, Colonel, and I will say it again: Your men are not doing their job. Every day I see drunken Sioux everyplace I go. It is perfectly obvious that whiskey is plentiful on this reservation, and I am here to repeat to you that Seth Bridges is involved. I know it now for a fact."

Gere sighed, leaning forward to rest his elbows on his knees. "And how is that?"

Evelyn glanced at McLaughlin, then back at Gere. "I visited an Indian village yesterday, then brought Black Hawk's son, Little Fox, back with me. He is going to live with me while he attends school. Because it was getting dark, Black Hawk accompanied me back. He took me along the Grand River to show me an area of the reservation I had never been before. It was there we were accosted by two men, whiskey smugglers! They rode out to us from the trees and threatened to kill Black Hawk and his son and carry me off. I don't have to tell you what they had in mind for me!"

Gere looked her over. "How do you know they were whiskey smugglers?"

She prayed she would not get Black Hawk in trouble. "Because Black Hawk knew them. He had seen them before, caught them bringing a whole wagonload of whiskey onto the reservation. He destroyed it, and he had every right to do so. If the Army had been doing its job, the whiskey would never have gotten onto the reservation!"

Gere glanced at McLaughlin. So, it *was* Black Hawk who destroyed the whiskey and attacked the men who had brought it. He decided to reserve judgment until he heard the woman out. "That's Black Hawk's word."

"It's *their* word! They *admitted* they were the ones who brought in that whiskey! They even admitted that Seth Bridges was with them that night! I am telling you that Seth is involved in whiskey smuggling, and, furthermore, there is more of it going on than you realize! And you cannot convince me that Sergeant Jubal Desmond is not involved in helping them. The man professes to have no special relationship with Seth Bridges, but he was seen with Seth's daughter, and it's a fact that the area where that whiskey wagon was destroyed is a spot where the sergeant was supposed to be keeping watch! How can you not see what is going on, Colonel?"

The man leaned back in his chair, scowling with irritation and anger. "I am a colonel in the United States Army, Miss Gibbons, and I didn't get this position by being stupid! I can't just go accusing someone of doing something wrong when I have no proof! The last time you tried to make trouble over this, we obliged you fully. If you will remember, we raided Seth Bridges's home and property and found nothing! *Nothing!* You can't say we didn't try, but there is simply no proof to your allegations about Seth Bridges *or* Sergeant Desmond!"

"But the smugglers admitted—"

"Did you *see* any of the whiskey with your own eyes?"

"Well, no, I—"

"And where are those men today? *Gone!*"

Evelyn could not help jumping slightly at the anger in the word. She struggled to keep her composure and not let the man bully her. "Only because if Black Hawk had tried to bring them in, they would have tried to twist the story and get *him* in trouble! You have to stop intimidating these people, Colonel, and give them some credit for their own intelligence and their ability to take care of themselves and this reservation."

"Then let Black Hawk join the Indian police," the man grumbled.

"The police do not have the freedom they should have to handle things their way!" Evelyn answered. "They have to kow-tow to Army regulations, do everything the Army's way. The Indian police are a farce, Colonel, and you know it! They're afraid to do anything about the smugglers because they might be accused of murdering white men, and some of them won't bother stopping them anyway! They *want* the whiskey!"

The man's brown eyes blazed with anger. "And you, Miss Gibbons, are a worse troublemaker than Black Hawk!"

Evelyn bristled even more. "I am trying to make things better here for the Sioux! Isn't that the whole idea? To keep the peace? What would you prefer, Colonel? To watch over six thousand sober, educated Indians, or six thousand drunken, belligerent ones? We have to keep out the whiskey and get these people educated, and we need the Army's help! I am telling you that there is too much smuggling going on, that Sergeant Desmond and Seth Bridges are both involved! Those men admitted yesterday they run whiskey, admitted they knew Seth Bridges! They threatened to murder Black Hawk and a seven-year-old boy in cold blood because Black Hawk knows too much; and they were going to drag me off and violate me, ship me down to Omaha and dump me off! They came downriver by flatboat from a bigger steamboat on the Mississippi. If you inspected the boats that come upriver from St. Louis and Independence and Omaha, you'd probably find plenty of whiskey on them!"

"We have no authority to go raiding trading ships that come upriver," McLaughlin told her. "We can only inspect wagons and supplies that actually come onto the reservation."

Evelyn turned her attention to the man, who was at least holding his composure better than the colonel. "Then more men should be assigned to doing just that," she told him.

McLaughlin rubbed at his white mustache. "We don't have enough men at Fort Yates to cover every inch of the Mississippi, the Grand and, the Cheyenne rivers, Miss Gibbons. It's simply impossible. The colonel does the best he can, and I will do what I can to see if the government will send us more troops."

Evelyn sighed. "I appreciate that much. I know we are talking about a very big area, Mr. McLaughlin, but something more must be done!"

"I'd like to know how you and Black Hawk got out of that situation yesterday," Colonel Gere asked. "Black Hawk is not allowed to carry any weapon but his knife."

Evelyn hesitated. This man was looking for any reason to arrest Black Hawk. She held his gaze steadily. "As I said, there were two of them, an older man with dark hair and beard who was called Luke Smith. His companion was much younger, clean-shaven and quite handsome if not for his despicable personality. His name was Marty Able. Luke was holding a rifle on Black Hawk, and Black Hawk realized he had to do something or take the chance that he and his son might be killed. He risked his life to save both me and Little Fox by bending down and charging his horse right into Luke Smith, knocking him from his horse. Luke dropped his rifle, and when I saw that Marty

Able was pulling a pistol to shoot Black Hawk, I picked up the rifle and I shot him!"

Gere's eyebrows arched. *"You* shot one of them?"

"I most certainly did, and I had every right! I hit him in the shoulder. I still have the rifle if you want to see it. Black Hawk was wrestling with Luke Smith and held a knife to his throat. He could have killed him, but he didn't. That should show you the man's wisdom. He knew what would happen to him if he killed a white man, no matter how much that person deserved to have his throat slit! I personally would have enjoyed watching it, considering what he had in mind for me. Black Hawk let him go, Colonel." She decided not to mention that Black Hawk had cut off half the man's ear. "Both men rode off and left on their flatboat. They are probably well on their way back downriver by now, and if they have any sense, they will not come back!"

The colonel got up and began pacing, and the room hung quiet while he gauged his words. "What were you doing riding alone with Black Hawk, of all people, and in that remote area besides? Why didn't you just go home the usual way, through other Indian villages?"

Evelyn sensed the man's thoughts. He didn't care one whit about the incident with the whiskey smugglers. All he cared about was whether or not a white woman was carrying on with an Indian. Perhaps he was looking for a reason to arrest Black Hawk as well. "I told you. Black Hawk wanted to show me the area—"

"I think you both just wanted to be alone awhile longer," he accused, turning to face her. "I think there is more between you and Black Hawk than just a friendship, and *that,* my dear, is how you get yourself in so much trouble. It makes you less credible because it reflects on your reputation. Anything you say in defense of Black Hawk is only because of your own prejudiced view! I suggest, Miss Gibbons, that you do what you came here to do, and that you take a good look at your personal choices of friends and lovers, if you intend to keep your position here on the reservation! I am sorry for what happened by the river, but you and I both know you shouldn't have been there in the first place. If you would quit putting yourself in dangerous situations, you would not be having these problems! It isn't wise for a young, unattached woman to be flitting about by herself on an Indian reservation, to be disobeying all the rules of protocol and to be seen time and again with an Indian renegade!"

Evelyn slowly rose to face him, fighting to keep from breaking down out of anger and humiliation. The man was trying to make her love for Black Hawk look ugly and sinful, and she would not allow it, nor would she let him turn attention from the problems with smugglers. She faced him squarely.

"I am not one of your soldiers, Colonel," she said calmly. "You have no right talking to me this way. Don't use rumors to invent stories just to make yourself look better. My relationship with Black Hawk, the way I teach, the fact that I happened to be at the wrong place at the wrong time yesterday—none of those matters give you an excuse for the fact that those men were on the reservation without permission, or that whiskey smugglers are running rampant all over this reservation! If you don't want me to tell you how to do your job, sir, then don't be telling me how to do mine! The point is to get Sioux children to school, and I have done a good job of that. More come every day, and soon we will need a bigger school. Keep the whiskey peddlers out, Colonel, and I will educate the children. Between the two, there can be total peace on this reservation. We can teach the Sioux to take care of themselves, let them govern themselves, rely on their own police to keep order so that one day the soldiers won't be needed at all." She turned to McLaughlin. "I thought I was doing my civic duty, Mr. McLaughlin. I do not deserve to be insulted and humiliated."

The man sighed. "I agree." McLaughlin looked up from his

desk at the colonel. "And I also agree that more must be done about the whiskey peddlers."

Colonel Gere's ruddy complexion turned even redder, making his white hair seem whiter. "I fully agree with you about working even harder to keep whiskey out of the reservation," he told McLaughlin. He moved his eyes to Evelyn. "But my comments were not meant as insults or an invasion of Miss Gibbons's privacy. Every word I said is true, meant to protect her job and her good name." He sighed with irritation, fingering his hat. "Let me ask you, ma'am, do you consider it an insult for a white woman to be hooked up with an Indian man?"

Evelyn hated him for putting her on the spot. "Not at all," she answered boldly, "except that I do not appreciate the term 'hooked up.' A man is a man, Colonel, and there are good men and some not so good. Black Hawk is a good man, intelligent and talented, and much more compassionate and brave than you will ever know. What I consider an insult is the meaning men like you put into your remarks, trying to make something dirty and ugly out of something beautiful and right." She turned, walking over to her chair and opening a blanket wrapped around something propped there. She took out Black Hawk's paintings and held them up. "This is the kind of talent Black Hawk has. This is proof that he wants to learn to live a new way. He is allowing his son to come to school, and he painted these pictures for me to send to my father to see if they can be sold. He hopes to be able to make money with his paintings."

Both men looked taken aback. McLaughlin leaned farther over his desk to get a closer look. "Those are remarkably realistic," he commented.

Gere sighed in unwanted resignation. "They are quite good."

"They're better than good," Evelyn told him. She looked at McLaughlin. "I want your promise that Black Hawk will not get in trouble over the incident with the whiskey smugglers, neither the first time when he destroyed their wagon, nor this last time. He had every right to attack those men. He was only protecting us. He is afraid you will try to have him arrested."

McLaughlin leaned back in his chair again. "He has nothing to worry about. He didn't use a gun, and both times he refrained from doing great harm to those men. Nor will I write any letters advising that you be removed from your position, Miss Gibbons. What Mission Services does is another matter, one over which I have no control. When they find out about your feelings for Black Hawk . . ." He shrugged. "Who can say? That is a chance you take on your own. I can certainly understand loving an Indian. As you know, my own wife is Sioux." He glanced at Colonel Gere rather scathingly, and Evelyn could tell Gere was embarrassed over his remarks. He had apparently forgotten about McLaughlin's wife for the moment.

"I *can* tell you that in the past Black Hawk has proved himself to be very unpredictable and sometimes dangerous," McLaughlin continued. "He has never been cooperative, and I still don't fully trust him not to use that knife of his in a meaner way if he's pushed."

"Maybe he's just afraid . . . of losing everything that is dear to him, of having his son taken away from him. He was at Wounded Knee. He saw his wife and baby son murdered! His whole way of life has changed, and he can no longer enjoy the freedom he knew as a youth. How do you *expect* him to feel? How do you expect *any* of them to feel?" Evelyn glanced at Gere, then back to Agent McLaughlin. "I trust him fully, Mr. McLaughlin. Never has he tried so hard to adapt to the changes, to accept what he knows he must accept. He has never felt before that he could trust anyone, but he trusts me, because he knows that I truly care. All *any* of them need is to know that. They need to see a little compassion. They need to be treated more respectfully on rations day. It hurts their pride to have to come for handouts, and it doesn't help when the meat they are offered is rotten."

"I am aware of the corruption, Miss Gibbons. I have written many letters to Congress about it. There is not much else I can do, and I have no control over what happens to rations between the time that they leave Washington and when they arrive here. They go through a lot of hands."

"I know you do your best. Many of the Sioux have a lot of respect for you." She glanced at Gere. "I can't say the same for how they feel about the Army. There is a lot the Army could do to remedy that, like getting rid of men like Sergeant Jubal Desmond."

Gere stiffened. "Desmond is a fine soldier, and so far I have not turned up anything about his personal life that warrants a reprimand."

Evelyn turned to wrap the paintings again. "Someday you will, Colonel. I just hope it isn't too late to repair whatever damage he has caused. I fear it is already too late for Lucille Bridges." She faced the man again. "One day I'm going to prove that man for what he really is, Bridges and Desmond both; and I will find a way to get poor Lucille and Katy out of what has to be a horrible situation."

"You're meddling in people's private lives, Miss Gibbons," the colonel reminded her.

Evelyn pulled on her fur coat, one of the few items of luxury she had brought along in her trunk when she came from Wisconsin. She picked up the paintings. "I have to take these to the freight office and get them wrapped for shipment." She met the colonel's gaze. "Any extra effort on your part against whiskey smugglers will help, Colonel. Have some of your men meet the riverboats. Take a look at what is being unloaded."

Lingering anger still showed in his eyes. "I do my best, Miss Gibbons. You stick to your work here, and I will do mine."

Evelyn felt spent, wondering if she had made any headway

at all. The only thing she had accomplished was to practically shock both men with Black Hawk's paintings. She could tell it had brought a new respect for the man from both of them. At least she had kept Black Hawk out of trouble . . . for now. The problem was that both McLaughlin and the colonel would be looking even harder for some sign that Black Hawk was the untrustworthy, dangerous renegade they claimed he was. She would have to go to his camp, talk to him, warn him to be extra careful.

Katy stood at the gate in the cold wind and watched for Many Birds to ride home from school. She had grown to like the Indian girl more than she thought she would. Whatever Seth's strange reasons for wanting her to make friends with Many Birds, she now looked forward to visiting with her. Perhaps Seth just wanted to show he had nothing against the Indians, or maybe it had something to do with how he got his whiskey.

She saw the girl coming, and she smiled, waiting faithfully, envying Many Birds for being able to go to school. She wished that Seth would let *her* go, and she had decided she would ask him again. Maybe if she convinced him it would mean she could get closer to Many Birds, he would allow it. If Seth was suddenly trying to put on a new front of being a good father, what better way to show it. Ever since the whiskey raid he had not been quite so mean, and he had not bothered Lucille.

Many Birds smiled when she waved, riding closer. Katy took a raggedy doll from under her coat and held it up. "Here is my doll. Did you bring yours?"

Many Birds nodded, taking a stick doll from under her own coat. She slid down from her horse and walked up to Katy to show it to her. "She is called Moonlight."

Katy frowned. "That's a strange name."

"She is my light in the night when I am alone. Old Grandmother says that since I have had my flowing time, I am too old to play with dolls, but I still keep her with me."

Katy smiled. "Me, too. Her name is Wanda. That's the name of one lady at the orphanage who was nice to us. I don't remember much about it, but Lucy does."

After they exchanged dolls, Many Birds studied Wanda. "I do not understand about these places called orphanages. With our people, when a child's parents die, the brothers and sisters take them in. If there are no brothers and sisters, one of the other families takes them, even if they are not related. They are never homeless."

"It isn't like that with us. They send homeless children to a big, ugly place where people aren't very nice to them. Sometimes they get adopted, like Seth adopted us, but he isn't very nice to us, either." She pouted. "I hate Seth. So does Lucy."

Many Birds glanced past her to the window, where Seth Bridges watched them. "I have heard talk of your father. He is not very much liked by my brother. I have not told Black Hawk that I come here. He would forbid it."

Katy realized Seth was watching her, and she remembered his warnings not to say anything bad about him. "Seth is just a lazy old man," she answered. "I wish he would let me and Lucy go to school, but he keeps us home to do all the chores while he sits around and dri—" She hesitated. She was not supposed to mention whiskey. "While he sits around."

Many Birds stroked the yellow yarn that made up Katy's doll's hair. "Indian women also do much work. Grandmother tells me that in the old days the men did much hunting and making war. Now our men have little to do. It makes them sad. Your people call them lazy, but they are not lazy. They just do not know what to do now. They hate farming, and their hearts are broken, so they just sit around. Some of them drink firewater and fall down and sleep."

Katy pouted, hating Seth even more for having something to

do with getting whiskey to Indians. Now that she had come to know Many Birds, she saw the Indians as just people, not the ignorant animals Seth made them out to be. "Are you going to get married soon?" she asked the pretty and smart Many Birds. "Seth says Indian girls get married young."

"Not me. There is no one I wish to marry for now. I just want to stay with Old Grandmother and help take care of her. When she dies, perhaps I will marry then, but he will have to be a very worthy man, or my brother will not allow it."

"I don't know what it's like to have a grandmother, or even a mother. I think I would like that very much." Katy held the stick doll close and ducked her nose under the collar of her frayed woolen coat because of a sudden sharp wind. "I like Miss Gibbons, the schoolteacher. Is she as nice as she seems?"

Many Birds smiled. "She is very nice. She is already married the Indian way to my brother."

"Married! Miss Gibbons? To an Indian?"

Many Birds nodded. "It is a secret for now. You must not tell your people. Black Hawk says she is Indian in her heart. They are going to be married the Christian way someday. She is already like a mother to my nephew, Little Fox."

Katy smiled. "That is exciting. I wish Seth would let me go to school. I would like to get to know her better. Someday I will be old enough to do what I want, and I will finish my schooling and be as educated as Miss Gibbons. But I won't live here. I will live in some wonderful big city, like Chicago or New York. Perhaps I will learn to play the piano. There are a lot of things I want to do."

Many Birds handed back the yarn-headed doll, shivering against the cold. Katy had invited her inside once or twice, but she had always refused because she was afraid of Seth Bridges. Now that the weather seemed to be getting colder every day and the season of wind had come, she knew she could not keep refusing. Katy handed her the stick doll.

"I must go. It is a long ride back to my village," Many Birds said, reaching inside the deerskin coat Old Grandmother had helped her make from hides Black Hawk had brought them. She placed the doll into a little leather pouch she wore over her shoulder under the coat, where she also carried her reading book. "It gets dark earlier now, so I cannot visit for long anymore."

Katy scowled with disappointment. "Do you ever ride to the agency for supplies or anything like that? Can you come over someday when there is no school?"

"I will try. I like being friends with you. I have never had a white friend before. But I am afraid of your father."

Katy shrugged. "Seth would never hurt you. I won't let him. He said it was okay to make friends with you, and now I'm glad I did. He's mean to me and Lucy sometimes, but he wouldn't be mean to somebody else, because he doesn't want other people to know. He pretends to be good. That's why he stands at the window and waves at you. I think maybe he's trying to get on Black Hawk's good side, so he would never bother you. Lucy and I don't get a chance to meet other people unless they come here. You come over someday when you can stay longer, and we'll go play in my room."

Many Birds smiled. "I would like that." She turned and walked her horse to a big rock outside the gate. She climbed up on the rock in order to get herself high enough to jump onto the back of her big roan mare. She was glad she had worn her knee-high winter moccasins today. She thought how soon the snow would be flying. She herself enjoyed the change of seasons, though the cold weather made Old Grandmother very stiff. "Good-bye, Katy."

Katy waved. "Bye, Many Birds. Please come back."

Many Birds turned and rode off, and Katy watched after her for a moment before turning to go inside. She noticed Seth looking out the window again. Whatever his reasons, her making friends with Many Birds had made him more amiable and a little more bearable, and that was fine with her. "You'd just better not have something mean in mind, Seth Bridges," she muttered. "I'll never let you hurt my new friend." She walked inside, looking forward to Many Birds's next visit, hoping she wouldn't wait too long.

Twenty-six

Evelyn was relieved that the week had finally ended so that now she could ride back to Black Hawk's grandmother's village. Many Birds had told her Black Hawk had come back from his camp and was staying with them again. He was ready to run, she had said, if he heard soldiers planned to come after him. In the meantime, he was hunting, trying to find enough meat for Many Birds and their grandmother to smoke and store for the winter.

She thought what a fine hunter he was. Bagging wild game was no longer an easy task in this part of the land, with so much of the wild game having been overhunted by outside settlers, by miners who came through the area on their way to Montana, and by the Indians themselves, who could not bear the rotten meat offered them by the government.

She wondered how much longer she could go on this way, aching for Black Hawk, forced to be apart from him. She knew that this time he was afraid to come to her cabin, for fear soldiers lay in wait for him. He would have to hear from her own lips that it was safe. Little Fox had come with her, since Evelyn knew his father hated being separated from the boy. Little Fox had brought some papers along to show Black Hawk he was learning to write. He had also brought his bow and arrow so he could give a demonstration on how skilled he was becoming with the weapon Black Hawk had made for him.

Evelyn felt no fear now when she rode through the Indian

villages. She thought what a long way she had come in the past several weeks, both with Black Hawk and with the Sioux as a whole. The schoolroom was full now, and the agency was planning to build a second room. Mission Services was sending another missionary couple to Oahe, a male schoolteacher to Standing Rock, as well as another missionary couple to help Reverend Phillips. So far there had been no reaction from them about the way she taught or the fact that she boldly went out alone to visit with the Indians . . . and that she was deeply involved with a Sioux man. She loved John Phillips for having obviously kept it all to himself. He could have written scathing letters, had her dismissed; but he had not. She knew that deep inside he realized she was reaching the Indians. Whatever her methods, they were working, and that was the only thing that mattered.

It would be another month before the help arrived, and in the meantime she had Beverly Evans to help her. Beverly had found a new peace within herself. Her waistline was beginning to expand with the child she intended to keep and love. Evelyn had noticed a new closeness between Beverly and Reverend Phillips, but after her disastrous experience with Herbert True, she knew Beverly was not eager to jump to conclusions about any man. Evelyn prayed it would lead to something good for both of them. Beverly needed a father for her child, and Reverend Phillips needed a helpmate and wanted a family. Since Anita's death, he seemed to judge people less and was more open to the opportunities of love. Evelyn liked to think she had in some way helped the man learn to be a little more forgiving and compassionate. He reminded her so much of her own father, whom she loved very deeply, not just because he was her father, but because he had embraced and forgiven her mother for loving another man that one brief summer back in Oklahoma. Now here she was with her own heart pounding for an Indian. She could almost feel her mother living through her. Perhaps, as she liked to imagine, Wild Horse really did live in Black Hawk.

She trotted her horse up to Old Grandmother's tipi, giving her greetings to the many Sioux who nodded to her along the way. She wore only a sweater, as it was unusually warm today, a teasing last taste of late autumn before winter would come roaring in. She carried her fur coat with her, realizing the weather could change drastically in only hours this time of year.

She dismounted, but not before Little Fox, who bounded past her to go inside the tipi and hug his great-grandmother. Evelyn followed him inside, half expecting to find both Black Hawk and Many Birds; but only Dancing Woman was there. The old woman looked up at Evelyn and smiled, showing only three teeth in front, her face breaking into thousands of wrinkles. Her snowy white hair was pulled back at her neck, but pieces of it had strayed and hung limply at the side of her face.

"My granddaughter chose to ride to the agency today," she told Evelyn in the Sioux tongue. "I think she has a friend, but she has not said for sure. Maybe it is some young man."

Evelyn grinned at her playful chuckle. "Where is Black Hawk?"

The old woman raised a thin arm and pointed to her right. "Outside. If you go that way, you will find a creek. He is there, painting. He brought us a deer and some rabbits. Isn't that nice?"

Evelyn nodded. "Yes, Dancing Woman. I am glad he found meat."

"He is a good young man, devoted to his old grandmother." Pride shone in the old woman's eyes. "Black Hawk thought maybe you would come today. You go to the creek and find him." The old woman looked at her Little Fox. "You be a good boy and stay here and talk with me for a while. Let the schoolteacher go and talk alone with your father."

Evelyn was grateful for the suggestion. "I will stay," Little Fox told her. He plunked down beside Dancing Woman and opened his parfleche. "I will show you my writing! And I will read to you!"

"Such a smart boy," Dancing Woman said, patting his head. She chuckled slyly, glancing at Evelyn. "Hurry to your lover."

Evelyn reddened at the words, but she needed no more prompting. She turned and hurried out, taking a blanket from her horse and walking swiftly to find the creek. She came to a little rise, and below she saw a stand of trees and the trickling creek bed, nearly dry, waiting for winter snows to fill it up again. She hurried down the hillside, looking back to realize that once below, no one from the village could see them. "Black Hawk!" she called out. "Where are you?"

She saw a movement over by a large collection of boulders that looked as though God had just casually thrown them there in a pile. She smiled when she realized it was Black Hawk, then ran to him when he opened his arms. In the next moment those arms enfolded her, and she felt safe and warm and loved.

"I missed you, *Wenonah.*"

"And I missed you. Black Hawk, everything is all right. No soldiers will come for you. I made sure of it."

She leaned back to look at him, and in the next moment his mouth met hers in a near-savage kiss. He held her close then, rubbing his cheek against the top of her head. "I was afraid, not so much for me, but for you. You had to tell them you were riding alone with me."

"I didn't care. I am anxious for everyone to know the truth, Black Hawk. I hate not being completely open about all of this." She met his eyes again. "I showed Agent McLaughlin and Colonel Gere your pictures, and I could tell they were almost shocked. I told them it was your way of discovering whether you could do something to make your own living a new way. I think they finally understand what you're trying to do. They're seeing you for who you really are."

A cool breeze blew some of his hair across his handsome

face. She marveled at how he fit in with nature and the land around him, his skin deep brown from the sun, his eyes brown like the earth, his hair loose and flowing like the wind. He was strong like the elements, sometimes fierce as a thunderstorm, yet gentle as a summer breeze. Even his clothes were a part of nature, and he shared his spirit with the animals, the earth, the hawk.

"I sent your paintings off to my father. It will probably take at least two months to get an answer. In the meantime . . ." She looked past him then to see a crudely made easel he had built for himself, on which sat another framed canvas. He had painted the creek, the trees around it, the dark hills far in the distance. Her heart rushed with overwhelming surprise to see he was painting a woman standing beside the creek. She had long yellow hair, hair that was blowing in the wind. "Black Hawk!" She left him and stepped closer, stunned at how he had been able to paint her face with such realistic detail, how accurate an image of her it was, except, she thought, it made her seem much more beautiful than she really was. "It's wonderful!"

"I missed you. It made me feel closer to you. I was going to paint a young Indian boy standing beside you—Little Fox. I have not gone that far yet. I wanted it to be finished before you saw it, but now I am just glad you are here."

She turned and faced him. "Please come and live closer to Little Fox . . . and to me. There is nothing to be afraid of. No one is coming after you. There is an empty cabin only about a mile west of the school. You know how most of your people refuse to live in the government-built houses. It is one of those that has sat empty. You could be closer to us, and at the same time, you could get used to living in a regular house, with a roof over your head."

He sighed, throwing his head back as though to think for a moment. "I will try it." He looked down at her then. "See what you do to me? I am going against all that is Indian in me, doing things I never would have considered only weeks ago. But I must warn you, when we marry, I will sleep in your bed, in your white man's house, but many times you will wake up to find me gone. I will have to go out, look at the stars, make sure *Wakantanka* can hear my prayers. I will be gone much, praying, hunting, sharing spirits with the animals and Grandmother Earth. I will take Little Fox often to teach him to hunt also. I wish to always be close to my son."

"I would never stop you from doing anything that makes you happy. Take your son off alone as often as you like. Do all the hunting you want. Join your people for their rituals." She touched his cheek with the back of her hand. "Just always come back to me, Black Hawk. Don't ever ride off without returning."

He studied her lovingly. "I would not do that."

Their lips met again, in a hungry but very gentle kiss that fed their aching hearts. Evelyn was hardly aware he was lowering her to the ground onto a blanket he already had spread out for himself where he could lie and take breaks from his painting and watch the sky.

"We do not always need to do this in a bed, or in a house or a tipi," he told her softly, licking at her neck. "We do not even have to be naked. Sometimes . . ." He rubbed his cheek against her breasts, feeling their swelling beneath her dress and sweater. "Sometimes all a man and woman need is to be one, to feel the beauty, to know they are together and alive and doing something that is more pleasing than anything they have ever done."

She had no desire to object. He pushed up her skirt and slips, curled his fingers into the waistband of her drawers, and got to his knees to yank them down over her knees and off her. She watched him unlace his leggings at the front, and she closed her eyes as he leaned closer. The air was chilly on her legs, but she did not notice, all her senses focused on that most pleasurable place when he eased himself into her, gently at first, then moving into hard, rhythmic thrusts that erased the present, all their troubles, all reality. There was only this, lying with her man beside a quiet creek, enjoying the cool, crisp day and a bright blue sky, joining bodies with her beloved. He met her mouth in a hungry kiss, filling her to ecstasy, and she thought how beautiful it was, doing what came naturally, like the deer or the horses, all of God's creatures . . . and Black Hawk was surely one of God's finest specimens.

Their lovemaking was quiet, sweet, yet refreshingly thrilling. She had never even *imagined* an expression of their passion out in the open, with fresh air and sunshine caressing her, birds singing nearby. Nor did she worry that someone from the village would come and find them, for they all knew what would happen here, and they would stay away. She herself had known the moment Old Grandmother told her Black Hawk was here waiting for her. It was right . . . and necessary . . . their bodies hungry, eager . . . their hearts beating with the same rhythm of love. She moved with him, now familiar with her husband's rhythm.

Husband . . . It hit her then that that was exactly how she had begun to think of him, papers or no papers. In her heart, her soul, in body, in the eyes of God, she was Black Hawk's wife, and she was not ashamed or afraid of it.

As his life spilled into her, for a moment they both lay there quietly. "You'll come back with me then?" she asked. "Stay closer?"

He kissed her eyes. "I will come."

"She gonna visit again next Saturday?"

Katy looked across the kitchen table at Seth. "Yes."

"I don't think you should be here."

Lucille slowly put down her fork, glancing at Seth, having her own suspicions as to his intentions for Many Birds.

"Why not?" Katy asked. "You said you wanted me to make

friends with her. I like her, Seth. We played dolls in my room. She's just like any other girl my age."

"She's Indian. I thought at first I wanted you to make friends with her, because I'm tryin' to get on Black Hawk's good side," he lied. "But now I'm not so sure it would look right for a young white girl to be seen around with an Indian."

"But, Seth, you told me—"

"I know what I told you! Now I'm tellin' you somethin' else! Black Hawk ain't never gonna change, so there's no sense in spoilin' your own reputation over it."

"She's a nice girl. We're good friends."

Seth's eyes squinted with anger. "You arguin' with me, girl?"

Katy blinked back tears of confusion. For the first time since coming here on the orphan train she and Lucille had a friend; someone to help fill the emptiness in their hearts, someone who was a connection to a world beyond the farm. She was also someone who was close to Miss Gibbons. It was fun to talk to Many Birds about school, about the pretty clothes Miss Gibbons wore, about Indian life. Although she was really Katy's friend, when she had finally dared to come into the house yesterday, they had invited Lucille to join them in Katy's room, where they had played and talked. It had been a refreshing change for the girls, a new joy in their lives.

"Don't make me be mean to her, Seth."

"You don't have to be." Seth stole a glance at Lucille, who had begun making him uncomfortable with the way she looked at him sometimes. He suspected that if he grabbed and forced Many Birds outright in front of the girls, they just might try to make trouble for him or put up a fight, in spite of how he'd beat them if they did. He had to be subtle about this, get it over with while they were gone, then convince them Many Birds was just a drunken, loose Indian girl just like he had already convinced them most Indian women were. If they dared to make a fuss then, he'd have at it with Katy once and for all just to get even, and he'd knock Lucille senseless, if necessary. Both girls were getting too big for their britches. If they got too out of hand, he'd get hold of Luke Smith and Marty Able. They could take them off his hands easy enough. There were whorehouses downriver that would pay plenty for two pretty young girls. He could just tell others he had decided to send them to his sister in Louisiana because they were getting old enough that they needed a woman's help and teaching. Who could prove otherwise?

"What do you mean?" Lucille was asking. "What is Katy supposed to say to Many Birds when she comes again next week? No matter *what* we say, it will hurt her feelings."

"You won't be here. I'll tell her for the both of you. I'll scare her off, tell her to scram, that I've decided I don't want my girls playin' with no Indian girl. That makes me the mean one and let's you off the hook."

Katy pouted, staring at her plate of corn and ham. She was sick of both. It seemed that's all there ever was to eat, and she had picked so much corn and slopped so many pigs, let alone seen Seth slaughter the poor animals, that she had little stomach left for the results. "Where will we be?" she asked, refusing to look at Seth.

"At the agency, buyin' yourselves somethin' nice. You girls have worked hard this summer. I'm gonna give you some money and you can go get yourselves whatever you want. You're always beefin' about wantin' to be able to go for a ride together, buy yourselves a new dress or the like. I'm lettin' you do it, next Saturday. It's payment for your chores."

Katy looked at Lucille, both of them sharing skepticism, afraid to get excited and believe Seth was telling the truth. He had never paid them for anything before. All he had done was expect more from them, threaten them, abuse them, bring horror to Lucille. Still, he *had* seemed to change some lately, allowing them to have a friend, leaving Lucille alone at night. He had even let Many Birds come inside the house today and go to

Katy's room to talk and play without bothering her the way they thought he might.

If they cooperated, maybe he would even let them go to school! Katy hated having to give up Many Birds's friendship, hated hurting her, but if it meant realizing more freedom, she would just have to do it it. Being able to ride off alone together to the agency and buy something pretty, to get away from this house and from Seth for a day—that would be like getting out of jail. She could think of nothing more wonderful at the moment, and she knew Lucille felt the same way. The only thing better than that would be to be able to go to school.

Seth leaned back in his chair, looking proud of himself. "I'm givin' you each three whole dollars. All the corn you picked, feedin' the chickens, takin' care of the pigs and horses, sweepin' out the stalls and all, you, Katy, cuttin' the grass, and you doin' most of the cookin', Lucy, you both deserve somethin' for it. I'm givin' you a little more freedom. Just don't betray me by goin' off and tellin' somebody about the whiskey in the barn and corn crib."

Neither girl found it easy to control their enthusiasm. Three whole dollars, and a day of freedom to ride to the agency and away from the farm!

"I just want your promise that you won't be talkin' to that fancy schoolteacher," Seth added. "Rumor is, she's goin' at it with Black Hawk, an *Indian* man. It's bad enough havin' an Indian for a friend, but for a white woman to lay with a buck is disgraceful. She's a sinful woman with no morals. All her fancy education and the way she dresses and all don't make her special, and if it's true about her and Black Hawk, I don't want you around her."

Lucille's heart fell at the words. If he didn't want them around Miss Gibbons, that meant he still would not send them to school. But then, maybe *another* school would be built, new teachers would come. She could hardly believe there was anything bad about Miss Gibbons. She was so beautiful and gracious, and she would never forget how the woman had stood up to Seth that day at the agency. She found it ironic that Seth would think the fact that the woman might be bedding Black Hawk was so terrible, yet he thought nothing of forcing himself on his own adopted daughter. She was grateful to be able to go away for a day and be paid something for all her hard work, but nothing Seth Bridges did could ever make up for how he had abused her and Katy, and her plans to someday take Katy and leave here and never come back remained the same. In fact, maybe she and Katy could find a way to save the money he paid them toward the day when they were on their own.

She wondered how far six dollars would take them on a riverboat. That was the only way she could think of to get away from here without heading into dangerous, wild country. They would be safe on a riverboat if they could afford passage. Once they reached a big city, like Omaha or St. Louis, they could find work and at last be rid of Seth Bridges. For now, they would cooperate in any way they could, if it meant continuing the relative peace they had been given of late.

"Don't be too mean to Many Birds," Katy was telling Seth. "*You're* the one who insisted I make friends with her. It doesn't seem right to turn her away now."

"I told you I'd be the one to tell her. I'll tell her it's not your choice, but mine, that it's best all the way around." Secretly, Seth could hardly wait for his turn at Many Birds. When she came next Saturday, he would invite her inside before informing her the girls were gone. He thought how delightful it was going to be to have a piece of Black Hawk's young sister, to shame her, and Black Hawk, too. He'd been leaving Lucille alone lately, and he was getting hungry for something new and fresh and young in his bed. Once it was done, he'd convince the girls Many Birds was willing. If it got out to soldiers, he'd convince them, too. No white man was going to punish another white man for bedding an Indian woman. Either way, Many Birds might like it and return for more, or maybe she'd be too ashamed to tell a soul. If she did tell, Black Hawk would come after him, and that was just fine. It was all the excuse he would need to use his shotgun on the bastard and be rid of him for good!

He put on a smile for the girls. "Eat up now, and start plannin' what you want to buy with your allowance money." He bit into another piece of ham, but his mouth did not water for the meat. It watered over the thought of having a new young virgin in his bed. She'd learn to like it quick enough, and by the time the girls got back from the agency, it would be done.

Twenty-seven

"Three whole dollars, Lucy . . . *each!*" Katy repeated for what seemed the tenth time. "I didn't know Seth had that much money!"

Lucille trotted Seth's only riding horse, an old mare called Sady, toward Bill Doogan's trading post. Katy sat behind, her arms wrapped around her sister's waist. The two girls seldom got to ride, except sometimes around a corral at the farm, and both were nervous about riding Sady three miles to the post, even though the horse was gentle. The main problem was whether or not Sady could even carry their weight for three miles. Seth's other four horses were big draft horses used for plowing and pulling the supply wagon. They were not accustomed to being ridden, and Lucille was afraid to try to handle any of them, either by horseback or with the wagon.

"He's got more money than you think," Lucille answered. "From whiskey smuggling." She paused thoughtfully. "I still worry that something isn't right. Seth has never done anything nice for us since we've known him."

Katy shrugged. "I think he figures Miss Gibbons suspects he mistreats us and he's afraid of losing our help. He's trying to show everybody he's a good father. I'll never like him one whit, mind you, but if he's going to start doing things like this, and if he keeps leaving you alone, maybe we can stand living with him."

Lucille halted Sady. "Climb down. We'll walk her the rest of the way in. It's not far." Katy obeyed, and Lucille also dismounted, glad that at least it was sunny today, even though it was bitterly cold. She held the reins and faced her sister, her breath showing in the cold air when she spoke. "Katy, we're still going to find a way to get away from there, soon as I'm eighteen. Let's make a pact. We don't spend our whole allowance, just enough to show Seth we're using the money and keep him from knowing we're saving it. If he asks why we didn't spend it all, we'll tell him we decided to be very careful. There are a lot of things we want, and we have to save some for Christmas. It's only a month away. We'll start saving some every time he pays us. We'll hide it somewhere."

Katy frowned. "I'm scared to try to run away, Lucy. Maybe bad people will get us, or we'll get lost, or—"

"Nothing is as bad as living with Seth. You know that. You're just happy for the moment because he gave us money. I think it's a payoff for something more than chores. You know Seth. Remember when he arranged my date with Jubal Desmond, said I could dress up pretty and go to a dance? You know what really happened. He was just paying a gambling debt, with my body!"

Katy studied her sister's hate-filled eyes. "I'm sorry, Lucy. I know it's been worse for you. And I know you've put up with it to protect me."

Lucille reached out and touched her shoulder. "It's not your fault. It's just a fact. It's also a fact that Seth could get drunk and sell me downriver any time and turn on you. He's been leaving me be, which means he'll be wanting a woman in his bed before long. I was scared he'd attack poor Many Birds last week, but I think he's afraid to bother with her because she's Black Hawk's sister. That means it won't be long before he'll be thinking about you, and I won't let that happen. We have to get out of there, and to do that, we need money. Promise me you'll only spend one dollar and you'll save the other two. You can get a lot for a dollar—candy, a new comb, a barrette, some ribbons, lots of things."

Katy blinked back tears. It seemed Seth always found a way to ruin her joy, even when he wasn't present. She would lose her best friend today. Many Birds would come to the house, happy, eager to talk and play, and mean old Seth would send her off and tell her they couldn't be friends anymore. She had at least thought she could come to the trading post and take some little pleasure in spending her hard-earned money, but she knew Lucille was right. Their new happiness might be short-lived. A long, cold winter lay ahead, filled with many days they would be cooped up in the house with Seth. If he drank too much . . . "I promise," she answered her sister.

Lucille smiled, putting an arm around her shoulder. "Good." They headed toward the trading post, Sady's hard breathing creating big puffs of white steam in the cold air. "We'll go someplace wonderful, Katy, a big city where there are big buildings and trains and such. I've looked at old newspapers Seth sometimes brings home. I can't read real good, but I remember enough from what I learned at the orphanage to make out some of the words. Some of the things I've read . . . there's a whole other world out there, Katy, big towns with paved streets, fancy buggies, ladies dressed all fine, like Miss Gibbons. There are places to eat where they serve you, and theaters, where you can go and watch actors and actresses put on a play that makes you cry, or where you can go and listen to music and to people sing. Back East are where all the big cities are, some of the most civilized places on earth. And out West there are gold fields and mining towns, where a woman can make a fortune just washing clothes or cooking for the miners! Someday we'll have the money to go to one place or another." She stopped walking again. "I have a secret to tell you, Katy. You're old enough now."

Katy's eyes widened in anticipation. "What is it?"

"Those nights when Seth comes to my bed and puts his filth

in me, I get back at him. In the morning, when he's snoring away from too much whiskey, I go through his pants and find money. So far I've saved up ten dollars without his ever catching me!"

"Ten dollars! That's a fortune!"

"He's so drunk half the time that he doesn't know how much he's carrying around. I've never found where he keeps the rest of it, but someday I will. There *must* be more, Katy. He gets paid good from the Army for the corn and ham, and he trades more corn and such for the whiskey, so he doesn't spend much, plus he gets paid extra by the whiskey smugglers." Her eyes darkened again with hatred. "That time he used me to pay off Sergeant Desmond, he probably had the money the whole time. He just didn't want to let go of it, so he used me instead."

"Let's not talk about it, Lucy. Let's hurry up and get to the post and see what we can buy."

Lucille realized that her sister would never fully understand the horror of what she had suffered until and unless it happened to her. She was determined that would never be. It was bad enough that she was dirty and soiled for life. Katy was prettier, smarter. She could go far, find herself a real nice man someday. She was not going to let Seth ruin that. She patted Katy's shoulder. "Okay."

They walked on in silence for a moment when Lucille noticed someone coming in a bouncing, creaking wagon. "Look!" She pointed. "I think it's Miss Gibbons!" They waited as the wagon came closer, recognizing the schoolteacher, who sat in the front seat with another pretty woman with dark hair, who in turn sat next to Reverend Phillips, who was driving the wagon.

As Phillips drew the wagon to a halt, Lucille was suddenly aware of her painfully plain gray dress and her ragged black wool coat. Both items had been picked by Seth from leftovers on rations day—hand-me-downs sent to the reservation by well-meaning do-gooders back East. The agency always let settlers go through items the Indians did not take. She noticed Miss

Gibbons wore a brown velvet dress, with a matching, fur-lined cape and a velvet-and-fur hat that was tied down over her ears against the cold air.

"Well, hello, girls!" Miss Gibbons greeted them.

"Hello, Miss Gibbons." Lucille put a hand to her dark hair, which she felt was much too straight. She had washed it, but it only hung limp—not like Miss Gibbons's golden hair, hair that today was twisted up under her hat, with only part of it hanging down the middle of her back. She supposed she could never be as beautiful as the schoolteacher, even with fine clothes and a fancy hairdo.

"Hello, ma'am," Katy said excitedly. "We're going to the trading post to spend our allowance! Seth gave each of us three whole dollars!"

Lucille touched her arm. "Don't be bragging, Katy." She looked at Evelyn Gibbons, saw the surprise in her all-knowing eyes. "We don't intend to spend it all at once," she told the woman, wanting to look wise and mature.

"Well, I didn't know your father was so generous," Miss Gibbons answered. Lucille caught the hint of sarcasm in the words. She wasn't sure what to say in reply. Miss Gibbons was so pretty and educated that the woman always left her at a loss for words.

"Seth said he's going to start paying us for our chores," Katy spoke up, always the bolder one.

Lucille gave her a nudge. "We aren't supposed to talk to the schoolteacher," she reminded her.

"Did Seth tell you not to speak to me?" Evelyn asked the girls.

Katy looked at the ground, embarrassed.

"Yes, ma'am," Lucille answered. "We don't get to go off like this often, Miss Gibbons, so I don't want to spoil it by him knowing we talked to you. He might not let us do this again."

"He actually let you come here alone?"

Both girls nodded.

"Your father should not be keeping you from church and school," Reverend Phillips spoke up. "It isn't right, no matter how much he pays you for your chores, and heaven knows you do more than your share of work to earn what little he gives you. Church and school are more important than money."

"Reverend, don't spoil their one day of escape from that miserable household," Miss Gibbons told the man.

Lucille looked gratefully at Miss Gibbons, who she sensed always understood her feelings. "I'm sorry, ma'am. We don't mean to be rude."

Evelyn smiled. "It's all right, Lucy. You just remember that if you ever need help, you come to me or Reverend Phillips. This woman beside me is Beverly Evans. She can help you, too, just the same as I or the reverend. You don't have to be afraid."

"Yes, ma'am." Lucille wanted to cry at the way Miss Gibbons smiled at her, was embarrassed at having to be rude. She so longed to be able to sit down and tell Miss Gibbons everything, to talk for hours, to ask her if she could ever hope to marry a decent man and have a good life. But then she would have to tell the woman about the ugly things Seth and Jubal Desmond had done to her, and she was not sure she could bear the shame of it. Maybe it was best to talk to no one, or she might end up telling them she planned to run away, and they might tell Seth. He would beat her senseless if he knew.

The reverend got the wagon into motion again, and both girls watched Miss Gibbons from the back as the wagon clattered away, the back of it filled with supplies for church and school . . . another world, another life . . . so close and yet so far.

"They must have come really early," Katy told her sister. "They're already going home." She looked up at Lucille. "Didn't Miss Gibbons look pretty today? Someday I'm going to dress like she does."

Lucille looked at her. Yes, there was still hope for Katy, and she was going to make sure that did not change. "Let's go see what we can buy," she answered.

Seth watched Many Birds ride up and tie her horse, then hurried to the front door to wait for her knock. As soon as he heard the timid tap, he waited for a second knock, not wanting to look in too much of a rush. He finally opened the door, greeting the pretty Indian girl with a smile. He had shaved and put on a clean shirt today, had rinsed his mouth good with whiskey. "Well, hello there, Many Birds."

The girl looked past him. "Are Lucy and Katy home? They told me to come back today."

"Sure enough," he nodded. "Come on in, honey."

Many Birds hesitated, looking up the stairs, back at Seth.

"It's okay. They're already upstairs in Katy's room waitin' for you. I told them I'd send you up soon as you got here. It's warmer up there. Heat rises, you know."

Many Birds smiled bashfully. "Yes." As she stepped inside, Seth closed the door.

"Let me take your coat." He grasped her wool coat by the shoulders, and Many Birds slipped her arms out of the sleeves. Seth hollered up the stairs that the Indian girl was here. "Them daughters of mine is so lost in their playin', I guess they don't hear me," he told her. "Come on. I'll take you up."

Many Birds looked around, thinking the house strangely quiet. Why didn't Katy and Lucy come out to greet her? Surely they had heard Seth call up to them. She heard no voices upstairs, felt confused. How many times had she been told not to trust Seth Bridges? Still, he had never bothered her before, and Katy and Lucy had become such good friends. Surely because of them, he would never harm her. She turned and went up the stairs, feeling Seth behind her. She could smell the whiskey on his breath, but then he always smelled of whiskey.

She took her stick doll from inside her heavy sweater and clung to it, feeling protected by the doll. She studied the now-familiar, faded rose pattern on the tattered wallpaper going up the stairs. The house smelled of wood smoke and tobacco . . . and of Seth's unclean body. She started for Katy's room when Seth grasped hold of her arm. "Over here," he told her. "I said they could play in my room today, on account of it's bigger and it's the warmest room up here."

Many Birds was filled with instant alarm at the almost painful hold he had on her arm. "I think I should go home," she told Seth. "I don't feel very good." Terror filled her when she saw the sudden change in Seth's pale-gray eyes, the hungry look of an animal that had just snared its prey.

"I don't think so, honey. You come on in here with me now, so's I don't have to hurt you."

She blinked back tears. "What do you want?"

He jerked her into his bedroom, where she saw ropes tied to each of the four bedposts.

"Let me go!" she screamed.

"You just have yourself a little drink, and you'll never feel a thing, little girl."

She started to fight him, but Seth was amazingly strong and mean. He grabbed both her wrists, jerking her over to the bed and forcing her down onto it. He managed to capture both her wrists in one hand, keeping his full weight on her while he reached over with his right hand and grabbed a bottle of whiskey on a stand beside the bed.

"Lay still, girl!" he said excitedly, grinning.

Many Birds twisted and struggled, screaming for help, yet knowing somewhere in the back of her mind that no one would come. Katy and Lucille were obviously not home, and the remote location of the farmhouse meant there was no one to hear her. Seth uncorked the whiskey bottle with his teeth and began pouring it over her mouth. She arched against him, turning her head to get away from the wicked firewater, but he pushed the bottle so hard against her lips, she was forced to open her mouth or let her lips be crushed between the bottle and her teeth. She felt the whiskey pouring into her mouth, tried not to swallow, but there was so much of it that it was impossible. Instantly, she understood why it was called firewater, as the liquid burned its way down her throat and into her stomach. She gagged, wondering how people could stand to drink the horrible stuff. She thought for a moment that she might even throw up.

In minutes it became more and more difficult to fight Seth Bridges, whose form above her began to blur, his words sounding more distant. She felt weak, and she had no strength to fight him when he held her nose then and forced more whiskey down her throat. Soon she felt as though she was floating out of her own body, and she imagined that what Seth Bridges did with her after that was happening to someone else, for physically she could feel nothing. Her clothes were being torn away. She tried to find her stick doll, but she had dropped it somewhere in her struggle against the ugly old man who hovered over her now. She closed her eyes then, allowing a blessed darkness to overcome her senses.

Lucille rode Sady quietly onto the back part of the farm and headed the horse into the barn, where she and Katy dismounted. "Let's go hide the rest of our money before I unsaddle Sady and brush her down," she told Katy. "I know a good place. It's in the corn crib, where I hid the other money."

Katy followed her sister, excited about their secret. She clung to the paper-wrapped packages that held candy and ribbons and two new pairs of stockings and two new flannel nightgowns. They had three dollars left, but were going to lie to Seth about how much they had spent.

"There's a loose board at the back of the corn crib," Lucille was telling her. "I've been hiding the other money there and stacking feed corn in front of it. We'll hide it before Seth knows we're back." They both ran to the corn crib, quietly opening the old wooden door and going inside. Lucille headed for the back of the building, then stopped short, noticing a movement to her left. She turned, and to her horror she saw her Indian friend's horse tied in the corner. It still had a blanket and small Indian saddle on it.

Katy nearly stumbled into her sister, in such a hurry she didn't realize Lucille had stopped in her tracks. She looked in the direction Lucille was staring, and a rush of dread moved through her. "It's Many Birds's horse!" She moved closer, clinging to her packages and shivering, in spite of the heavy woolen coat she wore. "What do you think it's doing here?"

Rage began to ripple through Lucille. "What do you think!" She walked over and felt the horse's rump. "She's cool. That means she's been here awhile." She shoved her hands and the money into the pockets of her own coat. "I *knew* it! I *knew* Seth was just trying to get rid of us! We never should have fell for it! We should have known!"

Katy's eyes started to tear. "What do you mean? What . . . what do you think he's done to Many Birds?"

Lucille met her eyes, hating the fact that her sister had to be aware of such ugly things at her age. "He's got her in there, Katy. He got rid of us and then tricked Many Birds into the house. He hid her horse in here so nobody would spot it. He's probably got her upstairs."

Katy shook her head, her breathing growing heavy. "No!" The tears began to fall. "No! He promised! He promised not to hurt her! She's my friend!" She jerked in a sob. "I'll *kill* him! I'll *kill* him!" She ran out of the shed and toward the house.

"Katy, wait!" Lucille ran after her, but a determined Katy managed to stay ahead of her sister, even though Lucille had longer legs. She ran to the back door of the house, shedding her coat and her packages on the way.

"I hate you, Seth! I hate you!" she screamed, charging through the back door.

Lucille was on her heels, and both girls barreled through the house and charged up the stairs. Lucille wanted desperately to stop her sister before she saw what she feared would be a dreadful sight, but Katy barged through Seth's bedroom door before she could catch her. Lucille followed her inside, where Katy stood transfixed, staring at a naked Many Birds, sprawled on Seth's bed, her wrists and ankles tied to the posts. She looked unconscious, and the room reeked of whiskey.

"You girls enjoy your shoppin'?" came a voice behind them.

Lucille and Katy whirled at the same time to see a naked Seth standing behind them in the doorway, a bottle of whiskey in one hand, a knife in the other. He grinned, his eyes bloodshot, his nakedness and the way he stumbled toward them indicating just how drunk he was.

"You bastard!" Lucille seethed, her hands moving into fists. "Why didn't you just pick on me, like always? Why did you have to do that to Many Birds?"

His eyes moved over her. "I'm sick and tired of you. And you kept hollerin' about me leavin' little Katy alone. A man has to have his satisfaction, girl. You know that. Besides, I haven't hurt her none. Only thing wrong with her is she's drunk. She was willin' enough to drink with me, like all of them are. She ain't no different from the rest of them Indian women, always ready to let a man make 'em feel good."

"You *forced* her!" Katy accused, unable to keep from crying.

"I didn't force nobody. I tell you, she was *willin'!*" He raised the knife. "You aimin' to argue about it?"

"If she was willing, why is she tied? And why is her face all bruised?" Lucille asked, her voice low and calm.

Seth met her glare. "She *wanted* to be tied. She thought it

was fun to pretend to be forced, slapped around a little." He
stepped even closer, waving the knife under her nose. "Now,
girl, I don't want no arguments from either one of you. She's
gonna wake up after awhile, and I'm gonna let her go, after I
have at her a couple more times. She ain't gonna tell nobody
because she won't want her Indian folks to know what a whore
she is. I'll remind her of that. And she won't want to get her
brother in trouble. She knows what Black Hawk would do if he
knew she'd been here. She ain't gonna say a goddamn word, and
neither is either one of you. If you do, it's Katy who's gonna be
strapped out on that bed, you little bitch! You understand me?"

"Never!" Katy screamed. "You'd have to kill me first, you
ugly, stinking rapist!" She charged into Seth, and his whiskey
bottle went flying. It broke against a wall as Seth stumbled backward, but even in his drunken state he managed to get hold of
Katy's hair and yank her off him. He jerked her head back and
laid the knife against her face.

"You're lookin' to get scarred, girl!"

Lucille lunged, grabbing at the hand that held the knife. "Get
away, Katy!" she screamed.

Seth punched Lucille in the side of the head with his left fist,
then jerked away the hand that held the knife. Lucille whirled
to grab him again, then felt the knife slash through her side as
Seth struggled to get away from her. She screamed and grabbed
her side, stumbling back. Katy was desperately trying to untie
Many Birds, but when she saw Lucille bleeding, she cried out
her sister's name and went to her side. She put an arm around
her, and both girls cowered back as Seth approached them, waving the bloody knife.

"You two keep quiet, or I'll sell you off to whorehouses, understand?" he roared. "If you tell on me, you just remember that
Many Birds is *Indian!* That means no white man will believe
she wasn't willin', which means *I* will go unpunished. That
means I'll be free to come after the two of you, and I'll by God

make your lives miserable for a long time to come! I know men who'd buy you in a second, and some of them like hearin' a gal scream for mercy! All I'd have to say is I sent you off to my sister in Louisiana, and nobody would know the difference! Now get out of here and keep your mouths *shut!* When I'm through with Many Birds, I'll let her go, and that will be the end of it!" He grabbed Katy's hair and slashed out again with the knife, whacking several inches off the end of her long tresses. The girl screamed, thinking he was going to cut her face. Again he waved the knife menacingly, as both girls stood there holding each other and shivering. "If I have to, I'll kill the both of you," Seth told them. "You get me in enough trouble, and I won't give a damn what happens to me. Understand? I'll *kill* you both!"

Katy broke into all-out sobbing, but Lucille just glared at him with deep hatred. She still grasped at her side, wondering if she was going to bleed to death.

"Get out of here!" Seth roared. "I've got a need!" He pointed the knife at Katy's chest. "Unless you'd like to take Many Birds's place."

He chuckled, backing away slightly, and both girls ran out of the room, still clinging to each other. They headed downstairs "What should we do, Lucy?" Katy sobbed. "Poor Many Birds!"

"Quiet!" Lucille warned. "Come outside." They headed out the back door, then ran to the barn. "I'm going for help!"

"You're hurt! I should go!" Katy told her sister.

Lucille shook her head. "We've got to hurry, and I'm the only one who can ride Sady. All you've ever done is ride on the back. She knows me, knows my commands."

"Take me with you! I'm scared, Lucy!"

Lucille grasped her shoulders, forcing herself to ignore the pain in her side. "Sady can go faster with just one rider. You hide behind that loose board in the corn crib. The space is big enough for somebody your size. Seth would never find you there. He'll only look in the barn, if he even gets the chance.

He's so drunk he's going to pass out pretty soon. I know the signs. He'll be out cold, and I'll have plenty of time to get back here with help. If he *does* come to the corn crib to look for us, you just keep real quiet behind that board, and he'll never know you're there."

Katy choked in a sob. "What about Many Birds? She'll be so ashamed. If we tell on Seth, her people will know what happened to her. Maybe they'll turn against her and treat her bad. Maybe her brother will come here and kill all of us!"

Lucille shook her head. "I think her people would understand. Seth just wants us to think Many Birds wouldn't want them to know. He thinks he'll keep us quiet that way, but he's got another think coming! I'm not afraid anymore, Katy. I've got a stab wound to prove what Seth is like, and if I can get somebody back here before he unties Many Birds, they'll see that she was forced. They'll arrest him! If we're lucky, Black Hawk will get here first and *kill* him! Then we'll be rid of him forever!"

Katy nodded, wiping at her eyes. "But the schoolteacher . . . Miss Gibbons . . . she loves Black Hawk, Many Birds said. I don't want Black Hawk to get in trouble, too."

Lucille stepped back, holding her side. "I don't care anymore who gets in trouble, as long as we're rid of Seth Bridges for good! Come on now! Hurry up and hide yourself in the corn crib before that drunken fool comes out here looking for us! I'm taking Sady and riding for help. I'll go to Miss Gibbons!"

Katy nodded. The sisters quickly embraced, then ran out to the corn crib. Lucille led Katy to the back wall, moving down two boards that each hung by a nail on only one end. "In here. You can fit because you're so skinny," she told Katy. "Seth will never find you if you're quiet."

A sobbing Katy squeezed through the boards, and Lucille moved them back into place.

"Don't be afraid, Katy. I'll be back."

She stumbled to the horse, praying she wouldn't pass out before she got to help. She managed to climb onto old Sady, then headed the mare quietly out of the barn. "Stay there, Katy, no matter what happens. Wait for me." She rode Sady out of the crib and kept the horse at a gentle walk at first, not wanting to break into a full gallop until she was well away from the farm so that Seth would not hear her.

In his room upstairs, Seth ogled Many Birds's young, naked body, climbing on top of her again and having his way with her. In his drunken state, he imagined she was enjoying it, that he was himself attractive and virile. All women liked this, didn't they? Even the ones who were forced. This was all women were good for. His own wife had learned that early on years ago, and his mother had learned it from his father. Besides, this girl was just an Indian. It didn't matter with an Indian woman. They didn't have the same feelings as white women, and white women just pretended not to like it.

He took a long time with her because the whiskey made it difficult for him to perform, although in his mind he was better than most men. When he finally finished with her, he climbed off the bed and stood staring down at Many Birds, taking another drink of whiskey. He had to concentrate to remember that Katy and Lucy had been in here. They had struggled, hadn't they? He'd cut Lucy.

He frowned, looking around. Where were they now? The house was too damn quiet. He stumbled to the door, looking out into the hallway. "Katy? Lucy? Where the hell are you?" There was no answer. He turned back inside and pulled on his wool pants with no underwear. He did not bother buttoning the fly. He clumsily pulled on a pair of old leather boots, then picked up his bottle and, still shirtless, went to the top of the stairs, clinging to the railing as he made his way to the bottom floor. "Lucy!" he called again. "Damn, stupid girls," he grumbled. He took his wool coat from a hook near the front door and pulled it on, then stumbled through the hallway to the kitchen. "Where the hell is everybody?" he hollered. "Hidin' in the barn, I'll bet!" he fussed.

He opened the back door and did not bother closing it as he made his way outside and stumbled over the girls' packages on his way to the barn. He looked around, taking up a pitchfork and stabbing into haystacks. "Where are you, you bitches! Come on out or I'll stab your guts out!" There was no reply. He took another good look around, feeling ready to pass out. He grabbed up his whiskey bottle then and walked back outside, glancing at the other outbuildings, then heading for the corn crib. He staggered inside, screaming the girls' names again. No reply.

"You'd better show yourselves," he warned. "You do me dirty, and you'll regret it! I'll sell you off to river pirates, and you'll be wishin' you was back home with ole Seth where you're safe! You think it's bad bein' with one man? How about ten men? *Twenty* men? Maybe more? Come on out, or that's how it will be for you!"

He stumbled around, moving bales of hay and sending them tumbling. He tore through piles of feed corn, still screaming their names. "I'll kill you little bitches! If you've gone to tell on me, I'll *kill* you! Ain't nobody gonna believe you, and they'll send you back to me! You know what that means!" He looked around again, waiting, listening. For a moment he thought he heard a little whimper, but he was too drunk to decipher where it came from or if he had even heard what he thought he'd heard. "Is this the thanks I get?" he said then. "I gave each of you three whole dollars! You had an exciting day, got to go riding alone to the tradin' post. Wasn't I good to you? Is this how you repay me for bein' so generous? It ain't worth it, girls, not over a damn Indian squaw! Indian women like layin' with men, don't you know that? Some of them are married by Many Birds's age. Come on out now, girls. Don't be frettin' over that Indian bitch!"

He slugged down more whiskey, vaguely aware Katy and Lucy might have ridden off to get help, but too drunk to do anything about it. It would all work out, wouldn't it? Nobody would think anything of a white man screwing an Indian. Hell, maybe Black Hawk would come here, and he could blow the man's guts out and be rid of him. Yes, sir, that was a nice thought. That's what he'd do. He'd go back to the house and wait with his shotgun.

He turned to leave, but his legs crumbled under him. He grinned as he fell to the floor. "Tomorrow," he mumbled. "I'll kill him tomorrow."

He closed his eyes and stretched out on the floor. The room began swimming around him, and he could not make himself get up and go back to the house. He lay there staring at piles of corn in the loft, unaware that someone watched him from behind loose boards that formed a double wall at the back of the corn crib.

Katy stared, terrified. She could feel a mouse skitter over her foot, but she dared not move or make a sound for fear Seth would find her here. The memory of how Many Birds looked sprawled on that bed with blood on her thighs was emblazoned in her young mind, and she feared the same thing would happen to her if Seth got hold of her. Maybe he would even stab her to death! Maybe right now he was just pretending to be passed out, hoping she would show herself. Lucille had told her to wait here and hide until she got back, and she was going to do just that.

She forced back the urge to break into tormented sobbing as she managed to slither down and sit on a piece of foundation cement. She told herself not to be afraid of the rats and mice and spiders with whom she knew she shared this dark hiding place. Compared to Seth Bridges, they were like good friends. They could never bring her the harm that Seth could. She would wait. Lucy would come. Her sister would not desert her.

Twenty-eight

Lucille was frustrated by how slow old Sady was. She could feel blood trickling down her side and over her leg, and she tried not to think about the fact that Seth had cut her, or the fact that she could bleed to death before reaching help. She couldn't leave Katy alone for too long. She had to tell someone what was happening before Seth came out of his drunken stupor.

She hoped she was headed in the right direction, because she couldn't think clearly, and her vision was blurred. She had to reach Miss Gibbons, but the three miles to her house seemed like a hundred now.

Surely Seth would get in terrible trouble over this, because she wouldn't tell just about him raping poor Many Birds. She would tell about the beatings, about his selling her to Jubal Desmond, and about the whiskey hidden in the corn crib. She would tell everything, and they would take Seth away for a long time. Miss Gibbons would take in her and Katy, she was sure, at least until they were old enough to be on their own. She had to believe that, had to trust in the schoolteacher's offer to come to her if they ever needed help. She was tired of being afraid of Seth. If he found her and killed her for this, so be it. That was better than putting up with life at the farm one day longer.

She leaned over and clung to Sady's mane, thinking she was riding fast; but in reality Sady was lumbering along at a slow walk, unresponsive to Lucille's weak kicks and still tired from the long ride to the agency and back. The horse headed to a stand of trees and stopped to graze. Lucille kicked at her sides. "Go, Sady, go!" The horse would not budge.

Lucille felt the tears of frustration wanting to come, but she refused to cry. It was almost completely dark now. Somehow she had to find her way to Miss Gibbons, even if she had to walk. She clung to the pommel of the saddle, managed to swing her leg around and dismount, but as soon as her feet hit the ground, she discovered her legs had no strength. She crumbled to the ground and lay there shivering. She curled up into her coat. "Miss Gibbons," she groaned.

Sady whinnied, and Lucille opened her eyes to daylight. She felt stiff and frozen, could not move one limb. Where was she? It took her a moment to realize how she had got here, where she was headed and why.

"Many Birds!" she whispered. And what about poor Katy? Was she still hiding in the corn crib, waiting faithfully for her sister to come with help? Had Seth found her and raped her? She realized she must have lain here all night! Sady whinnied again, and now Lucille could hear the sound of approaching horses. She managed to raise up on one elbow to see through blurry vision that soldiers were coming. Now she would have help! She managed to raise one arm and wave it, mustering all her strength to call out for help. She prayed that God had spared her life so that she could still help Katy and Many Birds. "Please protect Katy from Seth," she prayed.

An army patrol approached. To her dismay she could see that Jubal Desmond was with them. No, not Jubal. He would find a way to stop her. He would take her back to Seth, and Seth would kill her, sell poor Katy off to river pirates! Jubal knew everything. He would find a way to keep her quiet! She couldn't let that happen.

"Hold up there!" she heard a man shout. "What the hell—"

"It's the Bridges girl," she heard Jubal saying. "Looks like she's been hurt."

She heard horses all around her then. A man ordered others to dismount. Someone was bending over her. "Miss Gibbons," she said weakly. "Miss Gibbons!"

"What's that she's blabbering?"

It was Jubal's voice. She had to keep him from talking them into taking her to Seth. Someone looked her over. "She's bleeding! Looks like she's been stabbed," the man commented. "She's saying she wants to see Miss Gibbons."

"Maybe she was out riding and Indians got hold of her. We'd better take her to her pa, see what he wants to do about this."

There was Jubal's voice again.

"No! No!" she protested. "Miss Gibbons . . . got to find . . . Miss Gibbons!" She was lucid enough to realize she dare not say too much about how this had happened. Jubal might ride out and warn Seth, who could get rid of all the evidence before the rest of the soldiers got there. Jubal shouldn't know.

"Maybe her own pa did this to her." The words came from whoever was bending over her. "I've heard it's suspected he gets drunk and abuses his daughters. Let's take her to Miss Gibbons. Maybe the schoolteacher can get her to explain how she got here. Pick her up and we'll take her to the woman's cabin. The poor girl rode this far. We might as well take her to the closest place for help."

"Yes, sir."

That was Jubal's voice. Thank God he was apparently with someone who had more authority than he. She wanted to vomit at the thought it was Jubal who was carrying her now, holding her while he managed to mount his horse and place her in front of him. How she hated having to lean on him, but at least they were going to Miss Gibbons's house and not back to Seth's. All she had to do now was stay conscious long enough to tell Miss Gibbons what had happened. Once she knew, she would raise a ruckus, and Jubal couldn't stop anything then. He was with someone of higher authority, and he would have to obey the man's orders.

She was too weak to be aware of the worried look in Jubal's eyes. All kinds of possibilities over what had happened raced through Jubal's mind, and he wondered what in hell Seth was up to, how Lucille had come to be here, injured this way. And where was Katy? He worried that this time a drunken Seth had done something that would lead to the discovery of his whiskey smuggling, maybe even to his own involvement. He scrambled to think of all ranges of excuses to cover himself. Somehow he had to find a way to get to Seth before his new lieutenant and these other men did. At least Lieutenant Hart did not know his past, that he had once been accused of helping smuggle whiskey and of being in cahoots with Seth Bridges. That was one thing to his advantage. He had to find a way to shut Seth up. "Don't you dare get me in trouble over this, you little bitch, or I'll find a way to make you suffer," he growled close to Lucille's ear. The girl only groaned.

Evelyn cleaned up from breakfast, feeling warm and happy. Black Hawk had visited her in the night, a sweet, exotic liaison that had left her fulfilled. Surely it would not be long before he would be in her bed every night, and they could wake up in each other's arms. As it was, he had left before sunrise but had come back to share breakfast with her and Little Fox. He sat outside now showing Little Fox how to make his own arrows. In spite of the thirty-eight-degree temperature, both father and son preferred to sit outside rather than in the house.

She walked to a window to watch them for a moment. She knew now that she could share a life with Black Hawk. She understood that often he would have to be out in the fresh air, no matter what the weather, to ride off alone or with Little Fox.

Their Indian nature was part of what she loved about them both. Black Hawk wore winter moccasins and fringed leggings, as well as his deerskin jacket. Little Fox wore the woolen pants and coat a white boy would wear, but a red bandana was tied around his head.

She turned away, realizing she had to get busy. She would have to get ready soon for church services. She prayed that someday she could get Black Hawk to go with her. She placed a loaf of homemade bread in the breadbox, then heard the sound of several horses approaching. She hurried to the door to see Black Hawk standing on the porch with Little Fox, looking defensive. It was no wonder. A group of nine soldiers sat facing the house, and one of them was Jubal Desmond, who held someone in his arms. Evelyn hurried outside, not even noticing the cold. Had someone been hurt? Were they blaming Black Hawk? Was that why they were here? She recognized the man in charge, Carson Hart, a new lieutenant.

"Miss Gibbons!" Hart called out to her. "We have Lucille Bridges with us. She's been hurt and was calling for you when we found her!"

"Oh, dear Lord," Evelyn exclaimed. "Go and get her, Black Hawk. Bring her inside."

Black Hawk glanced at Evelyn curiously. She knew he was very wary, especially since it was Jubal Desmond who held Lucille.

"It's all right, Black Hawk."

He started over to get Lucille when the lieutenant balked. "Wait a minute! The sergeant can carry her in for you, ma'am. The girl might not want an Indian man holding her."

Evelyn folded her arms against the cold. "Lieutenant, Black Hawk is a good friend. He can be trusted." She glanced at Desmond. "More than your Sergeant Desmond." She looked back at Hart. "I assure you, Lucille would much rather be held by

Black Hawk than by the sergeant. I will not have that man in my house."

Hart frowned, and Desmond looked ready to kill.

"I don't understand, Miss Gibbons," Hart told her.

"I will explain later. Just let Black Hawk bring Lucille inside and we'll see if we can find out what happened. Where did you find her?"

Black Hawk walked up to Desmond with a look of victory in his eyes. He reached up for Lucille, and with a sneer Desmond shoved the girl's limp body into Black Hawk's arms. Black Hawk said nothing. He turned and carried her into the house, followed by Little Fox. By then the lieutenant had dismounted.

"We found her just about a half-mile from here," he was telling Evelyn. "She was lying nearly unconscious on the ground, with a deep cut in her right side. I think she's just weak from loss of blood. I suggested taking her back to her father, but she kept repeating your name, and this place was closer, so I brought her here. I hope you don't mind."

"Not at all. It's probably the best thing you could have done. Come with me, Lieutenant."

Hart ordered the rest of the men to stay mounted and wait outside. Jubal watched him, wishing he could go in and hear what Lucille had to say. He wanted to choke Evelyn Gibbons for her smart talk and for embarrassing him again in front of the other men. Hart didn't know about the accusations she had made against him earlier, but the bitch would damn well tell him now!

He took paper and tobacco from his supplies, rolling a cigarette while he waited, saying nothing to the others as they discussed among themselves what might have happened to Lucille. Was it Indians? Whiskey smugglers? Why was she so anxious to get to Miss Gibbons. *Yes. Why?* Desmond wondered privately. If Seth was in trouble, he would like to be able to go and warn him. And the state Lucille was in, she just might say too much—

about the whiskey . . . about his raping her. God, how he hated this waiting! He lit the cigarette and watched the house.

Inside, Evelyn ripped open Lucille's dress and inspected the deep gash in her side. At her instructions Black Hawk brought in a pan of heated water from a kettle that still sat on the wood-burning cook stove from breakfast. He set it on a stand beside the bed, then stepped back, watching and listening silently, Little Fox standing beside him. Lieutenant Hart glanced at him curiously. Black Hawk knew what the man was thinking. What was someone like him doing at Evelyn Gibbons's house so early in the morning? Someday soon he would be here every day, and everybody would just have to accept it.

"I don't think it's terribly serious," Evelyn was saying as she washed the wound. She left a damp rag on the cut and leaned closer to study Lucille's face and neck. She tore open the sleeves of her dress. "Little Fox, run and get Beverly Evans, will you? If Seth Bridges did this, I am going over there myself and take Katy out of there. Someone has to stay with Lucille."

"You think her own father did this?" Hart asked, moving around to the other side of the bed.

"You haven't been here long enough to know about every-one," Evelyn told him. "Seth Bridges is a despicable, filthy, abusive man who uses his adopted daughters like little slaves. God only knows what goes on at that farm. Look at her face and neck, and her arms. They're bruised. It looks like she's been in some kind of scuffle. She was probably running away from Seth when you found her." She gently stroked Lucille's hair back from her face. "Lucy? Can you hear me? It's Evelyn Gibbons."

Lucille groaned, then began tossing as though terribly afraid. She waved her arms, and Evelyn grabbed them, pushing them down. "Lucy! It's me, Miss Gibbons. It's all right, Lucy. You're safe. No one is going to hurt you. Where is Katy, Lucy? Is she all right?"

Lucille opened her eyes, staring at her with a blank look at first, then focusing her gaze to reality. "Miss . . . Gibbons?"

"Yes. You're here with me, and no one is going to hurt you, Lucy. What happened? You must tell us so we can help you. Lieutenant Hart is here. Who hurt you, Lucy? Where is Katy?"

"Katy . . ." Lucille's eyes rolled, then focused again on Evelyn. "She's hiding . . . from Seth. Somebody has to help her."

"Why is she hiding, Lucille? What has Seth done to make you run away?"

Lucille breathed deeply. "He'll hurt her . . . force her into . . . his bed. He's drunk. Many Birds . . . He's got Many Birds. She's our friend. She trusted us . . . trusted Seth." She started to cry. "Many Birds."

Quickly, Black Hawk was at Evelyn's side, bending over Lucille. "What are you saying?" he asked.

Already Evelyn could feel his rage building.

"Where is my sister?" he demanded louder.

"You'll scare her, Black Hawk," Evelyn warned.

Lieutenant Hart also leaned closer. "What's she trying to tell us?"

Lucille focused on Black Hawk. Yes. If he knew, he would kill Seth. She could be rid of him. "Many Birds . . . she is our friend . . . Katy's friend. She comes over . . . plays with us. We went away and she came over. Seth forced her to drink whiskey . . . tied her to his bed. We came home and found her . . . tried to help. Seth was drunk . . . pulled a knife on us. He cut me. Katy . . . she's hiding from him . . . waiting for me. You have to help them . . . help Many Birds. Get her and Katy away from Seth."

Black Hawk was out the door before she finished. Evelyn raced after him. "No, Black Hawk!"

Jubal Desmond watched curiously as Black Hawk came charging outside to his horse, not even wearing his coat. Evelyn was running after him, begging him not to go.

"Let the soldiers take care of it!" she screamed. "You can't go there! You can't hurt Seth Bridges!"

He whirled on her. "He has my *sister!*" he seethed, black rage obvious in his dark eyes and in his whole demeanor. "He has *raped* her! I told them! I told the soldiers he was bad! I could put up with his running whiskey, but he has stolen my sister's innocence, and he must *die* for it!"

"Please, Black Hawk!" Evelyn grasped at his leg as he mounted his horse. "He'll be punished. He can't get out of it this time. Let Lieutenant Hart go after him! Remember the vision!"

Desmond wondered again what the demented woman meant by "remembering the vision." Whatever it was, it was apparently important to both of them. From Black Hawk's words, it was not difficult to decipher what had happened. So, old Seth had finally got his hands on Many Birds, the dirty old bugger. Maybe if Black Hawk went there now, Seth would blow him away with his shotgun. Not one person would blame him for it. Here were a handful of witnesses ready to testify that Black Hawk went after Seth Bridges with the deliberate intent to kill the man. Maybe Desmond could finally be rid of Black Hawk, but he hesitated, looking down at Evelyn Gibbons, who apparently had tremendous influence over him now.

"I must do this," he said in a determined voice.

Evelyn was crying. "Please, Black Hawk, stay away from there. Let the soldiers arrest Seth and get Many Birds out of there. I'll tell the lieutenant to have her taken to Dancing Woman. Your people can help her. We'll work this out."

Black Hawk stiffened. "I cannot let this go. The man must die!" He whirled his horse and rode off, and Evelyn turned to the lieutenant, who was coming out of the house.

"Please, Lieutenant Hart, you've got to stop him! At least get over to Seth's before Black Hawk does! If he hurts or kills Seth . . . and once the Sioux find out about Many Birds, there could be an uprising on the reservation. The only answer is to keep Black Hawk from doing something terrible! We've got to find a way to reason with him!"

The lieutenant quickly mounted up. "I'll do what I can, ma'am."

"Wait! Let me go with you!"

"No, ma'am, it might be too dangerous."

Evelyn's head was spinning with worry and frustration. "You've got to find Katy, too. Bring her to me. Promise me!"

"Yes, ma'am. We'll do our best to find her and prevent any trouble." The man tipped his hat. "You stay here and watch after the other girl. We'll get this straightened out." He turned his horse and gave a signal. "Follow me, men!"

The soldiers turned and rode off after him. Jubal hesitated a moment to glance at Evelyn. He grinned, and Evelyn knew what he was thinking. It would be easy to make up an excuse today to kill Black Hawk. This was leading to something terrible, and he was enjoying every minute of it. The chilly morning seemed even colder as a deep fear pressed on her heart.

Lieutenant Hart rode his men hard. The nearly three miles out to Seth Bridges's farm was covered in fifteen minutes. "Spread out, men!" the lieutenant ordered. "Harkins, you and Smith come into the house with me to see if we can find the girl! Brady and Dinks, ride the perimeter. Watch for Black Hawk! Desmond, you and Johnston search the outbuildings. Bridges could be hiding by now, and we have to find the other daughter! Everybody look out for Black Hawk. He could be anywhere, and he's in a dangerous mood!"

Everyone obeyed without question, and the lieutenant and his two men headed for the house.

"I'll check the corn crib," Jubal told Private Johnston. He knew that was where most of the whiskey was hidden, and he didn't want to take the chance of anyone else finding it. If any-thing happened to Seth, perhaps he could at least find a way to come back and get it and sell it himself. He headed for the corn crib, his heart pounding, hoping he would not himself be found out today. If Seth was arrested, he might tell all, and God only knew what the girls might tell if they thought Seth was no longer a threat. He could always find a way to shut them up, threaten them, find a way to sell them off to river pirates. First he had to find Seth and warn the man to keep his mouth shut about his own involvement in whiskey smuggling and with Lucille. If he was lucky, Black Hawk had already been here and killed Seth. That would wipe out two birds, since Black Hawk would surely be hanged for murder, no matter what his reason for getting rid of Seth.

"Damn fool!" he muttered. He didn't really believe Seth would try for Black Hawk's sister like he had threatened to do. How did he think he could get away with that? But the old geezer was crazy when he was drunk.

He entered the corn crib, then stopped short. "My God," he muttered. There lay Seth, sprawled on his back, a bottle in one hand. He wore old leather boots and soiled cotton pants that gaped at the fly. His arms were sprawled out so that his coat fell open to reveal a bare chest. Jubal walked closer, wondering if he was passed out, or if Black Hawk had already killed him. He knelt beside the man. "Seth?"

The man only groaned, opening bloodshot eyes, then grinning through yellow teeth. "Hey, Jubal," he said, the words spoken slowly with a thick tongue. "Got to . . . find the girls . . . so's they don't tell. I've got Many Birds upstairs . . . if you want a piece of her."

"You stupid fool! You've got yourself in a lot of trouble this time, and I can't get you out of it!" Jubal growled. "Damn you, you drunken bastard!"

Seth just lay there grinning, unable to get up. It was obvious he was merely waking up from a drunken stupor, but not injured. The idea came to Jubal then like a bolt of lightning. It would be so easy to kill Seth and blame it on Black Hawk! Not one person would believe Black Hawk didn't do it.

He stood up, realizing there was not a lot of time to hesitate. One of the other men could come at any moment. He didn't like the idea of killing a man in cold blood, but then it would be best if Seth was out of the way; and what better chance would he have of also getting rid of Black Hawk? There were several witnesses to the man's threat to kill Seth, and his being a rene-gade Indian besides . . .

How he wanted to be rid of Black Hawk, to stop worrying about when or where the man might decide to kill him, or find a way to prove he was involved in whiskey running. Black Hawk had been a burr under his butt ever since Wounded Knee. He could sleep better and live with what he'd done to the man's wife and baby if he didn't have to look into those accusing dark eyes, and he would no longer have to live with the fear of an arrow or a knife in his back. The threat was always there, and he was tired of it.

He looked around, saw and heard no one. He reached down then and pulled a hunting knife from inside his boot, then knelt over Seth again. "I'm sorry, Seth."

Seth opened his eyes, and they widened when he saw Jubal holding the knife over his chest. "What—" He reached up and grabbed at Jubal's uniform. Jubal took a deep breath, looked around once more, then made the instant decision, ramming his knife into Seth's heart. He held it there for a moment, gritting his teeth in determination, already feeling the joy of realizing Black Hawk would be blamed for this and would never get out of it.

"Sergeant!" someone called from outside.

In a panic Jubal quickly yanked out the knife, jumping back when blood spurted from Seth's heart for a moment before trickling down to nothing as the heart stopped beating. Quickly, he bent down and wiped off the knife on Seth's pants, then shoved it back into his boot. "In here!" he yelled. "I found Seth Bridges. Black Hawk killed him!"

A moment later Private Johnston ran into the corn crib. He stopped short at the bloody sight. "My God!"

Jubal breathed deeply to keep his emotions in control. He was surprised at how elated he felt. "He's been stabbed in the heart, and there isn't a weapon anywhere on him. Looks like he was just lying there drunk. Black Hawk must have just walked in here and killed him in cold blood." He looked at the private. "We've got to tell the lieutenant. Somebody has to go after that damn renegade. It's too bad what's happened to his sister, but he can't get away with something like this. He should have left it up to the Army."

Johnston nodded. "I'll go get the lieutenant." He met Jubal's eyes. "They found Black Hawk's sister—pretty awful, Harkins says. She was drunked up, naked, tied to a bed upstairs, obviously raped. Lieutenant Hart had Corporal Brady take her to Miss Gibbons, figured maybe the schoolteacher ought to go along when they take her to her grandmother. The lieutenant thinks Miss Gibbons can help smooth things over. She's got a way with the Sioux." Johnston stared at Seth's body the whole time he spoke, feeling nauseous.

"Miss Gibbons isn't the saint everybody thinks she is," Jubal grumbled.

"This isn't going to go over too good with the Sioux," Johnston said, seeming not to hear Jubal's remark. He shook his head. "At least if Black Hawk got his revenge, maybe they'll be satisfied. Trouble is, Black Hawk's going to have to be hanged or sent to prison, and they won't like that. We're in for some trouble."

"We can handle it. Most of the Sioux don't even have weapons anymore. Go ahead and get Lieutenant Hart."

Johnston nodded and ran out, looking pale. Jubal stared down at Seth, feeling a great relief. In one slash of a knife he was rid of two men who were troublesome to his future and reputation. He was glad he'd done what he did. All he had to do now was make sure Lucy and Katy were properly threatened so they'd keep quiet. They'd be happy enough that Seth was dead. They had no reason to bother telling the Army or anyone else about his involvement with Seth, or what he'd done to Lucy. He breathed deeply, a smile crossing his lips. "Good riddance, Seth Bridges," he muttered.

He heard men running then, and the lieutenant and several others came into the corn crib. None of them was aware they were all being watched from behind some loose boards at the back of the shed. A pair of blue eyes stared at all of them through a crack in the boards, eyes that had witnessed Jubal Desmond stab Seth to death while he lay helpless.

Black Hawk rode his horse nervously back and forth on the low hill that looked down on Seth's farm. Where he had gotten the strength not to go down there and murder Seth Bridges, he was not sure, except that his love for Evelyn was so powerful that its force seemed to control him. He had felt as though he was going insane as he forced himself to stay back while he watched soldiers enter Seth's house and swarm around the outbuildings. Minutes later a man came out of the house carrying someone wrapped in a blanket.

Many Birds! Was she even still alive? What horrible things had Seth done to his sister? Again he wanted to charge down there and kill the man, but Evelyn's words and the vision kept haunting him. A white man would die, Night Hunter had said, and he would be in much trouble over it. Still, the old man's dream seemed to mean that it was not Black Hawk who would kill the white man, and that somehow the truth would win out.

Who would die? Seth? God knew he deserved it! He wanted to slowly cut the cruel old man into a hundred pieces himself, in all the right places, so that he would feel the pain but not die! Black Hawk's thirst for vengeance was great, but he would try to do this Evy's way. The soldier carrying Many Birds got onto a horse, holding her in front of him. Black Hawk watched and waited, anxious to see them bring out Seth. He wanted to be sure the man was arrested. If for any reason he was allowed to go free, *then* he would go and kill him! He would have no other choice.

He was prepared to ride down and see that justice was done and then take Many Birds to Grandmother himself, but it was then he noticed a soldier come out of one of the storage sheds at a run. When he stopped to vomit, Black Hawk felt a deep alarm. The soldier hurried off to get the others, and Black Hawk watched as he said something to Lieutenant Hart, who Black Hawk recognized, even from this distance, by the white horse he rode. Hart shouted some orders, and several of the men rushed back to the shed with the lieutenant.

Black Hawk kept himself hidden behind some bushes while he watched, and several minutes later four men carried out a body wrapped in a blanket. Black Hawk's blood ran cold. Who was it? The lieutenant ordered someone to take the body somewhere, as one man threw it over another man's horse. The man carrying the body rode north then with a second man. *They are taking the body to Fort Yates,* Black Hawk thought. What was happening? He wanted to ride down and get Many Birds, but something told him to stay away. *A white man will die.* Who was in that blanket? Seth? Reason told him that if Seth Bridges was dead, there wasn't one man on the reservation, even among his own people, who would not believe he had done it. Many had heard him threaten to take the man's life for what he had done to Many Birds.

The soldier who had taken Many Birds was already on his

way, and Black Hawk became anxious to be with her. He hoped perhaps they would take her to Evelyn first. She could go with them to Grandmother, where the women of the village would help her, purify her. She would be bathed, rubbed with special herbs that drove out evil spirits and washed away the touch of an evil one. She would visit the sweat lodge and be cleansed. She would be like a new woman, still untouched . . . except for the emotional scars she would bear. What had Seth put her through? How had he forced her? How cruel had he been to her?

He needed to know, needed to help her, be with her. Besides, he had done nothing wrong. He would go down there and talk to Lieutenant Hart, find out what had happened, where they were carrying his sister. He might be taking a great risk by showing himself, but, after all, Many Birds needed him, and by riding to the soldiers, they would know that he was innocent of any wrongdoing, or he would not make his presence known. Whoever had been taken out of the corn crib, it was not anyone he had hurt or killed. Surely the soldiers knew he had not had time to go down there and find Many Birds and then kill her rapist before they got there, if, indeed, it was Seth Bridges they had taken out of the shed. Maybe it was the other little girl. Maybe Seth had *killed* poor Katy!

He guided his horse through tangled underbrush and out into the open, his form barely visible before he heard shouting.

"There he is!"

"Don't let him get away!"

"Shoot to kill! That bastard renegade will only make more trouble if he slips away from us!"

Even from this distance Black Hawk recognized Jubal Desmond's voice on the last comment. Some of the soldiers shouted war whoops and began firing their pistols as they charged their horses up the hill toward him. What had happened! Why were they coming after him?

Bullets whizzed past him, and he turned his horse and kicked its sides, charging toward wooded hills to the west, soldiers hot on his heels.

Twenty-nine

Katy remained in her hiding place, rigid with terror. Who would believe her if she told them Jubal was the one who had killed Seth and not Black Hawk? Did she dare say anything? If Jubal got wind that she had witnessed the murder, would he come after her? Kill her? Maybe rape her like he'd raped Lucy and then send her downriver to other bad men?

After seeing him ruthlessly plunge his knife into Seth's heart, she was too afraid of Desmond to make her presence known until she was sure all the soldiers were gone. She had kept quiet when one of them said they had looked everywhere for her. She had seen a worried look on Jubal's face then, and her heart had pounded with terror when he looked all around the corn crib, his eyes resting on the back wall for a moment. Had he seen her? Would he know she had witnessed the murder?

She had watched men wrap Seth in a blanket and carry him outside, and she'd heard someone order another to throw the body over his horse. "Harkins, you and Private Smith take this man to the church for burial," someone had ordered. "I want everybody to report to Fort Yates after the Indian girl and the dead body have both been delivered. We've got to check with Colonel Gere about what to do about finding the other daughter, and if and how he wants us to go after Black Hawk."

"Yes, sir," someone replied. "Throw the body over the back of my horse, Jenkins."

Katy had waited several more minutes, stiff from standing

behind the boards all night waiting for Lucy. What had happened
to her sister? Was she all right? She was glad that at least Many
Birds would get help. She had waited awhile longer, but it had
seemed hours before she finally heard someone order the rest
of the soldiers to mount up; then suddenly a few of the men
began shouting.

"There he is!" someone yelled. She'd heard gunfire! Who
were they shooting at?

"Don't let him get away!"

"Shoot to kill!" Jubal shouted.

She had heard several horses riding off then, more shooting.
All the while she struggled against a need to burst into tears of
terror. She had seen so much horror since last night . . . the
vision of Many Birds's naked, abused body lying on that bed
haunted her, poor, innocent Many Birds, who had trusted her.
Maybe the authorities would arrest her and Lucy, thinking they
had a part in tricking Many Birds to come to the house. Then
there had been the long, dark night of terror, with rats crawling
over her, while she watched Seth, sure he would wake up and
find her any moment. Finally, morning had come, and so had
Jubal Desmond. She had never seen anything as awful as that
man plunging a knife into Seth's chest while Seth reached up,
grasping at him in what must have been a plea for mercy. She
hated Seth, but in that one moment, she had actually felt sorry
for him. She had thought about yelling for Jubal to stop, but
maybe he would have used that big knife on her!

Finally, the tears started to come. She made herself move,
slowly pushed away the loose boards and climbed out from behind the wall. She didn't bother to grab the money Lucy had
hidden there. It didn't matter now. All that mattered was survival,
and what she was going to tell others. She brushed cobwebs and
dirt from her hair and clothes and walked on stiff legs toward
the spot where Seth had been killed. She felt filthy and smelly,

for while waiting behind the wall she had wet her pants during the night.

She decided she had to go to the house first, wash and change. Then she had to decide what to do next. Go to the Army? To Miss Gibbons? Find Lucy? Run away? She didn't want to go anywhere without her sister. Should she tell on the sergeant? Would anyone believe her? She stared at the spot where Seth had been killed. There was still blood in the dirt. It was then she noticed something else . . . something shiny. She wiped at her tears, smearing more dirt on her face, then knelt to study the object. It was a button, a gold button that belonged to an army uniform. She picked it up, realizing this could be her proof that she had seen Jubal Desmond here, that Seth had grabbed at his uniform in a desperate attempt to stop the man from killing him. Surely she *had* to tell. Miss Gibbons loved Black Hawk. She couldn't let Black Hawk get blamed for something he didn't do. Was it Black Hawk the soldiers had chased after?

Maybe he would get away. Then she would never have to tell the truth. The thought of accusing Jubal terrified her. She knew how mean the man could be. Everyone would be ready to believe it was Black Hawk who had killed Seth. If they didn't believe her story, and Jubal was let go . . .

She clutched the gold button, shoved it into the pocket of her dress, and headed for the house.

Black Hawk rode at a hard gallop, still confused. The soldiers knew he was unarmed, yet they were firing at him! He leaned forward to create less of a target, opening his horse into a full, desperate run across open land. He could feel the soldiers behind him and had no way to defend himself if he was caught, except with his knife; but a knife was worthless against rifles and pistols. He cried out when a bullet slammed into his upper right shoulder, but he continued to cling to his horse's mane, as the animal sensed it must keep running.

He was not sure how far he had gone, how many minutes had passed. His horse was breathing hard now, and Black Hawk could feel the animal's sweat against his legs and arms. If he ran the faithful Appaloosa this hard much longer, it would kill the animal.

The pain in his shoulder intensified, and he knew he was bleeding badly. He felt his horse beginning to slow, even though it was trying hard to stay ahead of the soldiers. The animal was getting older. In the old days, every warrior had many horses, some for hunting, some for making war, some for the racing games, and always young horses to train for whatever purpose they were needed. All three of his horses were getting older. He needed new, young horses, but wild ones were few in number now, and the government made sure no Indian owned too many horses. Horses meant power for the Indians, a way of escape.

He deliberately slowed the Appaloosa, refusing to ride it to death. The soldiers would have him, one way or another. He felt them coming closer, and he slid off his horse, afraid that if they shot at him they would hit the animal instead.

"He's wounded!" someone shouted. "Hold your fire, men!"

Horses surrounded him, and someone walked up and kicked him over onto his back. He looked up at Jubal Desmond, who stood over him, pointing a pistol at his head.

"Make one move, Black Hawk, and I'll blow your brains out!"

Black Hawk looked around him, seeing that he was surrounded by six bluecoats.

"Back up, Sergeant!" someone else ordered. A man Black Hawk had never seen before stepped forward, wearing a lieutenant's uniform. "Get up, Black Hawk. We're taking you to Fort Yates."

Black Hawk rolled to his knees, holding his right arm with his left hand. "Why . . . are you doing this?"

"What?" The lieutenant came around and yanked Black Hawk's knife from its sheath. He studied it a moment, noticing some traces of blood near the handle. "For God's sake, man you must know you couldn't get away with killing Seth Bridges The man was lying there drunk and unarmed. I know how i must feel to know what he did to your sister, but—"

"Seth Bridges is dead?"

Lieutenant Hart frowned, sensing that Black Hawk truly was surprised. "What did you expect? When you bury a knife in a man's heart, he's going to die, Black Hawk."

Black Hawk grimaced with pain, his breath still coming in pants. "I . . . killed no one."

Hart held out his knife. "Seth Bridges was stabbed to death and there's blood on your knife."

Black Hawk frowned. "That is from a rabbit I cleaned last night. It is not human blood. I tell you, I did not kill Seth Bridges' Why would I have shown myself to you if I had? I was waiting on the hill. I decided to let the soldiers arrest Seth Bridges. I did not want any trouble. I just wanted to take my sister to our grandmother. That is why I was riding down the hill toward you."

"You lying sonofabitch!" The words came from Jubal. "Everybody knows what a renegade you are, and we all heard you threaten Seth's life. And when you saw us, you turned and ran!"

"You were shooting at me!" Black Hawk growled. "And I was unarmed! I did not know what else to do!"

"You rode off before the rest of us back there at the schoolteacher's house, and you got here first!" Jubal accused. "And nobody else had reason to kill Seth."

Black Hawk moved his dark, all-knowing eyes to look at the one person he hated even more than Seth Bridges. "I know one man who had reason to kill him."

Jubal reddened. "What the hell are you saying?"

Black Hawk looked at the lieutenant. "Who found Seth's body?"

Hart looked confused. "Why, the sergeant here did."

Black Hawk just nodded. "Just as I thought." He looked at Desmond. "The sergeant here had as much reason to kill Seth Bridges as anyone."

"Why, you—" Desmond pistol-whipped Black Hawk across the side of the head before anyone could stop him. "You filthy, lying Indian!" he roared. He raised his pistol again, but the lieutenant grabbed hold of his arm.

"That's enough, sergeant!" He ordered two other men to pick up Black Hawk and throw him over his horse. "Tie his wrists and ankles together underneath so he can't go anywhere. We'll have the Army medic look at him when we get him to Fort Yates." The man turned to Jubal. "What was that all about?"

Jubal rammed his pistol back into its holster. "That bastard hates me because I was at Wounded Knee, where he lost his wife and kid, that's all. Ever since then he's been trying to cause trouble for me, making up lies, accusing me of helping whiskey smugglers, saying Seth Bridges and I were into smuggling whiskey together. He's just looking for a way to turn the suspicion on somebody else, Lieutenant. For God's sake, I'd never shove a knife into somebody who's lying there helpless! But Black Hawk would, and we all know he went to that farm with the intent of killing Seth Bridges! Look at that big knife he carries. The bastard killed Seth. Anybody can see that. The blood on that knife isn't from any damn rabbit. It's Seth Bridges's blood! The Sioux have to be shown that they can't live the old way anymore, taking their vengeance whenever and wherever they like! Black Hawk's got to be hanged or sent off to prison! Things will be a lot more peaceful around here once he's gone."

The lieutenant sighed, looking down at Black Hawk's knife again. How could anyone doubt that the man had killed Seth? It was the nature of a man like that to kill first and think about it later. It was a way of life for the Sioux. "Let's get him to the fort," he told the others. "Johnston, you go tell Reverend Phillips what has happened here. Miss Gibbons will probably be gone with Many Birds by the time you get there. I told Brady to have her go with him to the girl's grandmother's village. Maybe the reverend can gather some people together and go back to the farm to try to find Seth's other daughter. She must have a hiding place nobody knows about, or maybe she ran away, after what she saw yesterday and all. We need to find her. We need both the girls' testimony in this."

"Yes, sir."

Jubal mounted up, still feeling a little uneasy that Katy had not been found, and worried about what she and Lucille might say about him. He hoped they had sense enough to keep quiet. Maybe he would visit Evelyn Gibbons later, just long enough to get a good look at Lucille, and Katy, too, if they found her by then. He'd make sure they knew by his eyes that they'd be wise to keep their mouths shut. "I'd be glad to go back and try to find the other daughter, Lieutenant," he volunteered, anxious to get to the girl before anyone else did.

"That's not necessary, Sergeant. We'll leave that to the reverend and his people. Let's get going," he ordered. "We have a lot to report to Colonel Gere and Agent McLaughlin, but we've got to walk these horses awhile after that chase."

They got under way, a bleeding Black Hawk draped over his own lathered horse. Jubal eyed him, hoping maybe he'd die from loss of blood before they ever reached the fort. That would be even better than a hanging. He wouldn't have a chance to defend himself, or say things better left unsaid. He had intended to kill him, if he could have got close enough without the lieutenant seeing him. He told himself that Black Hawk had no defense, that there was no possible way he could get out of this. Even if Lucy and Katy told about the whiskey smuggling and what he had done to Lucy, those things were a far cry from murder. He could claim Lucy was lying, that she was willing. After all, everyone at the dance had seen her walk off alone with him. And

ere was not one whit of evidence linking him to Seth's whiskey
muggling.

Yes, by God, he was in the clear, rid of Seth and soon to be
id of Black Hawk. Not one soul would believe Black Hawk was
ot the one who had killed Seth.

Evelyn ducked her head against a heavy wind that had come
p midmorning. Her heart was heavy for Many Birds, who lay
1 the back of the wagon that Private Brady drove to the village
vhere Dancing Woman lived. She had left Beverly with Lucille,
vho was sleeping from a dose of laudanum when she left. She
ad been too weak to do much talking so far, and Evelyn was
vorried about Katy. Had she been found yet? Lucille had not
tayed awake long enough to tell her where the girl was hiding.
he was anxious to talk to both girls about what was really going
n at Seth's house.

Her mind reeled with worry, not just for the girls and what
night have happened to Katy, but also for Black Hawk. Private
Brady had told her that when he left with Many Birds, Seth
Bridges still had not been found; but he thought he'd heard gun-
ire after he left with Many Birds. Poor Little Fox was beside
imself with worry when she had left, and she felt torn, realizing
hat he needed her, and so did Lucy and Katy, as well as Many
Birds . . . and Black Hawk himself, if he was still alive.

Who had been shooting at whom? Had Seth Bridges been
ound dead? Were the soldiers after Black Hawk? She did not
vant to believe he might have killed Seth. She'd been so sure
ie would realize killing the man would go entirely against the
rision. Had a white man died, just like Night Hunter had pre-
licted? If Seth was dead, everyone would think Black Hawk had
:illed him.

And what had happened to Katy? Brady said they still had
iot found her when he was there. They had called for her, but

she did not answer. Was the child capable of killing Seth herself
Perhaps she was, if driven too far, if threatened with rape. Mayb
that was why she was still hiding, or maybe she had run away

She ached to go to the agency and find out what had happene
but she knew Black Hawk would want her to first go with Man
Birds to Grandmother. Poor Many Birds, such a sweet, pretty
innocent young girl, saving herself for a worthy husband.

How could the morning turn from such blissful happiness t
such agony so quickly? Last night with Black Hawk had bee
like magic. They had lain and dreamed about the day when the
could at last be together every night, openly, happy in their lov
for each other. They had enjoyed breakfast with Little Fox, afte
which she had prepared for church. Now everything was in tur
moil. She prayed Seth had not got hold of Katy, that by som
miracle she would be found and she and Lucille would hav
some information to help put Seth Bridges behind bars for
long time.

They made their way through the village, and Evelyn coul
tell by the way some of the Sioux looked at them that the
already knew what had happened to Many Birds. Word travele
fast among these people. Most likely one of the Indians wh
lived near the church and had heard about Lucy and about Man
Birds had already ridden into some of the villages to tell others
In the old days, the Indians often sent messengers throughou
the villages by horseback to deliver news.

"I'm a little nervous," Private Brady told her. "Maybe they'l
take their anger out on us."

"No," she assured him. "They have too much respect for me
They'll wait to hear what Black Hawk wants to do about this
For now they know Many Birds needs their support. The wome
will help her." Her heart ached for Many Birds, who had becom
violently ill from all the whiskey Seth had forced into her. Now
she simply lay staring, refusing to speak, filled with horribl
shame for what had happened to her.

The cold air hung eerily quiet. No one from among the sullen onlookers said a word, and even the dogs were silent. A few flakes of snow fell, but they softly melted on the still-unfrozen ground.

"There is her grandmother's tipi," Evelyn said to the private, pointing. The old woman was already standing outside waiting, her eyes showing the inner pain she suffered over what had happened to her precious granddaughter. Evelyn felt ashamed that it was one of her own kind who had done this terrible thing to Many Birds. Why hadn't the girl told them she had been seeing Katy and Lucille? They could have warned her never to trust Seth, could have found some other way for her to continue her friendship without having to go into Seth's house. How cruel of Seth to urge the girls to be friends, then use that friendship to get his hands on Many Birds. What he had done would leave Katy and Lucy feeling responsible for the rape. Many Birds had grown to trust them. Scth had used their friendship to lure the poor girl into the house, had deliberately sent his daughters away so he could be alone with Many Birds. If only she had known that yesterday, when she stopped and talked to the girls on her way back from the trading post. She could have gone to the farm, kept Many Birds from going there. If . . . if . . . There was no changing any of it now. She felt guilty herself for not having done more to get Katy and Lucy away from Seth.

Private Brady drew the wagon to a halt, and Evelyn climbed down, walking up and hugging Dancing Woman, who she could see had been crying. "I'm sorry," she told the woman. She explained how it had happened, that it was not Many Birds's fault, nor the fault of Katy or Lucy, who treasured their friendship with Many Birds. She explained how they had been tricked themselves by their cruel adoptive father. Several women came to the wagon and helped Many Birds climb down. The girl threw a blanket over her head and wept as the women led her into her grandmother's tipi.

Dancing Woman looked into Evelyn's eyes. "This is what your people do to us," she said in her own tongue. "I do not blame *you*. My grandson loves you, and you are like us, in your heart. But the others . . ." She glanced up at Private Brady with hate and agony in her old eyes. "They bring only bad things to my people, take away our weapons, our game, our homeland. They violate Mother Earth, destroy the pride of our men, rob our young daughters of their innocence, reduce us to beggars. It is a sad time for us. The circle is broken."

Evelyn grasped her hands. "No, Grandmother. Some of us can keep the circle whole. Things will get better. I promise."

The old woman shook her head, tears slipping down her cheeks. "Can you mend my Many Birds? Can you give her back her innocence, take away the pain in her heart, the bad dreams she will have?"

Evelyn felt her heart breaking. "I wish that I could. All we can do is love and support her, and make her understand this is not her fault."

"And what will happen to my grandson? The messenger who came from your village said the soldiers found the man who did this to Many Birds. He was killed."

"What!"

"Already they think it was Black Hawk who did it, and they have gone after him. If they catch him, they will hang him, even if he did not do it. Maybe they will shoot him before he can defend himself. There is no justice for a man like Black Hawk."

Evelyn felt as though someone was shoving a knife into her own heart. Seth Bridges was dead! Had Black Hawk done it? Who else could have? Katy? She felt sick with panic. The soldiers were after Black Hawk! Visions of Wild Horse's death crashed vividly into memory, and she found it difficult to breathe.

"I am going now to find out what has happened," she told Black Hawk's grandmother. "You know I will do what I can to keep Black Hawk out of trouble, and to see that he does receive justice. If I have to, I will find a way to help him escape." She felt her own tears wanting to come. "I will not let them hurt him, Dancing Woman. I love him. I couldn't bear to live without him."

The old woman nodded. "You are the only one who can help him."

The two women embraced. "I will let you know what has happened," Evelyn told her. She turned away and climbed up into the wagon seat. "Hurry and get me back to my home." She told Private Brady the news Dancing Woman had imparted.

"Sounds like trouble." The man got the wagon moving, thinking how strange it was that the pretty Miss Gibbons seemed to be so close to Black Hawk's old grandmother, that she was so concerned about all these people. She even spoke in their language, a rarity among the whites who came out here to teach and spread the gospel. He headed out of the village, but drew the wagon to a halt when a young Indian man came riding into the village at a gallop. When he spotted Evelyn, he drew his horse to a skidding halt.

"Black Hawk!" he said urgently. "They have captured him and are taking him to the fort! He is wounded. They say he killed the farmer, Seth Bridges!"

Evelyn closed her eyes in agony. "Dear God," she muttered. She drew a deep breath for courage to face what she would have to face in the coming days. "Hurry, Private. We'll stop at the church first and see if they have found Katy. From there I will ride my own horse to Fort Yates. I have to talk to Colonel Gere, and to Black Hawk."

"Yes, ma'am." As the man got the wagon under way again, Evelyn told herself to keep the faith. All these months she had believed in the vision, believed it meant that she and Black Hawk would one day be together in peace. She did not want to believe that it could mean anything else, but she also could not imagine how Black Hawk could get out of this mess. She struggled against a feeling of hopelessness and began plotting how she could help Black Hawk escape if he was accused of murder. She would not let him hang, even if it meant risking her own life to free him!

Thirty

"You let me in there right this minute! I have papers here from Agent McLaughlin and from Colonel Gere allowing me to see Black Hawk!"

A young private studied Miss Evelyn Gibbons with a frown. "Lady, that's Black Hawk in there. He's already killed a man, stuck a knife right in his heart. Don't you know how dangerous it is for you to go in there? He might grab you and use you as a hostage to try to escape. I can't—"

"I happen to love him, Private, and intend to *marry* him, as soon as he is cleared of these charges, which he *will* be! Open that door and let me in. From what I am told of his injury, he is in no shape to try to use anyone as a hostage, and I have no fear of that happening anyway! Now, are you going to let me inside, or shall I have you reprimanded for disobeying orders? I have been riding since five o'clock this morning to get here, through snow and wind and cold! I am not leaving until I am allowed to see Black Hawk!"

The private blinked in surprise. *Marry* him? This pretty young schoolteacher was going to marry the notorious, murdering Black Hawk? He sighed, taking a set of keys from his pocket. If the woman insisted on being so demanding, the hell with her, he thought. She had to be a little bit stirred in the head.

"It's your own risk, lady." He turned and stuck a key in the lock to the thick wooden door that led into the tiny brick cell located in one corner of the fort grounds. The moment Evelyn saw it, she felt sick—so small, in such a lonely area of the fort, where a person could hear little of what was going on outside. The room had only one high little window at the side. Though she was glad it was no longer the middle of summer, imagining how hot such a cubicle must be, remembering Black Hawk had already been in here once when it *was* still hot, now she worried the opposite might be true. It was surely cold and damp inside, with the miserable December weather they had been having, and Black Hawk was wounded. He could get sick and die before a trial ever came about.

The private pulled his pistol and stepped back, then kicked open the door. "Stay put, Black Hawk, or there will be another bullet in you," he warned. "Go on in," he told Evelyn, without taking his eyes from the door.

Evelyn hurried inside, where it was so dark she could hardly see Black Hawk at first. The private closed and locked the door. It took a moment for Evelyn's eyes to adjust to the dim light, and for her nose to adjust to the damp smell, mixed with the smell of human waste from an untended chamber pot. She shuddered at what a hellish place this was for any man, let alone one who took pride in cleanliness and who was accustomed to freedom and fresh air and sunshine. And how was a wounded man supposed to heal in such a place? How dirty were the blankets on his cot? "Black Hawk?" She could barely make out the figure lying on a cot against the back wall.

"Go away," he told her quietly. "This is no place for you."

Her heart fell at the agony in his voice. The fight was gone out of him. "And if I were the one lying there, you would not come to help me? Support me?" She walked closer. She could see him now, lying on his back, staring at nothing. "Black Hawk, tell me in your own words you did not kill Seth Bridges. That is all I need to hear. If you say it, I'll know it's true. If you did kill him, you would tell me."

He slowly turned his head to look at her, and she saw the hopelessness in his dark eyes. "I did not kill him."

She nodded. "Tell me what happened."

He watched her sadly, his voice flat and lifeless when he spoke. "I did as you told me. I let the soldiers help Many Birds. I was riding down to meet them because I wanted to take my sister to Grandmother myself. They started shooting at me. I did not know why. I had no weapon for shooting back, and I was confused. I turned and rode hard, tried to get away." He looked back at the ceiling. "They say Sergeant Desmond is the one who found the dead body. I believe *he* killed Seth Bridges. He would enjoy having me blamed for it, and he knows there is not one person who would believe otherwise . . ." He looked at her again. "Except you. But you do not count. They think you are a foolish woman whose love for an Indian man would make her believe anything just to save him."

Evelyn felt a lump swelling in her throat. Black Hawk's situation seemed just as hopeless as he already thought it was, but she did not want to convey to him her own worry. "Black Hawk, the only evidence they have is that Seth was stabbed and you carry a knife. Surely they realize you didn't have time—"

"They will not stop to figure such things," he interrupted. "My knife had blood on it—rabbit blood, from that rabbit I cleaned for you the night before. I threatened to kill Seth Bridges, and I ran from the soldiers. That is all the evidence they need."

"But . . . the dream . . . the vision—"

"In the vision we reached out to each other, but always the other one disappeared. Now we know the true meaning . . . that we can never be together. Night Hunter said a white man would die, and I would be in much trouble because of it. Now we also know the meaning of his dream."

"He also said that I would somehow help you. I will find a

way, Black Hawk. Maybe I can get a lawyer to come here from Omaha. Maybe—"

He waved his left hand as though to shut her up. "You live in a dream, *Wenonah*. Rich white lawyers do not come to places like this to defend an Indian. Sometimes I do not think you realize just how your people really look at mine. I am nothing to them. If I die, they are simply rid of another troublemaking Indian, and the murder is solved—no questions."

Tears filled her eyes. "No. I refuse to believe this is all hopeless, Black Hawk." She knelt onto the cement floor beside his cot and touched his arm. "The doctor said you refused to drink any laudanum before he removed the bullet." He continued to stare at the ceiling. Evelyn knew he was ashamed of the putrid cell and the fact that he was a helpless prisoner. His pride had been deeply wounded, and like so many other proud Sioux men, his own spirit would soon be broken if she could not help him out of this situation.

"The laudanum is almost the same as whiskey. I will not drink something that makes my thoughts leave me, nor will I allow myself to be asleep while I am at the hands of a white doctor. I would rather feel the pain. Pain gives me strength."

Evelyn forced back the tears that wanted to come. "Are you in a lot of pain now?"

He sighed deeply. "It is not so bad." He deliberately bent his right arm, raised it a little. Perspiration broke out on his face. Evelyn could see that it brought him deeper pain than he let on, and she became aware of the old bloodstains down the back of the right sleeve of his buckskin shirt. "The doctor put something on it that burned. He said it would keep away infection. My shoulder is wrapped tightly." He let out a quick little laugh that rang of bitterness. "It is strange what your people do—operating on a man, saving his life so that they can hang him." His voice broke on the last words. "Do not let them hang me, *Wenonah*." The words were spoken softly but full of passion. "It is the worst way for an Indian to die. Shoot me yourself with a gun if you can."

She squeezed his arm. "You are *not* going to hang!"

"Promise me! If you love me, you will not let me hang. No one will punish you for shooting an Indian."

Her tears finally came then, and she rested her head against his arm. "I promise." Her head ached from holding back a need to vent her grief, a need to scream. "If only there was some way to prove your innocence," she groaned. "They found Katy hiding inside a kitchen cupboard. No one knows what she saw or heard, or why she didn't let her presence be known. They brought her to my house, but she just sits in a corner and won't talk. She is terrified of something. I don't know if it's from seeing poor Many Birds tied to that bed, or from Seth threatening her and Lucille with that knife, or waiting all night for Lucille to return with help. No one knows what she heard or saw after Lucille left."

"If she was hiding in the house, then she knows nothing. Seth Bridges was found in the corn crib . . . by Jubal Desmond." He closed his eyes. "What did Seth do to my sister?"

Evelyn wiped at quiet tears. "He forced whiskey into her so that she passed out. He . . . tied her to his bed. I don't need to explain what happened then."

Black Hawk let out a pitiful groan and rolled to his left side. The right back side of his shirt was ripped and bloodstained. Evelyn's heart ached for his pain, both physical and emotional.

"I took her to your grandmother," she explained. "Many women came to tend to her. She has so much love and support, Black Hawk. It's probably a godsend that she was in too much of an alcohol daze to remember much of it."

"That does not erase the shame of it."

"I know that, but at least she has little memory of whatever vile things that man did. And now he's dead. I'm glad of it, except for the fact that you were blamed for it. I'm glad Lucille and Katy no longer have to live with whatever hell he put them through. So far they won't talk about it, perhaps because of their shame. I would not have minded being the one to kill him, but the fact remains someone did, and we have to find a way to prove it wasn't you."

"That will never happen." He kept his back to her. "Please go. I am ashamed for you to be here. Go away and forget me. Go teach the children and live like a white woman. Find a white man to marry."

She rose. "Do you really think I could forget you? No man could ever take your place, in my heart or in my bed, and I won't listen to you talk this way. This is not the Black Hawk I fell in love with, the strong, rebellious fighter I met at Many Birds's puberty ritual. This is not the Black Hawk who defended me against those whiskey peddlers and has refused to bow to the soldiers or to give up his Sioux beliefs and customs. This is not the Black Hawk who has always been a good father to his son . . . a son who needs him, loves him, respects his father's courage."

On those words Black Hawk finally turned over again. He slowly sat up, then ran his left hand through his hair, pulling his hair behind his back. "How is Little Fox?"

"He is afraid for you. I promised him you would not die."

He raised his eyes and looked up at her. "You are a woman full of false hopes."

"I am a woman in love, and a woman who believes in her dreams. God did not direct me out here just to let me fall in love with you and then see you die. I believe His purpose was for me to be here for you when you needed me, and for me to be a part of keeping the circle. You represent the spirit of your people. If you die, *then* the circle will be broken. If you live, your people will take great hope in it, and our marrying and having children who carry the blood of both races will be a sign that the circle of life can continue, but in a new way. You must have faith, Black Hawk, faith in our love, faith in the God we share, the God who brought us together, faith in the vision we shared." She knelt once more and took hold of his hands. "We are going to get through this."

The guard outside pounded on the door then. "Long enough, Miss Gibbons. You all right in there?"

"I'm fine," she called out. She leaned up and kissed Black Hawk's cheek. "Pray, Black Hawk. Draw on the strength you've developed through the Sun Dance ritual and your closeness to Wakantanka. Don't give up hope. You and I and Little Fox will be together again."

She heard the sound of a key turning in the lock. Light filtered into the bare little room when the door opened. "Time to go, lady," the private outside told her.

Evelyn paid no heed. She searched Black Hawk's dark eyes, now that she could see them better, and her heart was crushed at what she saw there. New tears filled her eyes. "Don't forget who you are, Black Hawk. You are a Sioux warrior, proud, true to your heart. You have done nothing wrong, and it is the white man who is making himself a fool through all of this. They're all wrong, and God will help us find a way to prove it, and to prove who the real killer is. God will let us be together . . . one way or another." She touched his face, alarmed by how tired he looked, the circles under his eyes. "I love you," she whispered. Their eyes held as she rose. "Remember the vision."

She turned to the private, pulling her fur coat closer to her neck as she glanced at a potbelly stove in a corner of the room. "It is freezing in here, and I see no wood for a fire. Bring some wood so Black Hawk can build a fire to take away the dampness and chill. How can you expect a wounded man to survive in these conditions?"

"They're supposed to bring him some wood pretty soon now."

"It had *better* be soon! I will talk to Colonel Gere about this. The conditions in here are deplorable and inexcusable! In this country a man is considered innocent until proven guilty, and

every man deserves the right to be treated better than an animal."
Evelyn quickly left then, not wanting to break into tears in front
of Black Hawk. She waited for the young man guarding the door
to close and lock it again. "And see that his chamber pot is
emptied often," she told the young man, "and that he is given
clean blankets and is fed decent food."

"That's up to Colonel Gere, not me."

"I will take care of that. You had just better do as he says.
That man in there is a fine example of a proud Sioux warrior.
Treat him with the respect he deserves, Private. Even if he
were guilty, which he is not, give some consideration to why
he would want to kill Seth Bridges. What if a man did those
deplorable things to a sister of yours, Private? How would you
feel about that?"

The young man blinked. "Well, I . . . I—"

"Just as I thought! You would want to kill him, and you would
probably have every right to do it yourself!" She walked away,
heading for the colonel's headquarters to deliberately badger the
man. She intended to see that he took proper care of Black Hawk.
Perhaps the man could find a better place to put him, a room
where he had fresher air, some sunlight. With enough men
guarding him, he didn't need to be in that stinking hole of a
damp cell. The circuit judge who would listen to Black Hawk's
case was not going to make it to Fort Sully for another couple
of weeks yet. In the conditions under which he was living now,
a man like Black Hawk could die by then.

She closed her eyes for a moment as she walked. "God help
me," she whispered. "Don't take him from me. Not now."
Christmas would be here soon, but she felt no joy. A shadow
moved over her then, and she looked up to see a hawk floating
overhead, its wings spread in graceful beauty. She took hope
in the sight as a sign from God. The spirit of the hawk was
watching over the man she loved. God would surely help her
find a way to free him.

* * *

Jubal Desmond waited at the door to Evelyn's cabin, eager to get to Lucille and Katy before they said too much, if that was possible. What had they already told the schoolteacher and others? Now that they were rid of Seth, they should be glad of it. Maybe they would be willing to keep quiet about the whiskey, and about what he had done to Lucille. He knew only one way to shut them up . . .

His hands opened and closed into fists as he dealt with his anxiety and frustration. He knew Evelyn Gibbons was gone . . . at the fort visiting her Indian lover. The Widow Evans was at the school teaching, which meant the girls should be here alone. He'd like to kick his way inside, but he didn't want to draw too much attention. If anyone found him here, he would tell them he had orders to come here and question the girls about what they knew about Many Birds and what Katy possibly knew about Black Hawk murdering their father. He'd be damn glad when this was over and Black Hawk was dead and silent! Now if he could just make sure Lucille and Katy . . .

"Who is it?" came a timid voice from inside.

Jubal had deliberately left his horse behind the cabin so others would not notice it, and so the girls would not recognize it if they looked out a front window. He stood as close as possible to the door so that they also could not see him from the same window. "Reverend Phillips," he answered.

The door opened slightly, and quickly Jubal shoved it open wider and forced himself inside, closing the door again. Lucille, who had answered the door in her robe, gasped and jumped back, terror in her eyes. "You get out of here!" she shouted.

Jubal turned and rammed the bolt on the door closed. "Not just yet, young lady." He put out his hand as though to ward her off. "I'm not here to hurt you or Katy. Where *is* Katy?"

"What do you want?" Lucille moved farther back.

Jubal looked around the room, then noticed a pair of blue eyes watching him from behind the curtains that led to the bedroom. "Come on out, Katy. I just want to talk to you and Lucille."

Katy's heart pounded with terror. She had told no one, not even her sister, what she had actually seen. She had not spoken to one person besides Lucille, and all she had told her sister was that when Seth came to the corn crib and passed out, she ran out from her hiding place and back to the house to hide in a cupboard, where the reverend and Beverly found her. That had been two days ago, and she was too frightened of what could happen to her to tell the truth, even to Lucille, yet for some reason she had kept that button from Jubal's army jacket, slipping it into her little carpetbag when she packed to come here with the reverend.

"Talk about what?" Lucille asked, diverting his attention from Katy.

Jubal's hands went into fists again when he looked back at her. "What have you told everybody about me?"

Lucille studied him with hatred in her eyes. "Nothing . . . yet. All they know is what Seth did to Many Birds." Her eyes teared then. "I'm too ashamed to tell them about me and Seth . . ." Her lips moved into a sneer. "Or me and you, even though you both *forced* me! Miss Gibbons has been trying to get us to talk about it, but I won't, and Katy isn't talking at all. She's been too badly frightened by everything."

Jubal glanced over at the curtains again. There was something in those eyes he didn't like, not just hatred and terror . . . but *knowledge.* Was she thinking only of what she knew about him and Lucy, or him and his involvement with Seth in smuggling whiskey? It still made him uncomfortable to realize no one had been able to find Katy the day of Seth's murder. He could not get over the feeling that someone was watching that day when he looked around the corn crib, and he had lost sleep over it.

He decided it was probably his own guilty conscience. After all, Katy had been found in the house, hiding in a cupboard.

"Get out of here and leave us alone," Lucille told him. "I hope I never have to look at you again!"

"I'm not leaving until I get your promise that you won't say anything about me and you, or me and the whiskey smuggling."

"Or what?" Lucille sneered.

Jubal stepped closer. "Or you'll both find yourselves in a lot sorrier state than living with Seth! Neither one of those crimes will get me anything more than being kicked out of the Army! I'll still be a free man, and you had both better remember that I know every river pirate and woman slaver on the Missouri River! I'll get you! I'll get you *both* if you rat on me!" He pointed at Lucille. "You think about that, little girl! You think about what could happen to your sister. She's come through this unharmed, still a virgin. She can go to school now, make something of herself. Don't mess it up for her!" He glanced over at the pair of eyes watching him. "And don't mess it up for yourself, little lady! Don't think Miss Gibbons or that excuse of a man, Reverend Phillips, can protect you! If I want you, I'll *get* you!" He turned his eyes back to Lucille. "You're rid of Seth now. Be glad of it. You keep your mouth shut about me, and you can both have yourselves good lives, stay here with Miss Gibbons, go to school, wear pretty dresses. Nobody needs to know about you and Seth or you and me. Keep it to yourself and someday you'll be able to marry a decent man and he'll never know the difference! It's done now. Seth is dead, and you don't have to be afraid of him anymore."

He stepped even closer, his pale-blue eyes glaring with a determined threat that reminded Lucille of how Seth sometimes looked at her when he wanted to hit her. "But you *do* have to be afraid of *me,* if you get it in your head to tell everything you know! You think about that!" He turned his gaze once more to give Katy the same look, but she was no longer watching him. He took a deep breath to control his own anger. He wished he could strangle them both and be rid of them, and he hoped this little threat would do the trick. "I want your promise," he growled.

Lucille swallowed. How she hated this man, but she wanted only peace now, a chance to lead a normal life, unbranded by shame. "I promise," she answered.

Their eyes held, and he finally nodded. "Good." His eyes moved over her scathingly. "It's been nice knowing you," he said with a wicked smile. He turned and left, and Lucille just stood there shivering for a moment. She shuffled on weak legs to the bedroom, still not strong enough to get dressed and go outside. Seth's knife wound had not been deep enough to cause any serious damage, but it was enough to make her lose a lot of blood. She was still dizzy when she got up, and the stitches on her stomach were painful.

"Katy?" She called for her sister when she reached the bedroom.

"Don't let him kill me," Katy whimpered.

Lucille realized the words had come from under the bed. "Katy, come out of there. He's not going to kill us. He'd never get away with it."

"Yes, he could," Katy sniffled. "He could."

Lucille frowned with worry. She knew her sister well, knew when there was something Katy was not telling her. She was the only one who knew that Katy was originally hiding in the corn crib. She had told no one that first day, after waking up to learn that was where Seth's dead body was found. She even wondered if Katy herself could have killed the man. She was not about to give anyone else that idea, so she had never mentioned the hiding place. She had to protect her sister.

Besides, something else must have happened. Katy said she had run to the house after Seth passed out and had seen nothing of his murder; but Lucille had heard Miss Gibbons say she was suspicious of the fact that Jubal Desmond had been the one to find Seth's body. Did Katy know something she was not telling? She had suffered through a lot of Seth's abuse, but had always remained outspoken and defiant. It was not like her to be so terrified that she would speak to no one. And it certainly was not like her to hide in a cupboard from decent people like the reverend, or to crawl under a bed like a terrified animal. What was she so afraid of now, especially since Seth was dead and could not hurt them?

"Katy, is there something you aren't telling me? I'm your sister. You can tell me *anything.*"

"No! It's like Jubal said. We have to keep quiet."

Lucille folded her robe closer around her neck. "Don't worry about Jubal. We won't say anything, but we don't have to be afraid of him, either. He just came here to try to scare us because he's scared himself of getting into trouble. He can't do anything to us without getting caught."

Katy crawled out from under the bed, her eyes wide with terror. She nodded her head. "Yes, he can, Lucy," she said, tears streaming down her face. "Don't you tell on him. Don't you tell anything. He might kill us."

Lucille sighed. "Jubal is a coward and a crook and a rapist, but he's not a mur-" She frowned. "Katy, did you see Jubal *kill* somebody?"

Katy sniffed and shook her head. "No. I . . . I just think he could. He's an Army man. They killed all those Indians at Wounded Knee, remember? Women and children. And he knows bad men who would do bad things to us. Please don't tell on him, Lucy! I don't want him to come and get us!"

Lucille was even more sure her sister was hiding something, but she knew it would do no good to try to persuade her to tell now. Maybe after awhile, when she was stronger and had learned to trust Miss Gibbons and the others, she would get back her strength and courage. She moved her arms around her and let her cry on her shoulder. "I won't tell," she told her, petting her hair. "I promise."

Thirty-one

Evelyn glanced out the church window at snow. This was the first day in the past two weeks that there had not been a stiff, cold wind. Huge flakes drifted on still air, piling atop one another as they met the earth, the trees, the rooftops. She thought how her heart felt as cold as that snow. It had been nearly a month since Seth Bridges had been found dead, and Black Hawk was fast losing hope and life as he sat in that cold cell. She had not been able to convince Colonel Gere to put him in a warmer and more pleasant room, and each time she visited him she could see the desire to live was leaving him.

His wound had healed, but it was the inner wounds and the feeling of hopelessness that was killing him, the same things that killed other proud Indian men who were sent off to prison in Florida, the very things that led other Indian men here on the reservation to continue to pay any price for whiskey so that they could drink away the inner pain.

She was herself losing hope. Christmas had come and gone. She had made it as joyous as she could for Lucille, Katy, and Little Fox, had brought in a pine tree and let them decorate it with strings of popcorn and ornaments she had helped them make. She could tell it was the happiest the girls had ever been, and in spite of her own heavy heart and poor Little Fox's broken one, she was glad to see new light in Katy and Lucille's eyes.

Katy had blossomed, had gained some weight, and was completely changed from the silent, frightened child Reverend Phillips had found hiding in a cupboard. Still, she had said nothing about the day of the murder that might help Black Hawk. Evelyn had hoped the girl knew more than she was telling, but she'd had every opportunity to give her any helpful information she could. She stuck to her story that she had seen Many Birds tied to Seth's bed, and then Seth stabbing Lucille; that after that she had hidden in a cupboard the rest of the night, waiting for Lucille to go for help. Mention of that awful day and night never failed to wipe the joy off Katy's face, and every time Evelyn brought up the subject, the girl withdrew and became quiet again.

Evelyn had stopped talking about that day, afraid the progress that had been made with both girls would be lost. They were attending school, and they seemed content that Seth Bridges was dead and out of their lives. Neither girl would discuss what life had been like with him. They lived with her and Little Fox, and now Evelyn's concern was more for Black Hawk's son than for Katy and Lucille. The boy was not doing well in school, and Evelyn knew it was because his mind was on his father. She worried what would happen to him if Black Hawk was hanged or sent away.

So much was still so wrong. Her heart was torn with grief over Black Hawk's future and Little Fox's own broken heart; and then there was Many Birds to think about. She still refused to come out of her grandmother's tipi and return to school or even to everyday living. She had been allowed by the men to sit in the sweat lodge to help purge herself of Seth Bridges's filthy violation of her body. She had cut off all her hair, had fasted, cut her arms. It sickened Evelyn to think what the girl had suffered, and she prayed for her daily. Somehow, someday, she must get over what had happened. Perhaps she could renew her friendship with Lucy and Katy, come back to school. She knew the best hope for that happening was if Black Hawk were freed.

She tried to concentrate on what was taking place today. John Phillips was marrying Beverly Evans. How she wished it was she and Black Hawk getting married, but that might never happen now. Her heart ached at listening to wedding vows, and she thought of the beautiful Sioux wedding dress Black Hawk had given her—a dress that still lay waiting in her trunk . . . a dress that might never be worn.

She blinked back tears. Had they been wrong about the vision after all? How could she go on living if Black Hawk was sent away . . . or hanged? Her only reason for existing then would be to love and care for Little Fox, but the boy's spirit would be so broken, she wasn't sure he would ever be the same if something happened to his father. She was more and more suspicious herself that Jubal Desmond might have killed Seth Bridges, but how could it ever be proved? She had asked Colonel Gere to question Desmond, but the man had said that the sergeant had been harassed enough by her. He felt her suspicion was ridiculous and unfounded.

Evelyn looked to her right, where Lucy and Katy sat watching the wedding ceremony. She and Beverly had helped make new dresses for them, and with their hair washed and pulled up into fancy curls, new dresses and shoes, and wearing new woolen coats Evelyn had ordered for them from Omaha through Bill Doogan's trading post and given them for Christmas, the girls looked lovely. Rest, better food, and being able to socialize had brought them to life, put color in their cheeks. Evelyn thought how she had gradually come to have a family, responsible as she was now for raising the two girls and Little Fox . . . yet she was only just turned twenty-one, and she had no husband. If something happened to Black Hawk . . .

Katy turned to look at her. There it was again, that strange look of guilt in the girl's eyes, combined with sorrow. Evelyn was so sure she was not telling everything, but nothing she said could change Katy's story. Didn't they understand what it would do to her to see Black Hawk punished or hanged? Didn't they understand how much she loved him? Still, if letting an Indian man die somehow meant their own safety, or somehow saved their own reputations, she supposed to young white girls who had probably been taught all their lives that Indians were worthless, it mattered little that one Indian man would suffer. She had stressed to them that Black Hawk was Many Birds's brother, and that they owed Many Birds any kind of help they could give in helping Black Hawk, yet they continued to insist there was nothing they could do.

Everything would be perfect if not for Black Hawk's predicament. She was happy to be able to help the girls. The reverend had hired a few Indians and some men from the fort to add two rooms to her cabin so that she and the girls could have their own bedrooms. She put an arm around Little Fox. Somehow she would have to find a way to raise these children alone. She had to hold onto her teaching job but would have to find another way to earn a little extra money, perhaps through sewing. The girls could help her. They were very co-operative, pitched in with the cooking and cleaning, and were learning to sew and embroider.

She turned her attention to the wedding ceremony. She was happy for Beverly, but she knew the woman did not love John Phillips in the same wildly passionate way she had loved Herbert True. Still, she *did* love him. The reverend was a good man who would be a loving father to her child. Beverly loved him because he was willing to give her son his name and not allow him to be labeled a bastard. She loved him for accepting her just as she was, for understanding that anyone can make grave mistakes in their lives, just as he himself had made the mistake of ignoring Anita Wolf's sweet and innocent love for him.

So much had happened, so many changes since she first came here. A new missionary couple had finally arrived a week ago. They would live in the back of the church as Phillips had, until a home was built for them. John would move into Janine's old cabin with Beverly. The new minister, Reverend Gale Carter, conducted John and Beverly's marriage ceremony. His wife, Helen, who would help teach school, sat in the front pew now with the couple's three children, twelve-year-old Lynette, ten-year-old Johnny, and four-year-old Henrietta, and all three were well-behaved.

The Carters were a nice family, and it would be good to have them near. Another couple, Jeremy and Gladys Brady, had been sent to Oahe. They were an older couple, their children grown. The Carters' two older children would attend school, but what had happened to Many Birds had frightened and angered many of the Sioux, and again school attendance for Indian children was down. Evelyn was sure that all that was needed now to get most Indian children to school was for Black Hawk to be freed, but that seemed unlikely. She had considered how she might help him escape, but had given up the idea. Now that she had the responsibility of caring for Lucy and Katy and Little Fox, and because of the responsibility she felt to Black Hawk's people, she could not very well do something that could land her in jail or cause her to also have to flee, but she shuddered at the thought of possibly having to shoot Black Hawk as she had promised to do if he was sentenced to be hanged.

The ceremony ended, and Beverly and John embraced, touching cheeks. There were tears in Beverly's eyes when Evelyn walked up to congratulate her. "I pray this will happen for you and Black Hawk," she told Evelyn quietly as they embraced. "God will find a way, Evy."

Evelyn could not reply. A sudden, painful lump in her throat cut off her words. She thought how two years ago, just about this time, Black Hawk had suffered the loss of his wife and son, had seen the horror of Wounded Knee. He had been suffering ever since, and now might die himself. She blinked back tears as she turned to Reverend Phillips and shook his hand. He squeezed her hand warmly, and she knew he was thinking how there was a time when he would have wanted her to be the woman at his side. He finally had come to understand how much she loved Black Hawk.

"I've been told a Judge Hooper will be here in two more days," he told her. "I learned it from Agent McLaughlin just before the ceremony."

Evelyn glanced back at McLaughlin and his wife, who had come to watch the wedding. She took a deep breath to ward off more tears. "Good. At least something will happen soon. I just wish I could have found someone to defend Black Hawk. I don't see how he has much of a chance." Now the tears wanted to come again, and she had to stop talking. Beverly moved to put an arm around her.

"No tears on my wedding day," she scolded. "You are supposed to cut and serve the cake, Evy."

Evelyn nodded and moved to the front of the church, where a table was set up with a lovely cake baked by Helen Carter and decorated by her daughter. Lynnette was already at the table showing the cake to Lucille and Katy. Evelyn watched the girls talk and giggle, daydreaming, she supposed, about their own wedding day. Besides McLaughlin, a few Indians and several white settlers and Bill Doogan had attended the wedding. As people began to mingle, Evelyn heard a few of them talking about Black Hawk and how he had murdered "those poor girls' father."

Doogan came up to her then, holding out an envelope. "Old Dancing Eagle brought me this mail this morning, Miss Gibbons. He asked me to give it to you since I was coming here anyway."

Evelyn took the envelope, noticing the letter was from her father. She walked away from the others and quickly opened it. *Dear Daughter,* she read. *By the time you get this, Christmas will have come and gone. I pray yours was a merry one. I can tell by your letter that you are very much in love with the Indian called Black Hawk. Yes, you truly have your mother's spirit, and*

I worry that your heart will be broken as hers was. I pray it will all work out as you hope. Please do wire me before you marry, as I would like to come there and meet him and escort you down the aisle of your little church there, however humble it may be. Sometimes I think perhaps Wild Horse lives again through Black Hawk, and your mother through you, and the two of them will be together at last.

Evelyn stopped reading for a moment, overwhelmed by the comparison he had made all on his own, the very feeling she had had herself so many times. Her father was an insightful man who, through her mother, had learned so much about love and understanding and acceptance of all humankind. The man did not even know yet about Black Hawk's sad situation. She had not written to tell him.

There were so many times when I realized your mother was more Christian and caring than I, she continued reading, *even though I was the preacher and she held no official position with the church. You are very much like her in that way also.*

I am writing not just to be sure you ask me to your wedding, but also to tell you some good news. I took Black Hawk's paintings, (and I must say, they were remarkable) to an art dealer here in Waupun. He was quite impressed by them, and he took them on to Milwaukee to someone much more learned on such matters. That dealer in turn took them to Chicago, and he recently wired me, asking me if the artist would accept four hundred dollars for the paintings, two hundred dollars each. I need you to ask Black Hawk if that would suffice, and if so, the dealer will wire the money to me, and I will send you a certified check; better yet, I will bring you the check personally. In the meantime, the dealer wants to know if Black Hawk will agree to do more work for him. He wishes to send someone out to discuss a contract for Black Hawk to paint only for his gallery. He would supply the material and send someone periodically to pick up paintings. I have enclosed the man's name and address . . .

Evelyn had to stop reading. Four hundred dollars! She had expected Black Hawk to make money from his paintings, but she had not expected that much. It was wonderful . . . and heart-breaking. He might not live long enough or be able to stay here long enough to do any more painting. What wonderful news this would be if he were a free man and they could marry. Here was a guaranteed income for Black Hawk, doing something he loved. He could ride out into the land where his heart lay and paint pictures of it that would preserve it just the way it was. He could paint pictures of the old ways, of Indian life as it once was. And he could earn a great deal of money doing it.

She could not help the tears that came then over the irony of the timing of the letter. Now she would have to write her father back and tell him there might never be any more pictures . . . that her heart would, indeed, be broken, just like her mother's was when Wild Horse was killed. She gripped the letter tightly in her hand and walked outside, needing to breathe fresh air and get control of herself. Her cape was still inside, but she hardly noticed the cold. All she could think of was how perfect every-thing would be now if Black Hawk were free. Should she even bother to tell him the news about his paintings? Her heart pounded harder at the realization that a federal judge would be here soon, a man who would determine Black Hawk's fate; and Black Hawk didn't have one soul to stand up in his defense. She would try to get her own say in the matter, but she already knew no federal judge was going to put much worth in the words of a female, especially a white woman who was in love with the very Indian man who was on trial. Others would make sure the judge knew of her relationship with Black Hawk, which would only discredit her. Someone would probably bring up the fact that she had already harassed and tried to make trouble for "poor" Sergeant Desmond. There were plenty of witnesses to swear that Black Hawk rode out that day with the express pur-pose, in his own words, of killing Seth Bridges.

"Miss Gibbons?"

Someone touched her back, and she turned to see Katy standing behind her. She quickly wiped at her tears. "What is it, Katy?"

"What's in the letter? Why are you crying?"

Evelyn's shoulders shook in a sob, and she breathed deeply to stop her crying. "The letter is from my father. I sent him some paintings that Black Hawk did." She took a handkerchief from her pocket and blew her nose before she told the girl the contents of her father's letter.

Katy's eyes widened when Evelyn divulged the sum the dealer was willing to pay Black Hawk. "Two hundred dollars!"

Evelyn dabbed at her eyes. "It doesn't matter much now. I'll have them send the money and I'll use it for Little Fox. Black Hawk would want that. I doubt . . ." The tears came again. "I doubt he'll ever have the chance . . . to paint again." She turned away, sobbing. "I'm sorry, Katy. I can't help it. It all looks so hopeless, and I know Black Hawk is innocent."

Katy watched her, wanting to cry herself. *Yes, he is innocent,* she wanted to tell her. But what about Jubal Desmond? What if no one believed her and the man went free? And if she told about the murder, shouldn't she tell the rest of it, what Jubal did to Lucille? Tell about the whiskey? Poor Lucy wanted desperately to keep the years of rape and abuse a secret. She was so ashamed, and she had put up with it only to protect her little sister. How could she turn around and tell the truth? Besides, she would never forget the look in Jubal's eyes the day he came to the cabin, nor would she forget watching him stab that big knife into Seth's chest, as easily as if he was killing a chicken or a rabbit.

She hated seeing Miss Gibbons so unhappy. She had been so good to her and Lucy, had agreed to let them live with her, used her own money to buy material for new dresses, had bought them new coats, new shoes, made Christmas the happiest one she had ever known. She was teaching them so much, at school

and at home, and she and Lucy had found more peace and jc
with the schoolteacher than they ever dreamed possible. It didn
seem fair that their own happiness should be at the expense c
Miss Gibbons's. She could end all of this. She knew somethin
that even Lucille didn't know, but she clung to the hope tha
somehow Black Hawk would go free and she would never hav
to tell the truth.

"It will be all right, Miss Gibbons. You'll see."

Evelyn shook her head, her tears dripping onto the letter. "
don't think so, Katy." She wiped at her eyes again. "I'm jus
glad I have you and Lucy, and Little Fox, and my friends here
Beverly and the reverend. I think if I asked my father to come
he would." She blew her nose. "But nothing and no one can tak
away the pain of losing Black Hawk." She sighed deeply. "Th
judge will be here in two or three more days. I think you an
Lucille should be at the hearing. They might want to ask yo
some questions."

A sick feeling came to Katy's stomach. "Questions? Abou
what?"

"I don't even know. I am just supposing there will be ques
tions about Seth, what you saw that day." Evelyn watched a nev
terror come into Katy's eyes, and she grasped the girl's hands
"Katy, you must tell the truth. If there is anything you can sa
that could help Black Hawk, please say it."

The girl blinked, her cheeks growing pinker. "I can only tel
them what I told you . . . that I hid in the cupboard so Seth
couldn't find me. I heard him go outside, and that's all I know
I was too scared to come out, even when the soldiers first came
there looking for me."

"Why, Katy? Were you afraid of Sergeant Desmond? Ar
there things about him that you and Lucy haven't told us?" Eve
lyn noticed the girl stiffen, and she shook her head firmly.

"No." She put a hand to her stomach. "I don't feel very good

Miss Gibbons. I don't want any cake. Can I go back to the house and lie down?"

Evelyn grasped her arms. *"Please,* Katy! If we can show the judge the kind of man Sergeant Desmond is, it will shed doubt on him. It might show in some way that the sergeant had cause to kill Seth himself. It could throw *enough* doubt on the case that the judge might free Black Hawk!"

Katy wiggled free. "No!" She turned and ran from the church toward the cabin.

"Katy, you don't have to be afraid!" Evelyn called out to her. "We're all here to help you! No one can hurt you now!" She closed her eyes in a feeling of desperate hopelessness. "You and Lucy are our last hope," she murmured. *Our last hope.* Night Hunter had said that a white man would die, and that Black Hawk would be in trouble over it. He had also said that a white woman would help him. Maybe that white woman was not her. Maybe it was Lucille . . . or Katy.

The tension was heavy in the packed mess hall at Fort Yates, which had been set up as a hearing room. Both Indians and whites were present, and Colonel Gere had stationed soldiers all around the outside of the building as well as some inside, worried there could be trouble with the Sioux if Black Hawk was found guilty.

Evelyn could hardly bear watching Black Hawk, who looked gaunt from loss of weight, and whose dark eyes showed none of the fire they usually held. In spite of her urgings to him to eat properly, he'd had no appetite, and he hated the food that was brought to him. For the last few days he had refused food all together, deciding to fast and pray for freedom, although he feared Wakantanka would not hear his prayers from inside the brick jail.

Now he sat at the front of the room . . . alone. At least he had

clean clothes to wear. Evelyn had brought them for him so tha
he could make a decent appearance, knowing how much prid
he took in being clean. She had been given his belongings fror
the day he had been arrested, and she in turn had given Colone
Gere his best bleached buckskins, fringed pants and shirt. Bead
in diamond shapes decorated the sides of the pants and th
sleeves of the shirt. She knew he would want to wear his bes
Indian dress, not the white man's pants and shirt they were origi
nally going to make him wear. He would want to look the prou
Sioux to the end.

There would be no lawyer to defend him. His only defens
would be his word, and no white man in the room was going t
believe him. Evelyn could tell by the restlessness in the crow
that some were ready to hang him on the spot. It did not matte
to them that his sister had been cruelly violated. All that mattere
was that a troublemaking Indian had murdered a defenseles
white man.

She ached to go to him, but there was nothing she could d
for now. Seeing him sitting with a white woman at his side woul
only anger the crowd more. She could only watch from a fev
seats back, worried at what Black Hawk might try to do himsel
if found guilty. He would do anything to keep from being hange
or going to prison. His people believed that if a man is hangec
his spirit cannot get free and can never go to the great promise
land in the sky, where they found loved ones who have die
before them, where the grass grows green and high, and buffal
roam by the millions . . . and where there are no white men
Prison for an Indian was just another form of death. She feare
Black Hawk would deliberately attack one of the soldiers an
invite a shooting. Men like Black Hawk preferred to go dow
fighting the enemy, and to him, the "bluecoats" were still th
enemy.

Never had her memory of watching Wild Horse shot dow
by soldiers been more vivid than today. Would she see it happer

gain, this time to Black Hawk? How could she bear it? She had
) hang on to herself now, for Katy and Lucy, for Little Fox,
ho had been allowed to visit his father only once, and who had
ried all night afterward. She had left Little Fox home, against
is wishes, afraid of the violence he might witness against his
ather; but Katy and Lucy were with her. She was glad that the
olonel had ordered that they be there. It gave her an excuse to
ring them, and she hoped the reality of the hearing, the finality
f what could happen to Black Hawk, would force the girls to
pen up and tell the whole truth about Seth, and about Sergeant
)esmond, if indeed they still had something to tell.

Desmond sat to their right and one row ahead of them. Oc-
asionally he glanced back at the girls with a frightful look of
varning, and Evelyn was more sure than ever that the man had
omehow intimidated them. What was his hold on them?

It was the third day of January, 1894. Evelyn thought what
 miserable way this was to start a new year. The voices of
ie crowd quieted when a gray-haired, rotund Judge Hooper
ntered the room and sat down at a head table. He pounded a
avel and ordered everyone to be still, then read over a few
ages in front of him before asking Colonel Gere to explain
ie situation at hand. Gere told what had happened, why Black
Iawk was on trial. He made it a point to tell the judge about
:lack Hawk's obstinate refusal to come and live in one of the
illages on the reservation, or to come and collect his supplies
n rations day. He seemed to be doing everything he could to
et Black Hawk up as a troublemaker, a man who had on
revious occasions, by his own admission, attacked white
vhiskey traders. He called Black Hawk uncooperative and bel-
gerent. The colonel said he was sorry about what had hap-
ened to Black Hawk's sister, but as in the case with whiskey
mugglers, the man had refused to wait for the Army to take
are of the matter. He rode off to seek his revenge, in the

Indian fashion, by murdering Seth Bridges, just as he had sai
in front of several witnesses he intended to do.

It took all of Evelyn's strength to keep herself from jumpin
up and objecting to nearly everything the colonel said. Wasn
anyone going to point out that there had been no time for Blac
Hawk to do his dirty deed before the Army arrived? Wasn
anyone going to tell the judge that when the soldiers fired o
Black Hawk, he had been riding down to meet them, was makin
his presence known? Why would he do that if he were guilty (
murder?

More men came forward to testify, swearing they had hear
Black Hawk promise to kill Seth, that he rode off ahead of th
soldiers, and that he fled when the soldiers fired at him. Ther
had been traces of blood on his knife. The rebellious warrio
had gone one step too far.

Then came Sergeant Desmond's turn at the stand. He repeate
the same things the others had said, except he had something t
add. He was the one who had found the body. He seemed t
enjoy embellishing the situation, describing how it looked a
though Seth was lying there passed out from too much whiske
totally helpless and unarmed. No white person in the roor
seemed to care about what the man had done to poor Man
Birds. After all, she was just an Indian girl, and all Indian girl
liked to get drunk and lay with white men for more whiske
That was the picture most of the men presented, although on
man did seem very emotional as he described the state in whic
they had found Many Birds, tied to Seth's bed.

Desmond did a fine job of telling the gruesome details. Set
had been found with an ugly knife wound right in the middl
of his chest. He was covered with blood, blood that had spurte
from his own heart. It had been a vicious killing, as he put i
and someone capable of such a thing should not be allowed t
live. While he was giving the details, Evelyn sensed that Kat
was becoming very agitated. She noticed the girl sat there twist

ing her hands in her lap, and her breathing became labored. Was it because of the awful description of how Seth had died? Finally, she started crying, and Lucille put an arm around her, tears in her own eyes. Katy looked at her sister. "I'm sorry," she sniffed. "I have to tell, Lucy. There's something even you don't know."

Desmond was ordered to step down, but before he could, Katy stood up. "Wait!" she called out. "Sergeant Desmond is lying!" she spoke up.

The room broke into a rumble of voices, and Katy looked at Evelyn, tears running down her cheeks, but a new pride in her eyes. The judge pounded his gavel for order, and Evelyn glanced at Black Hawk, who had turned to look at Katy in surprise. The judge shouted that he would have order or the entire room would be cleared. Evelyn turned her gaze to Sergeant Desmond, who was gripping the arms of his chair and leaning forward, looking like a wildcat ready to pounce on Katy. The look in his eyes gave her shivers.

The room finally quieted, and Katy glared at Desmond as she swallowed back her tears and drew on all her courage to face him. She was stronger now, and she was tired of having to keep the secret. If she let this go, she would have to live the rest of her life with a guilty conscience. She couldn't bear the pain Miss Gibbons was suffering, nor could she allow Black Hawk to die for something as despicable as what Sergeant Desmond had done. Reverend Phillips and Evelyn Gibbons both had taught her about God, that she should trust in Him to guide and protect her. She had grown to like Little Fox very much, and she could not let the boy lose his precious father when there was something she could do to stop it. She looked down at Lucille. "I know the truth, Lucy. I have to tell. We *both* have to tell. I'm not afraid anymore."

Their eyes held, and finally Lucille nodded, taking her sister's hand and also rising. She also did not want to live in fear of

Jubal Desmond for the rest of her life. Something had to be done, and she took courage in her sister's bravery.

"Sergeant Desmond is lying," Katy repeated to the judge. "I can tell you what really happened. I saw it all." She pointed her finger at Jubal Desmond. *"He* killed Seth Bridges!"

Another uproar rose up from the crowd, and Desmond charged out of the witness chair. "You lying little sluts!" he shouted.

Katy stood firm, holding her chin high, and Lucille put a protective arm around her. The truth was going to be heard today, and Jubal Desmond was going to get his due!

Thirty-two

"She's a lying little bitch!" Sergeant Desmond repeated, his icy eyes blazing with rage. "Both of them are! And Lucille Bridges is nothing better than a whore!"

"They are innocent young girls who have been too frightened up to now to tell the truth!" Evelyn exclaimed, rising from her seat.

"You've prompted them to tell lies to save your Indian man!" Desmond shouted back. "That white whore is Black Hawk's lover!" he yelled to the judge, pointing at Evelyn.

The judge continued to pound his gavel. "I will have silence in this room, or you'll *all* be put in jail!" he shouted. "The rest of the public here had better quiet down, or you will have to leave!"

Evelyn ignored Jubal's remarks, determined not to let them stop her; nor would she allow herself to look or feel ashamed. She moved to stand behind Lucille and Katy, putting her arms around their shoulders. "Don't be afraid, girls," she said quietly. "Just tell the truth. Whether it helps Black Hawk or not, we can at least prove Sergeant Desmond for what he is. People will realize the truth in the end." She gave them a light squeeze. "God is with you."

The crowd quieted, and the judge turned to Jubal. "You will step down for a moment, Sergeant, and you will refrain from shouting insults to these ladies present!"

Jubal stepped away from his chair. "They're no ladies," he

growled. He walked over and took his seat, glowering threateningly at Katy and Lucille.

"I would like to say something before the girls tell you what they have to say, Judge Hooper," Evelyn spoke up.

The judge sighed. "Fine. Step up here."

Evelyn breathed deeply for courage and walked up to the judge's table. There was no jury. Evelyn took hope in the fact that the ultimate decision here today would be made by one man. "I prefer to stand," she told the judge as she approached the witness chair.

The judge leaned back in his chair. "Whatever makes you comfortable, ma'am. And you are?"

"I am Evelyn Gibbons, a schoolteacher here on the reservation. I am paid by the government and was sent here on the approval of Mission Services. I received my teaching degree from Ripon College in Wisconsin, and I speak the Sioux tongue." She moved her eyes from Judge Hooper to look at Black Hawk lovingly. "So far no one has said one word in Black Hawk's defense." She scanned the crowd then. "In this country all men are supposed to be equal, with equal rights to defend themselves. I am telling all of you that Black Hawk is not the man he has been made out to be. He is a gentle, loving father, and he is very proud."

She faced the judge. "Black Hawk is a good and honest man. He did attack whiskey smugglers, but only because the Army has not been properly patrolling this reservation. He wants the whiskey smugglers kept out because he knows that whiskey hurts his people and keeps them weak, destroys their pride. It should be noted that in those attacks, no white man was ever killed. Black Hawk knows he cannot kill a white man, and if anyone would ask him, he will tell you he did not kill Seth Bridges. When he got to Seth's farm, he knew the soldiers were right on his heels, and he decided to abide by the law and let the soldiers arrest Seth and take his sister out of that house. And do not forget that Many Birds was only thirteen. She was a sweet, innocent, pure young girl, *not* loose or willing! She was found tied to Seth Bridges's bed, stone drunk on whiskey he had *forced* into her. She was covered with bruises, *proof* of that force. The girl has been shamed beyond endurance, and to this day she still sits withdrawn and silent in her grandmother's tipi. I ask you, Judge, if it were *your* sister, wouldn't your natural first reaction be to want to kill the man who violated her?"

The judge sighed. "All right, Miss Gibbons, I understand what you are saying."

Evelyn looked out at the crowd. "There isn't one man among you who would not at first verbally express his desire to kill the man who would do such an awful thing to a young girl he loved. But *saying* you want to kill someone does not make you guilty of murder. No one has pointed out that Black Hawk would barely have had time to search the farm, find Seth Bridges in the corn crib and kill him before the soldiers got there. No one has pointed out the fact that when the soldiers started shooting at Black Hawk, he was riding down toward them, had made himself visible to them." She looked back at Judge Hooper. "He was going down there to get his sister from the soldiers so he could take Many Birds to their grandmother himself. The only reason he turned and ran is because the soldiers started shooting at him. He was confused, unarmed." She looked at the crowd again. "I know for a fact that Black Hawk has been trying to comply with this new way of life. And yes, to quell all the rumors, I *am* in love with him."

As gasps and murmurs filled the room, the judge pounded his gavel again. Evelyn glanced at Black Hawk, saw the love in his own eyes. She looked back out at the crowd. "I am not ashamed to love an Indian man. In my eyes he is just a man, strong, proud, brave and honest. Black Hawk is very intelligent and a fast learner. He speaks English, and you should all know that he has a marvelous talent for painting." Evelyn then related the happy news of her father making a successful contact for the sale of two of Black Hawk's paintings, ending with the generous price the dealer was willing to pay.

Black Hawk straightened in surprise as more murmurs and whispered exclamations moved through the crowd. This was the first Black Hawk had heard of this, and for a brief moment he felt new hope. Evelyn glanced at him and smiled. "This art dealer wants Black Hawk to sign a contract to do more paintings for his gallery. I have the letter from my father with me if you would like to see it," she added, turning to the judge.

"That will not be necessary, Miss Gibbons. I believe you."

"Black Hawk is too talented and too intelligent to get himself hanged or thrown in prison for killing the likes of Seth Bridges!" Again she turned to the crowd. "It should be noted that Black Hawk can testify that Seth Bridges was involved with whiskey smugglers, and I have a feeling Lucille and Katy Bridges, his two daughters standing over there, can verify that. I am sure they will also verify that Sergeant Jubal Desmond helped their father by looking the other way when whiskey smugglers came through reservation borders. They—"

"That's a lie!" Jubal interrupted. "She can't stand there and accuse me of such things!"

Again the judge pounded his gavel. "Miss Gibbons, I cannot allow you to accuse a man of such crimes without proof."

Evelyn faced Jubal. "Fine. I will let Seth's daughters give you the proof. They will tell you the kind of man Seth really was, and the kind of man Jubal Desmond really is. They have been afraid to talk until now, probably partly out of shame but also out of fear of the sergeant somehow finding a way to hurt them." She looked at the girls. "But they don't have to be afraid. God is with them, and they have friends now who will support and protect them." She scanned the crowd once more. "One more thing that has not been emphasized is the fact that Jubal Desmond is the man who supposedly found Seth's dead body. He was alone in the corn crib at the time. No one has asked how many minutes went by when the soldiers first arrived and began searching the grounds . . . surely plenty of time for Jubal himself to have killed Seth Bridges!"

"Goddamn you, you lying bitch!" Jubal swore, charging out of his chair.

Two other men jumped up and grabbed him before he had a chance to get too close to Evelyn. Evelyn smiled inwardly. The man was only showing the judge how despicable he was, what a temper and a foul mouth he had, while all through the hearing Black Hawk had sat quietly and calmly, saying nothing. She turned to the judge. "I only ask you, sir, to consider the possibility. For years the sergeant has hated Black Hawk. He is afraid of him." She told how Black Hawk had found the sergeant next to his own dead wife and baby son at Wounded Knee, and how there was blood all over the sergeant's sword. "Ever since then there has been bad blood between them," she explained. "Jubal Desmond knew that Black Hawk had threatened to kill Seth Bridges. He knew that if Seth Bridges was found dead from a knife wound, Black Hawk would be blamed. He is the one who came running out of the corn crib shouting that Black Hawk had killed Seth, just before Black Hawk himself came riding down to meet with the soldiers. Why would Black Hawk show himself like that if he had just murdered a white man? Wouldn't any intelligent man immediately run away from the scene just as fast as he could?"

As more mumbling filtered through the crowd, Evelyn turned to face Jubal with a look of victory on her face. He sat glaring at her, his face livid with rage. Evelyn walked back to her seat, giving Katy and Lucille a look of encouragement. She had set up the picture for everyone. She was certain that anything the girls told the judge would only make Jubal look even more guilty. All that was necessary now was to shed doubt on the theory that Black Hawk killed Seth Bridges.

As she sat down, Black Hawk turned to look at her, a new hope shining in his dark eyes. She gave him a reassuring smile when the judge called Katy and Lucille forward. Evelyn had made sure they dressed demurely, wearing simple, high-necked dresses, their hair in neat buns on top of their heads. She had hoped and prayed they would speak out today, would finally find the courage to tell the truth, whatever that truth was. She wanted them to look like the young, innocent children they were

"I don't care which one of you speaks first," Judge Hooper told them. "I just want you to tell the truth. Don't be afraid. No one is going to hurt you."

The girls looked at each other, Lucille still clinging to Katy's hand. She glanced at Jubal Desmond, and suddenly she was no longer afraid of him. He was showing his own guilt by his re- action to Miss Gibbons and his name-calling. She hated him even more than she had hated Seth, and now that she no longer had to be afraid of Seth or go back and live with him, she felt new courage. She looked out at the crowd. "Sergeant Desmond raped me the night of the social dance at Fort Yates," she said boldly.

More gasps and murmurs erupted from the crowd. Lucille gripped Katy's hand tightly, and she could feel the sweat break- ing out on her body. She had said the words, and it felt good. The judge pounded his gavel for quiet, and through fits of tears. Lucille spilled the truth . . . about Seth, what he had done to her, how she cooperated only because he threatened to do the same to Katy . . . that he allowed her to go to the dance with Jubal Desmond only because Desmond had won her in a bet . . how Jubal had raped her that night and other nights, coming to the house and paying Seth . . . how Seth continued to threaten to rape Katy if she did not cooperate. She told everything—that Jubal Desmond was involved in the whiskey smuggling, even to where the whiskey was hidden at the farm.

"You can go there and see for yourself," she told the judge.

"It's in the feed sacks in the barn and in the corn crib. Black Hawk was right when he accused our father of smuggling whiskey off the riverboat. It was in those feed sacks, and Jubal knew it, too."

Through more tears she told how suddenly Seth seemed to want to be nicer. They had hoped he was changing his ways so that they would not tell on him. He had even encouraged them to have a friend, suggested they make friends with Many Birds. She began sobbing then, saying she didn't know Seth meant to hurt Many Birds. She didn't know the day he gave them money and let them go alone to the trading post that he had plans to hurt Many Birds, who he knew would come visiting that day. The picture she painted left no doubt that Many Birds was forced to give her body. Her testimony also left no doubt that Jubal Desmond and Seth Bridges were more involved than anyone knew, and Evelyn's suggestion that Jubal had motive for killing Seth was now more believable. Jubal's shouts that Lucille was lying held no water compared to the honest tears the girl shed. The room hung silent so that all could hear. Evelyn noticed that the few women present were quietly crying, dabbing at their eyes with handkerchiefs.

Lucille told how Seth had attacked her with a knife and cut her, how she had gone for help and told Katy to hide in a special place she had found in the corn crib between two walls, where they had been hiding money so they could run away.

The corn crib! Everyone came more alert at the words, and Evelyn noticed Black Hawk straighten. She looked over at Jubal Desmond, whose red face had now grown pale. This was the first time she had heard any mention of Katy hiding in the corn crib. Lucille broke down into bitter sobbing, mortified at all she had had to tell those who listened. Evelyn rushed to her side and put an arm around her, helping her to a seat, while Katy stood glaring at Jubal, all the old feisty fire back in her eyes.

"Your name is Katy?" the judge asked gently.

She turned to look at him. "Yes, sir. And it's true I was hiding in the corn crib when the soldiers first came. After they left I ran to the house and changed my clothes because I was all dirty from hiding in the wall all night. I didn't know what to do then, because the soldiers had left, and after what I saw, I was afraid Jubal would come after me, so I hid in the cupboard."

"And what did you see? Why were you afraid of Sergeant Desmond?"

Katy swallowed. "Because he did bad things to Lucy, and he told us if we ever said anything about it, or about the whiskey, he would take us downriver and sell us to bad men who would make us do bad things with other men."

Whispers of shock moved through the crowd. Evelyn felt more relieved with every word Lucy and Katy told. Katy's small size made her seem even more pitiful. Evelyn could tell everyone in the room sympathized with her.

Katy turned to look at Jubal. "That's why I was even more afraid after what I saw in the corn crib. I was afraid Jubal would stick his knife in me, too."

Jubal's eyes widened in horror, and he gripped his chair so firmly that his knuckles grew white.

"Did you see Sergeant Desmond stick a knife in someone, Katy?"

Katy nodded, turning back to the judge. "Yes, sir. I was hiding behind the wall when Seth came into the corn crib looking for me and Lucy. He was real drunk, and he wasn't wearing a shirt. Just his pants and a jacket. He had a bottle of whiskey in his hand. He fell down and passed out from being so drunk. I was scared to come out because I was afraid he'd wake up and beat me, or do something bad to me like he did to Many Birds and to Lucy, so I just waited. Then the soldiers came. I could hear their horses and hear them shouting. Then Jubal came into the corn crib. He saw Seth laying there. Seth was kind of awake. He said something to Jubal about Many Birds, but he could hardly talk. Jubal was mad that he did that to Many Birds because he said it might get both of them in trouble. He said bad things to Seth, but Seth just layed there. Then Jubal looked all around, and he took a big knife from down by his boot. I remember it had a white handle. He looked down at Seth, and he said 'I'm sorry, Seth.' He raised the knife, and Seth reached up and grabbed at him, but he was too drunk to stop Jubal. Jubal stabbed him in the chest with the knife while Jubal was grabbing his jacket. Jubal jumped back when blood spurted out. Then another soldier yelled from outside, and Jubal hurried up and wiped off the knife on Seth's coat and put it back in his boot. Then he yelled that he was in the corn crib and that he had found Seth and that Black Hawk had killed him."

"She's lying!" Jubal shouted above a rumbling crowd. "She can't prove it. It's just her word, and she hates me because of Lucille."

Evelyn smiled. By those words, Jubal openly admitted having abused Lucy. The judge pounded his gavel again.

"Yes, I *can* prove it," Katy said boldly. She reached into her pocket and turned to the judge. She handed something to him. "This is a button off of Jubal's uniform jacket. Seth must have pulled it off when he reached up to try to stop Jubal from stabbing him, he must have grabbed it tight and pulled it off as he lay dying. I saw it happen, sir, and after they took the body away, I found the button on the floor of the corn crib and I kept it."

Jubal half rose out of his chair as the judge took the button. The crowd was again in an uproar, and while the judge pounded again for quiet, another man rose. "Sir, may I speak?"

The judge studied the button, then looked over at the man who had risen. "Only if you have something to say that will contribute to this case."

The man glanced at an enraged Jubal, then stepped forward. "I am Private James Johnston, sir. I was the first man in the corn crib after Jubal. I'm the one who called out to him."

"And?"

Johnston glanced at Jubal and swallowed, then looked back at the judge. "Well, sir, they loaded the body up to bring it here to the fort for burial, and that's when I noticed Sergeant Desmond had lost a button off his jacket. I, uh, I said something to him about it, and he looked down to see it was gone. He looked real upset, said he'd better go back into the corn crib to find it, but then Black Hawk, he rode out toward us and somebody shouted 'There he is!' and we all hightailed it after Black Hawk. I don't remember any more about the button. All I know is, it was missing when the sergeant came out of the corn crib."

Jubal was beet red again, looking ready to kill.

"And Black Hawk *did* ride toward you and the other men as though nothing was wrong?"

"Yes, sir. Before he had a chance to say anything, everybody started shooting at him, and he turned and rode off." The private glanced at Black Hawk. "I, uh, I have to say, when we caught him and said Seth had been murdered, Black Hawk really did look surprised, like he didn't know anything about it. I think Lieutenant Hart can verify that. I had the feeling that he really didn't know."

"Thank you, Private." The judge looked over at Jubal. "Do you carry a knife in your boot, Sergeant?"

Jubal looked around defensively. "Yes, sir."

"Will you please stand up?"

Jubal obeyed, and the judge looked him over. "I can see that you keep the knife hidden, which means Miss Bridges here would not know what color the knife handle is unless you pulled it out. Will you please show us your knife?"

People whispered, and Katy backed away, terror in her eyes. Evelyn realized that not one person there would believe either she or Lucille were lying. The fear in their eyes was too real. Jubal started to reach down toward his boot, but then he suddenly drew his handgun from its holster at his waist. People screamed as he raced over and grabbed Katy, holding the gun against her head.

"Katy!" Lucille cried, rising.

"All I want is a horse," Jubal shouted. "I'm taking Katy with me until I know I'm far enough away that no one can catch up with me!"

"Sergeant, for God's sake—" The words came from Colonel Gere.

"Get me a horse," Jubal interrupted, "or I swear, I'll blow this little bitch's brains out!"

Evelyn felt sick at the terror in poor Katy's eyes. What a fool Jubal Desmond was! He might have been able to talk his way out of the murder, since there was no one's word but Katy's. He might have been reprimanded only for what he did to the girls, and for being involved in the whiskey smuggling. But he had openly and foolishly given away his own guilt by what he was doing now. She wanted Black Hawk's freedom, but not at the cost of poor Katy's life.

"Get him a horse," the colonel ordered.

Jubal was so engrossed in watching the other soldiers because of their weapons that he had failed to keep Black Hawk in sight. An awful dread gripped Evelyn when she noticed Black Hawk quietly slink out of his chair and move around behind the judge, who apparently realized what Black Hawk had in mind and did nothing to stop him. Black Hawk moved closer behind Jubal, while at the same time Jubal backed up farther with Katy, who was breathing in whimpers from terror. A stunned audience sat frozen while one soldier ran outside to get a horse. All of them could see Black Hawk behind Jubal, but no one shouted any warning. By now their sentiments had fallen in favor of Black Hawk and of the terribly abused daughters of Seth Bridges.

"Let her go, Jubal Desmond," Black Hawk spoke up behind him.

Jubal whirled at the words, and Black Hawk took advantage

of his surprise by grasping his gun arm and pushing upward. Jubal let go of Katy, and she ran to Lucille while Black Hawk wrestled Jubal to the floor. He put a knee into Jubal's chest, pressing the breath out of him, while at the same time he bent Jubal's gun hand back painfully. Jubal grabbed at him unsuccessfully with his free hand, but finally he had no strength left. He dropped his pistol, and Black Hawk grabbed his other arm, pressing both wrists over his head, watching Jubal begin to turn blue from lack of air.

"It is done, Jubal Desmond!" he seethed. "You will *die,* and I will gladly watch the man who murdered my wife and daughter hang!" He moved off of Jubal, who rolled to his knees making choking sounds as he gasped for breath. Men surrounded Jubal and led him away. The room was in an uproar, the judge pounding his gavel, people talking to Private Johnston and Colonel Gere, Katy and Lucille hugging each other. Black Hawk walked up to Evelyn, reached out and touched her face gently.

"I will have order in this room!" the judge shouted.

Finally everyone quieted, and the judge ordered Black Hawk to face him. "Sir, do you have a Christian name?"

"I have never taken one," Black Hawk answered. He looked back at Evelyn. "Until now." He faced the judge again. "I wish to be called James Hawk."

The judge nodded, looking at Agent McLaughlin. "Let it be so recorded." He turned his gaze back to Black Hawk. "James Hawk, it is my decision that you have been wrongfully accused of murder, and you are hereby set free." He looked at Colonel Gere. "Hold Sergeant Desmond in the fort jail while I review the things I have heard and seen here today, Colonel. I will give my verdict tomorrow on what should be done with him." His eyes moved to Katy and Lucille. "As for you girls, I want to commend you for your courage and honesty. I hope the people who live on and near this reservation will understand the awful situation under which you have lived the past several years with a man who obviously adopted you only to have free help and to abuse you in a most despicable way. What you have done today took tremendous courage, and you deserve the respect and support of everyone here." He again turned to Colonel Gere. "Colonel, I want you to go to the Bridges farm and cut open those bags of feed and see if there is whiskey inside. I have no doubt the girls were telling the truth. I want all that whiskey destroyed."

"Yes, sir."

The judge pounded his gavel. "This hearing is closed."

Evelyn embraced Black Hawk and wept. He moved one arm around her, while with his other hand he reached out and touched Katy's hair. "You are as strong and brave as any Sioux warrior," he told her. "Forever you will hold a place of honor in my heart."

Katy blinked back tears. "Will you tell Many Birds how sorry we are? We would like to go and see her, to still be friends. Maybe it would help her to know what Seth did to Lucy, to know she's not the only one. I want her to be happy again. I . . . I saved her stick doll for her."

Black Hawk nodded. "I will tell her."

The room began to clear, Indians and whites alike gossiping and shaking their heads. Black Hawk grasped Evelyn's arms, looking down at her tear-stained face. "And you . . . such courage you have, to stand before everyone and admit your love for an Indian man. The things you said helped upset Jubal Desmond so that he lost control of himself and gave himself away. You are a smart woman, *Wenonah,* brave woman. I have never loved you more."

Evelyn took one of his hands and kissed it. "We can make it work, Black Hawk. We know that now. Night Hunter's vision was right, but I wasn't the white woman who ultimately ended up helping you. It was Katy."

He smiled sadly. "It was you who gave her the courage." He pressed the palm of his hand to the side of her face, rubbing at her tears with his thumb. "I wish to see my son. But first there is something I must do. I must ride away alone and pray. I feel weak from no air and no sun. I wish to go into the hills and touch Grandmother Earth, to feel the sun on my skin, to give thanks to Wakantanka for giving me my freedom. I wish to bathe myself and cleanse myself of the stench of that cell by going into the sweat lodge."

She nodded. "I understand. I will also give thanks, and I know we will be praying to the same God, Black Hawk."

He studied the beautiful blue eyes that set fire to his loins. "Perhaps you are right after all. If it is so, then by our union the circle will be complete. Be ready to marry me when I return, *Wenonah.*"

She smiled through her tears. "I have been ready to marry you since I first saw you in my dreams."

He leaned down and kissed the top of her head, then left her. Evelyn heard a soldier tell him he would get his horse for him. Evelyn noticed with secret joy that the soldier showed an air of great respect for Black Hawk. She looked at Katy and Lucille, hugged them both. "Everything is going to be all right now, girls. Let's go home and tell Beverly and Little Fox."

It took several minutes for them to walk out to the wagon in which Reverend Phillips had brought them. People kept stopping them, Indian and white alike, praising Lucille and Katy for their courage, asking how they could help the girls. Young Private Johnston seemed to appear from nowhere and helped Lucille climb into the back of the wagon.

"I never did like Seth Bridges," he told her, "or Sergeant Desmond. You don't know it, Miss Bridges, but the night of that dance, I watched you all night. I couldn't understand why your pa let you go with somebody so much older than yourself."

Lucille looked away, her face red with embarrassment.

"Hey, it's okay, Lucille. May I call you Lucille?"

She cast him a sidelong look, surprised at his attention. "I suppose."

"There's another dance coming in about a month, a little fling to break up the boredom of winter, if weather permits. Will you go with me?"

She pulled her coat tighter around her neck. "Maybe. I have a lot of things to think about, Private Johnston. I just want to concentrate on school and just . . . I don't know . . . just be normal and happy, I guess."

"Sure, I understand. I'll call on you, if that's okay."

Lucille wondered how having one man touch her, could be so ugly and horrifying, and yet the attentions of another could make her feel pretty and special. "I guess so. I live with Miss Gibbons."

Johnston nodded and tipped his hat. "Thank you, Lucille. I'll be paying you a visit."

While they talked, Reverend Phillips took hold of Evelyn's hands. "I'm happy for you, Evelyn," he said, calling her by her first name because of her intimate friendship with his wife. "I have tried to talk you out of your love for Black Hawk, but now I realize just how deep that love is. You have taught me so much about tolerance and acceptance."

Evelyn watched him with tear-filled eyes. "We have all learned a lot since coming here six months ago," she answered.

As Phillips helped her climb up into the wagon seat, she noticed someone ride off in the distance at a hard gallop. She recognized Black Hawk's horse. Her heart soared with joy for him. He was free now, more free than he had been in a long time. She knew he rode his spotted horse at a gallop so that he could feel the wind in his face. He was charging toward the distant hills with the bright sun on his shoulders, snow flying from beneath his horse's hooves. It was a very cold day, but he wore no jacket, and she knew it was because he wanted to feel the cold. He wanted to feel everything . . . and when he was ready, he would come back to her, and she would be Mrs. James Hawk. She closed her eyes and thanked God for her answered prayers.

* * *

A light wind blew snow in whispered rushes across the ground. Evelyn huddled closer under her fur coat. It had been a week since the hearing, and she had not seen Black Hawk. Jubal Desmond had been sentenced to hang, had been sent to Fort Leavenworth for the execution. The judge and Agent McLaughlin feared too much unrest among the Sioux if the hanging were to take place at Standing Rock. The girls seemed happier, and Little Fox, relieved over his father's release, was again doing better in school. Evelyn had sent for her father, who would bring Black Hawk's money; more important, she had sent for him so that he could be present when she wed Black Hawk in a Christian ceremony, wearing the beautiful bleached doeskin dress with the tiny pieces of tin tied to each tassel that made wearing it a mystical, musical event.

She could not wait to feel Black Hawk's arms around her again, to share her bed with him again, this time knowing they were both truly free to admit to their love. Their visions, and those of Night Hunter, were now a reality. There was only one last vision that must be realized to make the circle complete, and now she knew why Black Hawk had sent a messenger to bring her out here to the rolling hills west of the reservation. She was left standing here alone, the wind rippling the fur of her coat, the snow whispering to her of love and joy and new life to come.

She could see him now, riding toward her on a spotted horse, his long hair blowing in the wind. She could see the rippling chest muscles of the handsome Appaloosa as it ran, and as man and horse drew closer, a chill moved through her that did not come from the cold air. It came from the incredible reality of this moment. Here was her vision. Here was what she had dreamed, the vision that had compelled her to come here, where

she had found a most satisfying, sensual love, where she knew
she belonged and would stay forever.

He came closer, and she knew this was as important to Black
Hawk as it was to her—one last vision to be fulfilled. She smiled,
reaching out for him, and when he was near enough, he leaned
down and grasped her arm, swinging her up onto his horse in
front of him as though she weighed nothing.

Evelyn laughed, for he had not disappeared like in the
dream. This was real. This was what it had all been leading
to. He slowed his horse then. "My *Wenonah*," he said softly,
dropping the reins and wrapping his arms around her. His
horse slowed to an amble, and she turned and met his mouth
in a long, delicious kiss, her fur hood falling away to reveal
honey-colored hair that was brushed out long and loose for
her lover. The arms that held her were strong again, and there
was a bright happiness in his dark eyes.

"Now it is complete," he told her when he left her mouth and
moved his lips to nuzzle at her neck.

"No, there is one more thing," she told him, resting her head
on his strong shoulder and breathing in the familiar, masculine
scent of him. "A child of both bloods will make it complete,
Black Hawk, and I am carrying that child." She had not told
anyone. She had wanted to wait until after the hearing, wait until
he had gone off alone to find his strength and faith again, but
she had known since just after Black Hawk's arrest that she was
pregnant.

He moved a big hand to her belly, rubbing it gently. "This is
true? You are sure that you carry my child?"

"I am sure. My father will be here soon, and then we can
marry."

He smiled, moving his hand to the side of her face, studying
her beauty. "I am a happy man, but I do not want to wait until
after we are married to be one with my *Wenonah* again. Come
with me. I still have a camp in Eagle Canyon, by the creek. We

will build a fire inside the tipi, but we will not really need it. The heat of our love will keep us warm. Tell me you will come there with me."

She snuggled against him. "I was hoping you would want to go there. Beverly is watching the children. I told her not to worry if I didn't come back tonight."

He grinned. "You knew."

She studied his handsome face. "Of course I knew." She leaned up and kissed him lightly. "I love you, Black Hawk, now more than ever."

He grinned. "And I love my white woman who has an Indian heart."

He held her close as he guided his horse back toward Eagle Canyon. Evelyn gloried in the feel of his heart beating close to hers, the glory of love, and the life growing inside her. And she knew she would sleep well tonight and for many nights to come. She would be in Black Hawk's arms, and the dream would no longer haunt her.

I do hope you have enjoyed my story. For more information about me and other books I have written, just send a stamped, self-addressed, business-size (#10) envelope to Rosanne Bittner, 6013 North Coloma Road, Coloma, MI 49038. Thank you!